curvy girl summer

curvy girl summer

DANIELLE ALLEN

TOR PUBLISHING GROUP
NEW YORK

This is a work of fiction. All of the characters, organizations, and events portrayed in this novel are either products of the author's imagination or are used fictitiously.

CURVY GIRL SUMMER

A Bramble Book
Published by Tom Doherty Associates / Tor Publishing Group
120 Broadway
New York, NY 10271

www.torpublishinggroup.com

Bramble™ is a trademark of Macmillan Publishing Group, LLC.

The Library of Congress Cataloging-in-Publication Data is available upon request.

ISBN 978-1-250-33104-5 (trade paperback)
ISBN 978-1-250-33105-2 (ebook)

Our books may be purchased in bulk for promotional, educational, or business use. Please contact your local bookseller or the Macmillan Corporate and Premium Sales Department at 1-800-221-7945, extension 5442, or by email at MacmillanSpecialMarkets@macmillan.com.

First Edition: 2024

Printed in the United States of America

0 9 8 7 6 5 4 3 2 1

To Grandma and Grandpa

Forever

1

There were many reasons why I stopped dating Matthew, but a well-timed apology and his ten veiny inches had me bent over for him one final time. I was feeling good and was inexplicably horny, so it didn't take much for me to give in to his offer.

I normally wasn't the type to double back on someone I'd let go of. I didn't believe in second chances when it came to matters of the heart. But if I were being completely honest with myself, it wasn't the heart that was making the decisions. It was the six-month-long journey of singleness that I'd embarked on to start the new year. And while I wasn't proud of my decision, I was satisfied with it.

Thoroughly satisfied.

I was going to be thirty soon, and I was never really interested in casual hookups. It would've been easy to meet someone new to have sex with. Sex was easy. But there was no guarantee that a new man would take care of my needs. And the one thing that Matthew consistently did right was me.

"Matthew," I whimpered, feeling the tension between my thighs. My hands gripped the kitchen island. My fingers slipped across the freshly cleaned marble as he pushed my skintight skirt over my ass, bunching it at my waist.

"Do you know how much I've missed you?" he asked as he kissed the backs of my thighs. Slowly peeling my G-string down, he helped me step out of it. "Do you know how often I think about you"—he kissed my ass cheeks—"and this big . . . fat . . . ass?"

Without warning, his hand came down on my right cheek.

My skin tingled as the familiarity of his touch combined with the pain of the slap. The desire in his voice sent chills down my spine.

"How often?" I wondered breathily. "How often do you think about me?"

He trailed kisses across my lower back before he stood. "I've thought about you every day since you ghosted me."

The sound of his belt buckle hitting the laminate flooring was like a bell alerting me to what was to come. I grabbed the edge of the island countertop and braced myself. "I didn't ghost you."

"You did . . ." He positioned both of his hands on my hips, tugging me back so that I felt him hot and hard against me. "And I still couldn't stop thinking about our last time together and how hard you came on my face." His hands roughly pushed up my flowy top, exposing more of my back. "And how sexy you looked riding me and coming on my dick."

I was dripping wet.

"Yessssssss," I dragged out breathily. "But I didn't ghost you. We talked—"

"You talked," he interrupted. "I listened, but you talked." He took his tongue and licked up my spine. "And now it's time for you to listen."

I shivered. "I'm listening."

He wrapped his arms around my middle so that he could grip the fleshiness of my belly under my shirt. "You're so fucking soft."

He pulled me up so that I was standing upright. Running his hands upward until he reached my breasts, he cupped them and ran his thumbs over my hardened nipples. My head lolled back, resting on his shoulder as he continued to toy with me. When I felt his breath on my neck, I inhaled sharply.

"Spread your legs," he whispered.

I did as I was told and was rewarded with the feeling of his dick between my thighs.

Anticipating his next move, I held my breath when his hand moved from my breast to between my legs. The moment the pads of his fingers grazed my waxed flesh, I surrendered to his touch.

"You're already so wet for me," he murmured, massaging his way into me.

His middle and forefinger slid in and out of me, and I moaned loudly.

"Yeah, I've missed you." His voice was rough and needy. Pulling his fingers out, he rubbed my clit. "The fact that you're here tells me that you missed me, too."

I knew what he wanted me to say, but I couldn't bring myself to say it. It wasn't true. If anything, the only thing I missed was his dick.

"But how much did you miss me?" he wondered softly.

Instead of answering, I groaned, grinding against his hand. It felt like his dick got even harder as it pressed against my ass.

He slipped a finger back inside me. "Oh yeah? That much, huh?" Leaning down so that his lips brushed against the shell of my ear, he applied pressure while rubbing me. "It feels like she's ready for me."

Panting, my desire twisted my gut. I felt myself approaching the edge.

"Yesssssss . . ." I dragged the answer out as I gyrated against his hand. "I'm ready for you."

"What are you ready for me to do, Aaliyah?"

I wanted him so bad that I was starting to lose control. The only thing I could think about was how badly I needed to get off.

"I'm ready for you to fuck me," I whined.

He spun me around and then crashed his mouth to mine. Kissing me roughly and recklessly, he pinned me between the island and his hard body. When he pulled back, he yanked my shirt over my head and then cast his gaze over my body.

Running his fist over the length of his dick, he took another step back. "I missed your sexy ass."

"Show me," I murmured, staring at the reason I came over.

"Oh, I plan to." He grabbed his pants from the floor and took a condom out of his pocket. "I plan to show you a few times." The latex stretched over his dick. "Can you handle it?"

I nodded. "Yes."

"Good," he grunted, taking a step forward.

I gasped at the quickness with which he spun me around by my bunched-up skirt. Pushing me against the island, he put me into position. His hands moved up my back to bend me over and then down to my hips.

"So fucking soft," he whispered. With one hand, he held my skirt like reins and with the other, he palmed my ass.

Then he smacked it again.

"Ah!" I yelped, pleasure and pain spreading through my body.

"Stay right there," he breathed as I felt him lining up against me.

"Oh my God . . ." I moaned as he pushed himself into me.

"This pussy is so fucking good." He dug his fingers into my skin as he restrained himself. "And so fucking wet for me."

He wasn't lying.

It had been a long time since I'd been properly taken care of, so I was ready for him. Wet from anticipation and the pressure of him stretching me out, I didn't need him to be as gentle.

As he pushed inch after inch in me, I couldn't control the sounds that came out of me. The deeper he got, the louder I became.

He let out a low groan as he filled me to the hilt. He ran his hands all over me before returning his hands to my hips. "I've missed this pussy. I've missed how good you feel."

I could only moan in response as I started grinding against him.

"You remember exactly what I like," he rasped as I continued to throw it back on him.

His ragged breathing coupled with the sound of my wetness and our skin slapping together. The reverberation seemed to echo in his kitchen as he gripped me, taking back control. He moved in and out of me until I felt the tension tighten my entire lower body.

"You like that, don't you, Aaliyah?" His voice was desperate and needy.

"Yes, yes, yes, yes, yes!"

"Oh, shit," he groaned softly, picking up the pace.

His strokes consistently hit the right spot. It was like he knew which buttons to push and when. I held on to the edge of the island for dear life as he pounded into me.

"Right there, right there," I called out breathlessly. "Yes! Yes! Yes, yes, yes!"

"Come on this dick for old times' sake. Just like you used to. Let me feel that pussy."

I tried my best to hold it together, but I felt myself coming undone as soon as he said that. "Oh my God!"

He sucked in a shuddering breath before he let loose, ramming into me. "I know you missed it," he panted. "Even if you can't admit it, your pussy is telling on you. You're so wet for me. Do you hear that? Do you fucking hear how wet you are for me?"

As he continued to thrust his hips, I threw my ass back to meet him. Each and every word out of his mouth added to my building orgasm. He always talked a lot of shit, and I loved it.

"Matt," I panted, beginning my descent into pure pleasure. My muscles clenched, and I started clamping down around him. "Oh. God. Yes."

"That's right," he hissed. "You're coming for me."

The ache deep inside me exploded. Quivering, I came apart on his throbbing dick.

"Oh, shit!" His body jerked and shuddered as he reached his climax as abruptly as I'd reached mine.

I slumped against the island, completely worn out. My head rested against the cool marble and my breaths came out in heavy bursts. Matthew was bent over me, hugging me and panting on my back. My thighs were shaking and the only reason I was still upright was because I was pinned down.

"Wow," he exhaled before carefully pulling out of me. He turned me around and stared at me. "I almost forgot how good you feel."

"Yeah," I agreed lightly, still catching my breath. "That was good."

I let my head rock back, and I stared at the ceiling. Met expectations and pure satisfaction ran through my veins and quieted the noise my horniness had caused. The on-edge feeling had been replaced by calmness. The feral desire that started to cloud my judgment after months of abstinence had been replaced with quiet peace. Closing my eyes, I let out a deep contented breath.

"Now," Matthew started. "Can we just start over?"

I raised my head and looked into his hopeful brown eyes. The sinking sensation that I was hoping to avoid returned. Grabbing the paper towels that I'd pushed out of the way when he'd first bent me over, I tore off a few squares. Cleaning myself up, I started to move toward the trash can.

He took the juice-soaked paper towels from my hand and held them up to his nose, inhaling deep. "Do you even know what you do to me? You smell so good. Let me taste you again. Please."

Pulling my skirt down, I took the paper towels from his hand and tossed them in the trash. "I told you this was a one-time thing when I agreed to come over."

He removed the condom and then followed me to the sink while I washed my hands.

"You also told me that you weren't ever going to see me again, and here you are—seeing me again," he reasoned. "Things change, and I want you to change your mind about us kicking it with each other again."

"Matthew . . ." I shook my head before I tugged my shirt over it. "You and I didn't work out for multiple reasons. You already know this."

He twisted his face in confusion, pointing at my clothed body and then his naked one. "You didn't just feel that? We work. You can't tell me you didn't feel that."

I gestured between the two of us. "The only thing that ever worked between us was the sex. The more we got to know each other, the clearer it was that you and I aren't on the same page. You don't get me." He was giving me a little puppy-dog look, so I averted my eyes. "I told you this already."

I looked around, unable to find my G-string.

It was definitely time to go.

"Give me three good reasons why you and I aren't a good fit," he argued.

"This is exactly what I said I didn't want to happen if I came over here," I grumbled under my breath as I headed to the living room, where my bag was still on the couch. Grabbing it, I slung it over my shoulder.

"Please just talk to me. You can't give me a taste of that pussy and just roll out."

I looked at him as if he'd lost his mind. "What are you doing? You reached out to me and said everything was cool." I flailed my arms around. "This isn't cool."

"Because you're trippin' if you don't think there's something real here. You don't have a reason for not wanting to see this through."

"The thing is I told you the reasons why we ended when we ended. I didn't ghost you. I didn't lead you on. I didn't play you. I was honest with you, and that was that."

He shook his head. "But that wasn't that! You said what you had to say, and then you never responded to me again. We'd been dating for a while, and you just bailed on it."

"We'd been dating for two months," I corrected.

"I hit a bump in the road, and you just dipped on me."

My eyebrows flew up. "Is that what you've been telling yourself?"

He looked down with his lips in a tight line. "I mean, I know it was wrong that I accidentally called you someone else's name—"

"Your ex-girlfriend's name," I reminded him. "You called me your ex-girlfriend's name."

"And I apologized for that! It was a rough week. She had reached out—"

"And you said you thought you might still be in love with her," I reminded him.

"I was confused, and I told you that."

"And I told you to explore that and see how you feel." I shrugged. "It's standard advice."

"Okay, but I realized I wasn't still in love with her. I was just missing the life I had in Philly."

"Okay, and I told you I was happy for you for figuring that out."

"But then you didn't say anything else, and you weren't fucking with me anymore."

I blinked. "Yes," I said slowly, not understanding what he didn't understand. "Because I'm not obligated to hang around and wait for you to figure your shit out."

"All I've been trying to tell you for months was that if I would've known you were going to leave me, I wouldn't have even thought twice about hitting her up and seeing what was up."

Sighing, I walked to his front door.

"Come on, Aaliyah. You said we'd talk. I'm just trying to talk."

Turning to face him, I kept my hand on the doorknob to let him know I was still planning to leave.

"Just . . ." He ran his hands down his washboard abs and then rested them low on his hips.

I knew what he was doing. He was doing what he was used to doing: using his looks, his body, and his big-ass dick to get his way. But it didn't work on me then, and it wasn't going to work on me now. I only agreed to talk to him because of my needs.

"I don't know what to tell you." I lifted my shoulders. "You did what you wanted to do. It didn't work out the way you'd hoped. That's not on me."

I glanced down at his dick, hanging heavily against his thigh. *This is all your fucking fault,* I silently cursed the demonic dick. *I should've known this was going to happen.*

"When you responded tonight, you said you accepted my apology," he said, reaching out for me. "What changed?"

"I do accept your apology," I told him. "I accepted your apology back then, too. But at the end of the day, that doesn't have anything to do with the fact that I don't want to date you. We aren't compatible."

"It was because of my job situation, wasn't it?"

"Your job situation? You mean when you quit your job abruptly so you could pursue music."

His jaw tightened defensively. "You said I was talented."

"I said the song you played me was good. I never said you should quit your job—you know what . . ." I shook my head because I wasn't having that conversation again. "Matthew, I thought we could be cool, but it looks like it's still too soon and feelings are too raw." I opened the door to walk out.

"Are you going to honestly tell me you don't want me? You're really telling me that? Seriously?" He gestured to himself. His semihard dick was winking at me.

"Yes." Dragging my eyes back to his, I nodded. "That's what I'm saying. That's what I've been saying since we ended."

He sucked his teeth and shook his head. “Nah, I don’t believe you. You know what I do to your body. Your nipples are hard now just standing here. You want me just like I want you.”

“I’m going to go home now. Take care of yourself, Matthew.”

“Look at me. They always come back.”

Not this time.

With a tight smile, I nodded again. “Goodbye, Matthew.”

My eyes dropped back down to his dick before I left his place and closed the door between us. If that dick wasn’t going to keep me involved with him, nothing he could’ve said or done would’ve worked.

I jogged down the steps until I got to the first-floor landing. It was then that I remembered I’d left my panties. Looking up, I thought about it for a moment and then shook my head.

I’ll just buy some new ones.

It wasn’t worth the trouble.

As soon as I got in the car, I called the best friend that I was sure had experienced something similar before.

“Hey.” Nina Ford answered the call on the first ring. “Please tell me you got your itch scratched.”

“I did.”

She gasped. “I can’t believe you actually did it! How was it?”

“It was . . .” The flashback caused a dull ache between my thighs. “It was just as good as I remembered.”

“So why do you sound like that?” she wondered.

“Because you were right. I probably just should’ve found someone new.”

“What did Matthew do? He was still pressed, wasn’t he?”

“Yes.” I hit the steering wheel. “You called it. I just didn’t want to try my luck with someone new. But instead of being able to revel in my orgasm, he really wanted to talk about why I wasn’t trying to date him anymore.”

“That man has been pining away for you for months. He needs to let it gooooooo.”

I snickered at the way she said it and then sighed. “It’s my fault. I should’ve never responded to his message.”

"Well, he *has* been sending you a message every month for the last seven months. So, yeah . . . I think it was a little delusional to believe that man was just going to be cool with a one-night-only hookup."

"You're right," I admitted as I drove down the dark street. "You are absolutely right. I think I just went with something familiar because I'm ready to find my person. I'm not rushing it, but I can't continue on this drought."

"It's time for me to give you some real talk, my friend. It's going to be a long summer if you continue the way you're going," she warned. "You can't keep depriving yourself and thinking there will be no consequences. So, this is the perfect time for you to see what's out there. Hit these streets up with me."

"Nina, you know I'm just not the one-night-stand type."

"Well, I am. And let me tell you, I haven't been stressed about a thing! You, on the other hand, just spent months soul-searching and figuring out what you want—only to hook up with a dude working on his debut rap album."

"At forty!" I hollered. "Sir, it's too late."

"If anything, he needs to see if they'll give him studio time for a jazz album. Because nobody trying to shake ass to joint-pain jams and Roth IRA rhymes."

I laughed so hard I almost choked.

"These are your consequences for waiting too long," she continued as I cackled.

2

In the quiet moments before the house filled with people, I stared at the mocha-skinned beauty with the big almond-shaped eyes, full, plump lips, and perfectly placed, silk-pressed hair cascading to the middle of her back. She was shaped like a Coke bottle, and the angelic white dress that adorned her body looked flawless. Standing on our uncle's yacht, she looked happy, carefree.

And alive.

My heart twinged, and I knew it was going to be a long day.

Every year since my sister died, my parents threw a small birthday party honoring Aniyah at their home. But with the fifth birthday since her death falling on a Saturday, my parents decided to make it a family affair. The grill was fired up and slow-cooking slabs of ribs. The backyard was full of tents, tables, and chairs in anticipation of the cousins, aunts, uncles, and family friends who were all en route for the cookout. It was a beautiful summer day, but ever since I arrived half an hour ago, I felt unsettled.

I hadn't felt real peace since Aniyah died. If it wasn't one thing, it was another. Losing my sister when she was only thirty was traumatizing—mainly because it was hard living in her shadow. But there was something different in the air that day. I couldn't put my finger on it, but something was off. I knew in my gut something wasn't going to go as planned.

What's up, sis? I silently asked my sister as I stared at her portrait.

"Aaliyah," my mom called out in her "in front of company" tone of voice.

I turned around and was surprised to see her standing next to a woman who looked vaguely familiar and a man I'd never seen before in my life.

"Hello," I replied suspiciously. Glancing at the others and then back at my mom, I lifted my eyebrows. "What's going on?"

"You remember Liz, don't you?"

I reached my hand out to shake hers. "Hi, Ms. Liz. It's nice to see you again."

"Hi, Aaliyah. Don't you look lovely!" She released my hand and then gestured next to her. "This is my son Marcus. He's in town visiting for the weekend."

My mom's friend from church always talked about her son Marcus and all his military travels and exploits. I'd never met him, but the few times I'd encountered Ms. Liz, she'd tell me she had a son around my age. But the baby-faced man in front of me looked more like a twenty-two-year-old than a twenty-nine-year-old.

"Hi, Marcus," I said to him, shaking his hand as well.

"Hey. It's nice to meet you, Aaliyah," he responded in a husky tone.

I didn't expect that voice to come out of the khaki-and-white-polo-shirt-wearing man in front of me.

"Nice to meet you as well."

I looked back at my mother to find her staring at me expectantly.

"I need to get something for Liz that I left upstairs. Will you entertain Marcus for a few minutes?" my mom asked.

"Sure."

My mom and Liz scurried off before I had the word all the way out of my mouth. I looked at Marcus, who looked just as bewildered as I did.

He met me in the middle of the room.

"Do you want something to drink? The food should be done, but I'm not certain. I know for a fact there's plenty to drink though," I offered.

"I'm okay. Thank you," he replied, stepping closer to me. He lowered his voice and leaned forward a bit. "I really don't need a babysitter. I'm not sure why they interrupted what you had going on to ask you to watch me."

"I know, right?" Realizing how that came off, my eyes widened, and I put my hand to my chest. "I'm sorry. I didn't mean it like that. I just meant that you're grown."

He smiled.

He had a nice smile and kind eyes. He was a few inches taller than I was, maybe five feet, eleven inches. So, with my heels, we were pretty much eye to eye. For someone so young, he seemed to have wisdom behind those light brown eyes.

"That's a nice boat," he stated, gesturing toward the yacht in the picture.

"Yeah," I agreed. "It's pretty great."

"Is it your sister's?"

I twisted my lips contemplatively. "It's my uncle's. He gave it to my sister right before her engagement, but after she passed away, he reclaimed it."

He let out a low whistle. "That's some gift."

I nodded slowly. "Yeah, it was."

Aniyah and I loved that yacht. So many amazing memories took place on that thing. We were on it all the time growing up, and we had fun. But once Uncle Al gave it to her, it became more special to us. As adults, we'd drive to the ocean, where it was docked, and then spend the day catching up and discussing life. We left all our secrets out there on the water.

Those moments were the ones I'd miss most.

"I'll let you get back to . . . what you were doing," Marcus stated, putting his arms behind his back. "I'll give you some privacy."

"What is it that you think I was doing?"

"Talking to your sister."

My lips parted, and I froze. *How did he know that?*

I was shocked and couldn't bring myself to ask. So, I just stared at him.

I heard the people coming into the house. I heard voices yelling out for my parents. I heard my father and then my mother, but all of it was background noise as I stared at Marcus.

"How?" That was the only part of the question I managed to get out.

"A friend of mine died overseas a few years ago," he answered succinctly.

"I'm sorry to hear that. I'm sorry for your loss."

He nodded. "I'm sorry for yours, too."

Nodding, I gave him a tight smile. "Thanks."

"When I find myself thinking about him, I start having conversations with him in my head. So, when I saw you staring, and the way you were staring, I knew you were having a conversation or lost in a memory."

"It was a conversation of sorts," I admitted slowly, unsure of why I was sharing this with the stranger.

"Staring at a picture just makes me see missed opportunities and experiences we'd never get again."

"I get that," I told him. "I used to feel like that. I used to get really sad when I looked at her pictures. But I realized that as long as I have her in here"—I pointed to my heart—"Aniyah isn't gone. She just isn't here."

"That's deep." He was quiet for at least a minute. "I never thought about it like that. But that's deep."

Therapy. Lots of therapy.

After another moment of silence, the doorbell almost drowned out his next question. "How did your sister die?"

Grimacing, I shook my head.

I hated that question. Partially because I hated thinking about it. Partially because the wounds within the family were still raw. But mostly because it didn't acknowledge how she was still here. It made her physical demise seem like the end of her.

I knew people didn't mean any harm when they asked, so I took a deep breath.

"It's okay if you don't want to talk about it," he said gently. "I don't like to talk about how Keyshawn died either. I was just curious because she looks so young."

"She had a heart condition," I answered. "How did Keyshawn die?"

He cleared his throat. "He was shot."

"In the line of duty?"

He shook his head. "It was a non-combat-related death. He, uh . . . he was sleeping with a married woman, and her husband shot him."

My eyebrows flew up. "Oh, wow."

He eyed me for a moment before shaking his head. "I know."

Lifting my hands in surrender, I took a step back. "I didn't say a word."

"I usually just say, 'In combat,' and leave it at that. It becomes a fallen-soldier hero story that way. The moment someone hears the details, they're tuned out."

"I'm not tuned out. I'm listening. Maybe a little more closely than before because that was an unexpected twist."

"That's dark." He pointed at me. "I knew I liked you."

"What's not to like?" I tilted my head to the side. "Please let your mom know that your babysitter entertained you."

He groaned. "They did say *entertain,* didn't they?"

With pursed lips, I folded my arms over my chest. "Yep."

"Well, if it helps, you didn't just entertain me, you kept it real and shared with me. So, I felt like I should do the same with you."

"That's the only reason you told me the truth and didn't let me think your friend was a war hero or something? Now *that's* dark," I scoffed.

He smiled, seemingly amused.

"Do you have a phone number that we can exchange?" he asked boldly.

I gave him a quizzical look.

I wasn't interested, and I had my reasons.

He was cute, but way too young-looking for me. I was going to be thirty in a couple of months, and he looked like he was just able to buy drinks yesterday. He was forward and courageous, but his timing was off. He asked me how my sister died and then asked me for my number. He was employed, but I didn't do long-distance relationships or date men in the military. I needed too much time and attention for that. Regardless of all that, his mom was my mom's close friend. If anything were to go wrong between us, it would undoubtedly affect that relationship.

And if it's hard to make new friends as a twenty-nine-year-old, I can't imagine how hard it is to make friends as a sixty-year-old.

"You're asking me for my number at a memorial party for my

sister." I pointed. "In front of a picture of my sister." I twisted my face. "Really?"

"You're right," he agreed, frowning. "I don't know what I was thinking."

"It was probably all the emotions of us sharing our feelings," I guessed.

He smiled, but it didn't reach his eyes. "Yeah."

His smile faded as he stared at the picture of Aniyah.

"You want to talk about it?" I asked.

He turned to me. "About what?"

"About him . . . Keyshawn."

"There's not really much to say. He met a woman and thought she was the truth. Asked her for her number on a whim. She gave it to him, and that was that. When he found out she was married, he was already in love with her. So, even though he should've stopped seeing her, he didn't. They got reckless and sloppy, I guess. All I know is that the husband came home and found his Black ass on top of his wife." Marcus shook his head. "Ended his life right there."

Wide-eyed, I was uncertain of what to even say to that. "Wow. I'm . . . I'm sorry."

"Yeah, me too."

He was quiet.

We both were.

Staring at Aniyah's photo, we were in our own little worlds.

"There you two are," my mom said in a singsong tone. "I found them, Liz!" She turned back to us. "Glad to see you two getting along."

"Mrs. James," Marcus said politely. "You have an amazing daughter." Looking and then signaling down the hall, he gave my mom another smile. "If you could let my mother know I'll be waiting for her in the car, I would greatly appreciate it."

My mother looked absolutely stunned. "Oh, what? You're not staying? I thought . . . I think your mom thinks something different. Um, I'll get her."

She took off running down the hall.

Marcus turned to me. "It was nice to meet you, Aaliyah."

"It was nice to meet you as well."

"Maybe next time . . ." He let the sentence trail off.

I smirked. "Maybe."

By the time my mom had returned with Liz, Marcus was already gone. Liz ran out the door to her son, and my mom gave me a look.

"What?" I replied in an exasperated whisper.

"Everyone, come quick!" one of my cousins yelled, causing a stampede into the backyard.

She shook her head before taking off toward the commotion. I made my way outside last.

Two hours later, I was fully stuffed from grilled meats and vegetables, delicious sides, and mouthwatering desserts. I'd come in to get away from the nosiness and constant nitpicking of my life. It never failed to happen at an event celebrating Aniyah. But I was genuinely surprised by how I always became the hot topic.

Staring at the beautiful picture of my older sister, I reflected over the last six months of my life. I knew what I wanted. I knew what I deserved. I knew the path I was on was the right one. But a few hours at my parents' house with my dusty uncle and nosy aunts always managed to turn my life into a competition with my sister's.

I was never going to be Aniyah. I never wanted to be Aniyah. And the only person in my family who ever fully encouraged that was Aniyah.

I missed her.

I missed our chats.

I missed our days on the water.

Seeing pictures of Aniyah always put me in a reflective mood, but seeing the picture of her on the yacht affected me differently.

"This one was always my favorite," my grandmother said, startling me.

"Nana!" I gasped, putting my hand to my chest. "You scared me."

She was catlike. Her petite frame made her light on her feet. I'd been in the living room alone for almost fifteen minutes and hadn't heard her come in.

"What are you scared for, doll baby?" she teased, standing beside me. "You know that means you ain't living right?"

I twisted my lips into a smile and lifted my shoulders. "I mean . . ."

She playfully swatted at my arm. "Aaliyah!"

"I'm kidding, I'm kidding." With a sigh, I shifted my focus back to the large portrait I'd been staring at since I'd arrived. "This was my favorite, too."

"She loved that boat. You both did. I don't know how y'all could stand being in all that water." She shook her head. "But ever since you were little, you loved it."

My grandmother got seasick easily and never learned to swim. Needless to say, she was not a fan of boats. My mom didn't swim, but she wanted her daughters to be comfortable with water. So, we had swim lessons, and we spent a lot of time on Uncle Al's yacht.

"Remember when she wanted to get married on that thing?" Nana recalled, her eyes twinkling.

My lips spread into a smile. "You and Mom shut that down quickly."

"It wasn't going to hold all two hundred and fifty people! It barely holds eight!"

I laughed. "But I think doing a photo shoot on it for her bridal shower was a much better decision."

"Yes, it was. Even from the dock, people stopped and watched. All eyes were on her, and she was the center of attention," my grandma pointed out. "She was having her Cinderella moment."

"Yeah," I agreed.

"Everyone deserves to have a few Cinderella moments. Not just on your wedding day either."

"Aniyah definitely had plenty of those." I pointed to the picture. "I've never seen this picture this big before."

"Yeah. Your mama got it blown up for today. She didn't tell you?"

I shook my head. "No."

"I can't get over how much you two look alike," my grandma mused. "Like twins!"

I focused on the large portrait of my sister. "Twins is going a little far."

"Twins is *definitely* going too far," my uncle commented as he entered the living room. "Aaliyah and Aniyah ain't no damn twins!"

My grandma whipped around, glaring at her oldest child. "We weren't talking to you, Albert," she admonished him.

"Unless you're talking about that movie with, uh . . . what's his name? Arnold? Arnold from the *Terminated* movies and, uh . . . the other one. The short one." Uncle Al snapped his fingers. "Danny DeVine!"

Like usual, he was loud and wrong.

"You mind your manners," she warned as he took a seat in the leather recliner in the corner.

"Aniyah knew what was important, and Aaliyah doesn't," he complained. "I'm just keeping it real. Aaliyah knows."

"Mom!" my mother called my grandmother from the kitchen. "Mom!"

She started walking out of the room, her eyes fixated on her son. She wagged her finger at him. "You stop it right now!"

"Aw, don't be so sensitive! I'm just playing around! Aaliyah knows I'm playing around," he chuckled as she left the room. When he shifted his gaze to me, he leaned forward in the chair. "You know I like to joke. But I do want to get serious about something."

I crossed my arms over my chest. "What?"

"What are you doing with your life?"

I made a face. "What is that supposed to mean?"

"You two are completely different." He pointed at the portrait of Aniyah. "Your sister had a plan. We weren't worried about her. But you . . ." He shook his head. "You do have Aniyah's same beautiful face; I'll give you that. But your sister always watched her weight, and you are just . . ." He gestured to my size-twenty curves. "You're heading down a dangerous path."

My eyes bulged. "What?"

If I'm on a dangerous path, what path are you on? I asked him silently as I eyed his beer belly.

If I would've said what I was thinking, everyone would've said I was in the wrong. And while he always meant well, my sixty-five-year-old uncle never mastered the art of speaking to people. He didn't have tact or kindness at the forefront of his mind when he spoke. He always offered up unsolicited advice under the guise of jokes and tough love, but if someone did the same to him in return, he'd be mad. And if I advised him with the same jokes and tough love about his love life, everyone would say I was disrespecting my elder.

"A dangerous path?" I scoffed. "I went to the doctor for a physical last month, and I'm healthy. Documented and on file, I'm healthy. When was your last appoint—"

"Ain't no way," he interrupted loudly. His gruff voice was full of amusement. "You're a beautiful girl! But you're a big girl. And you've just been getting bigger and bigger. That can't be healthy!"

"That's a lie," I told him, putting my hands on my rounded hips. "I've maintained the same weight for the last few years."

"Well, for the last few years you should've been working on *losing* the weight. It gets harder to get it off after thirty, and at the rate you're going, you're going to end up on that show, living that one-thousand-pound life."

He had some nerve.

"Now, Uncle Al . . ."

"That was a joke. I don't mean no harm!" He threw his hands up and sat back in the chair. "But now I'm being serious, Aaliyah. I'm serious." He searched my face. "And I know you got something to say. So, say what's on your mind, but just listen first. I'm worried about you."

"There's nothing to be worried about."

"Yes, there is, and I'm worried!" His voice boomed, carrying through the house. "You don't have a husband or any prospects or anything. You don't think we sit around worried about what's going to become of you?"

"What?" My eyes widened because I couldn't have heard what I thought I heard. "What's going to become of me?"

He cocked his head to the side. "We're going to find you somebody."

"That's the last thing I'd want."

"Well, maybe it's what you need. Because it's looking like you're not having any luck on your own. And you know what it is, don't you?"

I sighed loudly and started to leave the room. "We're not having this conversation."

"If no one else is going to say it, I'm going to say it. It's your weight. Your weight has something to do with it."

I stopped in my tracks.

With family members joyously entertaining themselves outside, my uncle came into the house to tell me that I didn't have a man because I was fat.

To say I was dumbfounded was an understatement.

Turning to face him, I was ready to tell him off.

He pointed at the picture of Aniyah. "At thirty, she was married and pregnant. They were living in that big ol' house. She was running a successful business and making good money. That's why I gave Aniyah the yacht. She was ready to handle something like that, and she had somebody. She had a man to help her and to help her take care of the yacht. You'll be thirty in a couple months, and what do you have?"

I didn't know if I was more irritated by the pity in his eyes or the audacity of his words.

My jaw dropped. "You're not serious. You're *not* serious!"

The sharpness of my tone seemed to trigger something in him. He slowly pushed himself up. "Now don't get upset. I'm not saying this to hurt you." He took a couple of steps toward me. "I'm just worried about you. We're all just worried about you. That's all."

"What are we all worried about, Al?" Mom asked as she entered the room with my grandma in tow.

With a frown, he turned around and looked at my mother. "It's time to be honest with her, Alicia. Instead of you and Darryl silently worrying about her and her future, you should've been talking to her—"

"Al, what is the meaning of this?" my mom snapped, interrupting him. Putting her hands on her hips, she shifted her gaze between me and my uncle before she glared at her older brother. "Why are you in here running your mouth? This isn't your business!"

He poked his chest out. "Since you and Darryl haven't done it, I decided to have the conversation with her. Especially since Marcus—"

"Albert, you need to mind your manners," my grandma scolded him. "That's not your place."

"What is going on?" I questioned, looking around the room.

Everyone fell silent.

My uncle muttered under his breath and then turned to me. "It's not just me concerned about your condition."

"What condition?" I replied before turning to my mother. "What is he talking about?"

"Aaliyah, we'll talk about it later," she answered gently.

"You don't solve problems by ignoring them," Uncle Al said loudly.

"I said I'll talk to her about it later," Mom snapped at him.

The uneasy feeling settled over me. "No. I want to talk about it now. What's going on? What condition?"

My mom shook her head. "It's just something I wanted to wait until after the party is over to talk to you about."

I folded my arms across my chest. "No, let's talk now since all of you seem to know, and I'm the only one not privy to this 'condition' that I'm allegedly afflicted with."

She adjusted her glasses on the bridge of her nose. "Your uncle should've never brought it up. It wasn't his place." She took a breath. "We were having a conversation—"

"Who is 'we'?" I wondered.

"Your father and I." When I nodded, she continued, "And we were discussing how much we're looking forward to the period of our lives when we get grandchildren. We started talking about the fact that it's been a long time since you've mentioned dating anyone seriously—"

"Years!" Al chimed in unnecessarily.

"We questioned if that was in the cards for us if you aren't with anyone." She lifted her shoulders and looked around. "And then when your grandmother and uncle came into the kitchen, we got to talking about and reminiscing about Aniyah's plans."

"Ah. Okay." I nodded, connecting the dots.

So that's why Uncle Al was mentioning Aniyah being married and how they were planning for a baby.

My lip curled. "But I'm not Aniyah—"

"And that's all I was trying to tell you!" My uncle jumped in, interrupting me. "You need to get yourself together so that you can be on track like your sister. Which is why Marcus—"

"Albert!" My mother glared at her brother before turning back to me. Her face softened. "He had no right to bring that up to you. Especially not today. Like this."

"Why does he keep saying stuff at all? And what about Marcus?" I asked, my frown deepening as my mom and her brother bickered.

"Did either of you even ask the girl what she wants?" Nana looked between her children before looking at me. "Do you want a husband, Aaliyah? Is that what you want right now?"

All eyes were on me.

Last month's fiasco with Matthew flashed through my mind, sticking out like a sore thumb.

"Yes, I do," I admitted. "And I would love to have met the right man to be my husband, but I haven't. And I'm not willing to settle. There's nothing wrong with that."

"There's nothing at all wrong with that," Nana confirmed with a nod. "And do you want kids?"

"Yeah, one day." My biological clock ticked faintly in the background of my mind. "But again, I don't want to have kids with just anyone. I'd like to do that with my husband, and I'm not going to marry just anyone. So, it goes back to what I said before—I'm not willing to settle."

My grandma beamed at me. "That's my girl!"

I flashed her a small smile, but before "thank you" could cross my lips, Uncle Al opened his big mouth again.

"Your grandma was married before thirty. Your mom was married before thirty. Your cousins Tamara and Jonelle were married before thirty. Your sister was married before thirty. My first wife wasn't yet thirty when I married her," my uncle pointed out. "And

I'm telling you this because I love you. You need to get it together so you can get what it is that you say you want."

"Albert, that's enough!" Mom huffed, rolling her eyes.

"I'm just telling her the truth!" He threw his hands up in the air. "Sometimes we need a dose of reality. And her reality is that she's getting up there."

"She's just going to be thirty on her birthday," my grandma responded, dismissing him with a wave of her hand.

My uncle looked at her incredulously. "I'm not just talking about her age. I'm talking about her weight! How is she going to get a man who can take care of her at her size?"

My mom and grandmother looked horrified.

"Do not talk about her like that!" Mom snapped.

"I used to talk to you like that"—he pointed to her slim thick frame—"and you got the weight off you. And you managed to keep it off! Then you found you a good husband and had two beautiful babies. I want the same thing for my niece."

"Albert!" My grandma barked his name, and it wiped the expression off his face. Her body might have been small, but her voice was mighty. "Can I have a word with you in the kitchen?"

She turned on her heel and stormed out—slowly, but still.

"I'm grown now, Mama. You don't have to be yelling at me like this," he said as he followed her.

When it was just me and my mom, she shook her head. "If he weren't my brother, I would wring his neck!"

"Yeah, Uncle Al can be an ass—tronomical jerk." Remembering who I was talking to, I'd quickly changed my wording. "But why were you discussing my love life with everyone?"

"It wasn't with everyone. It was just with family."

I squeezed my eyes shut and exhaled. "Okay, that's not the point. You were telling them my business when you know I hate people in my business."

"It's not that big of a deal."

"To you. It's not that big of a deal *to you*."

"Well, I'm sorry," she apologized with a tone that seemed like she was indeed not sorry. "But honestly, we weren't talking about you.

Your father and I were talking about how excited we were to become grandparents. And when we lost that, we were hoping to have that opportunity again. So, by default, you are the only person that can make that a reality for us. So it wasn't that we were discussing you, per se. We were actually talking about us." She tilted her head. "But now that we're on the subject, how did you like Marcus?"

Confused as to what that had to do with anything, I balled my face up. "What?"

"Marcus will be back here in time for your birthday party. He's ending his military career and then moving to Richland. And since he doesn't know anyone in the area, I've extended an invitation to him."

My eyes bulged. "You invited him to my birthday party? The one I'm throwing for myself?"

"Yes."

"You invited him to the dinner or the party?"

"Both."

Because she didn't raise a fool, I didn't say what I wanted to say. But my mom had some nerve.

Taking a deep breath, I attempted a different approach. "Why?"

"Why what?" she asked.

"Why did you invite Marcus, a man I don't know, to my thirtieth birthday dinner, knowing it's an intimate gathering of people I'm close with?"

"Because he doesn't know anyone and"—she put her hands on her hips—"you could benefit from making a new friend. Especially one who is single and eligible . . ."

I stared at her for a second. "Was this supposed to be a setup?"

"Noooooo!"

My mother was always a terrible liar.

"Mom . . ." I pinched the bridge of my nose. "At Aniyah's celebration? I can't. I don't need your help finding a date."

"But it looks like you could use some help finding a *husband*."

My jaw dropped. *Wow.*

I was too stunned to speak.

"All I'm saying is that you aren't getting any younger," she continued. "Tomorrow isn't promised, Aaliyah. If you want the husband and the kids, you may need to look outside of your comfort zone. And from everything Liz has told me over the years, Marcus sounds like a good man. And I wouldn't be doing my job as your mother if I didn't at least try to make the introduction. He's looking to settle down. You're looking to settle down. So . . ." She gestured with her hands as if she wanted me to fill in the blanks.

I felt like my head was about to pop from my neck.

Closing my eyes, I exhaled roughly. "This is unbelievable," I muttered under my breath.

"What was that?"

My eyes flew open at the sound of my mother's stern voice. "Huh?" I played dumb.

She pursed her lips. "Young lady, you are not too old for me to get in your ass for that tone, so watch it."

"I'm sorry," I murmured, backtracking. "I'm just frustrated."

She made a face. "Frustrated that I'm looking out for you and your well-being?"

"Frustrated that you're trying to set me up by inviting a man I don't know to my birthday party without asking me about it. Frustrated that you tried to set me up on a blind date during Aniyah's celebration. Frustrated that we're even having this conversation! And you know what . . . how do you know I don't have someone?"

"She don't got nobody!" my uncle commented from the doorway with a hearty chuckle.

Mom and I both startled as we whipped around to face him.

"If she did, she would've said something," he continued. "Now she's just talking out the side of her neck."

"And you're talking out the side of your ass," I retorted, sneering at my uncle.

"Aaliyah!" my mom snapped. "Both of you need to stop this!"

He lifted his hands. "Listen, if you have somebody, prove it. Better yet, if you have somebody, I'll give you the yacht for your birthday."

My stomach lurched.

"Albert, enough is enough!" Mom yelled before I had a chance to respond.

"What? I gave it to Aniyah because she had a husband, and I'd be willing to give it to Aaliyah if she can give us hope that she can get a man."

Pointing and with narrowed eyes, she yelled, "Shut your mouth and get out!"

"Albert, you said you were going to help Darryl on the grill!" my grandma called from somewhere else in the house. "Go outside and help him! Stop being nosy!"

"She better hope that Marcus boy like 'em thick so we can get her married off," he muttered as he shuffled away.

I turned back to my mother.

Pointing in the direction of the door, I hissed, "To make matters worse, instead of talking to me and asking me if I was interested, you talked to Dad, Nana, and Uncle Al."

"Again, the topic wasn't about you, per se. But okay!" She sighed. "It all happened fast, but I can understand why you would feel that way."

It wasn't an apology, but it felt like an acknowledgment of some sort.

I nodded. "Thank you."

"But I've already invited him, so he *is* coming."

Closing my eyes for a second, I sighed. "My main issue isn't with him coming to the party," I relented. "My issue is with you inviting him to the dinner. It's with the setup in general and the fact that you're trying to marry me off as if I'm a burden on the family. So, I really hope you just told Marcus and Liz that this is an invitation from you and nothing more."

"You don't want to date him? Fine!" She tossed her hands up flippantly. "You said you were inviting a lot of people to the party—"

"A lot of people that I know," I interjected. "That's the difference!"

"Well, when you see him again, if it's not a love match, there may be someone else there for him. Either way, I think the party will be a nice way to welcome him to the area. What's the harm in that?"

"There's no harm in that."

"So why wouldn't you be open to giving him a chance? Why would you let someone at your party get first dibs on an eligible bachelor when Liz and I think Marcus could be a good fit for you?"

So, she has *talked to Liz about it. What the fuck?*

"Because there's someone else," I blurted out.

My mother's eyes narrowed suspiciously. "Who?"

"You'll see at my party."

My mother opened her mouth to speak, but the doorbell rang.

Rolling her shoulders back, she plastered a smile on her face. "We're celebrating your sister today. Let's focus on that."

"Gladly," I mumbled as she went to open the front door.

3

I left the cookout for my sister while my mom was in conversation with some family members and my dad was playing dominos with his brothers. Lifting my hand in a wave, I said goodbye to some cousins deep in conversation on the deck. With a to-go plate in hand, I eased my way back into the house. I stopped briefly in the kitchen to grab some aluminum foil and then I continued my trek out of the house.

"Your grandmama and mama are on my ass because of what I said to you," Uncle Al said just as I closed the front door behind me.

Turning around slowly, I saw him standing at the bottom of the stairs smoking a cigarette.

"Well, that's between the three of you," I told him as I stomped down the steps.

"Yeah, well, they'll cool off." He flicked his cigarette and then walked with me to my car. "I'm more concerned about you right now."

"I don't need your concern or your pity," I snapped irritably.

His face crumpled in confusion. "I'm coming from a place of love, Aaliyah. You know I love you"—he grabbed my arm—"don't you?"

I sighed. "Yes."

"I didn't mean no harm."

"Okay."

"I just want you to have a good life." He let go of my arm and searched my face. "Do you remember my second wife's daughter Macy? Big, heavyset one? She's about forty-five now, but the last time you saw her, you might've been ten. So, she was . . ." He looked like he was doing the math in his head. "About twenty-five. She was about twenty-five when you last saw her."

I nodded. "Yeah. I remember her."

"I done seen her at the store a couple months back." He shook his head. "I hadn't seen her in about seven years. She's struggling and raising up those two kids by herself. She ain't got nobody. And she was always a good girl. A real sweet one with a good head on her shoulders. And now that she's older, she may find somebody or maybe not. When men are younger, they're looking for someone a little fitter. She may find somebody soon, somebody who just wants companionship. But she's spent half her life without somebody to come home to. And do you know why she doesn't have a husband to take care of her?"

I put my hands on my hips. "No, I don't. And you don't either unless she told you. Did she tell you?"

"Yes! She told me she was depressed and lonely." He started listing off what she'd said with his fingers. "She said she didn't have help with the kids. She said she was struggling with her diet. She said she was going through a hard time. And when I asked her about a husband, she said she wished she could find a good one to date, let alone marry!"

"Okay, but she could be depressed, lonely, not have help with kids, going through a hard time, and not be able to find a husband if she were thinner. I have friends of all sizes who could say the same thing. Just because a woman is fat doesn't mean she can't get a man. She just may not have found the man she wants. Automatically assuming that she doesn't have a man because she can't get one because of her weight is the problem."

"No, Macy's weight *is* the problem!"

"So, she told you all that other stuff, but she didn't tell you that her weight was the problem. And yet you're *still* saying her weight is the problem?"

"She didn't have to tell me; I have eyes!" he exclaimed, his voice getting louder. "It's because of her size, and I don't want that for you. I mean it."

"Why are you convinced that it's her weight that's the cause of her depression and loneliness? How do you know it's not work stress, life stress, parenting stress, et cetera? It's—"

"What I'm saying is that I don't want that to be you," he interrupted me with a fierce sincerity. "You are the only blood niece I got left. You are the only child your parents have left. I just want you to have a real shot at life. I don't want you to be alone. That's all I meant. I don't mean no harm. I just don't want Macy's life to be your life. I'm worried about your future. I'm saying this because I love you."

I shook my head. "Uncle Al, I'm going home. I'm not doing this with you. You don't have a clue what you're talking about. I'm good. And you can either choose to believe that or not. Either way, I'm going home." I sidestepped him. "Now if you'll excuse me."

"I know you lied to your mama. You don't got somebody coming to your birthday party."

I unlocked my car door. "Have a good night, Uncle Al."

"I meant what I said about the yacht, Aaliyah," he restated.

My stomach lurched again.

I paused for only a second before I resumed opening my car door.

"If you don't have anyone, I can't give it to you," he continued. "So I'm going to sell it."

I shook my head and climbed into the driver's seat. "Goodbye, Uncle Al."

"Aight, Aaliyah," he sighed, sadness tugging at his words. "I love you."

"Yeah, love you, too," I said just before slamming the door shut.

I started the engine immediately. I watched my uncle make his way to the backyard before I backed out of the driveway and headed home.

Listening to music on the drive didn't help. The long, hot shower I took when I got home didn't help. Eating my cookout leftovers didn't help. Climbing in bed and watching a movie didn't help. No matter what I did, I couldn't shake what my mom and uncle said.

My uncle's fear was startling. I didn't subscribe to his line of thinking, but I was alarmed by the seriousness of his plea. It wasn't a surprise to me that people felt like being a fat woman meant lonely or desperate or willing to settle. Society pushed that narrative often. I grew up with a bigger body in the shadow of a slim sister. I went to a PWI for high school, so I didn't even realize the extent of how fine I was until I got to college. So, although my uncle's worry and concern blindsided me, that thought process wasn't new to me. But the fact that he felt like he needed to worry based off my mom's concerns bothered me.

Because when did my mom start having concerns?

My mother raised me to have unyielding high self-esteem, an abundance of self-confidence, and an independent spirit. I was well aware that I wasn't the beauty standard growing up. I was too fat, too smart, too Black. But I never doubted my beauty. And because I was happy with who I was on the inside and the outside, my mom assured me that I would find the person I was meant to be with. I just had to have faith and be patient.

And I believed that.

I'd always been a good person with a good sense of humor, so people gravitated toward me. But when I got to Hamilton University, I was quickly and immediately reminded that beauty comes in all shades, shapes, and sizes. It was no longer just my family and friends recognizing my beauty. It was everyone.

It was the boys at school actively hitting on me, asking me out, and complimenting me. It was the men at my internship and part-time job flirting with me. It was the older men wanting to take me out and fly me out. I was overwhelmed with attention, and when I got used to it, I figured out what I wanted and moved accordingly.

I dated.

I dated a lot.

And when I got my heart broken, I took a little break and then started dating again. And everything was cool until it wasn't.

Between college and my first job after graduation, I met men all the time, and I dated for sport. After things ended with my first love, I dated for security. But it got old quickly. Dating just didn't have the appeal that it once had. I was very clear on what I wanted, but I kept finding myself out with men who didn't want the same thing that I did.

Because of how invested my parents became in my love life after

Aniyah passed away, I stopped telling them about every little date. They were a little too hopeful when they heard the same name more than once, and they were a little too disappointed when I mentioned a new name. So, I made the decision to just wait until there was someone serious in my life.

It was better for everyone that way.

They hadn't heard about anyone new since my last boyfriend, because I wasn't taking any of the other ones seriously. After dating Matthew and figuring out we weren't compatible, I decided to start the year off by focusing on myself. I didn't want to date, but I did want to find a partner. And I'd just decided to start looking again after what happened with Matthew a few weeks ago. I would've told them that, but it wouldn't have made a difference. They didn't want to hear about the potential of a future boyfriend. They wanted to hear about the potential of a first grandchild.

That's their issue, not mine.

My family's comments got under my skin more than I wanted to admit. I spent the rest of the weekend in my head, replaying the conversations. I was going to forever be in Aniyah's shadow. She was always the perfect one, even more so after death. I'd made peace with that a long time ago. I wasn't where Aniyah was at this age. I hadn't achieved what she had achieved. I hadn't hit the benchmarks she had hit. It was clear that she did things the way they preferred; she did things the right way. But even still, they never made me feel like she was better or I was worse. I was never made to feel as though I was less loved or less accepted because of it. It was clear that I was just different from Aniyah. However, between the setup, the constant sibling comparison, and the collective effort to marry me off, it was unsettling, and I didn't know where it was all coming from.

I was irritated that my uncle didn't know how to talk to people at his big age. He was out of line, and his Christmas gift was going to reflect it. But it was my mom that really got to me.

I was irked that my mom was trying to hook me up with a man she didn't even know. I was bothered that she was talking about my love life with the family as if I were a lost cause. I was hurt by the fact that she seemed to have lost the faith and patience she sowed in me when I was younger. But on Sunday night, as I was stretched out in the middle of the bed, I realized why I couldn't shake the impromptu intervention of my love life.

I knew I wanted a husband, so I needed to find a boyfriend. I knew in order to find a boyfriend, I needed to date. And in order to find a date, I needed to engage with men in a more intentional way. But I wasn't really interested in trying anything new. So, to have my mom randomly throw the same sentiments to me that I'd been wrestling with was jarring, to say the least.

"Out of nowhere, my mom said if I wanted the husband and the kids, I may need to look outside of my comfort zone. And then she proceeded to tell me she invited a strange man to my birthday party," I told my best friends Monday morning as I drove to work.

Jazmyn Payne had called to ask about Aniyah's celebration, and I'd conferenced in Nina Ford so I could tell them both what happened. They were expecting a sentimental recap and ended up getting an earful about my family's assessment of my love life.

"Oh, wow!" Jazz reacted. "Your uncle was dead wrong. And your mom . . . called you out!" She paused. "I mean, she was wrong, but in reference to you getting out there again, wasn't she basically saying the same thing you were saying the other day?"

"Yeah," I replied, slapping the steering wheel while I sat at the red light. "And that's one of the reasons it got under my skin."

"The other reason is because she's kinda right, huh?" Nina suggested. The loud music from the gym speakers pulsated behind her question.

"Yeah," I admitted through gritted teeth. "She was wrong in her delivery, approach, and reasoning, but yeah."

She laughed. "So, if me and your mom said you need to get out of your comfort zone, maybe you should try . . . I don't know . . . getting out of your comfort zone!"

"I know I told you two that I wanted to find something real by my birthday, and I know getting out of my comfort zone is my best bet, but . . ." My voice trailed off as I flashed back to my exchange with my family. "The way my family made me feel like a failure because I'm not where Aniyah was in life by this age made me so mad."

"I know how family can be," Jazz offered sympathetically. "But you know you're not a failure."

"Not at all," Nina chimed in. "And while they were dead wrong for that and your uncle was on some bullshit, your mom wasn't wrong about you needing to get out more."

I took a left turn and frowned. "I know I *need* to do something different. But the issue is that I don't *want* to do anything different. I have eight weeks before my birthday, and I realized that I hate dating. I'm just ready to skip to the relationship part of it."

"If you hate dating, you're not doing it right," Nina commented.

"No, Aaliyah's right," Jazmyn agreed. "Dating sucks."

"Dating doesn't suck," she assured us both. "Aaliyah, you need to do something new, and, Jazz, you need to get back out there. Both of you took yourselves out the game and for what?"

"I got divorced," Jazz answered incredulously.

"You got divorced almost two years ago," Nina argued. "It's time to move on."

"Nina!" I gasped.

I mean, I agreed with the sentiment, but it could've been delivered more tactfully.

"What?" she wailed. "You know I'm right."

"Yes, but have some couth," I joked as I pulled into the parking structure connected to my office building.

They both laughed.

"What's funny is that my aunt said something like that to me yesterday." Jazmyn's voice had been sounding dejected lately. Even when she was amused, there was still a hint of sadness that remained. "She was in and out of sleep, and that was the last thing she said to me. It was time to move on."

Jazmyn's favorite aunt had been sick for the better part of two years. She'd been on hospice three times, and each time, she made a miraculous recovery. Jazz always spent a week of her summer vacation in her hometown. Up until her aunt got sick, she loved being there. Since then, whenever she'd call, she was just looking for a distraction and she would avoid talking about her aunt. So, the fact that she mentioned her was promising.

"How's your aunt doing?" I wondered as I pulled into a parking spot.

"She's the same," she answered.

"I'm glad she isn't getting worse. That's a blessing," Nina pointed out.

I nodded even though they couldn't see me. "Yeah, that is a blessing."

"It is. I don't know what I'm going to do when she goes. She's looking good, though, so hopefully I'll have her for a while longer."

"The time you're there with her will be good for the both of you. Time heals," I replied.

"And the advice that your aunt gives you is invaluable," Nina responded. "And I'm hoping that since you listen to her advice and she told you to get some new dick in your life, you'll actually do it."

Jazz burst out laughing. "That's not exactly what she said."

"But I'm sure it's what she meant," Nina reasoned. "I want both of you to reframe your thinking when it comes to dating. I've been telling both of you to get it together for years now, and this weekend, your mom and aunt also told you to get it together. That's a sign!"

"I just don't know—"

"You just don't know what?" Nina interrupted comically. "Because dick is literally everywhere. What are you looking for? Big? Medium? Thick? Curved? What? There are so many men who would happily throw dick your way. You both could have so many options, but y'all aren't dating right."

"Well, I want good dick," Jazmyn specified.

"And I want a good man," I chimed in.

"Well, I can't guarantee all that. You said you wanted dick, and you said you wanted a man. All I'm saying is that there are men out here, and you can't discover if the man or the dick is good if you aren't out there mixing and mingling."

"I'm not trying to mix or mingle," I complained, watching some of my coworkers enter the building. I lowered my voice, so I wasn't overheard. “There’s got to be an easier way than dating. I want the shortcut. I just want to find my person and start our lives together.”

“How are you going to do that if you don’t date?” she questioned. “It would be different if you didn’t want the husband and the kids, but you do, so you have to get out there and date, Aaliyah.”

“Been there, done that. Don’t want to do it again,” Jazz interrupted.

“I was talking to Aaliyah,” Nina countered. “But for you, you need to get back out there and knock the cobwebs off your pussy! You’ve been saying since your spring break that when school let out for the summer, you were going to get your back blown out. But you ain’t been nowhere or seen no one to make it happen. As far as I can tell, your back is fully intact, and a lone tumbleweed is blowing right across that cat of yours.”

I had tears in my eyes, and my body was slumped against the steering wheel. I was cracking up.

“Not tumbleweeds, Nina! You’re going too far now,” Jazmyn protested, amusement in her tone. “And I’m going to be working on it once I get back in town. It’s about to be July. I still have two full months of summer left.”

Nina clicked her tongue. “I don’t know what I’m going to do with you two! One of you wants dick. One of you wants a relationship. And neither one of you are out here doing anything about it. Just letting time, dick, and dates pass you by.”

“Nina, we get it! It’s too early in the morning for you to be coming at us like this,” I pleaded when I caught my breath.

“Well, rise and shine,” she laughed. “But let me give you some real talk—both of you have to get out of your own way to get what you want.”

Noticing the time, I opened my car door and eased out. “I hear what you’re saying, but—”

“Hello, Ms. James,” a familiar voice called out to me before I could finish my sentence. “I have a question for you.”

With my phone pressed to one ear, I hoisted my shoulder bag farther on my arm and turned my entire body toward the voice.

Knowing I couldn't finish my sentence, let alone finish the call, I smiled at the man who approached me.

"Hey, I just got to work, so I'm going to call y'all later," I said as I watched my supervisor get closer.

They said their goodbyes through giggles, and I disconnected the call.

Shoving my phone into the side pocket of my bag, I flashed him a smile. "Good morning, Jeremy." I waited until he caught up, and then he fell into step with me. "What's up?"

"That was a great save you submitted last week."

I nodded. "Thanks." I glanced at him suspiciously. "I appreciate it."

"I want to get your opinion on something." He grabbed the door and held it open for me to walk through. "Or, more specifically, someone."

My stomach turned at his request as we approached the elevator. "Opinion on what?"

"How do you think Grace Bowers is doing with the company?"

"Who?"

"She's a new developer." When the name and role didn't ring a bell, he cocked his head to the side. "She's the developer who created the design your team worked on."

"Oh! Okay." I nodded. "I know who you're talking about now."

"What are your thoughts?"

"She's only been with the company a month. I haven't gotten a chance to watch her work or work closely with her. So, I don't really have any thoughts on her, but she seems to be working out the kinks of what's being asked of her. She's still new and adjusting. It's only been a month."

He nodded thoughtfully. "Okay."

"Why? What's up?" I asked even though my gut told me what was going on.

"This is the second mistake we've caught, and now the manager's meeting is coming up and . . ." His voice trailed off as the elevator dinged. He gave me a curt nod to let me know the subject was closed. "Anyway, good work last week."

"Thank you."

He went to the second floor, and I went through the main door to my first-floor office space that I shared with four others at Encompass Tech.

"Good morning," I greeted the programming team.

There were a few low good-mornings and a grunt from the corner.

It was a typical Monday welcome from them.

With a tight smile, I went to my desk on the far right, near the window. I turned on my computer, unpacked my bag, and prepared for the workday. My desk phone rang, and I frowned until I saw who it was.

"Good morning, Ramona," I answered.

"Good morning! How are you? How was your weekend?"

I smiled. "I'm well, thank you. My weekend was nice. How was yours?"

"It was great! Are you coming to the second floor at any time today?"

My interest was piqued. "I can . . . Everything okay?"

"Yes, but something happened this weekend, and you are the first person I thought of."

"What happened?"

"It's not bad." She giggled. "Just come up here when you get a chance."

"Okay," I agreed. "Let me check my email, and then I'll be up."

I logged into my account, and somehow, I had almost one hundred unread messages. Every single one of them came after five o'clock on Friday, as if the weekend didn't exist. With a shake of my head, I started combing through each one.

Ninety minutes later, I finished going through my stuff, and the rest of the IT office seemed to wake up. They were a relatively quiet group of men, and since Constance was out on maternity leave, I was the only woman in the department. But my work environment was great, and my experience with them was far better than any other job I'd worked. We exchanged a laugh when someone pointed out an email that we'd all been copied on. We scheduled a meeting for eleven o'clock, and I smiled at the ease of everything with us.

My first job out of college, I was treated as if I were too young, too inexperienced, and too Black to successfully do my job. At the job I had prior to landing at Encompass Tech, I was told that my fatness was going to hinder my ability to move up in the company. And every day during my time there, I had to fight for my voice to be heard over the rest. So, I developed a thick skin, zero tolerance for bullshit, and the ability to make sure my voice was heard. I loved my career, and fortunately, for the last three years, I'd been happy with my coworkers and my employer.

Ahead of the meeting, I decided to go to the second floor and see what Ramona wanted. The finance office was toward the back, so I had to walk past the glass offices of the conference rooms. My supervisor was in a meeting with all the other supervisors, and it didn't look good. Averting my eyes, I continued to my destination.

"Oh, hey—you can't just walk in!" Bart Fender, Ramona's new receptionist, called out from somewhere behind me.

I glanced over my shoulder. "Okay . . ." I looked through the open door at Ramona and then back to Bart. "But she's looking right at me."

"It's fine, Bart!" Ramona yelled out from her desk.

"Oh, okay. Sorry," he mumbled under his breath as he slowed to a stop a few feet away from me. Lifting his coffee mug, he nodded at me. "You can go in."

With pursed lips, I walked into Ramona's office and closed the door behind me.

"Ignore him. Three months and he's still learning the ropes." She waved her hand in the air before her entire face lit up. "I was just about to call you again!"

"What's going on?" I asked, taking a seat across from her.

"So, remember when you stopped by my birthday party for a few minutes back in May?"

"Yes."

"Did you notice a man in black and red?"

I shook my head. "Not at all. I barely remember what you had on."

She laughed. "I understand. It's been a long month."

"Tell me about it!"

"Well, my friend in the black and red was Derrick. He asked me about someone at the party a few weeks ago, and I didn't know who he was talking about. But then he randomly brought it up again this weekend, and I realized he was talking about you. He's interested and"—she held up her hands—"no pressure. But he'd love to meet you. I told him I wasn't going to give him your last name or phone number, because I needed to check with you first. He said if you were interested in meeting him, just say the word, and he'll ask you out himself."

My eyebrows flew up. "What?"

"He said he wanted the ball to be in your court. He didn't want to put any pressure on you, so he said to let him know the time, date, and location and he'd be there. Oh! And he said that if you choose Friday, make it after five o'clock because of work."

I let out a stunned giggle. "What?"

I wasn't shocked that the man wanted to go out with me. I was more in disbelief at his approach. I loved that he knew what he wanted and wasn't afraid to go after it. But the whole thing caught me off guard.

"Yeah, I was impressed with the energy he was bringing, too. That's why I called you first thing this morning!" Grinning, Ramona swooped her relaxed hair behind her ears and leaned forward. "He's a good one. He's been single for a few months now, and I know he's serious about looking for the right woman to settle down with."

"I don't know . . ." As tempting as it sounded, I was a little hesitant about a blind date. "Do you have a picture of him?"

Her face crumpled in a sheepish expression. "I don't. And because I didn't show him anything of yours, I wouldn't feel right pulling up his social media to show you anything of his."

I nodded. "I respect that." I folded my arms over my chest and considered it for a moment. "Can I let you know?"

The phone on her desk started ringing just as she replied, "Yes, of course!"

"Saved by the bell," I joked as I rose to my feet. "I'll call you and let you know."

Lifting her hand in a wave, she answered the phone.

I made my way back to my office, and I couldn't help thinking about how all these signs were pointing to me finding my person. I took time to regroup, reflect, and refocus, and then I decided I wanted to start dating. The same week I said I was ready, my uncle said he was scared I'd end up alone, my mother said she was worried about my lack of relationships, and my best friend said I needed to get back out there.

Granted, Nina had been saying that all year, but still.

The fact that all those things happened within a few days and then my coworker tried to set me up with her friend out of the blue felt a little too coincidental. It was exactly two months, eight weeks, until my birthday. And I wanted to lock down a birthday boo.

God, is this a sign? I wondered as I sat down at my desk.

I was ready to date even though I didn't want to date. For me to get what I wanted out of life, I needed to do something. I'd taken myself out of the game. Maybe I got too comfortable during those months off because I was just not interested in doing what my friends suggested I should do to get back out there and meet men.

Starting July off with a date could be just the thing I needed to kickstart my boyfriend quest. I tapped my chin. Maybe meeting Ramona's friend was the perfect first step back into dating.

There was the potential that he was the man of my dreams. There was also the potential that he was the man of my nightmares.

I heard Nina's voice telling me to get out of my own way. I heard my mom telling me to get out of my comfort zone. I heard my uncle calling me out about not having a boyfriend or a birthday date. But most distinctly, I heard what I told myself when I started the new year. I was holding out for something real, something lasting, something magical. I told myself that when I was ready, I was going to find that for my thirtieth birthday.

And I was ready.

Before I could lose my nerve, I grabbed the phone and called Ramona. "I accept. Tell him to meet me at this new place downtown called Onyx," I blurted out. "Friday at seven thirty."

4

I hate dating.

I closed my eyes as the fruity cocktail swirled around my mouth, dancing across my taste buds. I savored it for a second before swallowing the last of the drink I'd been nursing for half an hour. Between the bartender asking me if I was still waiting for someone every five minutes and the fact that I was still waiting over thirty minutes later, I was in a mood.

"Men fucking suck," I grumbled aloud.

"Not all men," a deep voice interrupted my peaceful moment.

My eyes flew open, and my sights landed on the bartender with the toffee complexion, chiseled jaw, and goofy-ass look on his face. My cheeks heated under his gaze. I tried to look away, but the intensity of his eyes, or the intensity of my rage, kept us both locked in.

"Did I say that out loud?" I wondered.

With two long strides, he was standing directly in front of me with his arms crossed over his broad chest. I couldn't help but notice how his biceps flexed at the movement.

His smile grew as he nodded. "You did. And as a man, I'm offended."

"Well, take that up with the rest of your gender," I griped.

"Come on, don't be like that."

I eyed the bearded man warily. "I'm not being like anything."

"Do you want to order something? If you order another drink, maybe no one will notice you got stood up."

I glowered at him and his annoyingly perfect smile. "Who said I got stood up?" I snapped.

He put his hands against the bar and leaned toward me. "You've been checking your phone and the door since you got here."

"Why are you watching what I'm doing?"

"It's my job to notice things."

"It's your job to pour drinks."

He let out a chuckle and leaned a little closer. "What's your name?"

Glaring at him, I didn't immediately say anything. "Aaliyah," I finally answered.

"Aaliyah," he repeated, stretching out each syllable.

I readjusted myself on the stool and swallowed hard. A slight frown pulled on my lips. I was annoyed by how sexy it sounded as it rolled off his tongue.

I shifted my gaze for a moment, and when our eyes met again, he smirked.

"I'm Ahmad." He took a step back. "Are you going to order another drink, or are you going to keep taking a seat away from actual customers who want to drink?"

I looked around dramatically, opening my arms wide. "What customers?"

Onyx was a new bar conveniently located across the street from my luxury apartment complex downtown. It had only been open for a week, and the word hadn't spread about the place yet. There were maybe ten people in total in the building—including the bartender, a waitress, and someone hiding out in the back office.

"It's still early," he argued. "Most people don't start coming in until after eight o'clock."

I checked my phone. "Well, it's eight o'clock now."

"Just wait," he assured me. "This place will be packed."

As if on cue, the front door swung open, and two women walked in hand in hand.

"Are these all the customers you're waiting on?" I asked sarcastically.

"Yep," he replied with a smirk. "And it doesn't look like either of them is the date you're waiting on."

I sucked my teeth. "Asshole," I muttered under my breath.

Digging into my bag, I grabbed my wallet. When I saw that I never broke the hundred-dollar bill that I'd gotten from the ATM, I was even more frustrated. I wanted to throw my money on the bar and storm out. But I refused to give that man an eighty-dollar tip.

I watched him at the other end of the bar as he took the drink orders of the two women who had just entered. Shifting my gaze away from him, I stared at my reflection in the mirror that covered the wall in front of me.

What am I doing?

I'd spent two and a half hours finger coiling my thick hair. I wore a mauve dress that fit my full figure like a glove and complemented my rich mocha complexion. I wore black strappy heels that pinched my pinky toe but made my ass look incredible. I moved up my appointments, so my wax, nails, and eyebrows were fresh. All for a man that never even bothered to show up.

My phone vibrated and I startled. Seeing Nina's name dance across the screen immediately relaxed me.

"Hello?" I answered.

"What do you mean he hasn't shown up yet?" she shouted, replying to the text I sent her a few minutes prior.

"My coworker's friend hasn't shown up, and I'm about to leave," I told her. "This was a waste of time, energy, makeup, and an outfit."

"I'm sorry. Screw him. And honestly, screw your coworker, too."

"Yeah, I should've never agreed to go." I sighed, closing my eyes again. "I just wanted to meet someone, hit it off, and ring in my birthday with a man."

"And you still can. One man's fuckup is another man's opportunity. Write that down. That's quotable."

"Oh my God." I let out an amused groan. "I'm serious."

"I'm serious, too! Do you want a boyfriend, or do you just want a man for your birthday to prove your family wrong?" Nina asked.

"Both," I answered. "I mean, I don't want just anyone. And I don't want my first or second date with the guy to be my birthday party. I'm turning thirty. I'm trying to celebrate and then go to the house and get my back blown out."

I opened my eyes to find the bartender staring at me. I wasn't sure how long he'd been standing there or if he had heard me, but it didn't matter. After he called me out on being stood up, I had already decided that I was never setting foot in that establishment again.

"You don't need a boyfriend to do that," she pointed out.

"The way I'm trying to do it, it would be best if he was my man," I replied as I watched Ahmad walk over to help another customer.

She laughed. "I feel you. Well, listen, forget tonight. There's a lot that can happen in eight weeks."

"Technically seven because my party is on the eighth week."

"There's a lot that can happen in seven weeks," she corrected.

"I haven't had a boyfriend in almost three years, so the idea of me finding one this summer feels like a bit of a reach."

"Yeah, but now you're actually willing to try. All year, all you did was complain that you hate dating and refuse to go out."

"I *do* hate dating. And tonight is a perfect example of why."

"Being stood up sucks, so let's forget tonight. Go somewhere else and regroup. I already know you look good. Go to a new spot and let the men come to you. This could be a blessing in disguise. Maybe he was a troll and that's why your coworker didn't want to show you a picture. Maybe he saw you and left because he knew you were out of his league. Maybe he doesn't know how to parallel park and couldn't find a spot. Whatever the case, you look good and you're already out! I'm proud of you. And I'm glad you're back. I need you in these streets with me to take some of these men off my hands. So we'll go out when I get back and we'll meet some guys. Hell, if all goes well, I'll get back early enough for us to go out tomorrow night and Sunday night. We could end the weekend right."

I laughed lightly. "Thanks, Nina. I hope I'm not interrupting your hair appointment. I didn't text you so you'd call. I just wanted you to know I'd been publicly humiliated. You okay? How's the hair looking?"

She laughed. "You haven't been publicly humiliated. No one knows what happened tonight but us. And for all that asshole knows, you didn't show up for the date either. It'll be like it never happened."

"Thank you, girl. I needed that."

"Anytime. And I'll call you later tonight if I can."

"I'll be up," I promised before we said our goodbyes.

With a sigh, I dropped my phone back into my bag. I looked down the bar for Ahmad so I could pay for my drink.

His tall, muscular frame stood at the far end of the bar. It was clear he was engaged in a conversation with a woman who was clearly flirting with him. She was laughing hysterically, sticking her tongue out a lot, and pushing her breasts up every chance she got. He was admittedly handsome, and some of the jokes he'd made were moderately funny, but nothing was as funny as that woman was making it out to be. I couldn't see his face, so I just stared at the back of his sponge-curl fade. And as if he could feel my eyes boring into him, he turned to look at me.

With a quick word to the woman, he seemed to conclude their conversation. As he headed toward me, he rubbed his hands down the front of his shirt, and I noticed the black band on his left hand.

"Is that a wedding ring?" I blurted out.

He gave me a look. "Uh, yeah, it is."

I drew back, surprised. "Oh!"

He appeared to be thirtysomething, so I shouldn't have been shocked he was married. A lot of people were married by thirty. My lips turned downward as my mother's and uncle's words infiltrated my thoughts, reminding me of how I was not in that percentage.

"Why was that your reaction?" he wondered.

"It's . . . Never mind." I paused for a second, shaking my head. "It's a long story. But I'm ready to pay my tab."

He took the large bill from me and held it up to the light, inspecting it. Once he verified it was real, he brought me my change. "You want a little advice?"

"No," I answered, putting my money back in my wallet.

"I don't know why you got stood up, but I do know why you didn't get approached while you were in here."

"Because there are no people here?" I guessed.

"And you called me the asshole?" He let out a chuckle under his breath. "No, Aaliyah. It's because you don't look approachable."

"I don't take advice from random men," I informed him. But I didn't get up and leave. Something about the way his brown eyes pierced mine held me in place. "What do you mean I don't look approachable?"

"You're a beautiful woman—an asshole, but a beautiful woman." He moved out of the way so I could see my reflection in the mirror wall. "But look at the way you're sitting. You look like you'll knock the head off anyone who talks to you."

"And I will."

His eyes danced with amusement. "I believe it."

"It's not safe for women to be alone or inviting or approachable." I shook my head. "But I wasn't trying to look inviting or approachable, because I was supposed to be on a blind date."

He clapped his hands together. "I knew it!" he exclaimed loudly. "I fucking knew you got stood up!"

I stared at him, my mouth agape. "Wow."

"Oh nah, my bad. I just . . ." He nodded. "You're right. That was fucked up." His lips turned downward in a contemplative manner, and he tried to look serious. "Maybe he'll show up in the next few minutes."

"I don't like for my time to be wasted, so it doesn't matter if he does show up now. He's almost an hour late."

"Oh, shit, an hour? Yeah, he ain't coming."

I curled my lip in disgust. "Glad to know this is the place to come to when I want to be kicked while I'm down."

"If it makes you feel any better, I'll kick you while you're up, too."

Begrudgingly, my lips turned upward. "You're not funny."

He pinched his pointer and thumb together. "I am. A little bit."

With my head, I gestured to the right, in the direction of the woman he was speaking to earlier. "Don't let your *friend* hype you up. You're not that funny. I don't see it."

"You know what I don't see?" He gestured to the empty barstool beside me. "Your date."

My mouth dropped, and a stunned laugh coughed out. "I think I officially hate you."

"I'm just fucking with you," he said, amusement dripping from each word. "But serious question: Why the hell would you go on a blind date?"

I sighed loudly. "I don't even know. My thirtieth birthday is in a couple of months. I'm having a party at one of the houses over on Dowdy Lake—"

He let out a low whistle. "A house on Dowdy Lake? That's nice."

"Yeah. I'm having the dress-up dinner party portion to kick it off, and then the sun will set and we'll roll into the real party," I told him proudly. "I've been planning this for a year. I always envisioned having a date for it. But as of last week, I need to have a boyfriend for this thing."

"That's . . ." He shook his head and let the sentence trail off. "Why?"

"Why do I need to have a boyfriend?"

"By your birthday," he clarified.

I sighed. "It's a long story."

"Okay, but"—he twisted his face into a frown—"a blind date?"

"I know," I groaned. "I know."

He looked bewildered. He opened his mouth to say something, but a customer ran up to the bar a couple of feet away from me.

"Give me a second," he told me, tapping the bar and moving toward the woman.

"Can I have another straw, please?" she asked.

"Of course," Ahmad replied, grabbing one from behind him and handing it to her.

"I have another question." The woman tucked her hair behind her ear and leaned closer to him. "Um, well . . . are you single?"

"No, I'm married," he responded. "Happily."

"Oh, I'm sorry."

"Don't be sorry," he said kindly. "I appreciate you asking."

She giggled and then turned and left.

I tried to look away before he noticed.

Ahmad made his way back over to me and folded his arms over his chest. "So, what's got you out here going on a blind date to find a man before your thirtieth birthday?"

I didn't plan on ever seeing him again, so I told him the truth. "I told my family I would introduce them to my boyfriend at my birthday party and have my Cinderella moment," I admitted. "But there is no boyfriend, so now I have to produce a man and prove that I'm not the problem child they think I am."

"So, they think you're a problem because you don't have a man? Not because of your attitude or your personality or your general disposition?"

I narrowed my eyes. "I'm going to write a terrible review of this place online."

He laughed. "I'm just trying to understand what's going on." He straightened his face and tried to look serious. "So, let me guess—you're the only child not married and without kids?"

"Something like that. Which to them means I'm behind the curve or some shit." I made a face. "A boyfriend leads to a husband, and a husband leads to kids."

"And you think a boyfriend by your thirtieth is going to stop them from being on your ass about being behind?" he guessed.

"Yeah."

For a while anyway.

He gave me a long, contemplative look. "Then instead of blind dates, you'd be better off trying TenderFish."

It was my turn to frown. "I don't like dating apps. They aren't safe."

"You are stubborn, I see."

I narrowed my eyes and pursed my lips.

"You just don't like the idea of getting on TenderFish because I suggested it," he stated.

"I don't like the idea because it's not safe."

He balked. "How is it any less safe than you meeting someone you've never seen before? Not only that . . . meeting someone you've never seen before in a bar by yourself." He quirked an eyebrow. "I've seen some shit in my lifetime. You can't trust some of these men out here. Especially the ones you don't know."

"You can't trust some men you *do* know," I countered.

"So, what are you doing?"

"He came recommended by a coworker. So, at least someone I know knows he really exists."

Ahmad's brown eyes widened as he pointed to the empty seat beside me. "Who? Him?"

I bit my bottom lip to keep from laughing. "You think everything is a damn joke."

"Just hear me out . . ." He grabbed a shaker and started preparing a drink. "Create an account. Check out what's out there. And don't ever do this blind date shit again."

"The people I know who are on the apps always complain about the creeps on there." I made a face. "They meet some decent ones, too, but it's mostly creeps. It's not safe."

"It's not that bad," he scoffed.

I lifted my head and narrowed my eyes at him. "That's that male privilege. As a man, you don't have to think about all the things that could go left on a date in the same way as I do. Could you be set up and robbed? Yes. But outside of that, what do you really worry about on a date?"

He thought about it for a minute, pouring the mixed concoction into a glass. "Okay."

"And being fat, being Black, being a woman . . . all these things make it a little more complicated to date and feel safe."

"Well, what would make you feel safe?"

I shrugged. "I don't even know," I admitted. "But I'm scared of meeting a guy and him attacking me. I'm scared of someone slipping something in my drink. I'm scared of being assaulted. I'm scared of having phone chemistry, but no in-person chemistry. I'm scared of talking on the phone with a guy for weeks to get to know him and then meeting him and not being attracted to him. I'm scared of—"

"Okay, I get it," he interrupted. "I never really thought about it like that, but you're right. That's some heavy shit." He slid the drink he'd just prepared in front of me. "Here. It's on the house."

I touched the glass, sliding it closer to me. It was the exact same drink I'd had earlier. "Thank you."

He wiped his hands on a towel and then tossed it back down. "You're right. There are situations I don't have to think about when

I go on a date that you do. And you're right, that's bullshit. So instead of worrying about the things you can't control, focus on controlling the things that you can."

"Like . . . ?"

"I work here every Friday night. Set the dates for Friday nights and meet them here. I'll watch your back and make sure no shady shit happens."

Holding his gaze, I lifted the drink to my lips. After taking a sip, I cocked my head to the side. "What's in it for you?"

His brows furrowed. "What do you mean?"

"Why would you help me?"

"Why wouldn't I?" He turned away from me to take the order of the man who had just walked up.

I watched him as he grabbed various bottles and started putting a drink together. Unsure of why I trusted the man who had been roasting me for most of my time there, I pulled out my phone and downloaded TenderFish. Once I filled in the preliminary questions of my name, date of birth, gender, sexual orientation, and email, I switched to my photo album and selected a picture of me smiling.

"Oh, wow," Ahmad commented, leaning over the bar.

My eyes darted up, catching him staring at my phone. "What?"

"You're smiling. You've been frowning the whole time you've been here; I didn't realize you knew how to smile."

"I smiled when I first walked in here," I replied. "Back when I had hope."

He made a face. "Yeah, okay." He pointed to the phone. "Finish your profile. I'm going to go take care of them."

While he did his job, I lost myself in creating a bio that quickly and succinctly summed up who I was and what I wanted.

"Damn, you put your blood type and your credit score in there?" Ahmad joked as he approached me. "Why were you over here writing a novel? What did you put in your bio?"

I balked. "I just said a little about me and what I want. Now it's asking for my celebrity crush."

"Let me guess . . ." He squinted at me. "Your celebrity crush is probably Shaw Lockwood."

"From that superhero movie franchise? The one who just got arrested for fighting on set? That everyone's been calling mean and problematic?" My face twisted and my lip curled in disgust as the sexy yet troubled star came to mind. "You think my type is mean and problematic?"

He nodded. "You look like you like 'em mean. You know what they say . . . birds of a feather flock together."

I rolled my eyes. "And your celebrity crush is probably—"

Before I could get my joke off, he interrupted me. "India Davis."

Oh!

I loved India Davis. Her music resonated with my soul.

Because I had nothing bad to say about one of my favorite artists, I snapped my mouth closed.

"India Davis is the woman of my dreams." He beckoned to my phone before crossing his arms over his chest. "Now, let me hear what you put in your profile."

"No!"

"Come on . . ."

Once I'd added three additional pictures, my profile was complete. I shook my head as I hit Save and officially entered the world of online dating.

Even though he didn't ask me again with his words, he stood there, silently begging.

I could use the feedback from a male perspective.

I took a long sip from my glass before I relented. "Fine." I cleared my throat. "I'm an intelligent, communicative IT professional with no kids. I like to have fun, so karaoke sessions, museum trips, attending concerts, going skating, traveling the world, and trying new adventures are examples of great dates to me. Likes to drink, but no drugs. Likes dogs, but no pets. Likes sex, but no hookups. My ideal date is one that is planned for me with me in mind. So, if you are an honest, loyal, straightforward, funny, smart, thoughtful, single man with a successful career who knows how to plan a date, let's connect!"

When I looked up at him, there was a confused look on his face.

"What?" I asked. "What do you think?"

"I don't think anyone is going to read all that." He lifted his shoulders. "I mean, they might. Your pictures are fire, so they might . . ."

"So, you think I should change it?"

He shook his head. "If you think all of that is important for someone to know before swiping on you, then I guess you should keep it. But . . . it's a lot. I know I wouldn't read all that, but I'm sure someone will."

"What did yours say when you were on it?"

"Drug-free, disease-free, drama-free." He shrugged. "The app already had my age, education, and career posted. Everything else could be discussed in conversation." He gave me a look. "Short, sweet, and to the point."

"What would yours say now if you were looking?"

"Thirty-two-year-old professional looking for my match. Drug-free, disease-free, drama-free." He smirked. "So basically the same thing as back then."

I put my phone down and picked up my drink. "So you think mine is too much?"

He laughed. "That's not exactly what I said."

I groaned. "And this is why I didn't even want to do this. How did I let you talk me into it?"

"Because it's a good idea," he explained. "And you said you wanted a boyfriend for your birthday and your big lake party, right?"

I nodded, finishing my drink. "Yeah."

"Well, this is going to be your best bet." He gestured to me. "Because you're not the friendliest in person."

"That's rich coming from you."

He made a face. "What's that supposed to mean?"

"Ahmad, how many times did you ask me if I was waiting for someone? You knew I was, and you saw that no one showed up. Why would you keep asking me?"

"I was checking in on you."

"Yeah, maybe the first time."

"Okay, then after you had an attitude, I just did it to get under your skin."

I shook my head and frowned. "What kind of person does something like that? A sociopath?"

He chuckled. "In my defense, there wasn't much else going on to amuse myself." He gestured around the bar. "As you pointed out, there weren't many people here, and you were the only one sitting at the bar."

"Then use your time to clean glasses and wipe down your work area. Don't use your free time to harass me!"

He scratched his beard with one hand and gestured to my phone with the other. "And that's why I'm doing a good deed by helping you now."

I pursed my lips. "Mm-hmm."

"I'm righting my wrongs."

Amusement forced my lips upward. "Shut up."

"I'm serious. Forgive me."

"I do not forgive you," I told him.

"Yeah, you do. I can see the stress leaving your body."

"If anything, I'm more stressed because of you."

"Then why are you smiling?" he asked teasingly.

"Because you're ridiculous."

"Nah, it's because I'm the man with the master plan."

I got off my barstool. "Yeah, I'm leaving. And then you'll be down to nine people in here."

He chuckled. "Go home and swipe. I'll see you Friday."

"You might. There might not be anyone on the app."

"Well, there wasn't anyone here either, so it's worth a try."

My jaw dropped. "I think I hate you, Ahmad."

With a grin, he winked at me. "Back at you."

Laughing, I adjusted my cross-body bag. "I can't believe you said that." I looked around dramatically. "Where's the owner?"

"My father is at home."

"Ah, I see how you got the job. It all makes sense." I nodded. "Nepotism."

Snickering, he shook his head. "Just try out the app and see. Report back on Friday."

“I might,” I replied, turning on my heel and walking toward the exit. “Goodbye.”

“What’s the worst that could happen?” he called to my back as I left Onyx Bar.

“Famous last words . . .” I muttered as I walked across the street to my building.

5

"I can't believe you waited almost twenty-four hours to start swiping on this app," Nina stated in awe. "I would've started swiping the moment I created an account."

"This is stressful. I needed wine, popcorn, and moral support."

She laughed, folding her leg underneath her on the couch. "But weren't you curious?"

"Of course, but I felt like I needed an old pro by my side as I ventured into this. So, I spent the day cleaning, and now here we are."

She put her hand to her chest, feigning shock. "Did you call me an old pro? As in a professional?" She leaned forward. "Did you just call me a ho?"

I snickered. "That's not what I meant, and you know it! I just mean that you've been in these dating streets for a while, and you know the lay of the land. You could give me some pointers and help me get the hang of things."

"I mean, you're not wrong. I've been in the streets my entire adult life." With a smile, she closed her eyes. "These are my streets now."

"You are a problem," I cackled.

"For them, yes." She nodded. "I'll own that."

After a brief overview and the directive to swipe left to say no and swipe right to say yes, I was ready to begin. After a refill of wine, I started swiping through my app with Nina's guidance. We made a game of it, discussing each profile that came up.

"There's no way the type of man I'm looking for is on this app," I speculated. "I want someone who gets me, not someone who is out to get me."

Nina choked on her wine and coughed through a chuckle. "Liyah, please!"

"I'm serious!" I giggled.

"Just keep swiping and be for real."

"Oh my God," I gasped.

"What?"

I sat up and cleared my throat. 'I don't mean no harm, but women on this app are just looking for someone to spend money on them, and that ain't me,' I read with a deep voice, trying not to laugh. 'I make my own money. I got my own everything. I provide for me and mines. What do you bring to the table? What do you have to offer besides what's between your legs? If you're not a gold digger, swipe right.'

She groaned from the other end of the couch. "I hate it when I come across profiles like that—and you'll come across quite a few of them. This mindset is wild, and this approach is just so . . . just so negative! Does it say what he does for a living?"

I showed her my phone. "Of course not."

"And on top of that, he's not cute on the inside or the outside. That's a no." Pulling out her phone, she opened the TenderFish app. "On to the next one."

"Amen," I agreed, swiping left.

And then I kept swiping left.

"Well, hold on," Nina demanded, putting her hand on my forearm. "Slow down! You're swiping left so fast, you're not even savoring the experience."

I pointed at her phone. "I'm swiping just as fast as you are!"

"Yes, but I've been on apps before. This is month two of me being on this one in particular, and I know the drill." She gave me a look. "You are on it for the first time. Take your time. Experience all of its wonder."

"'George, thirty-six, twenty-two miles away. No fat chicks,'" I read aloud. 'I don't mean to be mean, but I like what I like. So, if you're big and fat, do not bother. I'm looking for someone fit—preferably between one hundred and fifteen pounds and one hundred and thirty-five pounds. If you're fat anywhere besides your ass, do not swipe on me. We will not match. I don't need that unhealthy, lazy energy in my life. Good vibes only.' I gave her a look. "Is this what you want me to savor? Because I would've swiped no on the picture alone, but the bio really solidified the no. And I could've done without this."

"The thing about dating while fat on an app is that you'll be minding your business and then—boom—you catch a stray for no reason." She shook her head. "You'll see profiles of men that are blatantly fatphobic, and then you'll see the ones that fetishize us," she explained. "The goal is to find the men who see us as normal people."

"Soooooooo, it's basically just like real-life dating?" I joked. "It looks like people are just being bold about their bullshit online." I sighed. "The beauty of being an internet gangster, I guess."

"And let's be honest, we know that George wouldn't have had a chance with either of us on his best day."

"Amen to that. But my issue isn't even just the fact that he doesn't like fat women. I mean, he probably couldn't handle all this anyway. My issue is that he spent his whole bio shitting on us instead of just highlighting who he wanted. Same with the guy who claimed to not want a gold digger. Why not just highlight what you want instead of talking shit about what you don't? I just don't understand."

"Because people suck." She held up the phone so I could see the man on her screen. "Men in particular."

I squinted my eyes. "What is he wearing?"

"A shirt that says NO FATTIES and a pair of cutoff shorts that don't fit well."

My lip curled in disgust. "Jean shorts? He has the nerve to say no fatties and he's wearing cutoff denim shorts?"

Nina's head fell back against the couch and she laughed. "Exactly!"

"But my thing is this—if you can't connect with or talk to anyone unless you mutually match, what is even the point of writing all that hate? I just don't get it."

"The world may never know."

With a shake of the head, I went back to my swiping.

"Jesus," I groaned, shaking my head.

"What's up?" Nina responded.

"No Blacks," I read before turning the phone toward her. "That's it. That's his only requirement."

"Wait . . . *he* said that?" The confusion on her face matched mine when I read it.

With pursed lips, I gave her a look. "Mm-hmm."

"Wow." She shook her head. "That's . . . problematic. And look"—she held up her phone—"this profile has more trash-ass energy."

I squinted my eyes. 'I'm down with the swirl and looking for some chocolate. Big booties to the front of the line,' I read the profile with a frown. "No. No, he didn't."

"Yes, he did. Audacity must be on sale somewhere."

"These can't be the men God sent down here for us to procreate with."

"Keep that procreating energy over there, bitch!" Nina squealed, dropping her phone on the couch and covering her pelvis with her hands. "The last thing I want is to get pregnant."

I giggled. "I know. And looking at these options, I'm questioning my future as a mother."

As I went through my options, there were a few people I was willing to take a chance on, and then I went on a left-swipe streak. Just when I was about to swipe no on the eleventh man in a row, my finger stopped in midair.

"Oh, hello," I murmured, taking a long look at each of his pictures.

"What do you see?"

"His name is Donte." I showed her the picture. "He's a thirty-three-year-old physical therapist. He has no kids. He likes to sing. And he's looking to date and see where things go."

She pushed her box braids over her shoulder as she leaned forward to inspect my phone. Nodding, she sat back. "That's a good pick. Swipe on him."

I swiped.

"It's a match!" I exclaimed.

Nina pumped her fist in the air. "Yes!"

"This is the first match I've actually been excited about. The others could be cool, too. But Donte feels promising."

She grinned. "I told you it could be fun. Sometimes it's annoying as hell. But sometimes, it's fun."

"You did say that."

"It's funny how your best friend can try to convince you to join a dating app for the last three years, and it takes a random bartender one conversation to convince you to take the leap."

"It wasn't like that. It was the whole situation. Being stood up. Hearing my mom's and uncle's voices in my head. Being ready to find my person. Realizing that you were right about me being in my own way. Having Ahmad give me shit. It was—"

"Who is Ahmad?"

"The bartender."

She turned her entire body and smirked. "The way you said his name makes me think that maybe there's more to the asshole-turned-cool-bartender story."

I scrunched my nose. "I'm saying his name the way it's pronounced. You are reaching!"

"Am I?"

"You always read too much into things," I told her with a laugh. "There's no more to the story. He was being an asshole because he said I had an attitude. When I broke down and told him what was going on, he told me that I wasn't approachable or friendly."

"Damn! My man didn't sugarcoat anything, did he?"

"He really didn't. But something about his realness just struck a nerve. So . . ." I shrugged. "He said he would look out for me if I did the first date at Onyx, so that's where I'm going to meet the guys I hit it off with."

"That's really cool of him."

"It was. I was surprised. Because the way he kept trying to embarrass me about being stood up, I thought I was going to have to fight him."

Nina burst out laughing. "Maybe he wasn't taking shots at you. Maybe he was shooting his shot."

I rolled my eyes. "He's married, and he was definitely not shooting his shot." I thought back to our interaction and frowned. "I think he might've felt bad for me." I put my phone down. "Did that man pity me?"

"No." Shaking her head, she waved her hand wildly. "Don't even go there."

I started to feel a weird mixture of embarrassment, indignation, and defeat. "I don't want someone pitying me. I don't want him or anyone else to feel like I can't find a man."

"Then swipe on men, and let's get these dates going!" She picked up my phone from my lap and handed it to me. "And for the record, it sounds like he was just looking out. Even if he felt a little bad because you got stood up, it could've been like how I felt bad you got stood up. You know damn well I don't pity you."

I nodded slowly. "That's true."

I was quiet for a moment.

I knew that recognizing that someone else was going through a tough time didn't always equate to pity. But whenever I was the recipient of the sad eyes and embarrassed look, it made me feel a way. Although it was irrational, the idea of someone pitying me made me feel like they were implying I'm inferior in some way.

"So, maybe you two got off on the wrong foot and he's actually a good guy," Nina offered with a shrug. "Bartenders are like therapists. They listen to people's problems all the time and then provide solutions."

"Well, he offered something, but I don't know if this is a solution." I held up my phone, showing her a man's bare torso. 'I am married and looking for something discreet,' I read before pursing my lips. "If this is a solution, I don't want it."

"Okay, real talk—there's some duds on there. But do you remember that guy I hooked up with around Christmas?"

"Oh yeah . . ." I nodded, recalling who she was referring to. "I remember that asshole."

"I met him at work, not on a dating site, and he lied about being single."

"I'm just glad he posted that Christmas pajama photo with his family, and you were able to find out the truth."

"Me, too, girl. Me, too. But my point is that if a man is going to cheat and lie and be a hot mess, he's going to do it regardless of if he's online or in person. So just swipe no and focus on the good ones that pop up. Honestly, online dating is a marathon, not a race. You'll have to weed through a lot of bullshit. But when you find what you're looking for, it's like you've struck gold."

I smiled at her. "Deep down, I think you're a romantic."

She frowned. "Ew, no. Romance is dead. I just want a handful of steady, reliable men to spend my time with."

I snickered. "I don't know, Nina. You've been saying this for years, but what are you going to do when you meet a man who brings all the things to the table?"

"In my thirty years of life, I've never come across one man who has all the things I'm looking for. So, I'm content rotating a few of them in and out to get my needs met. You're the one obsessed with finding *the one*. I want to find *the ones*."

We both laughed and went back to our phones.

"I can't believe you're spending your Saturday night inside instead of going out into the world," Nina said fifteen minutes later. "You know you could come out with me."

"I don't want to be a third wheel. And honestly, after last night's waste of an outfit, I think I just want to chill, watch a movie, and go to bed early," I explained.

"You can't let getting stood up shake your confidence. You need to make sure you secure a date for Friday night." She leaned over and looked at my phone. "You already have ten matches, and we really just got started. So keep swiping, and by the end of the weekend, you'll triple that. Depending on how picky you are, you may have fifty good matches to sort through. And talk to them all. Weed out and unmatch the ones that won't work, and then you'll have a solid handful to date."

"So out of fifty, I'll only have a handful of viable candidates?"

"Oh, honey . . ." She gave me an exaggerated pout as she reached over and patted my thigh. "You'd be lucky to find a handful that you actually want to meet."

My jaw dropped. "You can't be serious."

"You'll see." She winked before standing up. "Let's talk tomorrow. I need to get ready for my date."

"Okay, have a good time!" I rose to my feet and walked her to the door.

"I plan to." She gave me a hug and then pointed to my phone. "You have fun, too."

"I'll try."

We said our goodbyes, and then I plopped back down on the couch and continued browsing the single men of Richland and the surrounding areas. At some point, I'd stopped and got sucked into the movie I'd started. And the next thing I knew, I was asleep.

When I woke up at eight o'clock in the morning, my phone had died, and the bowl of popcorn had been knocked onto my freshly cleaned floors.

"Great," I grumbled as I dropped to my knees and picked up all the kernels.

I washed the dishes, vacuumed the crumbs, and then connected my phone to the charger. Instead of a shower, I decided I wanted a long, hot bubble bath, and I just soaked in the lavender-scented water.

I was in need of a yacht talk with my sister. She would've found a way to get the family off my back. She would've encouraged the online dating shenanigans. She would've been completely supportive of whatever it was that I wanted to do with my life. We would've been on the boat, talking everything out, and by the time we got back to shore, all of life's problems would've disappeared. I sighed.

I missed Aniyah deeply.

She felt like she could have it all. She felt like I could have it all—even if it didn't look like hers. We would've gone out on the boat and—

I stopped midthought.

Sloshing water, I sat up abruptly. It was almost as if my sister sent a message from heaven. Unless I made some moves, I was no closer to having a boyfriend or having the yacht.

And I have seven weeks to change that.

Motivated, I climbed out of the tub with a renewed determination.

"I should take myself out for brunch," I whispered as I dried off.

I mentally went over the list of restaurants that I wanted to try as I moisturized. And by the time I slipped into a cute pair of high-waisted floral pants and a pink top, I knew exactly where I was going.

I powered on my fully charged phone, and it started ringing instantly.

"Hello?"

"Do you want to meet me at Collective Kitchen?" Nina asked.

"Oh my God!" I exclaimed. "I just got dressed to go there!"

"No!"

"Yes!"

"I already know what I'm going to wear so let me get ready!"

"Yes! Okay, I'm going to finish my hair, and then I'll be on the way."

We squealed excitedly before deciding to meet there in forty-five minutes.

When I arrived at the popular brunch spot, it was packed. I was glad I decided to get there early. I made my way to the front so I could put our name on the list, and then I found a spot on the bench near the door.

I pulled out my phone to send Nina a text to let her know we were looking at a twenty-five-minute wait. After sending it, I noticed the notifications on the TenderFish app icon. My eyebrows flew up as I clicked on it and saw the number of messages I had.

Whoa.

My eyes breezed over the many "hey, beautiful" and "good morning, queen" messages and landed on the message from Donte.

Donte: Hello, Aaliyah. How are you doing this beautiful Sunday morning?

Aaliyah: I'm doing quite well. How are you, Donte?

Donte: I'm great now that I'm talking to you. What are you up to today?

Aaliyah: I'm getting brunch with one of my best friends, and then who knows. What about you? What are you up to?

Donte: Right now, I'm waiting for my bacon to finish cooking. I woke up, went to the gym, showered, and now I'm making breakfast.

Aaliyah: So, you can cook?

Donte: I can do a little something. If things go well, maybe I can show you what I can do. But I don't want to get ahead of myself. What do you do?

Aaliyah: I'm a computer programmer. What do you do? And do you like it?

Donte: I'm in marketing. I like what I do, but if I could do something else, I would.

Aaliyah: Why can't you?

Donte: I make a good salary, and the benefits are better than most companies. It's a risk I'm not willing to take right now.

Aaliyah: I get that. At least you like your job, though. Even if you don't love it and you would do something else, at the very least you like it and you're being paid well.

Donte: Exactly. But a risk I am willing to take is getting to know you better, if you'll let me.

Aaliyah: I would like that.

For the next twenty-five minutes, I sat outside grinning at my phone. When the waitress called me in, I didn't even realize how much time had gone by. I was seated in the booth and handed menus.

"You want me to give you a few minutes?" the waitress asked, gesturing to the empty seat across from me.

I nodded. "Yes, please." I checked my phone. "She's five minutes away. But I do want to place an order for two waters and two mimosas."

The waitress nodded and smiled. "I'll be right back."

> **Aaliyah:** I just got seated at the restaurant, waiting on my friend to get here.
>
> **Donte:** Somebody has you waiting? That's unacceptable. When we meet, I'm going to make sure you're not waiting.
>
> **Aaliyah:** If that was your way of asking me out, that was smooth.
>
> **Donte:** Good, because that's all the game I got! I would love to meet you in person and see if we click.
>
> **Aaliyah:** Would you like to meet for drinks on Friday at Onyx Bar? It's downtown.
>
> **Donte:** Yeah, that's cool. I never heard of it, but I'll look it up.
>
> **Aaliyah:** My friend just walked in the door. If you're free later, I can message you.
>
> **Donte:** I'm relaxing today, so definitely hit me up.
>
> **Aaliyah:** I sure will.

"What's all this about?" Nina questioned as she slid in the booth. "I know it's a man. Who is he?"

"Who is who?" I returned, placing my phone down.

She eyed me and held up one manicured finger. "One, you're smiling so hard; I can see your molars." She held up a second finger. "And two, I know for a fact that you put on your best outfits when you're trying to make yourself feel better." She narrowed her eyes, trying to read me. "So this could go either way."

I snickered because she wasn't wrong. "I was talking to Donte, and so far, I like him!"

"Good!"

I wiggled my eyebrows. "Hopefully, he'll give me reason to delete this app!"

Nina's expression was skeptical. "I hope so. But just in case, make sure you're talking to other people, too. Men start off promising and then—boom—trash."

I cackled. "Well, that was uplifting."

She pointed at me. "That's the truth."

Cocking my head to the side, I eyed her. The only reason I didn't say anything immediately was because the waitress brought our drinks. When she walked away, I leaned forward.

"Is everything okay? Did something happen last night?" I wondered.

"I was out with The Romantic One last night. Everything was cool, and guess who strolled up?"

My eyes widened. "Who?"

"The married man."

"No!"

"We talked him up!"

"What happened?"

"Let's order first, and then I'll tell you."

When the waitress came back, we ordered, and then I clasped my hands in front of me and was ready to listen.

"Before I begin," Nina started, grabbing her mimosa glass, "let's toast."

I picked mine up and held it in the air. "What are we toasting?"

"To the wild ride that is dating."

I smiled, clinking my glass against hers. "Wild ride?"

She winked. "Buckle up."

6

At Nina's insistence, I entertained conversations with some other men on TenderFish, too, but Donte had my attention. After we spent almost all day on Sunday texting each other through the app, I was quite smitten with his personality. Because of work, the conversation slowed during the week. But every night, we exchanged messages for a couple of hours before bed. And by the time Friday rolled around, my stomach was in knots.

"What do you think about the yellow dress?" I asked Jazmyn over the phone. "I just sent you a picture. It's hot today, and I think it's the perfect time to wear it."

"Oh, that looks cute on you," she approved. "Wear it."

"The only shoes I have to go with it are the gold, strappy ones. Do you think that's doing too much?"

"No, this is a meetup with a man you've been getting to know. First impressions matter." She let out a short, soft giggle. "I don't know why, but this reminds me of our days back at HU, getting ready for our first double date freshman year."

"Ahh, good ol' Hamilton University days." I smiled, thinking back to the carefree days of dating on campus. "The only thing missing is Nina loudly singing and dancing around the dorm."

"Wow, we've been talking each other through first-date jitters for almost twelve years."

"Yeah, we have. And one of these days, we'll talk each other through our last first-date pre-date jitters." I lifted my hand in the air. "Amen!"

"Oh, what did you decide to do with your hair?" she asked.

"I have my hair pinned up to show off my dangly earrings."

"Good. Don't forget to put the gold pins in your hair to give your 'fro some extra shimmer."

I didn't even think about that.

"Good call. Thanks."

I was quiet for a moment as I headed to the bathroom to add the pins. Jazmyn and I hadn't talked much since Sunday afternoon when I told her about my date. That night, her aunt took a turn for the worse. She didn't want me or Nina to come down, but we sent flowers. I knew she was just looking for a break from talking about everything with her aunt, so I answered all her pre-date questions. And even though she seemed in good spirits and at peace, I was worried about her.

"How are you?" I asked gently. "How is . . . everything? Are you sure you don't want us to come down?"

"Thank you again for offering, but no. It's already too much going on down here. And I'm fine. I'm sad, but I'm fine. There's so much stuff to do." She let out a sigh. "It's just a lot going on. Just have to take it one day at a time and everything will be fine."

"I'm sorry. And you're not alone. If you need help with anything or if you just want to talk about it? I'm always here to listen."

"I know. And I thank you. But I'm all talked out. I just needed a little distraction. What time is your date?"

"Eight."

"What time are you heading over?"

"Seven thirty. I want to make sure I get seats at the bar to start. If things go well, maybe we can grab a table or something."

"I like this plan. But it's seven, so you need to finish up and head over there."

"Yeah, you're right. Thanks, Jazz."

"Text me and let me know what happens. Even if I can't get back to you until Sunday, keep me updated. Good luck!"

"Thank you. You keep me updated, too. And if you need anything, don't hesitate to ask."

"I won't," she promised. "Thanks, Aaliyah."

"I wish I could be there with you, so you don't have to do everything alone."

"But if you were here, you wouldn't be able to go on hot dates in preparation for your birthday boyfriend. We'll talk soon."

I smiled as we concluded the conversation. My heart went out to her as she dealt with her favorite aunt's downward turn. She'd been sick for a while, so the fact that she only had a couple of months to live wasn't a surprise for Jazz. But it was still unexpected. Since Jazz was a teacher and she had the summer off, her five-day visit home turned indefinite.

With a final once-over and twirl in front of the mirror, I strolled out of my apartment with more confidence than I actually felt.

I'd underestimated how quickly I would make it across the street and walked through the door of Onyx forty-five minutes early for my date.

I briefly stopped in my tracks. Music flowed through the space, and there were about twenty people in the bar. I made a beeline for the spot I'd claimed last week.

"Welcome to Onyx," a woman with cute Afro puffs greeted me. "Can I get you anything?"

"Hi." I looked around. "Is Ahmad here?"

Her smile grew. "He is . . ." She hooked her thumb toward the office. "Would you like me to get him?"

"Yes, please."

"No problem. Let me take care of them"—she gestured to the couple on the other end of the bar with her head—"and then I'll go get him."

"Okay, thank you," I told her as I hoisted myself onto the stool.

Staring at myself in the mirror, I took a deep breath.

There's nothing to be worried about. It's a meeting with a man who seems perfect for me. That's it. Nothing to stress out about.

But I could see it all over my face.

"What's wrong with you?" Ahmad's deep voice cut through my thoughts and snatched my attention away from my image in the mirror.

"What? Me? Nothing!" I answered a little too quickly.

He made a face. "Well, smile or something."

My lip curled in disgust. "I hate for a man to tell me to smile."

"It was just a friendly suggestion." He grabbed a couple of bottles and started pouring them into a shaker. "You're sitting here looking like you're shitting yourself. I thought a smile might help.

But you could also frown. That seems to be your default setting anyway."

"Ha ha," I replied sarcastically. "You got a good little crowd in here, and now you don't know how to act."

His lips quivered as if he were holding in his amusement. "That's how you feel?"

I lifted my shoulders innocently. "You started it."

"You always have something to say, huh?" He shook the shaker and then poured the contents into a glass. "Just squawk, squawk, squawk."

His imitation of a bird was hilarious, but I refused to give him the satisfaction. Covering my mouth with my hand, I shook my head.

He pushed the drink in front of me. "This is for you, Tweety."

"Tweety?"

"Yes. Looking and squawking like a mean-ass yellow canary."

I looked down at myself. "You're such an asshole." I giggled.

"If I'm an asshole, you're an asshole."

"I guess it is what it is, then."

He smirked. "So, I take it since you're here, you have a date tonight."

I nodded. "I do."

"What's his name?"

"Donte."

"Nah, he's not the one. Dante? Journey-through-the-pits-of-hell Dante?"

I burst out laughing. "It's spelled differently, but yeah."

"Aaliyah and *Donte*." He shook his head. "I don't see it."

"Based on his name? Really?"

He grinned. "I'm just fucking with you. I hope it goes well. What made you pick *Donte*?"

"Stop saying his name like that!"

"My bad."

"Donte is really cool. Of all the guys I've been chatting with this week, he and I had the most in common, and we're looking for the same things in a partner."

"Top three things you're looking for?"

I held up one finger. "Intelligence." I held up a second finger. "Ambition." I held up a third finger. "Romance."

"Okay, so if he says some dumb shit, I'll kick his ass out." He pointed to the door. "If he slips up and we find out he doesn't have a job, he's out. And I don't know what you consider romantic, but if he gives me the vibe that he isn't romancing the fuck out of you, he's out."

"Thanks," I snickered. "Maybe a little aggressive, but thanks."

"I got your back," he assured me. "By any means necessary."

"When you were on the app, what did you look for?"

His brows crinkled and his brown eyes searched mine momentarily. "I like my women badass. Confident, sexy, intelligent, outgoing—"

"Ahmad!" the woman with the Afro puffs called out.

"Duty calls," he told me before heading over to the woman. "Yes, Asia?"

"Someone is here to see you," Asia replied, pointing to a pretty woman.

I took a sip of the Malibu sunrise and smiled. It was the same thing I'd ordered the week before. Glancing over in his direction, I smiled.

"Hey, Ahmad," the pretty woman greeted him. "You're looking mighty good behind that bar."

"Oh, shit, Shanita! What's up?"

"You tell me!" She cocked her head to the side. "And while you're at it, I'll take what you made for the girl you were flirting with over there," Shanita stated, pulling my attention from my thoughts. "She's cute."

I followed the voice and happened to make eye contact with Ahmad in the process.

"Nah, that's the homie right there," Ahmad corrected her. Pointing to me, he continued, "Aaliyah is drinking a Malibu sunrise."

"Well, I want what she has." She smirked. "But you already know that."

He chuckled to himself and shook his head.

I looked away immediately.

They were extremely comfortable around each other. She was flirting, and he was eating it up. There was something about the way they engaged with each other that made me feel like I was watching something more. The familiarity felt intimate.

Is that his wife?

The thought stopped me mid-sip.

As he made her the drink, I pretended I wasn't trying to listen to their conversation.

"You were on my mind, so I wanted to pop in and check on you," she said.

"I'm cool. How was your day?" he asked in return.

"Great. Busy," she told him before a wave of people came to the bar for drinks.

By the time the people had dispersed, I'd missed part of what they were saying to one another.

"I'm not ready. I'm good off that." Ahmad held up his left hand with his wedding band prominently displayed. "Drop it."

My head quirked curiously as I eavesdropped.

"Ahmad," she said gently. "All I'm saying is that—"

"Shanita," he interrupted. "I love you. But I'm working. Let's talk later, okay?" He moved to the other end of the bar to take an order.

I snuck another glance at the woman and saw her looking at me with a knowing smile.

I quickly shifted my gaze and took another sip.

Definitely must be his wife.

The fruity cocktail was delicious, and when I caught a glimpse of myself in the mirror, I noticed the stress and anxiety had melted from my face.

Everything is going to be fine. Donte is going to be fine. The date is going to be fine. Everything is going to be fine.

"You look better," Ahmad commented when he made his way back to me.

I narrowed my eyes at him. "What's that supposed to mean?"

His brows furrowed. "What?"

"You keep commenting on the way I look? You told me I need to smile, that I look like a bird, that I look better." I took another sip of my drink. "Are you trying to psych me out or something? I thought you had my back!"

He stepped forward and put his hands on the bar. "I suggested a smile because you looked like you were being held at gunpoint. I said you look better because now you look like you're here of your own free will."

I pursed my lips. "You still called me Tweety Bird."

"Because you have on a canary-yellow dress." He gestured to me. "I never said you didn't look absolutely beautiful in it."

A chill ran down my spine.

I tried to hide my smile, but my cheeks heated. "Oh, okay, then."

"See . . . look at you. You're always so ready to give me shit, but you can't handle it when I call you Tweety? You chose that color. You knew what it was."

"You're wearing a pair of jeans and a dirty shirt, so don't comment on how I look."

He laughed. "I just spent ten minutes using a bleach pen trying to get that cranberry juice stain out." He pulled his shirt up a bit, and I caught a glimpse of his abs as he inspected the stain. "I knew I should've double-checked to make sure that top was on. How bad is it?"

My eyes jerked up to his face. "It's not that bad. It just looks like something spilled on you. It doesn't look dirty. It looks like . . . maybe you shouldn't wear a white shirt behind the bar. But you don't look unclean."

"Yeah, but I came straight from work, so I didn't get a chance to change today." He pulled his shirt down and shrugged. "Ain't shit I can do about it, so I'm not going to worry about it."

"I like that attitude." I paused. "But do you see how someone can point something out and get in your head?"

"I'm not worried about this stain just like you're not worried about me calling you Tweety." He leaned forward and got into my eyeline. "You're just mad because you thought it was funny."

"You're not funny, Ahmad."

"You think I'm hilarious. And I don't blame you. I'm a funny dude."

"You're a Leo, aren't you?"

"I'm not telling you shit." He backed away. "Why would I give you more ammunition?"

I laughed. "I'll take that as a yes."

He grinned as he walked off to help the wave of people who'd just entered the bar.

As I finished the rest of my drink, it dawned on me to check my phone.

Donte: I'm here. I'm just looking for a place to park.

The message had just come through two minutes prior. I knew parking downtown could take a few minutes, so I used that time to calm my nerves. I needed a distraction.

"What do you do besides work here?" I asked Ahmad as he tossed cherries into the four glasses in front of him.

He served the drinks and took their money. When they walked away, he looked at me. "I work in IT," he answered just as a woman bounded up to the bar to get his attention.

"Really?" I mused as he conversed with the woman.

"Aaliyah?" a voice called from behind me.

I glanced in the mirror in front of me before turning to the side. A swarm of strangers entered, and the bar was getting kind of packed. But the man staring at me looked familiar.

Light brown skin. Light brown eyes. Bald head. Strong build.

"Donte?" I said cautiously, relieved he looked like his photos.

"Hi." He extended his arm, shaking my hand before bringing it to his lips. "It's nice to finally meet you."

"It's nice to meet you as well."

He took a seat next to me and smiled. "You look beautiful. Yellow is your color."

"Thank you. You also look nice."

"Thank you." He looked around. "I've never heard of this place before. How did you find it?"

"I'm in the area a lot," I replied, not wanting to tell him that I lived across the street.

"What's good here?" He pointed at my drink. "What are you drinking?"

"Malibu sunrise. It's delicious."

"It looks good, but I can't be seen drinking that."

I blinked rapidly. "Oh?"

"Yeah, I think I'll order a rum and Coke. I'm not trying to give you a reason to think I'm less manly than I am. I already let you catch me slipping when I told you I watched that reality TV dating show *InstaLove*."

I smiled. "I liked that you told me that. I've told you some of my TV guilty pleasures, too."

"Hey, can I get you anything?" Ahmad asked, catching me by surprise.

"Yeah, I'll take a rum and Coke," Donte ordered before pointing at my glass. "And another one of those for the lady."

Ahmad glanced at me, so I gave him a brief nod. "Okay," he responded with a grin. "Coming right up."

When he walked away, Donte turned toward me. "How was your day?"

"It was good! I've been excited about meeting you, so I'm sure that had something to do with the day flying by."

"Did you finish your project?"

"Yeah, I did. I didn't think I was going to, and I refused to work on it at home. So it all worked out, and I get to roll into my weekend without it hanging over my head." I pursed my lips. "Did *you* get all of your stuff finished?"

"Hell no." Shaking his head, he chuckled. "I'll be working a little tomorrow to finish. But it was crazy for them to think I was going to be able to get it all done in two weeks."

"I agree. I hope you talk to your supervisor on Monday. They get back on Monday, right?"

"Yes, thank God. I'm tired of doing his work and not getting paid his salary."

"Amen to that." I grinned. "How was your day overall, though?"

"My day was cool. I didn't push myself to finish the work. I ended up putting everything I needed together and left early since I'm planning on coming in tomorrow, too."

"Oh? That's automatically a good day when you leave work early."

"Yeah. I went to drop off some stuff to my older kids."

The record in my head scratched. *What?*

"Kids?" I questioned, confusion crumpling my face. "Y-you have kids?"

"Yeah, four."

"Four kids?"

"Here are your drinks," Ahmad interrupted slowly, placing the glasses in front of us.

When our eyes met, I could tell he'd heard the conversation.

"Thanks, man," Donte said, handing him a credit card.

I shifted my gaze back to the man sitting next to me. "Your profile said you didn't have any kids."

"Yeah, I like to let women get to know me before bringing up my kids."

I took a sip of my drink, trying to think of how I was going to approach the situation without being rude. "You lied on your profile, though," I blurted out.

"I didn't lie. I just want a fair shot."

I shook my head. "No, if you didn't say anything about your kids on your profile, I could see your point. But you straight up said you didn't have any children, but in reality, you have four."

He took a long gulp of his rum and Coke. "Is that going to be a problem for you?"

"Well, yeah."

He shook his head and let out an aggressive puff of air. "Great. You and I hit it off, didn't we?"

"Yeah. We did."

"So, why does this change anything? You hate kids or something?"

"Donte . . ." I couldn't hide my exasperation if I wanted to. "We've been talking all week, and you never said anything. How did you not bring up the fact that you have *four* kids?"

"Here's your card back," Ahmad said slowly, looking between us.

"Thanks." Snatching the card, Donte tipped his head back and finished his drink. "Are you really not going to give me a chance because I have kids? Really, Aaliyah?"

I was going to explain that he lied. I was going to tell him not to flip the script and make it my fault. I was going to respond with a lot of things, but I didn't have the energy.

"Yeah," I said flatly.

"Wow!" Donte exclaimed. "That's kind of shallow, don't you think? I didn't think you would have an issue with kids. But okay. It was nice meeting you, I guess."

"Yeah, you, too," I muttered as he left.

I was in shock.

It was such an unbelievable turn of events that I couldn't even get up from my seat.

"You good?" Ahmad asked as he was in the middle of mixing drinks.

I nodded but remained quiet.

"Brush it off," he told me before sliding the drinks to the waiting customers.

"I'm fine," I assured him quietly. "He wasn't it."

"Tell me something . . ." He returned to his position in front of me, placing his hands on the bar. "And I want you to say the first thing that comes to mind."

I gave him a suspicious look. "Okay . . . ?"

"How are you going to know when he *is* it?"

"Um—"

He shook his head. "Off the top of your head. Don't think about it," he demanded quickly. "How are you going to know?"

"Because he's going to look at me, know what I want, and take care of it," I answered honestly.

My stomach swirled as I imagined how it would feel to be seen in that way.

Ahmad held my gaze.

I inhaled and exhaled in time with him as we stared at each other over the bar. I felt him assessing me and my answer. His silence met my vulnerability, and even though it made me a little uncomfortable, I couldn't look away.

The sound of his name being called pulled us from the moment. He licked his lips and leaned toward me. "Ohhh, okay"—he nodded—"you want a mind reader."

Rolling my eyes, I held in a laugh. "You're such an ass! I'm not looking for a mind reader. I'm looking for a man who can read me."

Snickering, he glanced to some people flagging him down. "Don't leave yet," he ordered, moving down to take some more orders.

I waited a couple of minutes, and then my phone vibrated.

Mom.

Sliding off the stool, I tried to catch Ahmad's eye. He was busy, so I jotted down a note on the napkin that was near my drink.

See you next Friday. Thank you.

Turning on my heel, I answered my mother's call. "Hey, Mom, I'm walking out of a bar. Everything okay?"

"Everything is perfectly fine! I just called to say hi. I just got in from Bible study with Liz. She told me the funniest thing! Marcus called her earlier this week and told her that he's taking classes this fall—at Hamilton University!"

"Oh, wow, that's what's up."

"That's your alma mater!"

Smiling, I shook my head. "Yes, I know . . ."

7

Checking my watch, I rushed across the street before the light changed. My black-and-white-striped dress blew in the wind as I hopped up onto the sidewalk. I wasn't running late for my date, but I was hoping to get to Onyx before the Friday-night crowd showed up.

"Well, if it isn't the Hamburglar," Ahmad greeted me when I walked into the empty bar.

I stopped in my tracks.

For fifteen long seconds, I just glared at him. He had the biggest shit-eating grin on his face, and his big, brown eyes danced. With narrowed eyes, I bottled up the laughter that threatened to burst out of me.

"I think I hate you," I said finally, forcing my feet toward him.

"You know you love me," he returned with a smirk.

My stomach fluttered unexpectedly. "I don't."

"And you know that was funny!"

"You're a clown." I climbed up on the barstool. "If it wasn't too late to meet this guy somewhere else, I'd walk right out of here."

"Like you did last Friday?"

"What?"

He finished restocking the glasses and gave me a look. "I told you to give me a minute, and you dipped out."

"Oh!" I shook my head. "Nah, it wasn't like that. I tried to say goodbye, but you were busy."

Wiping his hands on the towel he had draped over his shoulder, he stood in front of me. "Well, if I'm going to look out for you, the least you can do is let me know when you're heading out."

I felt my lips curling upward under his gaze. "You're right," I acknowledged softly.

I opened my mouth to say more, but a group of people noisily entered, disrupting the quiet bar.

He greeted them and then focused his attention back at me. "So, who is the lucky guy you're meeting tonight?"

"Brayden Storm."

"Is he a weatherman?"

Confusion twisted my face. "No. Why?"

"Brayden Storm. He sounds like a weatherman." He changed his voice to a dry, nasally monotone. "Brayden Storm with the weather."

I rolled my eyes. "You just say anything. No common sense. You just have"—I pointed to my temple—"a couple of beans rattling up there and no filter."

Still using the voice, he said, "Sounds like a cold front is coming in from that side of the bar."

I pursed my lips. "I'm not talking to you if you keep talking like that."

He grabbed a stack of cups and moved them. "Fine. Tell me about this guy," he said in his normal tone.

"The conversation has been nice." I pointed at him. "He seems pretty cool. And the best part is that *he's* funny."

"Nah, I'm funny."

"I assure you, you're not funny."

He placed his hands on the bar and leaned toward me. "Then why do you have to try so hard not to laugh?"

"Anyway . . ." I hid my smile with my hand. "Why are you so dressed up today?"

Stepping back, he looked down at his green button-up shirt and black jeans. "This is dressed up to you?"

"Well, last week, you had a dirty T-shirt on, so this is a *vast* improvement."

"I thought you said it wasn't that bad."

"It wasn't, but I just thought about how you called me the Hamburglar and got mad all over again."

Ahmad chuckled under his breath as he left me to go take the orders of the people who'd just approached the bar. He was back and forth between checking on me and helping the ever-growing crowd. He moved so skillfully and effortlessly as he worked. Every time he would spend a couple of minutes making small talk with me, I felt myself loosening up.

But it wasn't just me.

He seemed to make everyone around him feel good. I watched the way he spoke to people, the way he smiled, and the way he entertained conversation while making the drinks. He was friendly without being too friendly. Cocking my head to the side, I couldn't help but notice how he seemed so respectful of his marriage.

I smiled.

And yet another reason why I have faith in finding my person.

Ahmad seemed like a really good man—exasperating, but good.

"Would you like a drink?" Asia asked me, stealing my attention from the other end of the bar.

"Oh, hey!" My voice was a little too loud, and the words came out a little too fast. "I didn't know you were here."

Her lips pulled into a taut pucker. "It happens a lot."

"What?"

"People forgetting I'm here when Ahmad's around." She leaned closer and lowered her voice. "He's the popular one—especially with the ladies."

I shook my head. "No, it's not like that."

With a smile, Asia took a step back. "Yeah, okay."

"No, I'm serious," I argued. "I'm doing my first dates here, and Ahmad's watching my back."

"Oh, I'm sure he is." She winked before turning her attention to the two men who had strolled up next to me. "What can I get for you two?"

She shifted gears so fast, I didn't have time to defend myself from the assumption she was making.

"We'll take you and your friend over there in the stripes," one of the men commented.

I looked over at them in confusion.

Now how did I get in this? I was minding my business.

The shorter of the two flashed me a toothy grin. "I don't mind taking the fat one."

"Yeah, well, I mind," I retorted.

"You're feisty," he commented, taking a step toward me. "Say it again. But this time, say it to my face."

"Get a step stool and I will."

"Oh, shit!" the taller one snickered. "You're not going to let some fat bitch diss you, are you, Frankie?"

"Not the guy with the Habsburg jaw talking shit about my friend," Asia commented.

I burst out laughing, which only made the two men madder.

"We're leaving this dump," the short one spat, pulling his friend back.

They started shouting obscenities when she pointed to the door. "Out. Now."

"What's going on?" Ahmad asked just as the two men stormed out. "You both okay?"

"Yeah, we're fine," Asia answered as I nodded.

He looked between us and shook his head. "One minute, I look down here and everything is cool, and the next minute, all hell is breaking loose."

"Those guys didn't know how to act, so I put them out. I don't tolerate that level of disrespect," Asia informed him. Crossing her arms across her chest, she smiled at me. "But this one right here can hold her own with the jokes." Noticing someone waiting to be served, she started walking away. "I see why you like her."

She tossed the comment over her shoulder like a grenade that neither of us were prepared for.

Like deer in headlights, we just stared at each other.

"I might have mentioned that you were cool," he mumbled before he noticed a woman waiting. "I'll be back."

What was that?

Turning my head, I looked into the mirror behind the bar and froze. My eyes locked with the light-skinned, curly-haired man who'd just walked in. The man who looked exactly like his profile picture smiled as he moved toward me. I waited until he was right next to me before I turned to greet him face-to-face.

"Aaliyah, it's nice to finally meet you." He extended his hand. "I'm Brayden."

I shook his hand. "I'm glad you could make it, Brayden."

"I wouldn't have missed the chance to meet you for the world."

A smile played on my lips. "Well, I've been looking forward to this all week." I gestured to the stool next to me. "Have a seat."

"What are you drinking? I hope I didn't keep you waiting long."

"I haven't been here that long," I lied. "I haven't ordered anything."

"What do you like?"

"I mostly like fruity drinks. I don't like to actually taste the alcohol."

"Hmm. I know just the thing." He lifted his hand and caught Ahmad's attention. "Yeah, man, can we start a tab?"

"Yeah, I got you," Ahmad replied, taking Brayden's card. "What can I get you?"

"Can we get two Amaretto sours? And add a couple of extra cherries for my beautiful date."

Ahmad glanced at me before he nodded. "Coming right up."

"This place is pretty cool," Brayden acknowledged, looking around. "I've never been here."

"Do you ever hang out in Richland? I know you live forty-five minutes away."

"No, never." He licked his lips. "But for you, I'm willing to make the trip."

Ahmad returned, sliding two glasses in front of us.

"Thanks, man," Brayden replied, picking up his drink. "A toast?"

I gave Ahmad a small smile before turning my attention back to my date. "What are we toasting?"

"The beginning of something special."

I cocked my head to the side. It felt like game was being run on me, so I was hesitant as I lifted my glass. "The beginning of something special," I repeated skeptically.

We tapped glasses and then took a sip.

I searched his face, looking for a tell. But his eyes didn't leave mine as he swallowed the tart drink.

Our first conversation started in the evening and carried on into the wee hours of the morning. After that, he talked to me on every lunch break he had since we exchanged numbers. After hours, we talked while he was finishing up things in the office. And a couple of nights, we spoke on his entire drive home. And with each conversation, he was attentive and charming. I enjoyed him, but I couldn't help the little nagging feeling in the back of my mind. I couldn't put my finger on why, but there was a bit of hesitation with him.

"I knew there was something special about you after our first conversation," he admitted.

"That was a really good conversation," I agreed. "Even though you seemed distracted by the end of it."

He shook his head. "I was working late, and my secretary had messed up some forms for me. I had to send it out before Wednesday's meeting, and because I didn't catch the error until after hours, I had to stay even later and work on it myself. But up until I noticed that, you had my undivided attention. Just like every night this week."

I stirred the straw in my cocktail. "I think I like having your undivided attention."

His smile grew. "Good. Because I like giving it to you."

Like he had all week, the man charmed me.

We sat on those barstools nursing our drinks and talking for an hour.

"You can get it," I told him as he checked his phone for the second time in ten minutes. "I won't deduct date points if you need to take the call."

"Nah, work can wait," he replied, shoving the phone back into his pocket. Turning, he flagged down Asia. "Can we get two more Amaretto sours, please?"

"I got it," Ahmad told her, coming from the other end of the bar. "Can you take care of the bachelorette party down there?"

I looked in the direction that he was talking about and spotted a group of five women giggling. They were staring at Ahmad as he grabbed two glasses and started making our drinks.

"They've had a lot to drink," Brayden pointed out.

"Who?" I asked, focusing back on my date.

"The women down there with the dick hats."

I laughed, noticing what they had on their heads. "Yeah, probably so. But that's the whole point of the bachelorette party, right? Have a good time with your friends for your last hurrah as a single person."

"Yeah, I guess. But the hats are a bit much."

I shrugged. "To each their own."

He looked surprised. "Would you wear something like that for your bachelorette party?"

"If it went with my outfit and my bridesmaids bought it. I wouldn't buy it myself, but one of my best friends would absolutely buy that and make us wear it." I smiled, thinking about Nina. "I mean, I could see her requiring us to do that for her birthday."

He chuckled. "Oh, wow!"

"What about you? Would you wear something crazy for your bachelor party?"

"Oh, hell nah."

"You wouldn't go out with your boys with little hats with . . ." I put my hand against the top of my head and wiggled my fingers, imitating the phalluses emitting from the hats of the bachelorettes.

"I can guarantee you I wouldn't have dicks on my head," he balked.

"Ooooookay," Ahmad intoned, sliding the drinks in front of us.

"Nah, man, it's not what it sounds like," Brayden tried to explain.

Ahmad held up his hands and backed away. "No judgment here."

I cackled.

"It's not funny," Brayden said with a laugh.

"It's a little funny," I returned. "But seriously, I don't think I asked if you'd been married before."

He cleared his throat. "No, I don't think you did. Yeah, I was."

Caught off guard, I took a tiny sip of my drink to mask my surprise. "Oh? Was?"

"Yeah. She, uh . . . she passed away."

I gasped. "I'm sorry to hear that."

He shook his head. "It's been a long time. But thank you."

"How long has it been?"

"About three years now."

"So, when you said you hadn't been on a date in a while, did you mean since she . . . passed?"

"No, no, no. I've been ready to date for about a year now. But over the last couple of months, I realized I'm ready for something more." Scooping my hand from midair, he ran his thumb over my knuckles. "Particularly, I'm looking to explore this connection with you."

My face flushed. And even though his fingertips were no longer brushing my skin, his touch lingered.

For the next forty-five minutes, we sipped and talked and laughed. Brayden was an engaging storyteller. He'd married young, and life had taken them on two separate paths. He said they were happy, and the relationship was strong until her undiagnosed medical condition seized her heart. He took time to work on himself, and then he dipped his toe into the dating scene. He recounted his attempts to date over the last year and his newfound commitment to finding the right woman.

"I believe in intentional dating," I told him, nodding in agreement. "No games. If there's mutual interest, compatibility, and both people want the same thing out of the relationship, there's no reason it shouldn't be a successful pairing."

"Exactly," he agreed.

"Do you feel like you're being intentional?"

"I do." He reached out and touched my hand again. "Especially as I get to know you better."

"You two still doing okay?" Ahmad asked, interrupting the moment.

Brayden let go of my hand and faced our bartender. "Can we get another round?"

Ahmad glanced at me and my still-full glass. "Okay. Would you like to switch it up?"

"No, two of the same," Brayden answered for the both of us.

Ahmad looked at my glass and then at me. When I nodded, so did he. "Another round, coming up."

Brayden focused his attention back on me. "The drink is helping my nerves."

"You're nervous?"

"Hell yeah. It's been a while since I've been on a date with someone and really cared that it went well. I always want the women I take out to have a good time, but with you . . . with you, I care if you want a second date." He gestured to me. "And also, you're fine as hell."

I didn't even realize I was grinning until Ahmad placed our drinks in front of us and I caught a glimpse of myself in the mirror.

"Well, rest assured, I am having a great time, and a second date sounds incredible."

"What's your favorite type of food?" he asked, picking up his fresh glass.

"Breakfast," I answered honestly.

A hearty laugh burst out of him.

My jaw dropped. "What?" I wondered.

"I was thinking you were going to say *soul food, Haitian food, Italian food, Mexican food,* something specific. But you said *breakfast.*"

"Why is that funny?" I asked indignantly.

He took a gulp of his drink and then grabbed my hands. "It's not funny. It's unexpected. Just like all the other things I've learned about you." He looked down at his hands encircling mine before meeting my eyes again. "You are completely unexpected."

Heat radiated from where he touched me and swept up my arms. "Unexpected in a good way?"

He leaned forward like he was preparing to kiss me. "Unexpected in the best way."

"Brayden," a woman roared, startling us apart.

I looked over and quickly located to whom the voice belonged. With brown skin contrasted with honey-blond hair, the tall, curvy woman was beautiful. And had it not been for her narrowed eyes, crinkled nose, and raised upper lip, that beauty would've been the first thing I noticed about her. But as her shoulders rose and fell rapidly, I couldn't stop focusing on the waves of fury that emanated from her.

Brayden dropped my hands, and I looked between the woman and my date.

He was stone-still with his mouth hanging slightly ajar. She was frozen in place with unmistakable rage. And I looked between them in disbelief.

Aw hell naw.

With both her fists balled up, she charged across the room.

I turned my entire body so that I could face her. I wasn't sure if she was going to try to swing on me or not, but I needed to be prepared. I didn't know how to fight. More than that, I refused to fight over a man. But I wasn't going to let someone just hit me without defending myself. Running through the moves I learned in kickboxing class, I prepared to bust out the jab-cross-jab-hook combo.

"What the hell is going on here, Brayden?" the woman yelled.

The conversations that surrounded us hushed. People turned to look. A few even stopped dancing. Only the mellow beat of the music carried over the tense atmosphere.

"I'm sorry," Brayden whispered before he rose to his feet. "Sierra, uh, what—" He blocked her path. "What are you doing here?"

"You said you had to work late, but your office said you left on time," she spat. "And since you wouldn't answer your phone, I used the tracker app."

"Well, I was just finishing up here. Can we talk outside?"

"Move! Get your hands off me!" the woman shouted as she tried to move around him to see me. "What? You don't want your date to know you have a *wife*!"

I balked. "A wife?"

"Yes, I'm his wife," she reiterated, trying to get around him.

"Come on, Sierra. Chill. I'm meeting with a colleague and—"

"A colleague? Are you kidding me?" she screeched, sidestepping him to point at me. Her hand was only a couple of feet away from me before he pushed her back a step. "You're lying and saying you're in a meeting, but you were holding this bitch's hand!"

"Calling me a bitch is a little uncalled for," I grumbled under my breath.

"What?" she growled, turning her anger toward me. "You have something you want to say to me?"

I frowned and shook my head. "Nah, you good."

That bitch looked strong.

"I know I'm good." She held up her left hand. "That's why he married me."

I stared at her in confusion. *Well, he asked me on a date and said he was a widower, so he really ain't a prize, sis.*

I lifted my hands. "You can have him," I assured her. "I didn't know he was married."

She glared at him and then looked at his hands. "Where's your fucking ring?"

He pulled it from his jacket pocket. "I must've forgotten to put it back on when I left the gym. You know I worked out after work today."

"Stop lying, you piece of shit!"

"I'm not lying!"

"How long have you been dating my husband?" She yelled the question at me. Each attempt she made to get around Brayden to get to me, he blocked her.

"This was a first date," I answered. "Again, I didn't know he was married. He said he was . . . single."

I decided at the last minute not to tell her what he really said. I wanted to avoid making a bad situation worse.

Brayden shot me a look over his shoulder before he faced his wife again. "Sierra, please—"

I gasped as the pop of her hand slapping his cheek reverberated through the bar.

Oh, she's trying to throw hands for real!

My eyes widened, and I didn't know if I should get up and leave or be prepared to defend myself.

I was shook.

She reared back and attempted to hit him again.

"Both of you! Out! Now!" Ahmad barked.

The authority in his voice seemed to startle them as much as it startled me.

I didn't realize Onyx had security until two men that I'd never noticed before appeared seemingly out of nowhere and corralled Brayden and the screaming Sierra out of the bar.

Since the two people who were causing the scene were escorted out, all eyes were on me. A couple of women were whispering and glancing over at me. A man was openly gawking with his friends. An older woman frowned, looking at me in disdain. I even heard someone call me a homewrecker. I wanted to leave, but I couldn't. I didn't want Brayden and his wife waiting for me. I didn't like how people were staring at me, but they weren't going to try to fight me. Unfortunately, staying put was the only option I had.

Exhaling loudly, I turned around on my stool and sighed.

When my eyes met Ahmad's gaze, I didn't see judgment or pity. "You good?" he asked.

"Yeah," I sighed.

He slid a Malibu sunrise in front of me. "You sure?"

I smiled appreciatively as he removed all of the Amaretto sour glasses. "Yeah." I took a sip of the drink he'd just given me. "I'm not worried about him."

"I'm not talking about him. I'm talking about her—the wife. She looked like she was going to beat your ass."

My eyes went wide. "Listen! Ain't no might about it. She would've definitely beat my ass."

He chuckled. "Ol' boy wasn't going to let that happen. He was doing basketball drills to keep her from getting to you."

"If I would've told her how he told me that he was a widower, he would've let her get me."

"Well, I wouldn't have let that happen. Can't let anything happen to that face."

A smile stretched my lips. "Aww, thank you."

"Because blood makes me squeamish," he continued.

My jaw dropped. "You asshole."

He laughed. "Nah, but for real, if I thought you were in any real danger, I would've stepped in sooner. You were always good."

I lifted my glass in appreciation. "Thank you."

"I told you, I got you."

"You did say that."

"By any means necessary." He paused for a second. "Wait, he told you he was a widower? So, he killed her off?" He shook his head. "That's cold."

"Right?" I put my elbows on the bar and let my head fall into my hands. "And now everyone in here thinks I'm a homewrecker. This dating app shit is the worst," I groaned.

"Hey. Look at me," he commanded gently.

I lifted my face and met his gaze.

"Everybody has shit," he pointed out.

"Yeah, but everybody's shit isn't on display. Everybody here knows I went on a date with a married man, and so they either think I choose bad men or that I knowingly and willingly date married men—which I don't."

"Don't worry about what anyone else thinks. You know the truth."

"And you know the truth."

He made a clicking noise and screwed up his face. "I mean, I know what you told me. But I couldn't vouch for you."

I gasped. "Ahmad!"

He laughed. "I'm playing. I got you."

"You said everyone has shit. Tell me something about you—something real."

He lowered his voice. "I don't drive."

"What?" I scoffed.

What thirty-two-year-old man doesn't know how to drive?

He was always trying to make jokes.

A look I couldn't quite place crossed his face.

Is he . . . is he serious?

"You don't have a car? You don't know how to drive? Or . . . ?" I asked carefully, trying to read him.

"I own a car. And I know *how* to drive. I just . . . don't do it," he explained.

"Why?"

"Long story."

I eyed him quizzically. "If you want to share, I want to know."

"Car accident fucked me up a couple years ago."

The vulnerability in his words gripped me tight. "I'm so sorry."

I was trying to get information about his dating life, his wife, his marriage. I didn't expect for him to share about a trauma. And as I sat with it, I realized I felt closer to him because of it.

"Everybody goes through stuff, and then they just figure it out. You had another bad date. You'll get through it." He looked over at a man patiently waiting. "What did I tell you?" he asked.

My face scrunched, and I lifted my shoulders. "To give the app a chance?"

"What did I tell you earlier tonight?"

"I don't know."

"I told you that cold front was coming." Changing his voice to that stiff news anchor tone, he added, "And I was right! Brayden Storm, signing off!"

The laugh bubbled up before I could stop it. "You get on my damn nerves."

Ahmad backed away to go take the man's order. "Are you going to hang around for a while?"

I picked up my drink and took a sip. "Yeah, for a little bit."

He smirked. "Good."

8

"You didn't get anything to eat," Ahmad noticed. "You can't drink on an empty stomach. Not that you were drinking much."

My stomach rumbled as I nodded. "Yeah, I guess I'll take a basket of fries."

"Our wings are good, too."

I shook my head. "You do not want to see me eat wings."

"Well, I'd rather offer you wings than a burger." He pointed to my striped dress. "Ol' robble robble ass."

I gasped as he made the unintelligible noise that the Hamburglar was known for. The unexpected joke caused a loud laugh turned cough.

"I hate you," I told him with tears in my eyes. Wiping away any eyeliner that could've smeared, I couldn't hide my amusement. "You're really showing your age with the Hamburglar reference."

He cocked his head to the side. "And yet, you knew exactly who I was talking about." With a smirk, he tapped his hand on the bar and backed away. "I'll put an order in for you."

I rolled my eyes, but my cheeks hurt from smiling.

"What's your name, beautiful?" a deep voice asked about a minute later as he took the seat next to me.

I glanced over at him.

He was cute and wore a nice suit.

"Aaliyah," I responded. "And you are?"

He flashed a smile. "I'm Ray."

"It's nice to meet you, Ray."

His gaze lingered on my lips. "The pleasure is *all* mine. I like to get to know the people I'm sharing space with."

"Oh, we're sharing space?"

"We are now." He grinned. "I came in here to celebrate, and

then I noticed this beautiful woman at the bar, so if you'll allow me to stay in your presence, I'd say we are sharing space."

"Hmm." I gave him a skeptical look. "Okay."

"Can I buy you a drink?"

I tapped my half-filled glass. "I have one, but thank you."

"What can I get you?" Ahmad asked.

I did a double take. *Damn! Did he sneak up?*

"I'll take a vodka martini, and you can get this beautiful lady another drink if she wants it."

"I told you, I'm fine," I replied with a soft smile. "But thank you."

"You are more than fine," Ray flirted.

Ahmad cleared his throat. "Okay, I'll get your drink." He glanced at me. "And your food will be out in a couple minutes."

My eyes connected with Ahmad's. "Thank you."

"Yeah, thanks, man," Ray added. "Now back to you . . ." He turned his attention back to me. "What are you doing here tonight? Looking all good and shit . . . you can't be here all alone."

"I had a date that ended early," I answered honestly.

"What happened?"

"Why?"

"I have to make sure I don't make the same mistakes he did on our date."

Smiling, I shook my head. "What makes you think I'm open to a date with you?"

"Because you keep flashing that gorgeous smile my way."

I cocked my head to the side. "Is that right?"

"Vodka martini," Ahmad interrupted, sliding the drink in front of Ray. He gave me a look before adding, "Your food will be out in a few."

Confusion caused my head to tilt as I held his gaze. "Thanks . . ." I said slowly.

When I tore my eyes from him, I found Ray staring at me. "Can I ask you a quick question?" He lifted his glass to his lips. "I wanted to at least buy you a drink before picking your brain, but here we are."

"Picking my brain? What's up?"

"I need a couple of suggestions. How can I move a random bar meeting to a first date with you?"

I let out a light laugh. "Okay." I put my glass to my lips and took a sip. "That was kind of smooth."

He turned on the barstool, so his body was facing me. "I'm real smooth if you give me a chance." He reached his left hand out to briefly touch my arm. "Let me get your number, and I can show you how smooth . . ."

I noticed the indentation on his ring finger and sighed. "You know what would be real smooth?"

"What's that?"

"Being faithful to your wife."

His eyes widened fractionally. "Wh-what? Wife? What are you talking about?"

"Where does she think you are?" I wondered. He looked like he was going to try to lie and defend himself, so I continued, "I'm genuinely curious."

He slid off the stool. "I don't know what you mean, but I'm here to celebrate." He picked up his drink with two fingers and pointed to me. "I thought you looked like someone I could celebrate with, but you're on some other shit."

"Everything okay?" Ahmad said in a deep voice as he placed my burger and fries in front of me.

"Yeah, this married man was just leaving," I said loudly.

Sputtering, Ray backed away from me. "Yo, what is wrong with you? I'm not married."

"Save your lies for someone who'll believe them," I called after him.

When I turned back around, Ahmad was staring at me.

"What are you doing?" he questioned.

My eyes widened. "What do you mean?"

"These"—he made a slightly disgusted face—"men. These dates."

I jerked my thumb backward toward the door. "That married man wasn't my date!" I scoffed.

"But the married man before him was. And ol' boy last week."

My mouth hung open for a moment. "You think they acted like

they didn't have any sense before I agreed to meet them?" I asked incredulously.

"No, but I think you need help."

"I don't need help," I balked.

He lifted his hands. "These dudes you keep linking with suggest otherwise."

I felt called out. "Wow, okay, Ahmad."

Leaning over the bar, he grabbed my arm. His fingertips seared my skin as soon as he gripped me. Even if I wanted to get up and walk away from him and those delicious-looking fries, I was rooted in place.

"Don't take it the wrong way," he said gently. "All I'm saying is come out with me and the fellas tomorrow night. Eight o'clock at Lava. We have a section under Ahmad Williamson."

I pursed my lips, but I didn't say no.

"I think you'd enjoy yourself," he continued.

"Are you trying to set me up?"

"No." His answer was firm, almost sharp.

"Because after what happened a few weeks ago, I'm not interested."

"A night out with some real ones might help you."

"I don't need help," I repeated with a little less conviction.

"Being around men who know how to act could help you spot the ones you need to leave alone. And maybe being around some real ones will help you loosen up so you're not sitting over here with your shoulders hunched up."

"My shoulders aren't hunched up," I argued.

He lifted his shoulders to his ears. "Looking ass," he joked.

My head fell back as I laughed. "I can't stand you!"

Ahmad ignored someone trying to get his attention as he responded. "But you know I'm right."

"Whatever."

"Prove me wrong at Lava tomorrow at eight."

I nodded, but I didn't verbally commit.

He smiled. "Your food is getting cold." He walked off to take an order.

I put some sanitizer on my hands and then popped a fry in my mouth. "Mmm."

I looked down at the thick-cut fries with the array of seasoning on them.

"Good, right?" Asia asked as she handed the couple next to me two beers.

"Hands down the best fries I've ever had," I told her.

"I told you," Ahmad said, overhearing our conversation as he carried a case of something behind Asia.

I watched his biceps flex under the weight of the case before jerking my eyes to his face. "You did say I'd like them," I admitted slowly.

"Stick with me. I'm right about a lot of things."

"You weren't right about the size of that shirt," Asia joked.

I snickered. "Ahmad *stay* wearing OshKosh B'Gosh."

"Gymboree!" Asia laughed loudly before heading to the other end of the bar.

"Baby Gap!"

Ahmad looked like he was trying his hardest not to laugh, which made me laugh harder.

"Both of y'all can kiss my ass," he grumbled with a huge smile on his face.

I ate my food and spent the next couple of hours exchanging jokes and laughing with Ahmad. I had such a good time that when I got home that night, I found myself feeling light and happy. Even after a few bad dates, it didn't feel as disastrous because of Ahmad.

I didn't even bother to open the dating app on Saturday morning. I saw the numerous notifications and I sucked my teeth. Even though I felt like I thoroughly vetted the men I met up with, I still was choosing the wrong ones. Between a man who lied about his kids and a man who lied about his wife, I was just done with the app.

Maybe I do *need help.*

Just the thought forced Ahmad into my mind.

He didn't take a break to spend time with me at the bar, but every chance he got, he checked on me, he talked to me, he made me laugh. His personality was so different from what I thought when I first met him. His conversation was engaging and intelligent, his personality was honest and funny. And I hated to admit it, but I liked him.

Not like that, I assured myself.

It was just that Ahmad had the type of reassuring presence that filled me with a sense of calm. He was obviously attractive, so my body reacted to the sight of him from time to time. And he was honest, so his frankness cut a little deep sometimes. But underneath that was a comforting calmness that made me feel safe with him.

It was rare.

I liked it.

I liked him.

He made a big impression on me last night. So much so that I spent the majority of the day laughing at things we'd said and jokes we'd made as I cleaned my apartment.

My phone had dinged and beeped and vibrated all day, but it rang for the first time around four o'clock in the afternoon.

"Hello?" I answered as soon as I saw who it was.

"So, you're going, right?" Nina questioned immediately.

Even though she was out of town, I'd texted her about Ahmad's offer when I'd gotten home. I assumed she was asleep or busy since it was almost one o'clock in the morning and a man had taken her on a weekend getaway. Because of that, I figured she was going to send me a text in response. But it was just like Nina to jump right into it.

"No hello or nothing, huh?" I replied with a laugh.

"Nope. I only have a few minutes before he comes back to the room. And since there's not much time, I'm going to give you some real talk. You need to go to Lava, and if I was home, I would be right there with you. You know who's going to be there tonight?"

"No, who?"

"Terra-Cotta."

My eyes widened. "What?"

Richland's very own Terra-Cotta was an R&B group that had been gaining national attention over the last few months. They were on the rise to superstardom, and they still did pop-up shows locally.

I was *really looking forward to seeing them again live.*

"You need to be there," Nina reiterated. "You need to get out more, and this is the perfect opportunity."

"I don't know . . ." I kind of groaned as I pulled my legs onto the couch with me. "Ahmad is—"

"You said Ahmad's sexy ass asked you to meet him in his section at Lava to see Terra-Cotta's pop-up show," she interrupted. "I'm not seeing the downside here."

"Ahmad is married."

"Girl, he invited you out with him and his boys. He didn't invite you to sit on his dick. Go to the damn lounge and stop playing."

"He's *married*."

"Maybe his wife will be there. Or maybe he invited you out because he thinks of you as one of the boys. Or maybe he wants you to meet one of his boys. Or maybe he wants to fuck you and he's just like these other cheating-ass dudes. Either way, you need to focus more on what you want and how to get it. Get out of the house. Go to Lava. See Terra-Cotta. Meet some men."

Laughing, I shook my head. "Nina!"

"You're laughing because I'm right. You claim this man is just your friend."

I readjusted my position on the couch and placed my feet on the floor. "He *is* just my friend."

"So, I don't see a downside. Friends hang out."

I silently pursed my lips.

She was right.

I wanted to go, and if I were being honest with myself, I'd been trying to talk myself out of it. But Nina was absolutely right. Ahmad was a friend who invited me out to do something that was definitely up my alley. There was no legitimate reason for me to not go if I wanted to go.

"Hey, I thought I had a few more minutes," Nina said suddenly. "I'm touching bases with my girl. I'll meet you in the shower."

I knew she wasn't talking to me, and I heard a deep voice reply in the background. She laughed at something before she came back to the line. "Hey, I'm back."

"You sound really happy right now. I see the Fun One is treating you right," I speculated, using the nickname she gave him.

"Absolutely. Details to come. But in the meantime, text me a picture of what you're wearing to Lava."

"I didn't say I was going," I protested quickly.

"Yeah, but we both know you are. Text me your outfit. Bye-eeeeeee!"

I laughed. "Goodbye, Nina!"

We hung up, and I immediately went to my closet to figure out what I was going to wear. After making a final decision and sending a photo to the group chat, I started working on my hair. When I was fully dressed and ready to leave, I admired myself in the mirror.

I look good, I thought as I did a little spin.

I snapped another picture and sent it to the group chat so Nina and Jazmyn could see my finished look. They said I was dressed like I had a hot date. I told them I didn't know what Ahmad's friends looked like, and I doubted that one of them could be my next boyfriend. They said I was giving date vibes, and I almost reconsidered my outfit.

Those were *not* the vibes I was trying to give.

I could still hear them teasing me about me trying to seduce Ahmad and his friends as the car I was in pulled up to Lava. I climbed out of the back seat still shaking my head at their jokes. Looking around, I was so glad I didn't let them get in my head.

I wiggled my toes in my gold strappy sandals before thanking the driver and closing the door behind me.

"I fit right in," I mused as I flounced out the white minidress.

My outfit had a flowy skirt that showcased my thick thighs and pretty legs. The sweetheart neckline was subtle in the way it brought attention to my cleavage. But the color against my skin was the main reason I wore it. It was a hot, late-July night, and almost every woman I saw in the parking lot and in line was wearing a short dress or short shorts. Legs were out everywhere. Skin was definitely exposed.

I took a picture of the line and sent it to the group chat before slipping my phone into my gold bag. When I got to the front, I showed my ID and asked them to point me in the direction of the sections.

"Whoa," I uttered as I entered the main space.

People were everywhere.

But it was crowded without being packed. I could easily maneuver through the crowd but not without brushing into someone. The DJ didn't have the music that loud, so there were some people dancing, but it seemed that most people were talking. The lights were bright, and the energy was positive and light. I could tell it was going to be a good night, and I'd just arrived.

I followed the directions the bouncer gave me and climbed the steps to the platform. As soon as I reached the top step, I stopped. Before I got a chance to survey the scene, I saw a tall man with broad shoulders and a sponge-curl fade with his back to me.

I knew it was Ahmad without him having to turn around. He was at the end of the walkway talking to someone I couldn't see. He had on black pants and a black short-sleeved collar shirt with stripes. My eyes danced over his muscular arms as he pointed to something, and I inhaled deeply.

Get it out of your system now.

The man looked good. I didn't even have to see him from the front to be taken by him.

"Hey, angel. You looking for me?" a man in the first section asked.

I shifted my attention to a short but cute man in a white shirt and white linen pants.

"We match," he pointed out as he rose to his feet and opened his arms. "So, if you aren't looking for me, you should be. Because I got room for your thick, pretty ass over here."

The three men in his section snickered at his antics.

"I'm good, but thank you," I replied.

"You sure?"

"Yeah, she's sure," a deep voice answered for me.

My head snapped toward it, but I already knew to whom it belonged.

Ahmad's voice sounded like thunder as it rumbled over the velvet rope toward the man in white. He looked good as he drew closer to me. The shirt was just as stylish from the front as it was from the back. I wasn't sure how he did it, but somehow, he looked even better outside of Onyx.

As he reached his arm out to me, I glanced at how his tattoo snaked down his bicep. He slipped his hand to the small of my back as he took his final step.

As soon as our eyes locked, my heart thumped in my chest.

Well, damn.

9

Placing his hand on my lower back, Ahmad escorted me down the walkway to his section.

"You good?" he wondered when we'd taken a few steps.

Still reeling from the array of emotions that interaction elicited in me, I didn't answer at first. I was concentrating on putting one foot in front of the other. "Oh, yeah, sorry." I cleared my throat and looked up at him. "I was fine. He seemed harmless."

He sighed. The disappointment pulled his full, luscious lips into a frown. "And this is exactly why I wanted you to come out tonight."

I made a face. "What?"

"Those guys have tried to get at every beautiful woman who has crossed their path for the last thirty minutes or so and because I knew you'd come looking like this and they'd try you—"

My skin heated as his compliment rang in my ears. In the midst of the point he was trying to make, my body clung to the fact that he was low-key attracted to me.

I'm glad I didn't change.

"I don't know what game they're playing, but they are not what you're looking for. And for a minute, it looked like you were falling for it."

My face scrunched up as I processed everything he was saying. "Do you really think I'm unaccustomed to being hit on? Do you think I give my number to anybody who asks?"

"No, I don't think that. But I do think those guys are the same type of riffraff you've been bringing into Onyx."

I balked. "Riffraff?!"

"Are you denying it?"

"I'm questioning your use of *riffraff*. How old are you?"

"Old enough to see someone in need and to help out." He leaned down so his mouth was close to my ear. "And you need help."

His breath was cool and minty, but it felt like fire as it danced across my skin.

I shivered.

"You need help," I countered, pushing him away from me. Hoping he didn't catch his effect on me, I glared at him. "And just because your shirt isn't dirty tonight doesn't mean you are qualified to give me advice, Ahmad."

He laughed. "Even though I *am* qualified, I didn't just invite you out to give you advice."

"Qualified, my ass! Ahmad, you are unlicensed without the first credit hour to your name."

Chuckling, he unlatched the velvet rope. "Shut up and get your ass in here."

Grinning, I stepped inside the three-couch section that had a perfect, unobstructed view of the stage. The brick wall and the dark cherry-red couches created a vibe. The glass table with champagne on ice, bottles of water, cans of energy drinks, and various juices created a mood. But the two handsome men sitting on two of the three couches made it a party.

"And you must be Aaliyah," the sexy, dark-skinned man with the taper fade and the long, well-kempt beard greeted me.

"I am." I slipped my hand into his outstretched one. "And you are?"

"Leon." He brought my hand to his lips. "But you can call me yours."

I laughed. "Wowwwwwww."

He laughed along with me. "You like that?"

"It was cute. Corny, but cute."

"Aight, that's enough," Ahmad interjected, grabbing my shoulders and shifting me in the other direction. "This is Darius."

I smiled at the light-skinned cutie with the curly hair and dimples. "Hi, Darius."

"What's up, Aaliyah?" He shook my hand. "I've heard a lot about you. It's nice to meet you."

"It's nice to meet you as well." I let go of his hand and looked between the three of them. "Thanks for having me."

"Glad you could make it," Ahmad replied, taking a seat on the empty couch. "Sit, drink, relax, enjoy yourself." He gestured to the other end of the couch he was on. "Make yourself at home."

I sat about a foot away from him. "Thank you." Sitting back, I crossed my ankles. "So, what brings you out tonight? What's the occasion?"

"My birthday was a couple weeks ago," Leon answered. "Darius finally had a weekend off. And Ahmad is a music head and wanted to see Terra-Cotta."

I smiled, shifting my gaze around the group. "Well . . . happy belated birthday."

"Thank you," he said, winking.

"I'm glad you got a weekend off," I said to Darius.

"You and me both," he replied, lifting his glass.

Turning my attention to Ahmad, I smiled. "I love Terra-Cotta."

Ahmad nodded. "Everybody is rocking with the hometown heroes now. I like that shit."

"No," I clarified. "I *love* Terra-Cotta. I've been rocking with them since they came on the scene."

He gave me a suspicious look. "What do you know about Terra-Cotta?"

"I was at the open mic where they launched their career six years ago! When they performed the original first verse of 'The Quickening,' I was there. I'm not some new fan who hopped on the bandwagon this year when their single got national attention. I've been following them since the beginning."

His eyes got huge. "No fucking way."

"Yes fucking way," I said, playfully mocking him.

"I was there."

My eyes widened. "What?!"

"I was at that open mic."

"No you weren't!"

"He was there," Darius confirmed. "We both were. We were on a double date with the Murphy twins and . . ." His sentence trailed off into a light chuckle. He took a sip of his drink and then shook his head. "We were there."

I looked between the two of them curiously. "I feel like there's more to the story."

"Oh, there's a lot more to the story," Leon snickered. "The Murphy twins had boyfriends they forgot to mention, and once they left the open mic spot, Darius and Ahmad almost got their asses kicked."

"You lying like shit now!" Ahmad exclaimed. His eyes danced with the amusement of his recollection of the event. Turning to me, he shook his head. "Don't listen to him."

I turned to Ahmad with a shocked expression. "You got your ass beat?" I poked at his bicep as it stretched the silky fabric of his shirt. "So, these are just for show?"

His friends hollered.

"I like her!"

"She's funny!"

His friends' amusement triggered my own, and I couldn't keep a straight face anymore.

"Mannnnnnn, y'all some assholes," Ahmad grumbled before he burst out laughing, too.

"After that beatdown, that's when Ahmad started hitting the gym. So, in his defense, he wasn't as brolic as he is now," Leon concluded. "Don't let them pretty boys fool you—they got hands now. They been training." He wiped down his white button-up shirt. "As a former football player, I *been* in fighting condition. I wasn't with them that night or I would've held it down. They wouldn't have been able to do anything with this." He flexed his muscles.

I smirked. "Ohhhh, so they're new to this, but you're true to this?"

He nodded emphatically. "Yes. Exactly."

"I hope you're not believing his bullshit," Darius said, refilling his glass.

I quirked an eyebrow. "So y'all didn't almost get beat up?"

Ahmad made a sarcastic noise. "Oh, nah, we absolutely got knocked the fuck out," he confirmed.

"But Leon's over there acting like he was a D-I college athlete and was headed to the pros," Darius continued. "He played flag football with the community league until he tore his meniscus."

Leon jumped to his feet and flexed again. "Okay, but is that not football?" He turned his attention to me and winked. "You see it."

"I sure do."

"I didn't think I needed to say this, but Aaliyah is off-limits. She's here to see how civilized men act, so act civilized, Leon," Ahmad stated while pointing to his flirtatious friend.

With a smile, Leon lifted his hands in surrender. "I hear you. I hear you." He then looked over at me and winked.

"Oh God," Ahmad groaned. "And on that note, I'm gonna need something stronger than this."

"Same," Darius agreed, lifting his hand to flag down the waitstaff.

"Oh, wow, is India Davis supposed to be here, too?" Leon wondered as he stared and pointed down to the first-floor level.

"Where?" Ahmad leaped to his feet, looking around in the same direction that Leon was pointing.

Leon stood up and slung his arm over Ahmad's shoulders. "Is that how civilized men act? Thirsty?"

"You was playing?" Laughing, Ahmad pushed Leon back, and he dramatically flopped onto the couch. "Don't play like that about India!"

"Why did you do him like that? You know he loves him some India Davis," I cackled.

After we placed orders for drinks and food, we easily fell into another conversation. They were all so comical and different. They all had attractive personalities to match their exteriors. But my eyes kept fixating on Ahmad. I enjoyed him behind the bar, but seeing him outside of Onyx, being fully himself, was captivating. Ahmad and I talked a lot, and I knew plenty about him, but seeing him with his friends felt different. It felt intimate.

"You good?" he asked.

"Oh, I—so sorry," I sputtered, realizing I was staring at him. "I was zoned out and . . . sorry."

He licked his lips. "It's cool. I asked if you'd lined up your next date on the app yet."

I rolled my eyes and sat back. "Not at all. I haven't been back on there. I don't think it's for me."

"Oh, what app are you on?" Leon asked.

"TenderFish," Darius answered before I got a chance.

I stared at him for a second. "You said you've heard a lot about me," I said slowly. Looking around at the men, I felt a flash of awkwardness. "Did Ahmad tell you that I needed help?"

"Yes," the two friends said in unison.

All four of us burst out laughing.

Reaching over, I shoved Ahmad's shoulder. "What the hell?"

"I *did not* say that!" he protested, barely moving from my effort.

"Nah, he didn't," Darius clarified when our amusement died down. "He just told us that his friend from the bar was coming out with us tonight. I asked him what your situation was, and he said you were single."

"Which tells me that you don't currently have a man in your life . . ." Leon chimed in. "And even though he said you were coming, he didn't mention how good you look."

"Because that's the least interesting thing about her," Ahmad responded. "I told you she was cool and that I'm looking out for her." He shifted his attention to me. "And right before you got here, I told them I wanted to expose you to the type of man you need in your life."

I searched his face for any indication of a joke. The sincerity was so pure that I felt myself holding his gaze a little too long. Something stirred within me.

I exhaled slowly, and a knot developed in my belly. "And what type of man is that?"

"Here are your appetizers," a woman interrupted, placing five plates of food on the glass table in the middle of the couches.

I ripped my eyes away from Ahmad and stared at the food. *What was that?*

As we grabbed plates and started to eat, the conversation circled back to my dating life.

"So, what's going on that Ahmad wanted you to be around some real ones like us?" Darius asked before biting into a wing.

"It's not me, it's the men I keep coming across," I explained.

"They seem cool at first, and then they end up being flakes, liars, or cheaters. Literally, the last three dates I went on."

"What questions are you asking them before you meet up?" Darius asked.

"And what pictures do you have on your profile?" Leon questioned.

"I ask the basics about their intentions with dating, goals, likes and dislikes, deal-breakers, beliefs, values." I shrugged. "The normal important details for me." I opened my phone and showed them three of my pictures. "And these are on my profile, and they are good—we have full body, we have face, we have natural beauty."

As they gave me props for my profile and questions, I noticed Ahmad was sitting back, saying nothing.

"Now all of a sudden, you don't have anything to say?" I wondered quizzically.

A small smile played on his lips. "It's not anything you're doing. It's the men you're picking." He gestured around. "You see how easy everything flowed here? Not one time have you looked like"—he hunched his shoulders to his ears—"this."

I slapped his arm playfully. "I do not look like that when I'm on the dates! You gotta stop lying," I giggled.

"No, but seriously, you have to trust your gut with these dudes," Ahmad told me. "You didn't know them"—he gestured between Leon and Darius—"before tonight, and you were comfortable, you read the situation, you had no expectations. You've been you. You've been the you I met when you had that . . . first date." He gave me a look, and we both knew he was talking about the time I was stood up. "When you're you, you'll see what it is you need to see and link up with what's for you."

"This muthafucka thinks he's Dr. Phil now," Leon joked, causing us all to laugh. "He's right, though."

"Yeah, you're cool as hell," Darius agreed. "If you can't relax around someone, they ain't it."

"I agree, and I thank you," I told them. "But this was different."

I was sitting around with three friends—all of them fine as

fuck—but still, it was a meetup with a married friend and friends of that married friend. It wasn't a date.

"Kinda, but not really," Leon replied.

"This isn't a date," I explained to the three confused-looking faces around me. "It's different because this is not a date."

Leon reached out for me. "We could leave these two and make it a date."

I laughed, swatting at his hand. "You're such a flirt! My point is Ahmad's my new friend. And you're Ahmad's friends. This was a no-pressure situation. There's no stress."

Darius looked at Ahmad, so I looked over at him, too. His chiseled jaw was set, and his full lips were in a tight line.

"Okay, it's not exactly the same," Leon relented, pulling my attention back to him. "But it doesn't change the fact that being comfortable is key."

"We know how men think, and so you're still going to come across the liars and the cheaters, but you should feel comfortable with the people you're around."

Ahmad put his hand on my back. "There should never be any pressure—even if it is a date."

I held his gaze, and for some reason, I felt a little choked up by the sentiment. It was such a simple statement. Swallowing hard, I nodded.

The lights flickered and dimmed, and everyone in the place started screaming. I tore my eyes from his and glanced at the stage.

"Please put your hands together for Terra-Cotta!" someone yelled through the speakers.

Clapping, the four of us got up to get a better view as the R&B trio made their grand entrance. Because it wasn't a concert, there was no opening act. The DJ left the booth, and Terra-Cotta got right to it.

From the first chord, I loudly sang right along with them. I was in the zone, dancing to the music and just enjoying myself.

"Let's go check out what's happening down there," Leon suggested, pointing to a group of beautiful women singing loudly on the dance floor below us.

"Yeah, they seem fun," Darius pointed out. "Y'all coming?"

"Nah, I'm good," Ahmad answered.

Darius's eyes widened, and he nodded. "Oh yeah, you're right."

I pretended I wasn't listening and snuck a fond glance at Ahmad. *He's such a good man.*

"Aaliyah, what about you?" Darius wondered.

I shook my head. "No, I'm going to stay up here."

"She doesn't want to go down there to meet men, because she's waiting for me," Leon explained humorously as they walked away.

"Don't mind him," Ahmad told me with a shake of his head. "That man plays too damn much. And—oh, this is my shit!"

The song that started was one of my favorites, too. We started crooning together as we appreciated the show that was being put on. We talked about the soul in their voices, the advanced choreography, and the energy in their performance. We were so caught up in the music and each other, I didn't even notice when the guys rolled up.

"Struck out?" Ahmad questioned, causing me to turn and look behind me.

"First of all," Darius started, poking Ahmad in the chest. "Yes."

I snickered behind my hand before turning back to the stage. I vaguely listened to their story for about thirty seconds before the group hit a high note that stole my attention.

I was transfixed.

"If you're celebrating something, I need you to go to the middle of the dance floor in five minutes," Jade, the primary singer of the group, called out about forty-five minutes into their set.

"Oh, they are going to do 'Round of Applause,' I think," I guessed excitedly, grabbing Ahmad's arm.

"I'm going down," Leon announced. "Y'all coming?"

I kind of wanted to, just in case they were going to get invited to meet the group afterward. But my gut told me it wasn't worth it. We had the best spot in the house.

"No, I'm going to stay here," I decided. "Have fun, though!"

"I'll go," Darius offered.

Ahmad shook his head. "Nah, I'm good."

The group started harmonizing, and I did a body roll as soon as the beat dropped. "We'll be cheering y'all on from here," I called behind them before turning my attention back to the stage.

I sang along, moving my body to the beat. Feeling eyes on me, I glanced over at Ahmad.

I narrowed my eyes. "What?"

"You're hitting all the notes but the ones you're supposed to hit," he joked.

"That's rich coming from someone who sounds like he's got a mouth full of marbles," I replied.

We laughed.

"Outside of my girls and my sister, I don't think I've laughed this much with anybody in my life," I told him, moving close since the music was loud. "Thanks for tonight."

When he leaned over so his forearms could rest on the guardrail, we were essentially the same height. We were eye level when he said, "You don't have to thank me. I invited you because I wanted you to be here, and I'm glad you came. I hope you got what you needed."

"A night out like this. A laugh with a friend. My dating profile being approved by your panel of friends. The best seat in the house." I sighed contentedly. "I got exactly what I needed tonight."

The harmonies of Terra-Cotta sounded like background music as his eyes dipped down to my lips. "I'm glad to hear that."

"And I appreciate what you said earlier."

His eyes flicked back up to meet mine. "I meant it."

The beat from their most popular party song dropped.

"For the people celebrating in the middle of the dance floor, are you ready?" Storm, one of the other members of Terra-Cotta, yelled out enthusiastically.

The crowd roared.

The third member of the group, Nubia, stepped forward with a huge grin. "Since they are ready, I need all of you out there to put your hands together and give them a round of applauseeeeeeeeeee!"

The song dropped and the entire place went wild.

"Look at Leon and Darius! They some damn fools," Ahmad said before he burst out laughing.

"Where?"

He moved closer, and I tried to follow his finger. "Right there."

"I don't see them."

He moved behind me and turned my head a quarter inch to the left. Leaning so his head was resting against mine, he pointed again. "Right there."

The silky material of his shirt brushed against my exposed back. His muscular chest made the silk feel warm against my skin. His closeness made the hair on the back of my neck stand at attention. My eyes closed and I gripped the metal railing tightly as his cologne infiltrated my nostrils.

"They're right near the pole," he said in a low tone that coursed through my entire body.

A shiver ran down my spine.

My eyes flew open, and I swallowed hard. I started to move out of his arms when I saw what he was talking about.

"Is that . . . Wait a fucking minute!" I burst out laughing.

My amusement triggered his, and he fell forward, the weight of him pressing me against the railing.

"These two-left-feet muthafuckas!" Ahmad chuckled. He moved to the side of me fractionally. He wasn't directly behind me anymore, but our bodies were still touching.

"Did they know they couldn't dance when they went down there?" I wondered with tears in my eyes.

"They knew!"

I gave him a look over my shoulder. "While you're standing here talking about them, can you dance?"

"Can I dance?" he scoffed, taking two steps back. "Hell yeah. Can you?"

As Terra-Cotta sang another up-tempo tune, I started rocking my hips. I put my arms in the air and moved to the beat. I started singing with them, and he joined me. His moves started to mimic mine, and as the song transitioned into the chorus, I turned my back to him and started shaking my ass.

"Oh, shit, Aaliyah, I see you," he said as he got up on me and started dancing with me.

Together, we sang loudly as we danced.

There was so much freedom in the fun we were having. There was lightness and joy in our movements. Even though our bodies were grinding against each other, it wasn't sexual. He wasn't just standing there letting me twerk on him. He was actually dancing with me—and he had rhythm. With his hands on my hips, he kept up with me. But when the beat slowed down and my movements slowed with it, something changed.

My nipples hardened, and the heat from his body permeated the fabric of my dress. He gripped my hips, his fingers digging into my fleshiness. As suddenly as the lighthearted fun washed over me, it left. A sexually charged energy crept up my spine, and desire coiled in my belly.

This needs to stop.

"Ohhhhhhh," Leon reacted loudly, causing me and Ahmad to separate hastily. He positioned himself in between us as we guiltily moved farther apart. With his arms crossed, he looked at me on one side of him and Ahmad on the other. "Now I see why you said Aaliyah was off-limits."

"Cut that shit, man," Ahmad responded.

"It's not even like that," I added quickly.

He's married, I finished the sentence in my head.

"It looked exactly like that," Leon countered before winking at me. "I mean, I get it. Aaliyah is the complete package. I just wish you would've said something before I got my hopes up."

"Ahmad and I are just friends," I asserted. My voice came out louder than anticipated. "That's it. That's all."

"And y'all coming up here with all this energy, where was that down there?" Ahmad pointed down to the first floor. "Both of y'all down there making a mockery of dance."

"Damnnnnnnnnnnnnnnn," Darius reacted with a hearty laugh.

"Why am I catching strays? I didn't say shit about Aaliyah throwing that ass back on you!"

My eyes bulged. "Wow! I was doing a little more than just throwing my ass back, Darius."

Leon smirked, rubbing his hands together. "You were doing *a lot* more than just throwing that ass back." He shifted his gaze to Ahmad. "You, on the other hand, weren't doing shit but grinning."

"You mean to tell me that you two were out there looking like Dumb"—he pointed at Darius—"and Dumber"—he pointed at Leon—"yet you are talking shit about us?"

"Gahdamn!" Darius threw his hands up dramatically. "Another shot? I don't think we were *that* bad. You thought we were bad, Aaliyah?"

"I wouldn't call you Dumb and Dumber. That's too far." I tapped my chin. "I'd say"—I pointed to Leon—"Rhythmless Nation and"—I pointed to Darius—"Tragic Mike."

The four of us cracked up just as Terra-Cotta started playing their biggest hit to date. Shifting our attention to the stage, we spent the rest of the night enjoying the music, drinking drinks, and talking. It wasn't lost on me that Ahmad kept his distance. But as the last song played, we caught each other's eye over Leon when he bent down. Exchanging small smiles, we continued singing.

It's cool. We're cool. It was just a dance. We're friends. He is clearly happily married, and he clarified that we were friends. Leon and Darius were just giving us shit. It's fine. Everything is fine.

The show ended, and the DJ started playing music to keep people on the dance floor.

"I think I'm going to call it a night, fellas," I announced as I finished my bottle of water.

"Nooo! Don't go!" Leon cried out.

"Really?" Darius checked his watch. "Already?"

"Yeah, it's my time. My ride will be here in five minutes." Picking up my clutch from the couch, I flashed them a smile. "But thank you all for such a fun night."

Ahmad rose to his feet. "I'll walk you out."

"Good luck with the dates. Let us know if you need any more advice," Darius said.

"And if the dates don't work out, I'm right here," Leon added.

I laughed. "I'll keep that in mind."

Ahmad sighed almost comically loud. "Okay, that's enough."

"Oh, we're just getting started," Leon joked, blowing kisses at me.

I waved. "Bye, guys!" Holding only my thumb and pinky to my face, I wiggled my eyebrows at Leon and mouthed, "Call me."

Putting his hand on the small of my back, Ahmad ushered me away. "Aight, let's go."

I cackled my way out of the lounge. As soon as we exited and the door shut behind us, the fun that was being had inside was silenced.

"I can still hear the music and the bass in my head," I commented, pulling at my ears. "It was loud in there."

"Not as loud as your laugh." Ahmad folded his arms over his chest. "That hyena pitch is going to haunt me."

Grinning, I pushed him. "You always got shit to say. But I'm going to let it slide this time because I had a great time tonight."

"I'm glad to hear that." He paused for a moment. "And next time we link up, you're more than welcome to come out with us."

"Well, thank you. I appreciate that." I swept my eyes around the parking lot. "You leaving soon, or are you guys pulling an all-nighter?"

"Probably leaving in about twenty, thirty minutes. Darius and Leon aren't gonna let that bottle go to waste. So, we'll probably head out when they're done."

"Do you have a ride?"

There was a shift in his expression, and his eyes left mine. "Yes."

I gave him a questioning look. "It's not Darius or Leon, is it? You had less to drink than those two up there and none of you need to be drinking and driving."

His jaw tightened and he swallowed hard. "Nah, never that. We're calling a car."

I searched his face. "Good," I said slowly. "Are you—oh, I think that's my ride." I stepped forward toward the curb as the red car slowed to a stop in front of us. I checked the license plate against the plate number on my phone. "Yeah, this is it." I turned to him and smiled. "Well, my friend, I hope you enjoy the rest of your night."

He licked his lips. "Yeah, you, too. You be careful."

"I will."

"Let me get that for you." Ahmad grabbed the back handle and opened the door for me.

A small smile pulled at my lips. "A gentleman!"

As soon as I was about to climb into the car, he reached for my hand. His touch took me by surprise and sent a sensation up my arm.

"I know I'm not your girls . . . or your sister," he started, holding my gaze intently. "But if you ever need a laugh, I'm here."

Emotion welled up inside me. I felt his words as much as I heard them. Caught off guard, I couldn't immediately find my voice. I looked down at his hand covering mine, and my heart skipped a beat.

"Thank you," I murmured as I got in the car.

He closed the door for me and then took a step back. Our eyes were locked until the driver pulled off. Letting out a breath I didn't realize I was holding, I put my hand to my chest.

What was that?

10

I felt like shit.

I wasn't hungover, but it was clear to me that I drank too much. The only thing that made sense was that the alcohol, the music, and the good time forced me to feel something I shouldn't have. It wasn't just harmless-attraction flutters in my belly. It was a prominent tugging at my heartstrings. Ahmad was just my friend—my *married* friend.

I should've never had that third shot.

Guilt had my stomach twisted in knots. I needed to get my shit together, so I spent Sunday trying to shake it off. I focused on me and my self-care. With a massage, pedicure, spa treatment, and no less than twelve hours of sleep, I rolled into Monday feeling good.

I felt like myself.

As I drove home from work, my phone rang. "Hey, Jazz!" I greeted her in a singsong tone.

"You sound like you're in a good mood," Jazmyn pointed out.

I glanced at myself in the rearview mirror as I eased around a corner. "I *am* in a good mood," I replied, picking up speed to beat the yellow light. "How are you? Is everything okay?"

She sighed loudly.

"I don't want to talk about it," she groaned. "Can we just talk about you? I need to take my mind off all the stuff here. Tell me about your date this weekend."

"Understood. But you know if you want to talk, I'm here."

"I know, and I appreciate it. I do. But right now, I need you to tell me about your date."

"Oh, well, that was a complete shit show." I launched into a retelling of what happened with Brayden and his wife. I concluded with how I spent the next couple of hours after he'd been tossed out, laughing and joking with Ahmad. "And then around midnight, it was way too busy for him to really have a conversation and I was getting tired, so I headed home."

"This Ahmad sounds like a good one."

My lips curled into a soft smile. "He is."

"His wife is lucky."

I cleared my throat at the sobering reminder. "Agreed."

"So, who's next on the roster?"

"Girl, I haven't even opened the app again. I just needed a break."

"I get that." She paused contemplatively. "But didn't you say you wanted a date for your birthday?"

"I did. But like I told Nina, I can't do the bullshit on the apps. I want to meet someone organically."

"But let's be for real, Aaliyah. The men on the apps are the same men who are out in the streets. They are the same."

I groaned. "I know you're right, but, girl . . . where are the normal ones?"

"I'll tell you where they aren't—this small-ass town I call home," she grumbled.

"You missing the city?"

"Hell yeah! It's been made painfully clear to me why I left home and never looked back."

"Aww, I'm sorry, girl. How much more do you have to do at the house?"

She grumbled under her breath, but I couldn't make out her response.

"Are there any men at that bar where you've been meeting your dates?" she asked, changing the subject.

Nodding in understanding, I rolled with it.

"I haven't noticed anyone at the bar," I answered.

"Hmm."

Looking at the Bluetooth speaker as if we could see each other, I made a face. "What? What's that noise supposed to mean?"

"I mean, you're looking for a man to lock it down with this summer, and you've been spending time in a bar not noticing the men in there. That seems counterproductive."

"Because I'm on dates with other men."

"I mean . . ." She stretched the word out skeptically.

"What?"

"You said you get to the bar early and you stay after the date ends."

"Yeah, but . . ." I cleared my throat. "You're right."

"So, if you're not trying to be on the app and you're not looking around in real-life settings, what are you doing?"

I groaned. "I don't know."

"You need help," she giggled.

Her words mimicked Ahmad's, and I shifted uncomfortably.

"I don't need help! Why does everyone think I need help? It's these men on the dates that need help!"

"Oh, believe me, I know," Jazmyn agreed. "I just want you to get what you want—whatever that is. And if you're not on the apps and not looking around at the bar and not wanting to be set up, maybe you need to go out and see what's up."

I was quiet for a moment. "Well, I did go out on Saturday night. Ahmad invited me out with him and his friends."

"Oh really?! So, you let Ahmad set you up with one of his friends?"

"Not exactly. He essentially said he just wants me to be around men who know how to act so that I can avoid the types of men I was attracting."

"Yeah, that sounds like a setup. Were the friends cute?"

"The friends were fine as fuck. All three of them looked good. But it was a friend linkup. Nothing more, nothing less."

"Mm-hmm."

I laughed. "I'm serious. It wasn't exactly like that, but it was a good time."

"You were out with three fine-ass men and you didn't flirt with any of them? You didn't get anyone's number? You didn't shoot your shot?"

I told her about the night, Ahmad outside of the bar, Ahmad's friends, and the fun we all had. But I held back on all the details because anything I felt was alcohol-induced and didn't mean anything.

"So, does that mean Ahmad's friend is going to be the next lucky bachelor in your summer of love?" she asked. "You're going to take him to Onyx next?"

"No! It was just harmless flirting. Leon was not actually trying to take me out."

"What if he was?"

I shook my head.

Something about going on a date with Ahmad's friend with Ahmad right there watching us didn't sit right with me. I couldn't put my finger on why, but it was uncomfortable to even think about.

"No, it wasn't like that. I assure you. But I'm going to have to figure something else out. Nina said I should get back on Tender-Fish."

"Like I said before, I want you to do what you think is best for you. And you're not going to meet anyone sitting at home. If I were in your shoes and I had your goal in mind, I probably wouldn't get on an app. But I would jump on being set up by friends."

"You and Nina haven't set me up with anyone since college."

"I was actually thinking about Ahmad. That's your friend, right?"

"Right, right," I said quickly.

"You said he invited you out, and even though he said it wasn't a setup, it clearly was. He's gotten to know you, and he's known his boys for however long he's known them. There was a reason he wanted you to come out with them. And it sounds like it was to hook you up."

I thought about what she said and how the night unfolded.

It made sense, but at the same time, it didn't.

Logically, the stage was set for a setup on Saturday night.

But that dance.

Swallowing hard, I shook off the thought and made my way into the parking garage of my building.

"I hear you. But I think I'll pass on Ahmad's friends," I told her.

"So, that means you're going to go out more or you're going to get back on the app?"

"Yeah, I guess I'm going to have to do both."

We talked for about fifteen more minutes before we said our goodbyes. I spent the next hour thinking about our conversation. I'd talked to Nina over my lunch break, and she'd said something similar—more vulgar, but similar.

With the encouragement of my best friends, I sat on my couch after dinner and finally opened the app. I read through all the messages, deleting and ignoring most of them. But a few stood out.

"Mike," I whispered to myself as I eyed his profile.

He was a good-looking firefighter with a decent bio page. But it was his opening message to me that caught my attention.

Mike: Aaliyah, I run into burning buildings for complete strangers. Imagine what I would do for you.

Aaliyah: Nice line.

Mike: Nice? That's all I get? That was my best line!

Aaliyah: Oh, so that must be the one you use on all the women you contact. Let me get another one.

Mike: You promise not to block me?

Aaliyah: I can't make that promise. It depends on how bad it is.

Mike: I can't risk it!

Aaliyah: Fine, I won't block you.

Mike: In my line of work, I put out fires. But say the word and we can start one.

Aaliyah: Ha! That one actually made me laugh a little bit.

Mike: Just a little? You're tough.

Aaliyah: I am.

Mike: Well, it's a good thing I like tough.

I spent the next few days getting to know Mike. We had a great rapport. He said he liked to dance, and the first thing I thought of was my Cinderella moment on the dance floor at my party. We didn't exchange numbers, so we alternated between texting and video chatting through the app. It didn't bother me that he didn't ask me for my number. But after the incident with Brayden being married, I was a little cautious. When he asked me for a date, I suggested Friday at Onyx. And even though my hopes weren't high, and I didn't even feel that excited about the date, I still took the time to get cute.

Wearing a sundress and a pair of sexy sandals, I entered Onyx almost an hour before my date. There were a few people already in the bar, and Ahmad was taking an order when I sat down on the barstool that had become my favorite.

"Hey!" I greeted the woman with the cute Afro puffs. "Asia, right?"

She gave me a beaming smile. "Hey! Welcome back. What can I get you?" She glanced down the bar to Ahmad, who was looking our way as he prepared drinks. "Or are you waiting for my brother?"

"Oh, wow, wait . . . Ahmad is your real brother?"

I assumed when they said *bro* and *sis*, they meant it colloquially. I had no idea they were actually siblings.

She laughed. "Yeah. He looks like our dad. I look like our mom."

"So, gorgeousness just runs in the family, huh?"

She giggled. "Thank you. You need anything while you wait?"

I twisted my lips. "I'm good for right now. Thank you, though. And I'm not waiting for him. He's just watching my back and helping me out."

"So, you two are just friends?" she asked, a curious smile played on her lips.

"Yes," I assured her. "I don't date married men."

"I think last week determined that was a lie," Ahmad quipped, hearing the latter part of my statement.

Asia laughed, patting Ahmad's shoulder and walking to the other end of the bar.

"Why must you always have something to say?" I wondered, staring up at him. "You're an asshole, you know that?"

He flashed me a smile. "Come on. You know that was funny."

"It's not funny that I was tricked into a date with a married man."

"A widower," he clarified with a serious expression. "He said he was a widower."

Shaking my head, I stifled a laugh. "You know what? I'm done."

"No, we're just getting started. You want a drink, or are we waiting for bachelor number three to get here?"

"I'm going to wait." I eyed his muscular frame. "What's going on with your smedium shirt? You trying to get extra tips or something?"

He crossed his arms over his chest. "It isn't that tight."

"Whoa, slow down with all those quick moves, Hulk."

His head tipped back, and he let out a hearty laugh. "Don't do that."

"Listen, I'm just looking out." I tried to keep a straight face as I watched his body quake with laughter. "I wouldn't want you to have to work in tattered cloth and scraps of fabric because you reached up for a top-shelf bottle."

"What's so funny?" Asia asked as she grabbed a couple of bottles that were behind him.

"Aaliyah said my shirt was tight," Ahmad answered.

She pulled a face. "She's not wrong, bro."

His mouth opened, and he stared at her in disbelief. "This is some bullshit."

"No, what's bullshit is that I can see your heart beating through your shirt," I joked.

The three of us were cracking up.

They left to go take more drink orders and greet other guests, and I checked my phone.

"So, what do I need to know about this one?" Ahmad asked a few minutes later.

"Um, his name is Mike, and he's a firefighter."

"Mike, huh?"

I pursed my lips. "Let's hear it. You had something to say about the names of the other two. What do you have to say about Mike?"

He shook his head and lifted his arms. "I got nothing. I hope he's a good dude."

I eyed him suspiciously. "You do?"

"Yeah. You're cool. Mean as hell, but you're cool."

"You're cool, too. Not funny at all, but cool."

"Ha ha." His tone was dry, but his lips still turned upward.

I looked around and then met his gaze again. "I have a serious question . . ."

"What's up?"

"How long were you on the app? How long did it take you to find someone decent?"

"When I was on the app, I wasn't looking for someone decent. I was looking for someone compatible," he answered before a slim woman with long hair rushed up next to me, commanding his attention.

Bumping me, she didn't acknowledge me or excuse herself. "I want to give—I mean *get*—a blow job," she announced, batting her eyelashes. "And can you put it on my tab?"

"Just one shot?" he asked, not flinching.

"That's all it'll take," she flirted.

"Coming right up." He pointed at me. "To be continued."

When he walked off to get the ingredients, the woman tossed her hair over her shoulder and eyed me.

"You come here a lot," she stated.

It wasn't a question, so I didn't feel an obligation to respond. Slowly, I nodded, unsure of why she was even talking to me.

"I've seen you around," she continued. "You know the bartender. Are you his cousin or something? A friend?"

"Yeah," I replied, glancing down to see Ahmad bend over to put the whipped cream back into the refrigerator. "I mean, I met him here."

"Do you know anything about his situation?" She pointed to her hand and wiggled her ring finger.

I could feel the perplexed expression on my face. "Other than the fact that he is wearing a wedding band?"

She looked around guiltily. "Never mind," she snapped.

"Here's your shot," Ahmad announced, sliding the small glass over to her.

She grabbed her hair with one hand and pulled it back. Leaning over, she wrapped her crimson-slathered lips around the rim of the glass, securing it before she lifted her head and downed the drink with no hands. She set the glass back on the bar and then licked her lips.

There were about five people actively watching in awe. But based on the way she was eyeing Ahmad, it was clear she was doing it for his benefit. Unfortunately for her, he wasn't paying attention. He had already moved on to take someone else's order.

A frustrated grunt escaped her, and she stamped her foot. Catching my eye in the mirror, she turned to me. "How do you get him to pay attention to you?"

I lifted my shoulders. "We just talk."

"I wish it was that easy for me!" She started to turn around, and then she looked back at me. "And I love your confidence, by the way," she commented, pointing at what I was wearing. "That actually looks really good on you."

My lips parted, but words didn't come out.

What the fuck?

It wasn't the first time that backhanded compliment had been thrown at me. It always held the tone of condescension. But each time, it grated on my nerves more. Because it wasn't about my confidence. It was about their perceived judgment of my body and their disbelief that I managed to be confident despite what I looked like in their opinion. And it usually came from people who would swear up and down they were being complimentary.

Between the confidence comment and the use of *actually,* I imagined slapping her across her face like Brayden's wife did to him. But because I couldn't fight, I just had to settle for a verbal confrontation.

My lip curled in disgust. "What do you mean this *actually* looks good on me?"

"I'm just saying that it's really flattering on your figure. And your confidence pulls it off."

"My confidence? What are you talking about?"

"You know."

"I don't."

She shrugged. "Your whole look. The way you carry yourself. You just look so . . . confident is all," she explained. "The way you just chat it up with someone like him. I wish I was as confident as you."

"How am I confident?" Even though I knew exactly what she was insinuating, I wanted to put her on the spot. "And why would it be difficult for me to talk to someone like him?"

"You just . . ." She gestured to my body and flashed me a fake smile. "Never mind."

I stared at her, making her sit in her discomfort. "Commenting on my confidence and all I'm doing is sitting here is weird."

"Or you could've just said thank you because I was being nice to you," she snarled.

I shook my head. "You were being condescending, not nice. And to be clear, I'm beautiful, funny, and he enjoys my company. That's why he chats it up with me."

Turning on her heel, she stormed away. "Whatever."

Existing in my body and not being ashamed of who I was and how I looked was only an act of confidence to people who viewed me as if something was wrong with me.

And there was nothing wrong with me.

"What's wrong with you?" Ahmad asked.

My eyes jerked up to his. "Nothing!"

"Then why do you have that look on your face?" His eyes pinged over me. "You good?"

"I'm fine."

"You look stressed."

"I'm not stressed. I'm . . ." My sentence trailed off with a sigh.

He stared at me, waiting with anticipation. But I didn't feel like explaining the interaction I'd just had with his fan.

He checked his watch. With a serious expression, he asked, "Are you getting stood up again?"

I pursed my lips. "No."

"You sure?" He lowered his voice. "It's happened before."

"Shut—"

"Is that him?" Ahmad interrupted me, nodding to a confused-looking man standing at the door, staring at his phone.

I didn't feel anything as I watched him.

"Yeah." I nodded slowly. "I think so."

"You good?"

I forced a big smile. "Yes."

"You're full of shit."

"And you're full of yourself."

Snickering, he backed away to go help someone a few seats down. "Okay, I'll be back."

When Mike looked up, he craned his long neck until he saw me. His lips pulled into a tight smile. His eyes roamed my body as he approached.

"Aaliyah?" he asked, extending his hand.

I shook it in return. "Mike, hi."

He sat down on the stool beside me and then looked down at his phone. When he looked back at me, he laughed under his breath. "Wow, you look different in person."

My stomach sank. "Um . . ."

Ahmad strolled up just in time. "Can I get you two something to drink?"

Mike turned to face him. "Yes, thanks. Two IPAs?" He pulled a twenty out of his pocket and then turned to me. "I know you said you didn't like beer, but trust me."

I shrugged. "If I don't like it, I'm not going to finish it."

"If you don't like it, I'll finish yours, and then you can get a cosmo or some shit. But you have to just try it. It's different. It'll change your mind."

Being a good sport, I smiled. "Okay . . ."

Ahmad looked at me for a second. "Okay."

When he walked off to prepare our drinks, I noticed Mike looking down at his phone again.

"So . . ." I started. "I'm glad you asked me out. It's nice to finally meet you."

"Yeah." He slipped his phone in his pocket. "It's nice to actually see you in person."

Ahmad placed two mugs in front of us and then immediately went to take another order.

"You ready to try this?" Mike asked.

"I'm as ready as I'll ever be," I replied, sniffing the drink.

He lifted his mug. "Let's do this."

I took a sip while he took a gulp.

It was not good.

"It's bitter," I told him, sliding the drink away from me.

"You don't understand," he argued before taking another gulp. "This isn't that bad, but it isn't the best. Now if you want the best . . ."

For thirty-four uninterrupted minutes, that man explained India pale ale, hops, and his quest to brew his own beer. It did not matter to him that my eyes had glazed over or that he was having a conversation by himself. When he did ask me questions, they seemed rhetorical because while I was in the midst of answering, he would interrupt me and tell me how I didn't like beer, so I didn't know. As he finished his IPA lecture, he'd managed to finish his beer and half of mine.

"You know . . ." he began. "You're bigger than you look in your pictures. I didn't know."

"What?" My entire body tensed. "No. I don't think so."

He nodded. "Yeah, you are."

"The pictures on my profile are very recent, and we'd had a few video calls where you saw my full body. So, no, you knew." I shook my head profusely. "You definitely knew—"

"Don't sweat it. It's okay. I don't usually date fat chicks, but you're actually pretty," he offered with a straight face.

My forehead crinkled as my eyebrows stretched to reach my hairline. There was that word again. *Actually*.

His words came out of nowhere and I felt like I'd been slapped awake. He'd gone from droning on about brewing to giving me my second backhanded compliment of the night.

"What?" I managed to reply.

"You're pretty." He downed the rest of the alcohol and placed the glass back down. "Fat isn't usually my thing. I love thick. I'm cool with big. But fat isn't really my type. But I'm glad I decided to give you a chance."

"Are you serious?"

"Yeah. I like my women thick, but not . . ." His eyes zeroed in on my belly. "I don't know. But something about you made me want to give you a try. Like I said, it's not usually my thing, but with you . . . I'm willing to make the exception."

"Don't. I'm going to save us both a lot of time. If fat isn't usually your thing, don't let me be the one to change your mind."

He frowned. "What?"

I looked down the bar to see how close Ahmad was to us. "I'm not interested."

"You aren't interested. You? With your big back? Aren't interested? In me?" He let out a scornful laugh. "I was the one giving *you* a chance."

"And now you can take your chance and give it to someone else. Because I'm *actually* not interested in you."

His face hardened and he stood up abruptly, almost tipping his barstool over. "I didn't want you anyway, fat bitch," he snarled.

"Yes, you did," I replied, rolling my eyes.

I knew it was coming.

Fat bitch was a go-to term when people with bruised egos lashed out—especially if they're attacking anyone my size. And even though I felt it coming, the public setting made it worse.

"But this fat bitch doesn't want you," I continued.

"Whatever," he spat before stomping away.

Anger and embarrassment enflamed my cheeks as I glanced around to see if anyone overheard the interaction. Ahmad was already on his way down to my end of the bar, ignoring the people waiting to place an order.

"What happened?" he asked.

I nodded, forcing a smile. "I'm fine. I'm just going to head home."

"What happened?" he repeated, more forcefully.

I hooked my thumb toward the people waiting for him or Asia to take their orders. "You have customers."

His eyes pierced mine. "Did he touch you?"

"No, he just said some shit I didn't appreciate, and I told him I wasn't interested. He got mad and left."

His eyes pinged my face. "What did he say?"

"It doesn't matter." I shook my head. "We just weren't compatible, and he didn't like that I was the one to point that out."

"The next time some shit goes down, you let me know. That's the whole point of this."

I nodded.

"I said I was going to look out for you, so you have to stop being stubborn and let me," he continued roughly.

"Excuse me!" a woman called out, trying to get Ahmad's attention.

Ignoring her, he held my gaze, causing my stomach to knot. "Okay?"

I nodded. "Okay."

"You want a drink?"

"Nah, I think I'm going to head out."

He opened his mouth and then snapped it shut. Assessing me quietly, he nodded. "Okay. See you Friday?"

I gave him a small smile as I got up. "See you Friday."

I honestly didn't know if I was going to see Ahmad on Friday. I was close to giving up on the TenderFish app after the string of dates I'd dealt with. I had a lot on my mind, and giving up on dating, on the boyfriend, on the yacht was at the forefront.

"Aaliyah," Ahmad called after me. "What are you doing on Monday?"

I turned and looked at him. "What?"

"Monday . . ." He grabbed a glass and shifted it from one hand to the other. "What are you doing?"

"Working . . ." I cocked my head to the side. "Why?"

"Meet me here. Seven o'clock. I have something for you."

My eyebrows shot up. "For me?"

"Ahmad, I need some help over here," Asia called out from the other side of the bar.

He glanced over to her and then back to me. Pointing his finger, he said, "Monday."

He turned away before I could respond. So instead, I lifted my hand in a wave and left the bar.

11

"Even though you couldn't come back for the concert, I hope you're finding something to do with your time," I told Jazmyn as we were concluding our call. "Getting out would be good for you."

"I know. I know," she sighed. "It's just been a long summer."

"I'm sorry, girl. Let me know if you want us to come down for a weekend."

"I appreciate it, but it's just a lot of work to be done. It wouldn't be any fun, and I wouldn't want you to waste a trip."

"It wouldn't be a waste. I'm here if you need me. And Nina feels the same way."

"I know. Thank you."

"If you change your mind, just say the word."

"Okay. Thanks. I really do appreciate it. Now you go shake off that date with Mike and just enjoy the concert."

"Yes, ma'am. And I'll send you pictures and videos."

"Thank you." She paused. "For everything. I'll talk to you later, girl."

She sounded sad, tired, and maybe a little overwhelmed.

I resigned myself not to push the issue and let her conclude the call. My heart went out to her. I knew she was dealing with a lot, and going back home for the entire summer was the last thing she wanted to do. I felt bad that while she was dealing with such heavy stuff, Nina and I were going to a surprise concert by one of our favorite artists.

The pop-up event featuring India Davis would've been just the Saturday-night thing that Jazz, Nina, and I would've been first in line to attend. But Jazz was out of town and Nina was meeting me at the venue after her date, so I dressed in a formfitting, shimmery pink dress and headed out alone.

My phone vibrated just as I was about to toss it into my bag.

"I know you're not calling me from the date," I answered with a smile.

"Girl," Nina replied.

I stopped in my tracks. "Everything okay?"

"I'm dressed like a fucking video vixen right now, and after being an hour late, this dude just texted me and canceled."

"What?"

"Yeah. So, he's done."

"Did he give a reason?"

"No. But honestly, it doesn't matter. If you cancel on me, I'm over it. If you cancel on me after being an hour late, you're dead to me. Because honestly, why did you even reach out?"

I snickered. "Dead to you? Really, Nina?"

"Really," she confirmed with finality. "But everything happens for a reason. Because of that man's death, I will be able to catch the whole India Davis show with my best friend."

"I'm sorry about your date, but I'm glad you won't miss the opening acts, and we can be there together. His loss is my gain."

"Look at God!"

"Rest in peace to . . . what was his name?"

"The departed," she deadpanned.

I cackled.

Nina and I met at the Lyric Lounge twenty minutes later. She was five foot ten without heels on, so I could spot her in a crowd easily. But not just because of her height; her bold style stood out. Her full figure was scarcely covered in a two-piece outfit. The bra-like top could barely cover her large breasts, and as she made her way toward me, men gawked. She paid them no mind as she passed by them, but I knew her well enough to know she was loving the attention.

After a quick hug and an exchange of compliments, Nina and I got in line. We were only waiting for about ten minutes before they let in the first wave of people. Because we were early, we got a great spot on a platform to the right of the stage. Everyone assumed rushing the stage and trying to be in the front row was the best place to be. But as I swept my eyes over the room, it was confirmed that we had the best vantage point in the building.

The Lyric Lounge was one of my favorite venues. The sound quality was amazing. No matter who performed, their voice was magnified and beautifully highlighted in the state-of-the-art sound system. We could be anywhere in the building, and it would sound great. But my favorite spot offered a bird's-eye view of the stage, of the artist performing and feeding off the crowd, of the crowd engaged and vibing with the artist. Sometimes I'd come to shows and just people-watch, taking it all in.

"I left my umbrella in the car!" I realized with wide eyes.

"I didn't think it was going to rain until after midnight, so I didn't even bring one." She pouted. "Hopefully, it won't rain until late, and we'll be good."

"I hope so."

She wiggled her eyebrows. "You know what'll fix this?"

"Drinks!" we said in unison.

"I'm going to get us drinks. Two each," Nina announced. "I'll keep my head on a swivel to see if there are any potentials for us on the way to the bar."

"Oh!" I gasped. "That reminds me." I pulled my phone out and opened the TenderFish app. Showing her the man who had messaged me a couple of days ago, I filled her in. "This guy asked me to meet up with him on Friday, but because I already have a date with Silas, I had to push him to next week. But on the way here, look what he said."

I watched her face as she read the message from the sexy and poetic Lennox.

With an open-mouth smile, she glanced up at me. "If you give me the opportunity to know you, I'll make the most of it," she read. "Oh, he's smooth! I like that energy."

"Yeah." I took the phone back from her. "He's talking a good game."

"Well, I'm still going to keep an eye out for potentials. There's nothing wrong with having more than one in the mix. A little competition never hurt no one." She winked. "Gotta have at least four on the roster."

Amused, I shook my head. "I'll hold our spots," I said, widening my stance and taking up more room.

She rushed off to the bar and not even two minutes later, a group of people stormed the platform.

"Excuse me," a woman said, nudging me gently.

My nose wrinkled and my forehead creased as she was trying to wedge herself between my body and the rail I was leaning against. "Uh . . . what are you doing? This is where I'm standing," I told her.

"You could move over."

I tightened my grip on the railing. "My friend and I are here. You can find a different spot."

She huffed and looked over at her friend—a man—and stamped her foot. "She won't move, Stephen!"

The man she was with approached. "Can you please let her get your spot? Please. India is her favorite artist."

"No. I'm not going to give up my spot." I turned my back to the both of them.

She mumbled something inaudible.

"Talk as much shit as you want. You're not getting my spot." I tossed the words over my shoulder with a shrug.

"It's not fair!" the woman wailed loudly as I continued staring down at the growing crowd. "It's not like I can see around her."

"Then go somewhere else," I retorted even though she wasn't talking to me.

My fingers tightened around the metal rail. It took everything in me not to turn around and curse her out. Because even though she wasn't saying exactly what she meant, I could read between the lines.

"Just great! Another one," she grumbled as Nina appeared next to me. "How am I supposed to see with the two of *them* in the front?"

Nina, not missing a beat, handed me my drink and then turned to glare at the woman. "What was that?"

Nina towered over the shorter, smaller-framed woman. I glanced over my shoulder and watched her cower slightly. She looked unsure if the verbal confrontation was going to turn physical.

Because I knew Nina wasn't going to fight, I smiled at the fear that flashed in the thin woman's eyes.

Even though she ignored Nina's question, she continued complaining to Stephen and the others in her group. "Let's just go somewhere else. It's not enough room for all of us over here."

"It sure isn't!" Nina yelled behind them. Turning, she flashed me a confused look. "What was that all about?"

"She wanted our spot," I answered with pursed lips.

"Don't they always?" she replied.

We both laughed.

The crowd below was packed to maximum capacity, and the crowd behind us was just as tight. The air-conditioning was working overtime, but it was as if warm air was being blown around. I looked at the people below and shook my head. If it was hot where we were, I could only imagine how the people down there felt.

"Oh!" Nina exclaimed. "Look at him."

"Who?" I wondered.

"The one in the white shirt. He's walking through the crowd toward the exit sign. Right there! Walking with the girl with the ponytail."

I followed her pointed finger toward the speaker on the far side of the stage. "I don't see . . ." My sentence trailed off as I laid eyes on the man she was talking about.

"He looks good as fuck," Nina observed, bumping me with her hip.

I swallowed hard as I watched him disappear through the doorway. He did look good. He also looked very familiar. "I think that was Ahmad."

"What?"

Blinking rapidly, I nodded. "That was Ahmad."

"That was Ahmad who?"

"From Onyx. The bartender."

"The one who you said was like your wingman?"

I nodded.

"Shiiiiiiiiiiiit." Waving a dismissive hand, she gawked at me.

"That's not what wingmen look like. That's a damn leading man. You said he was giving wing, and the whole time, you should've been giving him thighs and breasts."

I howled.

She pointed again even though he was long gone. "You mean to tell me that you've been chatting it up with a man who looks like that, and you haven't shot your shot? Or at least called me to come down to the bar with you so I can shoot mine?"

Amused, I shook my head. "He's married."

"Oh, I forgot you said he was 'married'"—she did air quotes—"and therefore off the market. Damn shame. I didn't know he looked like that. Mm-mm-mm." She paused for a moment. "Is he happily married? Openly married?"

"Nina!"

"Fine! You got dibs. It's only fair since you saw him first."

I waved her off. "I'm not calling dibs on a married man."

"I wouldn't go after a married man, but a girl can still look. What's the name of the bar again?"

I shook my head. "What is wrong with you?"

Before she could answer, the lights dimmed, and a strong voice pierced through the noisy crowd. Everyone went wild before quieting and enjoying the opening act. Even though I was enjoying the unknown performer's vocalizations, I glanced toward the exit where I'd last seen Ahmad.

My mind kept filtering back to him—wondering where he'd disappeared to, wondering if the woman he was with was his wife, wondering if he got the backstage pass to meet India Davis. It hadn't hit me how little I knew about his marriage. His drinking preferences, his favorite foods, his weird quirks, his dynamic with his friends, and his thoughts on various songs, I knew. We talked about life and laughed about everything, but I didn't know much of anything about his romantic life.

Was the woman he was with his wife?

The thunderous applause at the end of India Davis's set was well-earned and well deserved. She killed her performance. The entire show was a good time, and I'd almost forgotten about the incident over our spot until we were leaving.

"If I didn't just get my nails done, I would've slapped that bitch," Nina commented loud enough for the woman to hear. When she glanced over her shoulder at us, Nina pointed. "Yes, you."

It took everything in me not to laugh out loud. Because of Nina's stature, some people found her intimidating. Nina talked shit, but she didn't actually fight. She often described herself as a lover, not a fighter. And for as long as I'd known her, she had never so much as gotten angry enough to want to physically assault someone—which is why I was so amused by Nina's posturing.

"—talking like you want me and my girl to address the situation outside," Nina continued.

Snickering, I had to cover my mouth with my hand and turn my head.

While Nina chose not to fight, I was 100 percent certain I couldn't fight. If anyone in our group was going to fight a battle, it would've been Jazz. But it was just us, and I didn't know why she was starting stuff.

"You're going to feel funny if that girl tries us in the parking lot," I whispered, still laughing.

"I already have my phone out ready to call the police if she does," she returned as we exited the building into the light drizzle.

The two of us cracked up.

"I thought I heard your laugh," a deep voice commented just as we stepped onto the sidewalk. "It's funny because I was just thinking about you."

My stomach flipped, and I stopped in my tracks.

"Watch it!" a lady cried out as she bumped into me.

"Sorry," I distractedly called over my shoulder as my eyes stayed locked on the man staring at me. My pulse quickened, and there was a distinct throb between my thighs. "Ahmad, hi!" Moving out of the way, I stood in front of him. "You were here?"

It was a dumb question. I knew it the moment the words left my mouth. But I was so caught off guard by his presence that it was the first thing that came to mind to say.

"No, I just hang around outside of venues and wait for people to come out," he replied sarcastically.

"Ah," Nina mused from beside me. "A parking lot pimp."

"Exactly." With a light chuckle, he popped open the umbrella in his hand and positioned it between me and Nina. "Here."

Our fingers brushed as I took it from his grasp. The sensation spread through my entire body. His touch lit something within me, and I wasn't expecting that. Ignoring the softness of the gesture and the way my stomach flipped, I squared my shoulders.

"I was just surprised to see you. I know you love India Davis, but in general, your taste is usually so questionable, I didn't expect to see you," I retorted, trying to recover from earlier.

"I told her I like chitterlings, and she's been on my ass about it ever since," he told Nina before looking back at me. "But the only questionable thing I've done recently is associate with you."

I quirked an eyebrow. "Best decision of your life."

His grin grew. "Hardly."

Resting my free hand on Nina's arm, I introduced the two of them. "Ahmad, this is my best friend, Nina. Nina, this is—"

"Your wingman from the bar," she interjected, taking his outstretched hand. "The bartender. You never mentioned how sexy he is."

"He aight," I lied, rolling my eyes.

"Thank you, Nina. It's nice to meet you." He stepped back, crossing his arms over his chest and directing his next comment at me. "Just aight, huh?"

I ignored the way the slightly damp material stretched across his biceps as he smirked at me. "Yeah, you aight," I confirmed. "You're not bad. You cool." I made a face. "Don't fish for compliments. It's beneath you."

He chuckled. "See . . . and I was going to say you look incredibly beautiful. But now I'll just say I hope you and Nina get home safely. Although I have no doubt you will." He paused. "Nobody is fucking with the Pink Panther."

My jaw dropped. "You know what . . ."

Nina stifled her open-mouth laugh. "Too far!"

He started humming *The Pink Panther* theme song, which only added to Nina's amusement. I tried my hardest not to laugh as I glared at him.

"Ahmad!" a woman called out from the corner of the street. "Ahmad! It's here!" She pointed to a car stopped at the intersection.

I recognized her.

It was the woman from the bar. She was too far away for me to see the details of her face, but I knew it was the woman Ahmad had so much chemistry with. I didn't recognize her with the ponytail at first, but I remembered her voice.

Damn. That is *his wife.*

My gut twisted with guilt and an unnamed emotion.

He looked back at her and held his hand up. "Okay!" he yelled back as he took a couple of steps away from us. "Nice meeting you, Nina. Aaliyah, it was tolerable as always."

"Barely," I replied with a smile. "Don't forget your umbrella."

He shook his head. "Keep it. Wouldn't want you to get wet."

There was a throb between my legs as I pushed off the thoughts his words provoked. The second drink I'd had was strong, and I wasn't doing a great job keeping my hormones in check. I just prayed my face didn't betray me the way my body did.

I didn't want him—he was a married man. I was just physically attracted to him and having an incidental reaction to being caught off guard by the sight of him.

I cleared my throat. "Thanks."

He smirked. "See you Monday?"

I nodded. "See you Monday."

Turning on his heels, he jogged over to the woman standing at the crosswalk.

Silently, Nina and I watched him take her umbrella and open the door for her. After they both climbed into the vehicle, we watched it disappear around the corner before any words were spoken.

"Ah-mad is ah-sexy-ass man," Nina observed, looping her arm with mine and taking the umbrella from me. "You weren't holding it high enough."

"Sorry."

"It's cool. Tall-girl problems." She let out a whistle. "No, but seriously, Aaliyah. He's the total package."

"Yeah," I agreed. "Lots of good qualities."

"He's sexy *and* he's funny. He really called your ass the Pink Panther." She snickered. "That was funny as fuck."

"It wasn't *that* funny." I rolled my eyes with a smile. "That's how it is with him, though. Just nonstop jokes and good vibes."

"I saw a spark between them jokes, though."

"You didn't see no damn spark!"

"I did!" She tightened her grip on my arm. "He couldn't keep his eyes off of you."

"He was roasting me."

"Nah, but he *wanted* to roast you."

"What?" I sputtered, making a face. "What does that even mean?"

She wiggled her eyebrows. "Oh, you know."

Laughing, I swatted at her. "You always make everything sexual!"

"Everything *is* sexual. And if you didn't see that man checking you out, you are blind."

"First of all, he's married. Second of all, I'm not his type."

"What's his type?"

"His wife," I answered. "And India Davis."

"You know what? If that was his wife, she kinda looks like India Davis. She has the same shape," she pointed out.

There was a tightness in my chest as I nodded.

I'd noticed that, too.

"But you know what else I find interesting?" Nina continued.

I cleared my throat. "What's that?"

"There might be trouble in paradise."

My face crinkled in confusion. "Huh?"

"Ahmad was over here talking to you while his wife continued walking."

"She was obviously looking for their ride." I shrugged. "And I'm sure she trusts him. I've witnessed him turning down women and respecting his marriage."

"But he also gave you this"—she shook the umbrella—"on some knight-in-shining-armor shit."

"He also offered to watch my back while I meet random men from the internet. He's just a good guy."

"And the most damning evidence," she continued as if I hadn't combated her other arguments. "You two have crazy chemistry."

I thought back for a moment. "Our friendship is why we have chemistry. We're really comfortable with each other. That's all."

"Nah, this was not friendship chemistry. This was romantic chemistry. This was sexual chemistry. This was AP chemistry."

I laughed it off. "You are seeing what you want to see. This man was literally with a woman, and he faithfully wears a black band on his left ring finger."

Her lips twisted contemplatively. "So, maybe that woman wasn't his wife." She sucked in a sharp breath as if she had an epiphany. "That's probably why he didn't introduce you to her! That's why they kept their distance! He was waiting at the door, and she was down the block. She was playing her position! Oh, she's good."

"No, no, no." I waved the speculation off. "That can't be it. He wouldn't do that."

"He's a man. Men cheat." She made a face. "I mean, women cheat, too, but men cheat like that"—she jerked her thumb back behind us—"all out in the open with no finesse. Just sloppy."

"But Ahmad isn't like that. He's . . ." I searched for the right word to describe the man I'd come to know and genuinely like. "He's not like that."

"If you say so . . ."

"He's a happily married IT guy—"

"Some of the worst offenders are in IT! Have my dating stories taught you nothing? Behind professional athletes, doctors, nurses, call-center employees, truck drivers, military members, and *bartenders,* the top cheating-ass man is in IT."

"You've named damn near the whole workforce."

She opened her arms, leaving us both exposed to the almost

nonexistent drizzle coming down. "Exactly. Cheating-ass men are everywhere."

"And what fields are cheating-ass women in?"

"We are in the field of minding our business and not getting caught."

I laughed. "What is wrong with you?"

"I'm just telling it like it is."

I got home from the concert, and I felt that familiar throb between my thighs reminding me that I hadn't taken care of myself in a while. It had been a long week, and I just wanted to take a bath, relax, and get myself off before bed.

But as I placed the umbrella next to the coatrack, my mind went to Ahmad. Even after the long, hot bath and the glass of wine, I still couldn't stop thinking about Ahmad for some reason. Seeing him out of context at the concert really threw me for a loop.

Nina spent an hour and a half trying to convince me that Ahmad would leave his wife for me. After reminding her that I don't break up happy homes, I explained the content of his character. Even without knowing him long, I knew for a fact he was one of the good ones. For all the shit we talked, I liked him, and I respected him, and I respected his marriage.

After the wine and the bath, I still didn't feel as relaxed as I wanted to feel. While I moisturized my body, Ahmad briefly crossed my mind again. Even though I knew he wasn't into me romantically and I knew he was happily married, flashes of how he looked at me, how he spoke to me, how he looked out for me rushed in. While I knew Nina was being extreme, I had to admit that Ahmad and I had chemistry. But we were just friends, and our relationship was just friendship.

Nothing more, nothing less.

Remembering how he looked standing outside that concert venue, I had to admit that I was attracted to him. There was no way I could lie and say I didn't see the artwork God put in when he created Ahmad. That was just a fact. That wasn't inappropriate. That was just a fact of the matter—Ahmad looked good as fuck.

My mind drifted to how he always looked good at the bar no matter what was going on, how good he looked at the concert, and how good he looked in general. That was a normal observation. That made sense.

What didn't make sense was the intensity of the throb between my legs as I thought about Ahmad's physical appearance.

Yet another reminder that I haven't been taken care of in a while. Not by me or anyone else. I looked down at my naked body and then over at my nightstand drawer.

No time like the present.

I checked the time.

If it took me half an hour to find porn that I was in the mood to watch and that was going to get me off and then another fifteen to thirty minutes to masturbate, I was looking at an hour. Glancing at the clock, I sighed.

It was one o'clock in the morning.

On one hand, I'm tired and it's late. On the other hand, I need to de-stress.

And the way I was feeling, the amount of stress and tension I needed to release, it was feeling like I was only going to need fifteen minutes instead of thirty.

I pulled out a vibrating toy as opposed to my dildo because I had business to take care of.

I stretched my naked body across my bed. Closing my eyes, I let my fingertips brush my skin.

My body stirred.

Grabbing my laptop, I clicked through porn clips until I found a dirty-talking amateur couple. The sound filled my room with want and desire. Palming and massaging my breasts, I tried to clear my mind. Pinching my nipples harder, I just wanted to dull the ache and feel good.

The couple on the screen was putting on a show, but I just needed them as background noise. My intent was to stay focused on me and my pleasure.

I closed my eyes, and Ahmad's strong hands popped into my

mind. As I caressed my belly on the way to my thighs, I saw more and more of him. It wasn't intentional and I was still not interested in anything more than friendship with him, but the more I tried to think about another man, the clearer Ahmad's face became. And unfortunately, fantasizing about him touching me seemed to heighten my arousal.

Butterflies fluttered deep in my belly as my fingers brushed against my lips. Realizing how wet I was, I sucked in a ragged breath. Adding another finger along my slit, I spread my wetness around, giving more and more attention to my clit with each pass.

Hit with a wave of arousal, I froze.

What am I doing?

I shook my head and told myself to think about the man who had messaged me on the app. He had movie-star good looks, a great profile, and really good energy. But as soon as I forced the man's face into my head, it quickly changed to Ahmad's.

I tried to shake it off and look at the computer screen.

"Do it, do it!" the woman on-screen cried as her partner threatened to smack her ass. "Do it, do it."

As the encouragement to "do it" rang in my ears, I closed my eyes and let nature take its course.

I moved my hands to my thighs and then spread myself wide again. I wanted to tease myself before bringing the toy in. So, I coasted my hands all over every surface area of my body before cupping my breasts and fondling myself. I began tweaking my hard nipples again, and that time, I didn't reject the mental image that played in my mind.

Ahmad was standing at the edge of the bed watching me, wanting me, waiting for me. He was stroking his dick as I caressed my body.

"You want to touch me, don't you?" I murmured aloud.

When the fantasy Ahmad admitted to it, he climbed on the bed and started to feel all over me.

Those weren't my fingers. They were Ahmad's.

Those weren't my hands. They were Ahmad's.

That wasn't my touch. It was Ahmad's.

"Mmm . . ." A gentle sigh came from deep within me as I fantasized about what I needed, and from a sexy someone who could never give it to me.

My body was on fire as the thought of being touched by him took over. I kept one hand fondling and twisting my nipples as the other hand roamed back down south. With my middle finger, I parted my lips and used my wetness to tease my clit. I moaned as I imagined it was his tongue pressing against me. With a fresh image of him licking his lips in my mind, I sank into the sensation of him using his tongue on me.

It felt so good that I started to get lost in the fantasy.

My eyes were shut tight as I visualized him between my legs. "This is exactly what I need right now," I whispered aloud.

He licked exactly where I needed him to.

The mental image of his head buried between my legs and his face covered in my juices rushed me to the brink of an orgasm.

"That's the spot," I murmured as Ahmad looked up at me. He kept his tongue on my clit as he watched me react to his skills.

"You want me to come for you?" I whispered aloud, imagining Ahmad groaning into my pussy.

I gasped, knowing I wasn't going to last much longer. The idea of Ahmad was making it impossible to take my time.

Turning on the vibrator, I placed it inside me, coating it with my juices, and then I ran it up and down my slit.

"Ahmad," I moaned loudly.

The moment the vibrations met my clit, I thrust my hips upward against my hand.

The thought of Ahmad getting up from eating my pussy and sliding his dick into me was all it took. My orgasm crashed over me, and my body shook uncontrollably. That image combined with the steady, constant vibrations against my sensitive bundle of nerves pushed me over the edge before I'd had a chance to really wrap my mind around it.

With perseverance, I kept the vibrator in place even though my legs fought against it. Clamping my thighs together to lock the toy in place, my too-sensitive, yet extremely horny pussy reacted immediately. Ahmad was fucking me, and just the thought of it consumed me. My body became rigid as another wave of pleasure pulsed through me.

My eyes flew open, but I was too far gone to stop. The idea of Ahmad watching me, joining me, eating me, and then fucking me overwhelmed my senses. A third shudder ripped through my body, and I almost knocked my laptop onto the floor.

Crying out loudly, I shook with pleasure, knocking the vibrator away. When I regained control of my body, I grabbed the toy and turned it off.

Breathing hard and unsure of what I'd just done, I stared at the ceiling.

It was just a fantasy.

It wasn't real.

It didn't mean anything.

I'd convinced myself that thinking about Ahmad while masturbating was simply because my unconscious mind reverted back to the last man I'd interacted with. It wasn't a secret that I found him attractive. But he was my friend . . . just my friend . . . just my married friend.

Shit. What did I just do?

12

My weekend had a shaky start with that poor excuse for a date. And even though I had a great night with Nina and the concert was amazing, I was discombobulated by my Ahmad fantasy. So I had no clue how seeing my family for the first time since Aniyah's birthday was going to affect me. I knew it was going to push me over the edge if things went anything like the last time. After the weekend I'd had, I was in no mood to talk about my relationship status.

I'd talked to my parents, and everything seemed cool over the phone. But pulling up in their driveway on Sunday afternoon, I was brought back to the irritation I felt a few weeks ago.

"Now why is he here?" I wondered aloud as I parked behind my uncle's car.

They did not tell me he was coming.

I was thankful I had plans after my lunch with my family to pick my spirits back up if they got on my nerves.

Using my key, I didn't bother to knock as I entered my childhood home. "Coming in," I called out.

"There she is," my grandmother greeted me with open arms.

I enveloped her in a tight hug. "Hi, Nana. How are you?"

"I'm all right, doll baby. How are you?"

"I'm not bad."

She released me from the hug and eyed me. "I haven't seen you in a few weeks. I know we talked on the phone, but I just want to put eyes on you and make sure you're okay."

I nodded. "I'm okay."

"You look good." She gestured to my outfit. "Is that new?"

The bright orange tropical shorts with the matching tank top were cute and kept me cool on the hot summer day.

"I got it at the end of last summer, so this is my first time wearing it," I informed her as we walked into the kitchen.

"Your father and your uncle are outside on the grill." She pointed out the kitchen window. "Your mother is upstairs. We were getting the food ready."

I looked around. "This is a lot of food for just the five of us."

"Some of it is for us. Some of it is for the church."

"Ohhhh, okay."

My mom jogged down the stairs, her footsteps pounding against the wood. "Is that my daughter I hear?"

"Yes," I called out before she made her way into the kitchen.

With a bright smile and open arms, my mom rushed over to me. "Well, don't you look beautiful!"

"Thank you. You, too."

When she pulled out of the hug, she asked, "How is everything? Any update about . . . anything?"

"Anything like what?" Nana wondered. She pulled the macaroni and cheese from the oven. "Good news, I hope."

I frowned a bit. "Update about . . . ?"

"About life. About work. About your friends." My mom's smile grew. "About that man you're seeing . . ."

My grandma turned around and gave me a look.

I was just as confused. "I'm not—"

"Aaliyah!" My dad called my name with such enthusiasm that I jumped. "When did you get here?" He carried a plate full of burgers and gave me a one-armed hug. "I hope you're hungry."

"Hey!" I greeted him. "I am. Good to see you, Dad."

"How's everything going?" he asked with a grin. "I see you're overdressed as usual. You look good, though!"

"Thanks," I laughed, gesturing to his salmon-colored shorts and matching shirt. "I get it from you."

"Is that Aaliyah I hear?" my uncle asked my dad as he carried in what looked like hot dogs and bratwursts. "There's my niece."

I pursed my lips. "Hey, Uncle Al."

Making small talk, we washed our hands and fixed our plates.

We sat down at the dining room table, and my mom filled us all in on her big news.

"I'm going to be co-teaching Bible study starting this fall," she revealed with bubbly excitement. "They made the announcement at church this morning. Me and Liz are going to lead it together!"

"Congratulations, Mom," I said after swallowing some of the best macaroni and cheese I'd ever had.

"What's your schedule going to look like?" Dad wondered.

"You might as well get paid for something because you already spend all your goddamn time at that church," Uncle Al commented.

"Albert!" Nana admonished him from across the table. "Don't use the Lord's name in vain."

We spent the next hour talking about Mom, the church gossip, and Uncle Albert's need of prayer.

"And that's how they found out she was sleeping with the associate pastor," Uncle Al finished.

"For someone who doesn't go to church that often, you sure know all the gossip," my mom quipped.

"For someone who goes all the time, you sure don't know nothing," he retorted, causing us all to laugh. "Unless Liz told you, you don't got no information. What are you in there doing?"

"I'm getting the Word . . . like I'm supposed to," she argued. "You're listening to everyone's business when you should be listening to the Word."

They bickered back and forth like they always did. Nana lovingly complained about them going at it. Dad and I laughed and egged on the situation. It felt like old times. After the last time I'd spent time there, it was exactly what I needed.

"I think I'm about to head out in a few minutes," I announced, patting my full belly. "This was delicious, thank you."

"Worth the thirty-minute drive to the outskirts of town?" Nana teased. "You can't get home cooking like this in the city."

"The best restaurants wish they could do this," I agreed, swallowing the last bite of my food.

"Well, let me tell y'all this one last thing . . ." Mom started talking, and I listened intently as my food digested. "But that's just what Liz told me," Mom concluded.

"Oh, speaking of Liz," my uncle started, turning his head in my direction. "When does Marcus move back here?"

My nose crinkled. "I don't know."

"Next month," my mother answered him quickly. "He's already lined up a really good job in the city. At Franklin Financial. So, he's looking at places to live downtown." With a quick peek at me, she continued, "I told Liz I would ask you for suggestions . . ."

"I thought we were leaving the Marcus thing alone," my dad said, bemused. He looked over at me. "Your mom told me that you're bringing some boy you're seeing to your party."

The last thing I wanted to think about was a date. I wasn't sure if I had it in me to keep dating after the past few weeks.

Trying to change the subject, I asked, "What about asking me about my job? My friends? The rest of my life?!"

My father made a face. "Because you told me about the other stuff. You ain't say nothing about this new boyfriend, so that's what I want to talk about." He crossed his arms. "And I'll ask my daughter whatever I damn well please," he added with a chuckle.

"Now, Darryl, leave Aaliyah alone," my mom chastised with a catlike smile. "She'll tell us about him when she's good and ready."

"There's nothing to tell," I told them.

"Because she ain't got nobody! I done tried to tell you!" Uncle Al exclaimed. He shifted his body and his attention to me. "Now this Marcus fella sounds like a good one, Aaliyah. He got a few dollars on him, too."

"I'm not having this conversation," I told them, picking up my empty plate to take to the kitchen. "I have to get back to the city."

My uncle's lips turned down into a frown. "You ain't gotta run off."

"If she says there's someone, there's someone," Mom argued, standing up for me.

I appreciated my mother defending me and I felt bad about not being completely honest about my situation. Just as I opened my mouth to tell them all the truth, my uncle interrupted me.

"She can't head into thirty alone," he warned. "And at the rate she's going . . ."

"Now hold on, Al." My dad turned his chair to face him. "What are you trying to say?"

He lifted his arms. "All I'm saying is that I want to see Aaliyah married off just like you do." He gestured around the table. "Like we *all* do."

"It's her life. Let's let her live it," Dad replied.

"Exactly," I agreed. "It's my life. Why does it matter to you?"

My uncle dropped his hands with a loud thump against his thighs. "Because I know you ain't got nobody, and I'm just worried is all. With Aniyah—"

"Let me worry about me, please," I sighed, standing up.

Nana put her hand on my arm. "As long as you're seeing someone and not settling for someone, I'm happy to hear it."

"We want the same thing," Mom spoke up.

"Yeah," Dad added.

"Well, I mean, either way—see or settle with somebody with a few dollars in their pocket soon. You're not getting any younger," Uncle Al mumbled.

Mom swatted at him. "Can you shut your mouth for once? For once? One time?"

"Fine! But if there's not a man at this birthday party, I'm going to say I told you so," he replied. "This is why at the end of the summer, the yacht's going to be put up for sale."

"What does that have to do with anything?" Nana reacted.

"Aaliyah knows," he stated.

"I don't know what you're talking about, but you are antagonizing her, and it needs to stop," Dad said firmly. "It's not happening again. Not in my house."

I heard a low-toned argument between my dad and uncle while I threw my trash away in the kitchen. With my keys in hand, I returned to the dining room to officially say goodbye.

"I'm sorry, Aaliyah," my uncle apologized as I got to him.

"I accept your apology, but you have to stop, Uncle Al. I mean it. You're doing too much."

"You know I don't mean no harm." He looked like he wanted to say something else, but he looked over my shoulder at my father.

"Okay." My response was dry because I knew he didn't get it. Whether he didn't mean any harm or not, he didn't get it.

He grabbed my arms and squeezed them. "And you know I love you."

"I know. I love you, too."

"And I look forward to meeting your boyfriend at your party," he continued.

I pursed my lips. "Mm-hmm."

Turning on my heel, I marched out of the house more determined than ever. After I prepared for work in the morning, I spent the rest of Sunday swiping and researching local events. I needed to put myself out there to find what I was looking for by my birthday. I didn't just want anyone. I wanted the one for me. And while my uncle got under my skin and my family's meddling got on my nerves, I wanted a boyfriend for my birthday for me—not for them.

I mean, yeah, I wanted to shut them up, and I wanted the yacht. My uncle's problematic takes needed to be proved wrong. My parents' unsolicited matchmaking needed to be stopped. But it was more than that. I wanted to show them that I was fully capable of living a happy, fulfilling life—with or without a man, with or without marriage, with or without a child.

Because I wanted a man, they would argue that we want the same thing for me. But that's not true. I wasn't just looking for someone to fulfill a role. I was looking for the man for me. And in order to get that, I needed to be open to meeting him. I needed to be open to opportunities to meet him. And just maybe I needed to be open to receiving help meeting him.

And for that reason, I walked over to Onyx on Monday after work.

Still wearing my yellow dress with the black zigzag print at the bottom, I opened the door and cast my eyes around the room. There were two people I didn't recognize behind the bar and about fifteen people spread about the place. Over toward the back hallway that led to the bathrooms, I saw a broad-shouldered man in a red shirt standing near a booth. I knew it was Ahmad from his muscular physique. But it was his sponge-curl fade that confirmed it for me. His hand was pressed to his ear as he turned to the side. I eyed his profile as he stared down the hall.

I walked over and overheard his voice.

"I'll be here for about thirty minutes, and then I'll be home," he said into the phone. "I love you, too."

I stopped in my tracks.

His wife.

I never heard him talk about his wife, let alone talk to her. I suddenly felt uneasy about meeting him one-on-one. We were just friends, but he was a married man.

A married man who said he had something for me.

A married man who never talked to me about his wife.

I took a step back just as he turned around.

"She just got here, so I gotta go," he concluded, ending the call.

He told her about me?

It made me feel better about the meetup.

He slipped his phone into his pocket. "Charlie Brown, you made it."

Rolling my eyes, I held in a laugh. "You're not funny."

"Good grief!"

Twisting my lips, I hid my amusement. "You're an asshole, and you're not funny."

"You know it was funny." Pointing at the booth next to him, he continued, "We're right here."

I slid into the booth. "What's wrong with you?" I cocked my head to the side and waited for him to sit. "You're so bored at home that you invited me here to try out your jokes?"

His eyes danced. "I didn't know you were going to come here dressed like Charlie Brown! How is that on me?"

I glared at him because now that he'd said it, I couldn't unsee the comparison he was making.

I pointed dramatically toward the exit. "I will walk out of here and never look back."

His head tipped back, and he chuckled. "Aight, my bad. I'll stop. You look good. You look like wah wah wah wah wah."

My eyes narrowed at his imitation of Charlie Brown's teacher. I bit the inside of my cheek to keep from laughing. "Cut the bullshit, Ahmad."

Amused with himself, he sat back in his seat. "I just wanted to talk to you, check in with you. You enjoyed yourself at the concert?"

"I did. India Davis's voice is impeccable. We were up top, so we had a great view of the stage. She puts on such a great show," I gushed.

He nodded. "Yeah, she did her thing. She has the voice of an angel."

"Aww. It's cute watching someone with a crush."

He rolled his eyes. "Here you go. We didn't really get a chance to talk about it much, but my boys overexaggerated my thing for India Davis."

"Bullshit!" I exclaimed. "I think it was in our very first conversation you said that your dream woman was India Davis." He opened his mouth to dispute it, but I pointed at him. "Lie if you want to, but I know you got it bad."

He burst out laughing. "Maybe I'm telling you too much because I don't remember telling you that, but it's true. You got me."

With a self-satisfied grin, I wiggled in my chair. "I know. Oh!"

"What?"

I put my hands to my chest. "I'm so sorry. I forgot your umbrella at home, but I can go get it after we leave here."

He shook his head. "No, you don't have to do all that running around. You can just bring it on Friday."

"I live really close. It's no problem at all."

A smile played on his lips. "How close is close?"

"Across the street."

He froze. "The Manor?"

I nodded. "Yeah."

He laughed.

"What's so funny?" I wondered.

"I just moved there about six months ago."

I gasped. "No!"

It was a big building with at least sixty luxury apartments in the restored space. I barely knew my neighbors on my floor, let alone other people within the building. But for some reason, the idea of Ahmad living in my building made me squirm.

He smirked. "Yes."

"You're really my neighbor?"

"If you really live there, then yes, I'm your neighbor." He searched my face. "Why does that surprise you?"

"You live in my building. You work in IT. You like the same music as I do." I lifted my shoulders and twisted my lips. "I'm starting to think you're just copying me at this point."

"You wish."

"*You* wish."

As we grinned at each other across the table, there was a level of comfort that almost made me giddy.

"We didn't really get a chance to talk much after you came out with us. The fellas think you're cool."

I smiled. "Well, I am."

He chuckled to himself. "You're so humble."

"I really am."

"They liked you, though. A lot."

"Good," I replied. "Nina liked you, too. She said you were funny. So that's one person."

"You can deny you think I'm funny all you want, but I know the truth."

"Nina had a few drinks when she made that assessment, so take that with a grain of salt."

"Leon and Darius also had drinks in their system, now that we're talking about it."

We were both laughing and when it trailed off, he held my gaze. His face became serious, but his eyes remained soft. "How are you? Everything okay?"

"I'm fine. Everything is fine," I said slowly. "How are you?"

"I'm cool. It's Monday, so you know how that goes."

I nodded. "Yeah, I hear that."

He paused for only a second before he blurted out, "Okay, so what happened on Friday?"

Caught off guard, I didn't immediately answer. "Uh . . . nothing. What do you mean?"

"You didn't seem like yourself when you left. That giraffe dude said something that got to you?"

"Giraffe?"

"That long-neck dude you met up with on Friday."

A loud cackle rang out of me. "You are so dumb!"

When our amusement died out, he looked at me expectantly.

"Nah, but seriously. What happened?" he wondered.

"It just didn't work out. He said some bullshit I didn't like, and I ended the date. So, he got mad that I ended it and said what they all say when a fat woman has the audacity to reject them." I shrugged. "It really wasn't that serious."

"So, why did you leave?"

"Because I was over it. Between him and that woman, I was just ready to go."

"What woman?"

I shook my head. I really didn't feel like going through the incident with the backhanded compliment. "Just someone at the bar that rubbed me the wrong way. But what did you want to meet up about? It can't be this."

"It was exactly this."

Surprised, I sputtered. "What? Why?"

"I didn't like the way you looked when you left on Friday," he answered. "I know you can take care of yourself, but I always keep my eye on you while you're at the bar. Even when it's too loud for me to hear your conversations, I try to keep tabs on the body language."

"So now you're a body language expert?"

"Nah, but I can read your body language."

"What's it saying now?"

My insides tingled as a slow smile crossed his lips. He stroked his chin as if he were contemplating. My narrowed eyes softened, and my cheeks felt flushed. I shifted my gaze and folded my arms across my chest.

The last thing I wanted him to do was read me.

"You're guarded," he answered. "You tensed up on me the minute I asked."

I lightly cleared my throat and tried to relax. He was absolutely right.

"But it was your body language on Friday that made me want to check on you," he continued. "Are you good? For real?"

"Yeah. Why?"

"Because you looked . . . stressed."

"I wouldn't say I was stressed."

"Well, what would you say? Because you took off before I could really ask you anything."

"I told you—the guy I was with said some slick shit, and I didn't like it."

"Yeah, I got that. But you've had bad dates before, and you didn't take off. And I'm gonna be honest . . . I don't like seeing you upset."

"I wasn't upset . . . I was more annoyed than anything."

"Well, upset, annoyed, stressed, whatever the fuck it was, it wasn't good." He sat up, resting his elbows on the table. "So, are you ready to take my advice now?"

I sighed loudly. "Fine, Ahmad. What is your advice?"

He picked up a small box and slid it across the table. That was the first moment I noticed that he wasn't wearing his wedding band.

"Take this," he encouraged.

Eyeing the small white box suspiciously, I ran my fingers over the pointy edges. It looked like it could perfectly fit a bracelet or earrings. But Ahmad wouldn't be getting me jewelry. There was no logo to give me a hint, so I had no idea what it could be.

I glanced up at him. "What is this?"

"Open it," he insisted. His brown eyes sparkled, and his perfect lips spread into an endearing smile.

Tearing my eyes away from him, I broke the seal and lifted the lid.

It looks like something a spy would use.

My eyes flicked up to his. "What's this?"

"Earbuds."

"I . . . appreciate it. Thank you." I took the thick plastic package out and held it in my hand. I noticed a QR code. "But what is this for?"

"It's for you." He reached over, took them from my hands, and opened it. "They're so small, you could wear them on the date. Put them in. Scan the code. And then listen." He handed them back to me. "Guaranteed to calm your nerves and get you out of your head."

"Ahmad," I whispered, surprised by the thoughtfulness of the gift. "That's . . . Wow, thank you for this."

He just smiled. "But this"—he pointed to the QR code—"is key. It takes you to a playlist. Everything is slower tempo, so it quiets your mind and releases the stress of the day."

"How do you know?"

"Actually, my, uh, my therapist put me on. It worked that first time, and I've used it ever since."

"So, you've been stress-free since you started?"

He chuckled. "I wouldn't say all that. But it helps. Especially with the heavy shit."

I searched his face, intrigued by the glimpse of himself he'd just offered me. "Heavy like what?"

He shook his head. "Nah . . ."

"You've had a front-row seat to my dating disasters and then paraded me in front of your best friends as a case study." I pointed at him. "You owe me a personal story or something."

He let out an amused grunt. "Okay, you're right." He sat back in the booth and stared at me across the table. "The car accident I told you about . . . a drunk driver ran through a light. Car was totaled, but I survived it, so you know . . . gotta take the good with the bad." He forced a smile, but I could still see the incident haunted him. "Life is short."

My hands went to my chest. "Ahmad, I'm so sorry—"

"Yeah, I appreciate that," he interrupted. "But don't give me that look."

"What look?"

"Be the same asshole you've always been. What happened a couple years ago doesn't change anything."

"Damn, I was just saying I'm glad you made it through that!"

"Well, channel that energy into making it through a date."

My jaw dropped. "Wowwwwwwww . . . That was a low blow."

His eyes widened as if he were listening back to his statement. "I didn't mean it like that."

"Yes, you did."

He laughed. "I really didn't."

I playfully glared at him.

"You need a drink?" he wondered, ignoring my glare. "You look like you need a drink."

He jumped up, went to the bar, and returned a couple of minutes later with two drinks.

"Sweetie's tea," he announced, sliding my drink in front of me as he took his seat. "And Omar is going to bring burgers and fries over in a minute. You want to order anything else?"

"I'm good with just the fries for now. Thanks," I said, bringing the glass to my lips. "Mmm."

"You like it?"

"Who made this?"

His lips pulled into a smile before he took a swig of his drink. "It's a secret family recipe. My grandma's nickname was Sweetie. It's her recipe."

"This is really good," I told him.

"You would do better on dates if you were like this."

His random assessment kind of blindsided me, and I took a second to process it. Moving my glass to the side, I clasped my hands in front of me. "What's going on?"

"What do you mean?"

"I mean what are you doing?"

"I'm trying to help you out. Just . . ." He sighed, pushing his drink to the side as well. "Maybe you're out of practice. Pretend I'm that giraffe ass—"

"No," I interrupted, amused.

"Fine. The one with the wife—"

"No."

"Okay, I'm going to be some random man you haven't met yet." When I didn't say anything, he continued, "What is it going to hurt?"

I sighed. "Fine."

"It's nice to meet you," he started.

I pursed my lips. "Yeah, you, too."

"Come on, Aaliyah. You said you already asked the basic questions before agreeing to meet with them. So, how do you want to start the conversation with them now that you're on the first date?"

"I'd typically let him take the lead and initiate the conversation in person. How a man breaks the conversational ice tells me a lot."

Ahmad nodded. "Okay . . . tell me about yourself. Tell me something you love about yourself. First thing that comes to mind."

"I love my sense of style." After the words left my mouth, I held up my hand. "And if you say some shit about me looking like Charlie Brown, I'll air this bitch out."

His head fell back as he let out a loud, hearty chuckle. "I'm not Ahmad right now. I'm your date. And your date will only say you look beautiful."

"What do you love about yourself?"

"My sense of humor."

With a dramatic sigh, I rolled my eyes. "If you're not going to take this seriously, neither am I."

Still laughing, he shook his head. "Let's start again . . . What was the best and worst advice you've ever gotten?"

"Worst? To get on a dating app."

He narrowed his eyes at me. "Aaliyah."

"I stand by it," I laughed. "What was your worst advice?"

He rubbed his hands together and then dropped them in his lap. "Play it cool."

"Play it cool?"

"Yeah. Acting like I'm not affected by whatever is going on. Acting like I'm too cool and calm to act or react . . . or pursue. Middle school advice that I'm still outgrowing."

I was intrigued.

"Very interesting." I leaned forward. "I need an example of the adult you playing it cool."

"Well . . ." He took a sip of his drink. "I was passed over for a promotion, and I acted like it didn't bother me. Whole time, I'm hitting the gym twice a day for a week because I'm pissed. I'm online looking for new jobs because they had me fucked up."

I snickered a little. "I feel you, though!" Cocking my head to the side, I watched him. "Why do you think you were passed over?"

"I honestly don't know. That's the part that fucked with me. There's no good reason they could give me."

I shook my head. "That is some bullshit, and I understand why you'd feel a way about it. Is this at the job you're at now or was this in the past?"

"This was in June," he laughed. "I'm still looking to get out of there. But yeah, I played it cool with everyone in my life. Pretended I didn't care when I did." He made a face. "Now, you're the only person who knows the truth."

I felt special.

My lips parted, and air rushed out. I wasn't sure why words weren't forming, but the longer we stared at each other in silence, the louder my heart pounded in my chest. Warmth crept up my neck and flushed my face.

I was so focused on the man across the table from me, I didn't notice the waiter sliding two baskets between us until the scent hit my nostrils. Breaking eye contact, I looked at my food, over at the waiter who was halfway back to the bar, and then back up at Ahmad.

I cleared my throat. "If you ever need someone to not be cool or calm around, I'm here for you. I already don't think you're cool, so no harm, no foul."

"Yooooooo." He chuckled. "You're an asshole for real."

I grabbed a fry and winked at him.

"And you didn't finish answering the question," he continued. "Best advice you've gotten?"

I finished chewing. "To never let anyone get in the way of me being me."

"That sounds like something I'd tell you."

"No, that wasn't you," I informed him. "That was something my sister would tell me."

"That's good advice."

"It is." I looked into my glass and then took another sip. "She always had good advice."

"Are you taking that advice?"

"I live by that advice." I felt his eyes boring into me, and I felt myself wanting to say more. Instead, I shifted the focus to him. "What's the best advice you've received?"

"The best advice I was ever given was from my father. It was simple, but he basically said to keep going."

"Look at us with our basic advice." I lifted my glass and waited for him to clink his against mine. "Cheers to us."

"Cheers." He took a sip. "It was basic, but it was powerful. For a long time, that kept me going. Those two words from my father put the battery in my back, and I didn't give up on anything I wanted. Life happens, and you can kind of lose yourself, lose that momentum. Just as long as you don't stop. So day by day, I push myself forward. I keep going."

"I like that," I murmured thoughtfully. "That type of mindset keeps you from being stuck."

A look flashed across his face. Instead of responding, he picked up his glass and took a gulp.

"I'm glad you like the tea," he said, his expression back to normal.

"Wait, what was on your mind?" I wondered, eating another fry. "You looked like you wanted to say something."

He shook his head. "Nah, it's nothing."

"Ahmad." My firm tone and twisted lips reiterated my skepticism. "First of all, I don't believe you. Second, how do you expect me to keep telling you all my business and you don't tell me the realness of yours?" I gestured between us. "There should be an equal exchange of information."

It looked like he was about to argue, but then he exhaled. "I was just thinking about how the other day someone said something about if my motto is really to keep going, I wouldn't currently be stuck, so it kind of tripped me out that you said that. That's all."

"Stuck . . . ?"

He held my gaze but didn't say anything. I felt stirring within me, and a tenderness flooded my system out of nowhere.

Is he talking about his marriage? Oh, wait . . . no, he's talking about his job. That makes sense.

After swallowing, I started to ask to get clarity. "So, you—"

"Sorry, I have to take this." He grabbed his phone and put it to his ear before I could see the name that flashed on the screen. "Hello?"

I watched him look everywhere but at me as he gave short answers to the questions he was being asked. "Yes . . . Yes . . . Cool . . . Yeah, I'm leaving now . . . I love you, too."

His wife.

"Sorry about that." He slipped his phone back into his pocket. "I have to head out, so that's the end of our practice run. I can get a box for the rest if you want me to walk you out?"

"No," I answered. I needed time to gather my thoughts, and more importantly, I didn't want it to look like I was meeting up with a married man. "I'm going to chill for a little bit." I pointed to the fries. "And I want to eat these while they're hot."

He slid out the booth and stood. "You're going to be okay here by yourself?"

"Are you going to be okay heading out by yourself?" I tilted my head to the side. "You need me to walk out with you?"

"Asshole Aaliyah is back."

"Asshole Ahmad never left."

He smirked. "I'll see you Friday."

Before he turned to walk away, I put the earbuds in the box and then tapped it. "This was really nice. Can I ask you a question, though?"

"Yeah, what's up?"

"Why do you care?" I wondered. I slipped the gift into my handbag.

"Because I'm invested at this point." He paused and then added, "And no one wants a front row seat to a shit show."

My jaw dropped. "That was rude as fuck! My dating life isn't a shit show."

He frowned. "Isn't it?"

"I hate you," I giggled. "You're living in the past, and even if it *was* a shit show, it won't be for long. I'm not giving up on what I want."

"Good. You shouldn't."

"I'm not."

"Listen to the playlist."

"I will."

He paused for a moment. "I love how you're all in. You're committed. You're going for it. I respect that. I respect *you*. I don't know if it's because you want to spite your family or if it's because you really want a man, but watching you go on these dates reminds me to keep going. *That's* why I'm invested. *That's* why I care."

"Ahmad," I breathed, putting my hand to my chest. "That . . ." I poked my lip out. "I love that."

"Now if only you'll listen to me about these clowns, you'll be on your way."

"Here you go," I groaned. "You see how you go from sweet to sour in one fell swoop?"

"You have to start taking my advice. I know things."

"How do you get your small-ass shirts over that inflated ego of yours?"

His lips twitched. Slowly walking backward, he said, "That long-neck muthafucka walked in here, and I knew instantly that he wasn't the one for you. And you knew it, too. But you didn't listen to yourself. Or me. You just sat over there like . . ." He hunched his shoulders up in his exaggerated imitation of me.

I cackled. "Goodbye, Ahmad."

"Bye, Aaliyah."

With a smile on my face, I watched him walk away. He dapped up the people behind the bar, and then he left Onyx without a glance back.

As soon as I was sure he was gone for good, I pulled out the earbuds and the QR code. I scanned it with my phone and queued up the playlist. For the next fifteen minutes, I just sat there listening with tears in my eyes.

The music wasn't particularly sad.

I was just touched.

13

They said the dating pool had pee in it, but I was convinced there was shit in there, too.

No chlorine—just shit, algae, and bacteria.

I listened to the playlist Ahmad had given me on repeat. I felt connected to him, with him, through the music. The earbuds were so discreet, I even got away with listening at work. But no amount of musical good energy could combat the men who had been attempting to connect with me on the app.

I was already on a mission to find the man for me. But after my last interaction with my family, I was more determined than ever to find my someone special. I knew it was a stretch, but I'd hoped to find my person. Or at the very least, I'd hoped to have a date and my back blown out to ring in my thirtieth birthday. But even after dodging the obvious creeps on the app, I was still running into the bottom of the barrel. So I was trying to think of ways outside of TenderFish to meet men. Until a promising message and flirty conversation led me back to Onyx on Friday night.

Wearing a pair of jeans, a cute green top with a plunging neckline, and sexy sandals, I felt good as I strolled into the bar. There were a few more people inside than I expected at that time, but it was still relatively empty.

"Hey!" Asia greeted me with a wave. "I'll be right with you."

I climbed onto the barstool and looked around. Pulling my phone out of my bag, I started thumbing through social media. I'd posted a couple of selfies that seemed to be catching the attention of men from my past—none of which I wanted to bring into my future.

"So, another date tonight?" Asia asked, pulling my attention from my phone.

I nodded. "Yeah. I'm hoping it goes well, but honestly . . ." I shrugged. "It is what it is at this point."

"I hear that. I've gone on a dating hiatus. I'll try back again in the fall." She scrunched up her nose. "Maybe."

"Good call." I paused for a moment, a memory washing over me.

She wiggled her eyebrows. "When I get back out there, I'll hit you up for some tips. I need to be quick and efficient. Get in and get out."

"I know someone who went on a dating hiatus and literally met her husband the day after she told me she wasn't dating anymore. I think you'll be fine."

She looked at me suspiciously. "You made that up."

I lifted my hand. "I swear. It happened."

"To who?"

"My sister."

Her eyes lit up. "Really?"

I nodded. "Really."

"It makes me more optimistic when I hear it's happened like that before."

I nodded in agreement. Aniyah's trajectory in life was awe-inspiring. She found her soulmate quite quickly and easily. For anyone who had been in the murky waters of dating, the idea of finding that special someone was already difficult enough. But to find someone so quickly and to marry them soon thereafter was unheard of.

But that was how life played out for Aniyah.

She had it easy. Whatever she wanted landed at her feet. She truly lived a charmed life.

But she didn't make it beyond thirty.

I swallowed hard and tried to push the thought away.

Asia glanced over to a man who was flagging her down. "I'll be back."

Just as she walked off, I got an alert on my phone. Thinking it was my date, I prepared for a cancellation, postponement, or delay of some sort.

My eyebrows flew up as I recognized the name across my screen—and it wasn't my date.

My ex-boyfriend, my first heartbreak, had commented on my photo and sent me a message. Hesitantly, I opened it and read it. Rolling my eyes, I went back to the picture in question and studied it. I looked good. But I was not expecting to hear from someone who swore he'd never speak to me again. Holding my phone at eye level, I zoomed in.

I mean . . . I do *look good, though.*

It'd been a month since my first TenderFish date and five weeks since I'd been stood up, and I was no closer to being booed up on my birthday. And while I could've responded to my ex, that wasn't the energy I wanted to usher into my thirties. Tremaine was my ex for a reason. But I couldn't deny that the others in my DMs were tempting as my birthday loomed a few weeks away.

"That picture is fire," Ahmad commented from behind me.

His voice sent a chill down my spine.

I lurched forward, bringing my arm down and my phone to my chest. "Why are you creepily looking over my shoulder?"

"Why are you holding your phone up with the picture zoomed in like it was on a jumbo screen? Your eyes bad?"

"They must be if I'm just now noticing you're a creep."

He chuckled as he made his way around the bar to the back office. When he returned, he grabbed a crate of clean glasses and started putting them away in front of me.

"You look good in green," Ahmad stated with a straight face.

I narrowed my eyes suspiciously but decided to take the compliment. "It's my favorite color."

As soon as I opened my mouth to thank him, he continued, "Over here looking like the sexy M&M."

I suppressed a giggle, but I couldn't cover the smile. "I can't stand you."

"You look a little more relaxed today. Did you listen to the playlist?"

I nodded. "I did. And I love it. It's a vibe."

Ahmad grinned. "I hate to say I told you so . . ."

"Don't look so impressed with yourself. Not with that outfit on."

He laughed, looking down at himself. "Damn, what's wrong with what I have on?"

My eyes swept his body. *Not a damn thing.*

I frowned and gestured from his head to his feet. "Where do I start?"

When he smoothed his hands down his shirt, from his chest to his stomach, I was eye level with his wedding ring.

I cleared my throat and shifted my gaze away from him. "I'm playing. Your outfit is fine. I see you went up to a full medium shirt, so that's a nice change. Now I can only see two of your ribs through the threads of fabric."

"Aye yo, you are an asshole for real!"

We snickered.

"Who's up to bat today?" Ahmad asked after taking an order. "You're the queen of first dates."

"I don't know about the *queen* of first dates . . ."

"Well, you for damn sure haven't lined up a second date yet."

My jaw dropped. Reaching over and grabbing a napkin from the stack on the corner, I tossed it at him.

"Too far?" he guessed, catching the soft white projectile.

"I hate you," I told him, pinching my thumb and pointer finger together. "Just a bit. There's hate there. Growing by the day."

He pointed at me. "But I keep that smile on your face."

"It's a grimace," I corrected.

"Spell *grimace.*"

"You want me to spell the word for 'snarled-up frown'?" I cocked my head to the side. "A-h-m-a-d."

He chuckled. "Nah, for real. What's up with your date tonight?"

"His name is Silas. He seems cool." I shrugged. "But don't they all?"

"Nah, not really. That first one looked like he was being interviewed for *The First 48.*"

I laughed. "No he didn't!"

"I'm serious! I know what your type is . . . random."

My head fell back, and my shoulders shook. "Shut up!"

"I'm serious. He came in here with a zoot suit and—"

"Ahmad!" Asia called out, pointing to a group who had just gathered.

My amusement slowly dissipated as the minutes ticked by and the conversations I'd had over the week replayed in my mind. Silas was cute and flirty. He seemed both genuinely interesting and interested. But if I was being real with myself, it was his thirst-trap photos that pushed me into conversing with him in the first place.

"So . . . Silas, huh?" Ahmad pondered as he returned to his post in front of me. "Tell me about him."

"No, because you're just going to make jokes." I put my elbows on the bar and leaned forward. "Tell me about when you were in the streets. You probably didn't know how to act."

"Who said I was in the streets?"

My eyes bulged. "You told me to get on this app, so I know you were in the streets."

"I knew how to act, though." His lips pulled upward. "I went on a few dates. Met a few women. Had a good time."

I eyed him suspiciously. "No, no, no. You've had a front-row seat to my dating life for the past month, so it's your turn to spill. What's your type? What type of dates did you go on?"

"Beautiful women who can keep up with me," he answered with a shrug. "Spontaneous, crazy—good crazy—and smart. I don't know how else to explain it. And if I met the woman in person, I'd pick a restaurant to get to know her a little better. If I like her, the second date is something specifically tailored to her. If I met her online, I'd meet her at a bar or coffee shop first, and then the second date would be someplace legit."

"So basically, what you're saying is that if you already know there was physical attraction and chemistry, you'll spring for the meal. If you haven't seen her in person yet, you'll pay for a drink."

He lifted his shoulders. "Pretty much. At the end of the day, if I'm not attracted to her, it's not going anywhere. And I don't just mean that physically. I need to be attracted to her conversation just as much as her physical appearance."

I nodded. "I feel you."

He held my gaze. "I know you do."

"How many dates did it take you to determine she's the one?"

"By the end of the fourth date, I know what's up."

"So, on the fourth date, you knew you found the one?"

"On the fourth date, I know what I want to do. If it works out, it works out. If it doesn't, it doesn't. But by the end of the fourth date, I know if I want to focus my time exclusively with that woman."

I nodded as I mulled over his thought process. There was something incredibly refreshing about a man who knew what he wanted and followed through with it. As evidenced by the ring on his finger, he didn't just talk the talk. He walked the walk, too.

By Ahmad's logic, if I hit it off with Silas tonight, we'd know where we'd want to take it on my birthday.

"When do you know?" he asked, interrupting my thoughts.

"Depends on the man," I answered honestly. "I've known I was interested in more on the first date. Sometimes it took a little longer. But from this point forward, I'm just trusting my gut."

"Smart. You have a good head on your shoulders." He put his hands a few inches from his head. "That big head of yours will serve you well."

"I do have a big head," I acknowledged. "That's not the first time I've heard that. Sorry you can't relate."

It took him a second before he burst out laughing. "Yooooooo."

A couple of women approached the bar, and instead of going to Asia, they stood next to me and waited for Ahmad.

After he served them, he turned to me. "What does this Silas do? Please tell me he has a job."

"He's a tattoo artist."

"That's what's up. He any good?"

I frowned. "I don't know. He showed me pictures of some of his work, but honestly, he could've taken those pictures from anywhere on the internet."

Amused, he shook his head. "You don't trust nobody, do you?"

"I sure don't!"

"You trust me, though."

I rolled my eyes, but I didn't answer him.

Funny enough, I did trust him.

As if my silence gave him confirmation, he smirked and moved on. "Well, if you get to know him and verify his work, let me know what's up. I was thinking about turning this half sleeve into a full sleeve next month."

The black ink dancing across his arm was mostly hidden by his shirt sleeve. But every time he reached over to mix a drink, wipe down the bar, or put something away, an intricate design peeked out. Even when I tried not to look at his muscles as he stretched out the fabric of his shirt, I noticed. I wasn't checking him out, but I had eyes.

"What do you have and what are you thinking about getting?" I asked, studying his arm like it was the first time.

"I have prayer hands up here"—he pointed to his upper arm—"a Bible verse, a, um . . . a quote, and a design that goes all around my bicep. I want to get the design connected down to my wrist to make a full sleeve."

I nodded slowly. "Did all that hurt?"

"Not as much as I thought it was going to. Do you have any?"

I shook my head. "No, but I'm getting one for my birthday."

"Of what?"

"Aaliyah?" a voice interrupted the conversation, and instinctively, I knew it was Silas.

Caught off guard, I hadn't had a chance to brace myself for the meeting. A jolt fired through me before I turned to face my date.

Oh, okay!

Silas was just as sexy as his pictures. Tall, slim, square-jawed, he had a cool vibe about him. He looked like a stereotypical artist.

"Hi," I greeted him as he took his seat.

"You're beautiful," he complimented me. His eyes swept up and down my body. "Wow. You look good and you smell good."

I grinned. "Thank you."

"What would you like? How should we start off the night?" He cocked his head to the side. "With champagne?"

A slow smile crept across my face. "Sounds good."

He lifted his hand to signal to Ahmad, who had taken a few steps away and was pretending not to be watching in the mirror.

"What's up, man? What can I get you?" Ahmad greeted him.

Silas ordered a bottle of champagne and proudly pulled out a black card to pay for it. The way he was holding it made it clear he wanted me to see what it was. Once it was securely back in his pocket, he turned to me and engaged me in conversation. He leaned in close to me, inhaled deeply, and then started asking me some questions about myself.

A drink and a half later, he seemed to get a little too comfortable.

"Big women are my type—always have been and always will be." He held up a finger. "The best hugs are from big women." He held up a second finger. "The best cuddling is from big women." He held up a third finger. "The best . . ." His sentence trailed off, and he let out a small chuckle under his breath. "The best skills."

"Skills?"

"Yeah. Skills in the kitchen, in the home, in the bedroom—you asked," he pointed out quickly, lifting his hands as if I were going to call him out. When I didn't speak, he continued with a smile, "Big women are mad cool. And I might not look like it, but I eat a lot, and I need a woman with a big appetite, too. So naturally, I love a woman that can cook. Big women know how to treat a man because they can cook, they clean, and they're the freakiest. So, if I'm being completely honest, there's nothing better than a big, sexy woman who will match my energy."

I was quiet for a moment as I assessed the self-satisfied look on his face. "Every woman who is big isn't like that. You know that, right?"

His forehead creased. "What do you mean?"

"Big women aren't just one thing. If you want these qualities in a woman, that's one thing. But to say that you like big women because all big women are like this . . . is just not true."

"Yo, chill . . . I'm just naming some things I like." Confusion crumpled his face. "I'm trying to give you a compliment."

"These aren't compliments," I explained. "These are stereotypes."

He rolled his eyes and exhaled loudly. "You're blowing shit way out of proportion."

"No. I'm just trying to get clarity and making sure I'm not a fetish."

"Ain't nobody say nothing about a fetish," he replied indignantly. He shook his head. "I'm going to keep it real with you, baby girl, this ain't going to work if this is your attitude."

"I agree. This isn't going to work. We should call it a night," I told him.

"Because I told you how sexy you are?"

I made a face. "That wasn't exactly what happened." I lowered my voice. "It feels like you're fetishizing me, and I'm not interested in being someone's fetish."

His face contorted expressively. "What? How?"

"All of the assumptions and generalizations you were making about women with fatter bodies."

"Aw, come on now! We were talking, and I was complimenting you." He looked me up and down. "I think your body is sexy."

I nodded, shifting my gaze to Ahmad, who was laughing loudly as he put on a show preparing a cocktail. "Okay," I sighed. "I'm glad we got a chance to meet, but let's not waste each other's time. Let's call it a night."

His eyes were as big as saucers. "Are you serious?"

I nodded. "I'm very serious."

"Wow, really? I don't understand."

I didn't respond.

There was no reason to respond.

He didn't get it, and I didn't care enough to explain further. Instead, I stared at our reflection in the mirror until he stood up.

Looking me up and down, he leaned forward and inhaled deeply. "When you get over yourself, come find me. I'd still fuck the shit out of you. Fat bitches have the best pussy. And you look like—"

"You good?" Ahmad asked me, interrupting the bullshit coming out of Silas's mouth.

I gave him a look, but I nodded.

He shifted his eyes to Silas. "What were you saying?"

Even though the bar separated them, the color drained from Silas's face, and he took a step back. He lifted his hands, and his mouth opened and closed a few times. "I-I-I was just say-saying good night."

Anger flashed in Ahmad's eyes as they narrowed. "Yeah, I think that's for the best."

"She's all yours," Silas muttered before walking away.

Ahmad glared at Silas's retreating form until he shifted his attention to me. "You good?"

"Yeah."

"I didn't like that one."

An amused smirk bent my lips. "Me either."

"I came over because of the look on your face. I could see you weren't feeling it, but then I got over here, and I caught the tail end of what he said and . . ." He shook his head. "He's lucky I'm behind this bar."

The protectiveness made me feel warm inside.

"Yeahhhhhhh." I let the word stretch out in tired resignation. "But I was over him before he even got to the part you heard."

"You looked like you were cool in the beginning. What happened?"

"We weren't compatible."

He stroked his chin. "You know what?"

"What?"

"I'm starting to think you're the problem."

Reeling, I felt my reaction consume my whole body. "What?!" I screeched.

"I'm just saying . . ." Grinning, he lifted his arms. "It's just starting to look like it might be you. I mean, *you* are the common denominator."

Reaching for a napkin, I crumpled it and threw it at him. "I can't stand you!"

"Well, tell me what happened or I'm going to just have to assume you're the problem." He glanced at a man who was waiting to order. "Hold that thought," he told me. When he came back, he crossed his arms over his chest. "Let's hear it. Why weren't you compatible with this one?"

I glared at him. The expression on his face was comical, but I held firm with my pursed lips. "If you must know, we weren't compatible because he didn't have a genuine interest in me."

"That's too bad. He was clearly attracted to you. Every time I came down to check on you, he was staring you down."

"Yeah, well . . ."

"But he wasn't here long enough to get to know that behind your beauty, you're the Grinch."

I let out a loud, unexpected laugh. "You know what? This is why I don't talk to you."

"Come on," he chuckled. "Now what happened? I thought you two were hitting it off."

"Yeah, I thought so, too, until he got that liquor in his system, and I realized he was fetishizing me."

His face froze. "What?"

"His interest was based on stereotypes he has about 'big girls'"—I did air quotes—"and what we like, how we act, what we're willing to do."

"So instead of getting to know you, he was just telling you who he assumed you were?"

"Pretty much." I chewed my bottom lip for a second. "And it didn't sit right with me."

He shook his head. "Well, it looks like you dodged a bullet. Man couldn't handle his liquor, and he didn't see what he had in front of him. To hell with him."

My lips curled into a soft smile. "Thanks."

"And besides, I think he was smelling you."

I burst out laughing. "You saw that?"

"Hell yeah! And I saw some shit like that on a documentary about serial killers once, and that just hadn't sat right with me since. It's one thing if someone smells good and you catch their scent. It's a whole other thing when you're trying to put your nose on somebody you just met."

"That was wild, right? I'm so glad I have a witness!"

"Even when I'm busy, I keep an eye on you. I told you I got you," he assured me.

His brown eyes were as kind as his words.

"I appreciate you," I told him, ignoring the flutter in my belly. I lifted my glass in his direction. "Thanks!"

He grabbed a glass. "And you're not talking about giving up on dating this time, so that's a good sign."

"Yeah, well, my birthday weekend is in a few weeks, so I don't have much time." I pulled out my phone. "I've been having conversations on the app here and there with this other guy. He asked me out, so I'll accept his offer." Typing as I spoke, I said, "For next Friday at seven thirty."

"That's my girl," Ahmad cheered. His eyes flitted over me. "You want to stick around and have a drink?"

I nodded. "Yeah. That'll be cool."

The crowd at Onyx grew, and with all the tables packed, every stool at the bar was occupied. Sipping my drink, I busied myself on the app between conversations with Ahmad. When it was time to go, I leaned over the bar and caught his attention.

With a smile, he stopped what he was doing and came to me.

"You're not leaving, are you?" he asked.

I nodded. "I am. I'm hungry—"

He jerked his thumb toward the kitchen. "I can get someone to make you whatever you want."

"I took out chicken earlier, so I'm about to make that," I told him.

"You can't make chicken better than I can," he teased.

"Well, I didn't know it was a competition, but since you want to go there—we can do a cook-off anytime."

He leaned closer, bringing his face inches from mine. "Just name the day and time, and I'm on it."

"You don't intimidate me. Not with your chicken"—I lightly bumped my forehead to his—"and not with your big-ass head."

He cracked up.

The sound gave me butterflies.

Standing up straight, he pointed to the door. "Okay, Green Arrow, I'm tired of your shit. Get out of here," he joked.

My eyes widened. "You're going to play it like you're kicking me out when I was already leaving?" I snickered. "Wow, Ahmad."

"I invited you to stay longer, but you're playing—pretending like you're going to cook chicken at midnight."

"You're in my business."

He gestured down the bar. "I have work to do. You good?"

"Yeah, I'm good."

"See you Friday?"

I took a step back. "If I'm the highlight of your Friday night, just say that."

Grinning, he shook his head. "You're so full of yourself."

"See you Friday," I called behind him.

He winked at me and then proceeded to take the man's order.

Despite how my date went, I felt really good as I walked out of Onyx. I'd just gotten to the corner and pressed the crosswalk button when I heard my name called.

"Aaliyah?"

Startled, I turned. "Asia! Hey!"

"Hey!" She switched her bag strap from one shoulder to the other. "Are you heading home?"

"Yeah, it's late." I gestured to her cute bag. "Are you leaving early tonight?"

"I am. I'm tired and I have to be back here tomorrow, so I told them I'm not closing."

"I know that's right!"

The signal indicated we could walk across the street. "I'm parked over there," Asia informed me, so we both crossed. "So, I have a question. As I was leaving, you and Ahmad had your heads smushed together."

Shit. I got a sinking feeling in my stomach, and it took everything in me to not trip over my own feet. *Shit shit shit shit shit!*

I knew how it looked, and that was the last thing I wanted for either of us. I would never knowingly get with a married man. And Ahmad had been nothing but a good friend to me and a loyal—as far as I could tell—partner to his wife.

"He just had jokes because I have on green. He called me the green M&M and Green Arrow. You know how he is. Just jokes all the time," I explained in a rush. "And he said he could cook better chicken than I could, so we were going back and forth, and then he got in my face. It was to be intimidating. It wasn't . . . I'm sure it looked wild from the outside looking in, but it was innocent."

"Innocent, huh?"

I glanced over at her.

Her smile made me uncomfortable. "He hasn't been wearing his ring all the time, and I know it's because of you."

I shook my head profusely. "No, I don't know anything about that. He's just been looking out for me because we're friends. That's all," I continued, stepping onto the sidewalk. I knew I was talking too much, but I couldn't stop. "He gave me some therapy tips and helped me get more comfortable with dating. He's been an example of what I'd want in my future husband—kind, loyal, funny, hardworking, thoughtful, interesting, giving . . . He's truly a great man, and I treasure our friendship. We're just friends. That's all."

"Are you sure that's all?" Asia hit the button to start her car. "Are you absolutely positive?"

"Yes, of course. I would never . . ." I let my sentence trail off because of the way she was looking at me.

"Hmm. That's too bad, because you've been really good for him. He's different with you, and the way you two light each other up, I just thought maybe . . ." She moved her hands around as if she were searching for the word. "He doesn't talk to me about his love life anymore, and he doesn't take my advice. But I know my brother, and I haven't seen him like this in a long time." She bit her lip and nodded. "It's been really good to witness."

Confusion enveloped me, and my mind was racing. I actively fought the urge to take off running into my building. "We're just friends."

She gave me a knowing smile. "Okay. The chemistry is undeniable, but okay."

"Asia, Ahmad is married!"

Her brows furrowed, and she made a face. "No, he's not."

14

"What?" I sputtered. "What?"

Asia's eyes slowly widened, and she took a step back. "Wait, you didn't know?"

"Didn't know what?" I was having trouble understanding what she was saying. I felt like my brain wasn't functioning correctly because nothing was making sense. "Ahmad is married."

She looked as stunned as I felt. "I thought you said he told you about therapy."

"He did tell me about therapy. He also wears a wedding band like most married men. So, I'm not understanding what you mean."

Pinching the bridge of her nose, she closed her eyes and exhaled. "So, he didn't say *why* he was in therapy?"

"No, but he did say out of his own mouth that he was happily married." I let out a humorless laugh as I tried to put the pieces together myself. "So, you're saying he's lying about being married?"

"It's like a defense mechanism. It's . . . complicated. It's really not my place to say anything. I didn't know you didn't know. I'm sorry."

I turned toward Onyx and contemplated marching over there and giving Ahmad a piece of my mind. But a myriad of emotions kept me rooted in place.

"Hey . . ." Asia grabbed my shoulders and turned me toward her. "If he hasn't told you yet, he will. Just . . . ask him."

I swallowed around the lump in my throat. "I don't know what to say."

"I'm sorry. I shouldn't have said anything. But if y'all are friends like you described, talk to him about it. He's different with you. I know he'd tell you. Maybe it's just hard at the bar with all the people around." She covered her face and let out a loud groan. "He's going to kill me."

My throat burned, and I felt like I was going to choke. "I'm not going to tell him you said anything," I told her, taking a step back. "I might not say anything at all. He didn't tell me for a reason."

"Aaliyah—"

I looked at my phone. "It's getting late, so I should really get going." I lifted my hand and forced a smile as I headed toward my door. "See you later, Asia."

"Give him a chance to explain," she called out after me. "See you Friday!"

I waved but didn't say anything.

I couldn't.

I was still reeling from what she'd just told me.

I damn near ran through the front door and to the elevator. When I got to my floor, my vision was blurry, but I managed to get inside my apartment before a tear squeaked out. My chest burned and my heart hurt. A hundred and fifty-seven thoughts ran through my mind, and I felt betrayed and lied to.

I walked right past the kitchen and straight to the bathroom. I wasn't even hungry anymore. I needed to clear my mind and slow everything down. Stepping into the hot shower, I lathered my body in a daze. It wasn't until I rinsed off that I allowed the tears to fall freely. I didn't cry because I was sad. I cried because I was in shock.

I really thought I knew him.

Wrapped in a towel, I called up Nina. She didn't answer, so I called Jazz. When she didn't answer, I went to my music app and started to play music. Unfortunately, it was set to start from the last playlist, and the last playlist was Ahmad's. I tried to keep my composure, but I was sick.

I'm not talking to him about it, I decided as I pulled on my pajamas. *I might not talk to his ass ever again. Wait, didn't I already tell Lennox to meet me at Onyx next weekend? Shit . . . well, it's still early. I can switch locations. It's probably for the best anyway—*

"Nina!" I answered the phone on the first ring.

"Hey, how was your date?" she responded in a singsong tone.

"Oh, he was problematic. But, girl, that's not even the most shocking thing that happened. I have something to tell you. I haven't even fully processed it yet, and honestly, I don't know how to process it. I feel—"

"You are killing me! What's going on?"

The worry in her voice rushed me to my point.

"Ahmad isn't married," I told her.

"He left his wife because he's in love with you," she gasped. "I knew it!"

"No." I shook my head even though she couldn't see me. "He was never married."

"Wait, what?"

"Exactly!" I yelled into the phone. "His sister, Asia, works at Onyx, too, and she thought I knew. She said something about our chemistry, and I was telling her that I would never because he was married. She looked baffled, okay? Baffled! She looked confused as to why I would even think he was married."

"He wears a wedding ring!"

"Exactly!"

"Men who aren't married don't wear wedding rings. Hell, men who are married be slipping theirs off from time to time. So, what is going on?"

"That's what I'm saying. I don't know, and I'm sick about it."

I could hear Nina starting to move around as if she were pacing.

"Now wait a damn minute!" she exclaimed. "I'm confused."

"Same, sis! And not to mention that I've just spent the last five weeks getting to know this man only to find out I don't know him at all. He lied to me."

"Not to sound like Jazz, but there has to be a reasonable explanation. It doesn't make any sense. What did he say when you asked him?"

"I just found out like an hour ago. I haven't talked to him. But the more I think about it, the more I don't think I *want* to talk to him."

Nina was silent for a few seconds. "Now I'm really confused. What do you mean you're not going to talk to him about this?"

"He clearly wanted me to think he was married. He isn't interested in being honest with me. He isn't interested in me knowing. He isn't interested in . . ."

Me.

I let my sentence trail off and continued it in my head. The pang in my chest punctuated the sentence.

He isn't interested in me.

"No," Nina uttered firmly. "The dots aren't connecting. I watched you and him together. There's no way he's not interested. And from everything you've ever said about him, there has to be more to it than what it looks like. Because this really doesn't make any sense."

"It's the only thing that makes sense," I reasoned.

"So, you're just not going to talk to him? Really?"

"Not about this." I swallowed hard. "If he wanted to talk about it, he would've brought it up. So, I'm going to respect his lie and keep doing what I've been doing. I'm going to have to reach out to Lennox and tell him that our date needs to be relocated."

"I mean . . . I'm all for you seeing what's up with Lennox because variety is the spice of life. But are you sure you want to give up on the bartender without at least hearing him out?"

I sat up abruptly. "I didn't give up on him!" My tone was indignant, as my best friend clearly didn't listen to what I'd told her. "Nina, he gave up on me! He was pretending to be married so I didn't hit on him. He let me believe he had a wife so that I would leave him alone."

"From what I saw at the concert, that man did everything *but* make sure you'd leave him alone."

"There were ample opportunities for him to tell me the truth, and he didn't."

"Liyah," Nina sighed.

I climbed under the covers. "I don't understand what you don't understand. Ahmad lied about his relationship status to let me down easy or whatever. And then I thought we became friends, and he still didn't say anything. I've told him personal stuff, and he just . . ." I shook my head and rolled onto my side. "I guess he's not who I thought he was."

"I can understand that," Nina said carefully. "That's valid."

I could hear the *but* in her tone.

"But what?" I replied with a sigh.

"You know my motto is 'On to the next one,'" she reminded me. "And ordinarily, I would be completely on board with you leaving one man in the dust and seeing what's up with the next one. Because really, I'm still struggling with why you want one boyfriend when you can have several."

"Nina," I laughed, shaking my head at the unexpected comment.

"I'm serious. But since you're not trying to live a beautifully carefree life like me, I have two questions I want you to answer and sit with before you make moves."

"What's that?"

"Think about why having a boyfriend on your birthday is important to you. And then ask yourself if you're willing to settle for a boyfriend just to have one on your birthday."

"No," I answered quickly.

It was a no-brainer. I wasn't willing to settle, and that was why I spent most of the summer running through so many dates.

"Exactly!" Her voice was elevated and sharp. "So of all the men you went on dates with, talked to, and connected with on the app, none of them were boyfriend material. *For you.* Some of them seemed cool, but they weren't it. *For you.* And that's fine. But at the end of the day, forget your family's expectations, forget trying to prove something to them, forget what you think you should do. What do *you* want? *For you.* Not for anyone else. *For you.*"

"I—"

"No," she cut me off before I could respond. "I don't want you to answer right now. I want you to really think about it, so sleep on it. I'm serious."

I nodded even though she couldn't see me. "Okay."

"And my second question for you circles back to this thing with the bartender, and this time, I want an immediate answer from you."

I stared at the ceiling fan as I replied, "Okay . . ."

"Why are you really mad at Ahmad?"

"Because he lied! I was completely honest with him, and he lied to me."

"Aaliyah, let me give you some real talk . . . You weren't completely honest with him either."

"What?" I sat up, indignant. "Yes, I was! I told that man my business, and the whole time—"

"Did you tell him you had feelings for him?"

My mouth hung open for a second. "I—so—it—the—I don't," I sputtered, completely flustered.

"Give it up, girl!" Nina laughed lightly. "I commend you. You tried not to like him, because you thought he was someone else's husband. But you are not about to sit on this phone and deny you have feelings for him. I saw the two of you looking at each other with hearts in your eyes. It was sickening, to be honest."

It took me a full thirty seconds to find my words. "You're right. Maybe I did have a little crush on him, but that doesn't change the fact that he lied."

"Did he come out and tell you a lie? Or did he let you believe a lie?"

"As my friend, he shouldn't have let me believe a lie," I argued, feeling my case becoming increasingly shaky.

"Was it a lie that he told or a lie you assumed to be true?"

I balled my face into a frown and remained quiet. Nina was cutting a little too close, and I wasn't ready.

"Exactly," she stated. "Because if I'm remembering correctly, he never told you he was married. You saw his ring and you overheard him telling someone about his wife. But he never looked you in your face and told you specifically that he was married."

Groaning, I rolled onto my side. "Okay, this conversation is over."

"This conversation might be over, but the conversation you need to have with yourself needs to start. And here's what I want you to think about . . . you assumed he was married, and he let you run with that assumption. I get why you'd feel a way—so again, that's valid. But are you really mad at him because of that? Because I don't think that's it at all. I think you're mad at him because of your feelings for him."

My chest hurt as my card was pulled. In that way that only a best friend could, Nina cut to the chase and forced me to look at my situation differently.

And I wasn't ready for that.

"No, it's just—"

"No," she interrupted me again. "I'll make it easier for you. Just answer this question. Do you have feelings for him?"

My heart thumped as I heard the question I'd been avoiding in my mind for days. "Nina."

"Yes or no?"

I made a face. "Whose side are you on?"

"The side of truth. Yes or no?"

"Nina."

"Do you have feelings for him? Yes. Or. No."

"Yes," I answered through gritted teeth.

"So, now that you've gotten to the root of the problem, what's the solution? Because—and I'm going to be real with you—there's something between you and Ahmad. I've heard it in your voice the last few weeks, and I saw it firsthand at the concert. You denied it because you thought he was married, and now that you know he's not, you're not even going to talk to him about it?"

I felt a burning sensation coat my throat. Tears pricked my eyes as I held in my emotion. The silence between us grew.

She waited for my answer, and I choked on my truth.

I was mad that he wasn't honest and forthcoming with me. But the real reason I was in my feelings was because of what it meant. If he were interested in me, he wouldn't have continued with the charade of being married. If he were attracted to me, he would've made a move by now. So, I felt a way because of the feelings I developed for him. But more than that, I felt a way because of the feelings he obviously didn't have for me.

I wasn't ready to admit any of that out loud.

"But hey, what do I know?" Nina conceded after my extended silence. "Sometimes my real talk can be a little too real, so I'm going to give you a chance to digest it. But know that I love you and I want what's best for you. And you're not going to get what's best for you if you're not honest about what's for you. And, Liyah, let me tell you . . . living your life for others isn't what's for you. You don't have anything to prove to anyone about anything. Okay?"

"Yeah," I whispered, swiping the tears that fell from my lashes. "Love you, too, Nina."

"Think about what I said and call me tomorrow."

We said our goodbyes, and I buried my face in my pillow to stop the tears that wanted to flow freely. I kept hearing Nina's question over and over again. And it wasn't that I didn't have an answer to her question. I had one. I'd just been avoiding it for the last few days.

A man not being interested in me didn't make me feel insecure. It didn't make me feel bad about myself. It didn't hurt my ego. It didn't hurt my feelings.

But Ahmad not being interested in me hurt my heart.

And I wasn't ready to deal with that.

I tossed and turned all night, and when I finally got out of bed Saturday morning, I still couldn't do anything about the heaviness on my chest. Every time I thought about Ahmad, I felt such a volatile cocktail of emotions. I had so many questions. And all night thinking about Nina's questions forced me to one conclusion.

Maybe I do need to talk to him.

I didn't have his number. I didn't know where to find him except on Friday nights. But I knew his full name, and I knew he lived in my building. I grabbed my phone and hesitated for only a second. When I felt that pang in my chest, I called down to the leasing office.

"Hi. Is Angelique available?" I asked as soon as someone answered.

"Yes, one moment, please."

I nervously paced from one end of my apartment to the other.

"Hello. Angelique speaking," the property manager answered.

"Hi, Angelique. It's Aaliyah! How are you?"

"Aaliyah! How is the woman who saved my ass?"

I laughed. "I just fixed your computer. You are too funny."

"You saved my ass. What can I do for you? You don't have any maintenance issues, do you?"

"No, no, nothing like that." I stopped in the living room and stared at my coatrack. "I have something that belongs to Ahmad Williamson, and I don't know his apartment number."

With my fingers crossed, I waited to hear what she would say. I heard keys clicking and tapping.

"We usually don't give out that information," Angelique started. "Even though if you have something of his, it would be quicker for you to put his correct address on it and place it in the mailroom room." A few more clicks. "Oh, and it makes sense why they got it confused. You're 303, and he's 503." She paused. "So just address it to 503, and then it'll get worked out."

Biting my bottom lip, I stared at Ahmad's umbrella. "Okay, perfect. Thank you."

I showered, and pulled on a pair of black yoga pants and a matching black racer-back tank top. My hair was pushed up into a high puff, and I put in a pair of white-gold hoops. With no makeup, no plan, and no invitation, I marched to the elevator and took myself to the fifth floor. Armed with his umbrella and a need for answers, I knocked on Ahmad's apartment door.

It wasn't until after I heard the shuffling on the other side of the door that I had doubts about my actions.

I look like a stalker.

It's nine o'clock in the morning.

I should've called Nina and Jazz and run this plan by them.

What am I doing?

What the fuck am I doing?

You know what, no . . . I deserve answers. I demand answers!

I shouldn't be the one nervous. He should be the one nervous!

With a confused expression on his face, Ahmad opened the door. "Aaliyah?"

Shook, my mouth went dry.

Reality hit me: I really just showed up at this man's place.

Even in a pair of gray sweatpants and a disheveled white T-shirt, he looked good. It was hard to look into his eyes, so I found myself staring at his lips.

Realizing I was just staring, I quickly greeted him. "He-hey!" Holding up the umbrella, I awkwardly announced my decoy reason for being there. "There's a chance of rain, so I wanted to make sure I got this back to you."

With crumpled brows, he chuckled lightly. "Oh, really? The news just said it's supposed to be sunny all week, but thank you."

I opened my mouth to begin launching into the real reason I was there, but he spoke first.

Stepping back, he opened the door a little wider. "Come in. I actually have something for you."

It was my turn to be surprised. "Oh! Okay . . ." I dragged the word out.

I came to demand answers, and curiosity and the unexpected gift kind of took the wind out of my sails a bit. Rolling my shoulders back, I walked into his home as if I hadn't shown up unannounced.

"Don't mind the stuff in the living room. I wasn't expecting anyone, and I was reorganizing," he mentioned.

"Oh, this is nice," I commented as I looked around.

"Thank you," he said, closing and locking the door behind us. "How did you know which apartment was mine?"

I glanced over my shoulder. "A lady doesn't reveal her secrets."

"Well, it's a good thing I'm not speaking to a lady," he joked.

"Ha ha," I replied dryly. "The internet has way too much information out there."

"Facts," he agreed.

"Your layout is like mine," I told him, changing the subject.

His apartment looked almost identical to mine, but it had a lot less stuff. The living room was just a nice leather couch that took up the whole back wall, a glass coffee table with a few books and coasters, a bookshelf in the corner, an entertainment center, and a huge hundred-inch TV mounted onto the wall. There were no wedding pictures, no pictures of him with any woman, and no photo indication that he was in a relationship. There was no décor with any extra touches that made it look like a married couple lived there.

Not that I thought Asia was lying, but seeing Ahmad's bachelor pad confirmed his single status. Again, a mix of emotions bubbled up in me.

I didn't know how I was going to bring it up, but I knew I needed to do it right. If I wanted answers, I couldn't let my frustration lead the conversation.

I looked around, craning my neck. "That's a lot of albums," I pointed out as I noticed the mess on the floor.

"Yeah." He gestured to the couch. "You can have a seat. I need to go to the back and grab the thing."

He disappeared down the hall, and although I took a few steps toward the butterscotch leather sectional sofa, I stopped. The bookshelf in the corner didn't have books. Instead, it had photos, awards, degrees, and trophies. I gravitated to it.

Asia was right. They look just like their parents.

There was a childhood photo of the four of them that was adorable. I'd never met his parents, but there was no denying who they were in that picture. Ahmad and Asia looked to be elementary school aged in the photo, and Mr. and Mrs. Williamson looked almost identical to present day Ahmad and Asia. There was another family photo that looked like it was taken within the last year. There was a picture of Ahmad, Leon, and Darius all dressed up in tuxedos. And then, in the back corner, I saw a photo of a beautiful brown-skinned woman with a radiant smile.

"Oh!" Ahmad reacted as he returned. His eyes flickered toward the couch and then back to me. "Everything okay?"

"Yeah," I said, quickly turning around. I quirked an eyebrow as we made our way toward each other. "What's that?"

With a wide grin, he ceremoniously presented me a folded T-shirt. "It's for you."

I came here to call him out, possibly cuss him out—and he has a gift for me?

I got nervous all over again. "What?"

"Here." He shook the olive-green shirt until I took it from him.

Our hands brushed against each other's, and the sensation from his fingertips rippled through my entire body. I took a small step back, hoping he didn't notice his effect on me.

"Thank you," I murmured. When I held the shirt open, I realized it was an India Davis concert T-shirt. "Oh, wow—" I balked. "Is this signed?"

Grinning proudly, he nodded. "Yeah."

My mouth was agape. "How?"

"At the concert, you could buy shirts outright or you could pay to get them signed and then they'd ship it to you. So I ordered a couple to be signed. When we met, you said you loved India, so when they said they only had one in green left, I . . ." He shrugged. "I ordered it for you."

"Ahmad!" I clutched the shirt to my aching chest and looked everywhere but at him. "This is really cool, but I can't accept this."

"You can," he insisted.

I shook my head and tried to hand it back to him. "I can't," I whispered.

"Your birthday's in less than three weeks. Think of it as an early birthday gift."

When I looked back up at him, our eyes locked again, and I felt something.

"Aaliyah—"

"Do you have a wife?" I blurted out.

He froze momentarily. "What?"

The emotions he brought out of me shook something loose. Unable to rein it in, I kept going. "You were wearing a wedding band. Are you married?"

He brought his left hand up and rubbed his ring finger. "Oh! I, uh . . . No, I'm not. It's . . ." Shaking his head, he pinched the bridge of his nose. "I'm not."

"Okay, so then . . . I don't understand." I pointed to his hand again. "You were wearing a wedding band last night, and you said you were married. So, none of it is true?"

Panic crossed his face. "No, no." He gestured to the couch.

"Come sit and talk for a minute." He reached out for me, and I backed away.

"So, you lied to me?" I sputtered, trying to hold back the tears. "Everything I thought I knew about you was a lie?"

He shook his head. "No, I didn't lie—not to you. I'm sorry if I misled you, but I never told you I was married."

"You alluded to it! What was all that bullshit you said about online dating and meeting your person on TenderFish? Why did you make it a point to be my wingman? Was the whole thing bullshit?"

"It wasn't bullshit. It's just"—he ran his hand over his beard—"a long story. Can you just sit and talk to me?"

He stared at me with fierce intensity as I warily crossed my arms over my chest.

"Answer one question for me. Did you intentionally lie to me about your marital status? Yes or no," I replied dryly.

He exhaled. "I bartended during my last couple years in college," he started. "And long story short, I learned it's easier to be unavailable than it is to be single and not interested."

I just stared at him.

So that's why he was my wingman . . . It was easier to pretend to be married than to just tell me he wasn't interested in me. This is why he was so invested in helping me find someone.

I felt like I'd been kicked in the chest. The breath I sucked in hurt.

"So, I started wearing a wedding band, and it worked," he continued.

"Got it. Loud and clear." I bit the inside of my cheek to keep any tears from falling. "I'm going to go," I announced even though I didn't attempt to move my feet.

Ahmad took a step toward me. "Aaliyah, please sit down and talk to me."

I moved to the other side of the room. "I don't even know you."

He stopped in his tracks. "Aaliyah."

"What?"

"Don't do that."

"Don't do what?" I put my hands on my hips. "I don't know you—"

"You do know me. We're . . . friends." He looked like he had to search for the word before he let it out.

That rubbed me the wrong way.

"No, I *thought* we were friends, but friends don't lie to each other, so . . ." I lifted my shoulders and then headed out of the living room.

"I didn't lie to you," he said, continuing to follow me. "I didn't . . ."

I spun around. "You did lie," I stated before I realized how close he was to me. Tipping my head back, I stared into his eyes. "I've told you a lot about me. I've divulged personal stuff about me and my life. And you"—I poked him in his chest—"were pretending to be someone you're not."

His face scrunched up, and he took a step back. "I've told you a lot about me, too! What are you saying? I've talked to you, confided in you." His voice rose passionately. "And because of this one thing, you're going to act like you don't know me?"

"I don't know you!" My tone matched his. "That's what's sad, Ahmad! That's what's so messed up about this whole thing! You just—ugh!" Frustrated, I backed away from him. "It doesn't matter. I'm just glad I know the truth."

"And what do you think the truth is?"

My heart thudded in my chest, and I felt that sick, sinking feeling that had been plaguing me since I'd found out. "The whole story . . . your whole story. . . . who I thought you were . . . it was all a lie. You—you've been lying since day one."

His eyebrows flew up, and he looked taken aback. "Wow. Okay. Again, I'm sorry I misled you, but I would really like the chance to explain myself, because I didn't lie to you. I just don't like dealing with a lot of the bullshit that can come with being a bartender, and I've found that wearing a ring keeps unwanted attention away. It lets me let people down easy without having to do much of anything. And I didn't clarify my relationship status when we first met because I didn't know you."

His reasoning wasn't easier to digest the second time around.

My stomach was in knots. Blinking rapidly, I shook my head. “No, no, it’s okay, Ahmad. Really.”

“So, it’s not even—”

“No, I’m serious,” I interrupted, not wanting to hear more of his explanation. “It’s okay. Because the more I think about it, the more I realize this is on me. I was the one telling all my business and getting all this dating advice from a man I met in a bar. I was the one coming to you like you were someone I could trust. That’s one hundred percent on me. It’s like you said in our first conversation. You can’t trust some of these men out here. Especially a man you don’t know.”

“Aaliyah—”

I tried to hand him back the T-shirt, but he wouldn’t take it. Shaking my head, I turned around and opened his front door.

“My fiancée died,” he uttered.

15

I flinched.

His words felt like cold water thrown on my back. My hand tightened on the door handle as his words played in my head over and over again. I dropped my arms to my sides, and the door clicked softly as it closed. Taking a breath, I turned to face him.

Ahmad's face was serious, and his eyes were downcast.

I swallowed hard. "What?" I whispered.

He turned and headed toward his couch, and I followed. He took a seat on one end of the couch, and I was on the opposite end. We sat in silence for a minute. I stared at the cushion separating us while I gathered my thoughts. When I was ready, I looked up to find him already staring at me.

Pulling on every emotion within me, his eyes bored into mine.

My heart beat faster with each passing second.

"I, um . . . Sorry. It's been a long time since I've talked about this." He rubbed his hands together and then tried starting again. "Up until recently, I wore that ring every day for three years." He cleared his throat. "You want something to drink?"

Watching him chew his bottom lip, I felt his anxiety on the other side of the couch.

"No, thank you," I said quietly.

It was as if I were afraid that if I spoke too loudly, it would scare the truth from the room. It was obvious what he was trying to share with me was difficult. I didn't want to make it harder for him. I also had no intention of letting him off the hook. I needed to know what was going on.

"I met Kayla on TenderFish when I was twenty-six," he said after a slight hesitation. "She'd just turned thirty. We dated for two years, and then we got engaged. I gave her a ring, and she got me that black band to wear a week later. She said if everyone knew she was off the market, everyone needed to know I was off the market, too." He smiled at the memory. "Our relationship was pretty good, but . . ." He paused, scrubbing his face with his hands. "Our relationship was good, but after we got engaged, we hit some bumps. Our lives didn't really come together as cohesively as I would've liked, but overall, we were good. Uh . . . one night, we ended up getting into an argument over kids. She was ready, and I wasn't. She made plans with her girls to blow off some steam. I stayed home because it was a Thursday night, and I had a big presentation in the morning."

He fell silent, and his eyes dropped from mine. His chest rose and fell, and I watched each shaky breath he took. I wanted to wrap my arms around him. I wanted to hug him tight. I wanted to let him know that everything was going to be okay. I wanted to be there for him.

Instead, I sat there watching him, waiting for him to finish.

"She had too much to drink, and she called me at almost two o'clock in the morning to come get her. I was irritated. Nah, I was pissed. She knew I had that presentation. She knew I was still mad about how our conversation earlier in the night went. So I felt like she called to wake me up on purpose. But I still went to get her because I loved her, and I didn't want her driving."

He let out a big breath, and then his gaze met mine again. "I picked her up, and we immediately got into it. I called her selfish for going out and drinking and then expecting me to pick her up. She said I was selfish for not wanting a baby, knowing she was thirty-two and her biological clock was ticking. I told her I loved her, but she was on some bullshit, and I didn't have anything else to say. She started crying and yelling. I just ignored her because it was two o'clock in the morning and I didn't want to say some shit I didn't mean. We were at a red light, and I remember looking over at her and shaking my head. I knew ignoring her would only make her madder . . . and it did. So, then she screamed, 'Say something!' at the top of her lungs." He swallowed hard. "And that's the last thing I remember before a car slammed into the back of us, pushing us into the intersection and causing us to get T-boned."

I gasped, bringing my hands to my face.

"I woke up in a hospital. I had a broken leg, bruised ribs, a busted lip, and a concussion." Anguish pulled at his lips before he was able to continue. "They told me what happened. They said they'd arrested the drunk driver—who, oddly enough, didn't have a scratch on them. They were telling me everything except for where Kayla was. Finally, Kayla's mom and sister told me what happened to Kayla, and they said . . . they said she died on impact."

"I'm so sorry, Ahmad."

He shook his head. "For a long time, I blamed myself."

I searched his face. "You weren't the one drinking and driving. You did everything you were supposed to do. She was drinking and you were her designated driver. You got up in the middle of the night and were there for her. You came to a complete stop at the light. You didn't cause the accident."

"For a long time, I couldn't shake the fact that if we wouldn't have gotten into that argument, she wouldn't have gone out with her friends. But I worked that out in therapy. So now I don't blame myself for her dying—but I still can't get behind the wheel. I haven't driven in almost three years because of it." He exhaled. "That whole thing fucked me up."

"Losing someone unexpectedly can fuck you up in ways you never saw coming," I reflected sorrowfully. "I overstand."

He looked like he was waiting for me to continue, but when I didn't, he sighed. "I haven't been driving. I haven't been in a relationship. I haven't . . ."

"Healed?" I guessed quietly.

"I wouldn't necessarily say that. I just hadn't felt compelled to do either. So I wore the ring because Kayla gave it to me. And then as time went on, I wore the ring because it kept me from having to explain my situation. I didn't have to be rude. I didn't have to reject anyone. I could just deal with my shit and mind my business. Apparently, I was using it as a defense mechanism."

I nodded. "Yeah. I can see that. What did your therapist say about that?"

"Dr. Mary knows I'm at peace with that relationship, and she said that the ring would come off when I was ready. But she's been more focused on getting me back behind the wheel. And like I told her, a relationship is a choice. But driving . . ." He let out a low whistle. "You can do everything right, and some asshole who drank too much can knock your shit back."

I understood where he was coming from. I understood that his loss impacted him. I wanted to tell him that, but I didn't want to make the conversation about me. We were talking about him and what he had going on, so I wanted to give him the space to share.

My heart went out to him.

"When was the last time you got behind the wheel?" I wondered.

"Maybe six months after the accident. I had a panic attack, and Asia ended up picking me up. I told her what happened, and she had me linked up with a therapy appointment that next week." He let out a short laugh. "Before that, I wasn't the therapy type. But getting my cast off and thinking I was going to drive over to Mom and Dad's real quick put things into perspective. I had shit I needed to deal with."

"I'm so glad Asia had your back like that. Being in therapy can be a game changer. Your friends and family are good to talk to, but when you're dealing with grief, loss, PTSD, trauma, guilt, you needed Dr. Mary."

"Hell yeah, because I wasn't talking to anybody about what I had going on. And then I didn't even want to tell them I was in therapy. I didn't tell my boys. I didn't tell my parents. I didn't tell anyone until I was a year in with Dr. Mary."

"What made you tell them?"

"Asia let something slip to my parents, and then they asked me about it. And with Darius and Leon, Darius was going through something, and I suggested he go to therapy. After they got their jokes off, we talked about it, and he went."

"That's good," I told him. "Thank you for sharing with me. I could see that it wasn't easy for you, and you did it anyway."

"Because I couldn't let you walk out of here thinking I lied to you." His eyes darted around my face. "I wouldn't lie to you. And you do know me."

"I'm sorry," I apologized.

"I'm sorry, too."

I nodded, feeling petty.

He turned his body on the couch, resting his arm along the back of it. "Now I have a question for you."

"Anything."

"Did you look for my apartment to give me back my umbrella, or was there another reason?"

"I wanted to give you your umbrella since I forgot it on Friday. Andddddd because I wanted to ask you about your marital status," I admitted.

Chuckling, he shook his head. "Okay, because you showing up here first thing in the morning with an umbrella is wild shit."

"Valid. But in my defense, you inviting me in and having a gift for me is right up there with wild shit."

"Nahhhhh, don't try to turn this around on me. You could've just given me the umbrella on Friday. You looked for me. You hunted me down—"

My face screwed up. "Okay, 'hunted' is a little far."

"You out here pretending to be a meteorologist is a little far," he joked, pointing to the window, where the sun was shining bright. "There's not a cloud in the sky, yet you show up before ten o'clock on a Saturday with an umbrella."

I glared at him. "I should've let it rain on your head."

He laughed, pulling his phone out of his pocket. "I was going to head up the street to get something to eat. You want to come?"

"Oh, I'm not dressed for brunch," I told him.

He looked me up and down. "You look good to me."

I felt my cheeks flush.

"I'm changing my shirt, but I'm wearing this," he continued, getting off the couch. "I just threw this shirt on because I'd just gotten out the shower when you started banging on my door like the police."

I rolled my eyes. "I knocked like a normal person."

"You knocked like I was getting evicted."

"Whatever," I called after him as he left the room.

When I was alone, I pulled out my cell phone.

Aaliyah: I have an update.

My heart went from hurting from Ahmad to hurting for Ahmad. The thought of him choosing to lie about a wife in order to reject me made me mad, embarrassed, and hurt my feelings. But the knowledge of his own heartbreak, his own healing journey, and his not being ready for a relationship made me love him more.

Not love as in in love. Love as in friendship love.

I bristled uncomfortably as the L-word snuck into my psyche. Because I didn't mean that.

There were a lot of emotions that I needed to unpack, but hearing Ahmad out really helped. I felt better. And now that I knew where he was emotionally, romantically, and I didn't feel completely rejected, we could go back to our friendship.

Nina: Text me the update. Don't just announce the update!

I giggled quietly at Nina's reply. Just as I was about to text, I heard footsteps coming down the hall.

"Checking on your next date?" Ahmad asked as he walked in with a navy-blue-and-white shirt with navy-and-white shoes to match.

"You look good," I blurted out.

The words tumbled out of my mouth quicker than I realized, but it was the truth.

He made a face. "That was a dig at my wrinkled shirt, huh? You always got shit to say."

My eyes widened. "Me?! That's literally you! In the time that I've known you, not a day has gone by without you commenting on my outfits."

"I didn't say anything about you coming in here dressed like *The Omen*."

It took me a second, and then I burst out laughing. "Okay, Lil' Kim."

"Come on. Let's go. I'm hungry."

I stopped by my apartment to drop off my shirt, and then we were on our way.

We joked our way out of our building and up a couple of blocks to a little hole-in-the-wall restaurant called Miss Mama's.

"When did they start serving brunch?" I wondered as we walked in the door.

"They've been doing it all summer," Ahmad told me before he asked the hostess for a table for two.

As soon as we sat down, we reviewed the menu and then ordered.

"Your chicken last night must not have been like that if you're ordering chicken this morning, too," he pointed out.

"For somebody whose chicken is definitely not better than mine, you have a lot to say."

"Who taught you how to cook?"

"My grandma. Who taught you?"

"My mom."

I tilted my head to the side. "Will your mom be disappointed with you when she finds out my chicken kicked your chicken's ass?"

"Yoooo, what is wrong with you?" He snickered, shaking his head. "You know, you're pretty funny. You dress nice. You're smart. You're beautiful. I can't understand why you can't get a second date."

My jaw dropped. "That was a low blow."

He sat there with a self-satisfied grin.

I pointed at him. "You're proud of that, aren't you? You shouldn't be."

We spent the entire brunch going back and forth. And after the seriousness of our conversation in his apartment, the uninterrupted good time was welcome. It wasn't until the waitress brought the check that it became a little awkward.

"One check or two?" the waitress asked.

"One," Ahmad answered.

At the exact same time, I said, "Two."

The waitress looked between us and then just slowly placed the bill on the table and walked away.

"I got this," Ahmad offered, checking the total before placing his card down.

"You should let me pay," I argued. "I popped up at your place unannounced and delayed your brunch. Let me pay."

"No, I got you. I invited you to eat, so I'm paying."

"Ahmad."

"Aaliyah."

"You're so stubborn."

"Me?" he chuckled. "Nah, that's you."

The waitress came back to collect the payment, and then we were about to head out.

"Oh!" I stopped in my tracks.

Ahmad bumped into me from behind.

"Damn, Ahmad, you're trying to run me over?" I joked, pushing his shoulder.

Amused, he grabbed me and forced me onto the sidewalk. "Why would you stop walking?"

"I just got a text saying that my dress has arrived." I raised up on my toes and bounced. "It's right up the street. I need to go try it on real quick. Do . . . you want to come?" I pointed to the next corner. "It's right there."

"Oh, shit, that's close." He lifted his shoulder. "Yeah, I'll come."

We started walking farther from our apartment complex. There were more people out and about than when we'd walked to brunch. Ahmad had one hand on my shoulder and one on my hip, and he shifted me in front of him as we made our way down the sidewalk. It was a gentlemanly touch that was very on brand for him. But when the horde of people dissipated, he didn't remove his hand from my hip immediately.

My entire body was hyperaware of his touch.

When his hand dropped away, I could still feel the heat from it through my yoga pants.

Not that I was negating his situation or what he had going on, but the man was sexy as hell. Mentally, I knew we were just friends. Emotionally, I knew he wasn't trying to be with anyone. But when he touched me, my body wasn't trying to acknowledge any of that.

"This is it," I said as we approached the boutique.

With his hand on my hip again, he kind of pulled me into him as he reached around me and opened the door.

I sucked in a sharp intake of air. "Thank you."

Marching in and trying to put some distance between the two of us, I made my way to the counter.

"Hi, Charlotte," I greeted the owner of Charlotte's Webb as I got closer to her.

Her eyes lit up. "Aaliyah!" Her eyes darted behind me, and her smile grew. "How are you?"

"I'm great! Can't wait to see my birthday dress."

"I can't wait to see it on you." She shifted her gaze to Ahmad again, so I knew she was waiting for an introduction.

"Charlotte, this is Ahmad. Ahmad, this is Charlotte."

He reached his hand out toward her. "Hey, what's up, Charlotte? Nice to meet you."

They shook hands.

"It's nice to meet you, too." She looked between us with a twinkle in her eye. "You two look really good together."

"Thanks," he said.

I kept my mouth shut.

She turned around and grabbed the large garment bag that was on a rack behind her. "Okay, you two, follow me." As we got to the back, she pointed to a chair in front of a huge mirror. "You can sit right over here," she told Ahmad. "Aaliyah . . ." She went into the dressing room and hung the dress on a peg and then unzipped the bag. "If you need any help getting it on, I'll be right out here."

As soon as Charlotte walked out, I peeked at Ahmad. "It won't take me long, and then we can leave."

"Take your time," he said, relaxing in the chair. "I'm curious about what's in that big bag."

I smiled and closed the door.

After I shimmied on the dress, I took a step back and looked at myself in the small mirror in the room with me.

I love it.

It was the perfect birthday dress.

"You good?" Ahmad asked. "You've been quiet for a minute."

"I'm so, so, soooooooo good," I called out to him over the door. "So, what are your plans for the day? I should've asked earlier."

"I'm not doing anything except finishing organizing my albums and getting my living room back in order. Tonight, I'm linking up with Leon."

"Tell Leon I said what's up."

"I definitely won't do that."

"Why are you trying to stand in between what Leon and I have?"

He laughed.

I did one more spin before I opened the door to look at the dress in the big mirror.

The moment I walked out, all the amusement left him. He sat up straight, and his lips parted as he took me in. "Wow."

"Right?!" I squealed.

"You look . . ." He gawked unhurriedly as if he were committing me to memory. "What's this for?"

"My birthday!"

"That makes sense. You look absolutely beautiful."

Beaming, I turned and watched the way the dress moved in the mirror. When I caught his eye in the reflection and I saw the way he was looking at me, my breathing hitched.

"That was made for you!" Charlotte cheered, yanking my attention away from Ahmad.

"I love it," I gushed. "It's even better than I was expecting."

As Charlotte excitedly ran down information I needed to know, I snuck a glance at Ahmad, who was still staring at me. When he noticed me noticing him, he didn't look away. He held my gaze and forced me to be the one who looked away first.

That was a little harder to shake off than his touch.

When we left the store, Ahmad insisted on carrying my dress for me.

His phone started ringing in his pocket.

"I'll take the dress. You get your phone," I instructed.

"You just watch where you're going," he said, grabbing me and pulling me into him.

"You're so annoying," I complained, remaining tucked in his arm as the group of teens made their way past us.

When his phone started ringing again, I disengaged myself from him so he could answer it.

"Yo, what's up, Leon?" he answered.

I wiggled my eyebrows. "Tell him I said hey!"

Ahmad shook his head, ignoring me. Then he twisted his lips. "That was Aaliyah. She said hey." He paused. "No, she doesn't want your number. Take that shit somewhere else. I'm not giving her your number either." He started laughing. "We're on the way back from the store. That's it. Anyway, what's up?" He looked at his watch. "Yeah, I can be ready early. But honestly, man, I can just meet you over there. You don't—I know." He sighed. "Aight, I'll be ready. Give me an hour."

When he slipped his phone back into his pocket, I just stared at him.

"Soooooo . . ." I started. "You're just not going to pass along my messages."

"Stop playing," he laughed. "Are you looking forward to your thirtieth birthday?"

"I am. Don't think I'm going to let you get away with just changing the subject. We will be circling back."

He grinned. "I have no doubt. So, are you looking forward to the party?"

"I am. All the RSVPs have come in. The caterer has been paid. My dinner dress is here. Really, I'm just waiting on one thing."

"The boyfriend."

"I was going to say my party dress, but damn, Ahmad." I let out a little snicker. "Rude!"

"What? I thought that was a good guess!"

I shook my head. "You're so full of shit."

"How are things going on that front? You lined up your date for this week?"

"I actually have. We've been having good conversation on the app. We'll see how that translates in person."

"You have what? Three Fridays left?"

"Yeah, don't remind me. What did you do for your thirtieth?"

"I went to Jamaica."

"Did you have fun?"

A slow smile spread across his face. "Yes."

I elbowed him. "See, I knew you were for the streets."

He shook his head. "Nah, nothing like that."

I teased him the rest of the way back. When we got off the elevator on the third floor, he followed me to my place.

"Would you like to come in?" I asked.

"I would like that a lot. But Leon is about to be on his way, and I still gotta get my shit together."

I nodded. "I understand." I reached for my dress, and he held it out of my grasp.

"I didn't say I wasn't going to carry your dress in for you. I just meant I couldn't come in and stay."

"It's too late," I laughed, reaching up again. Grabbing at his arm, I tried to pull it down so I could get to the hanger. "I've rescinded the invitation."

"It's too late. No take-backs," he returned, amused. "I guess it's my dress now."

I started trying to tickle him under his arms, but it didn't work.

Chuckling at my feeble attempts, he used his free arm to wrap around me and keep me away from the arm holding the dress. It was about the third jump that I noticed his eyes dipped to my chest. My nipples were hard, straining against the spandex. My body was pressed against his, and although I was legitimately trying to get the dress, I was suddenly very aware of how close we were, how good he smelled, how strong his body felt, and how firm his grip was on me.

His face hovered over mine, and his eyes bored into me with such a fierce intensity that I didn't know what was coming next.

Breathing heavily, we stared at each other. There was so much longing, so much passion, and so much unchecked desire between us that I was certain he was about to kiss me.

My next-door neighbor loudly came out of his apartment with two garbage bags. We startled away from each other as if we'd just gotten caught doing something we shouldn't. I stared at my neighbor because I didn't—I *couldn't*—look Ahmad in his eyes.

My heart was racing. My door was against my back, and I was thankful for something solid to hold on to.

"Good afternoon," the neighbor greeted us with a curt nod.

Ahmad and I spoke in unison and then stared at each other until the neighbor disappeared through the door leading to the stairwell.

"I should, um . . . I should probably go get ready," Ahmad said, breaking the silence.

His breathing seemed to be just as irregular as mine. He held the dress out to me, and I was scared to grab it. I was scared to touch him. I couldn't even hide how my breasts were excited by the moment we'd just shared. I was fortunate he couldn't see other parts of me.

I forced myself to speak. "Yeah, you should," I agreed. Timidly, I reached out for the dress, and our fingers brushed. I sucked in a quick breath as we shocked each other. I brought the dress to my chest to cover myself up. "I hope you have a good time."

He took a step back. "Thank you. I hope you have a good night as well. I enjoyed you today."

As he was talking, my eyes dropped down to the prominent print I saw etched in his gray sweatpants. Three whole seconds ticked by before I forced my eyes back to his face.

"I enjoyed you, too," I said breathily.

Did he see that? I know he saw that. Oh. My. God.

"See you Friday?" he asked.

Lifting my hand in a wave, I confirmed, "See you Friday."

For my date.

I'll see you Friday for my date.

I had to repeat it a couple of times in my head to try to force the print outline from haunting my thoughts.

16

Between working on a big project for work, chatting up a bunch of men on TenderFish, and getting to know Lennox, I had a full week. When Friday rolled around, I realized that I hadn't been that excited about a first date in a while. I wasn't nervous, but meeting him felt different from when I met with the others.

Maybe because I've been thinking about Ahmad's dick, and now I'm going to have to face him for the first time since he watched me eye-fuck him.

I shook off the intrusive thought.

The thing with Lennox seemed like it could be something real. The fantasy with Ahmad was just that—a fantasy.

Ahmad and I are friends. Lennox is trying to be more than that.

Lennox was the kind of man who just sucked me in. Talking to him was so interesting and fun that a quick hello would turn into a three-hour conversation. The way he told stories was so engaging that he'd have me hanging on to his every word. He lived an interesting life and had a story about everything. In his thirty-six years, he'd gone to college, served in the military, started a business, and almost won the grand prize on a popular game show.

Wanting to make a good first impression, I wore a low-cut floral romper with a pair of pink slingbacks and the matching bag. The necklace I chose was a thin gold chain that dropped two strings between my breasts. It was a subtle attention-grabber. Gold pins adorned my picked-out 'fro, which added a little razzle-dazzle. I walked out of my apartment looking as good as I felt.

It wasn't until I was about to open the door to Onyx that I felt a few nerves.

Because of Lennox or Ahmad?

"Hey, Aaliyah!" Asia chirped as soon as I walked in. "Ahmad should be out in a few. He's finishing up inventory."

"Okay, cool. Thanks." I took a seat in my same spot at the bar. "How are you?"

"I'm fine. How are you?" She looked around and lowered her voice. "Did you talk to him?"

I nodded. "I had to."

She put her hands together. "Thank God. I was so scared I'd have to tell him that not only did I tell his business but I also scared you away." She shook her head. "I don't think he'd forgive me for that."

"He'd forgive you. Your brother loves you."

"My brother also loves—I said I'm coming!" Her outburst to security, who was waving her over to the other side of the bar, interrupted her sentence to me. She smiled at me. "Duty calls."

Her brother also loves what?

I didn't want to speculate, so I cast my gaze around the after-work crowd that had started to creep in. I spun around on the stool to see if I recognized anyone in there. Each week, the number of people seemed to grow. Although it wasn't crowded yet, there were about twenty-five people spread out over the space. Usually, I was the first one there, so it was a little noisier than normal. I was happy that people were finding out about it because I wanted it to succeed. I'd grown attached to the place.

"No!" I gasped as my turning caused my bag to knock my phone off the bar. Face down, it hit the floor hard.

I hopped off the stool, and as I bent to pick it up, I prayed that my screen wasn't cracked. Still standing and with my eyes closed tight, I took a deep breath.

Please. Please. Please.

Letting my fingers slide over the glass, I braced myself for the worst. Slowly, I turned it over in my hand and opened my eyes.

"Oh, thank God," I sighed with relief before spinning around.

Caught off guard, I inhaled sharply when I found Ahmad's eyes on me. My body tingled under his gaze and my heart thumped against my chest as soon as I realized what was happening.

"You're here early," he greeted me as he continued carrying a crate behind the bar.

"A little." Climbing back on my seat, I eyed his biceps as they bulged under the weight of what he had in his hands. "That looks heavy. You need some help?"

"Nah." He hoisted it onto the shelf against the mirror. "I can handle the weight."

It seemed my body took what he said differently from how my mind did. Even though his back was to me, I looked down in hopes he couldn't tell my cheeks flushed. I was so in my head, I missed part of what he was saying.

"Leon?"

"What about my boo?" I joked.

He was taking the bottles of top-shelf liquor out of the crate and placing it on the shelves. He stopped what he was doing and gave me a look. "Yoooo, you two are both on some bullshit."

"I'm just kidding," I laughed along with him. "I wouldn't date your friends."

He looked like he wanted to say something, but instead, he turned his back to me to continue restocking the alcohol. "So, who is the lucky guy tonight?"

"Wait." I waved off his question. "What were you about to say?"

"Nothing. I was just thinking about something Leon said."

I watched his body move as he reached over to grab an almost-empty bottle of tequila and replace it. "Are you going to share?"

"He just said that I might be scaring off your dates and that maybe I'm a little too protective."

"You don't scare off the dates," I assured him. "Let Leon know that the dates talk a good game online and just don't back it up in person."

"That's what I told him. From their attitude to their clothes, they just haven't been good enough for you. I haven't even had to flex on most of them."

"That's true," I agreed.

"Like that one dude with the suit," he continued. "He came here on a date looking like a shifty pastor."

"Ol' taking-money-from-the-collection-plate-looking ass," I joked.

"Ol' tabernacle-ministries-looking ass."

We both burst out laughing.

He rested his hands flat on the bar and leaned toward me. "You're so fucking childish," he told me, eyes dancing.

"Not the man in the child-size shirt calling me childish."

"That's rich coming from the woman in the onesie," he joked.

I looked down at my romper and bit my lip to keep from laughing. "You think you're so fucking funny, don't you?"

"You want to laugh so bad."

"No." My shoulders shook as I denied it. "I don't."

"Yeah, okay." He grabbed the empty crate and hoisted it on his shoulder. "I can tell when your eyes do that little twitchy thing that you're trying not to laugh."

"Stop studying my face and mind your business!" I called out to him as he walked away.

He disappeared around a corner, and I shifted my gaze to the mirror, noticing the smile plastered on my face. I looked as giddy as I felt. Shaking my head, I looked down at my phone. Punching my code to unlock it, I viewed the unread text message waiting for me.

Nina: I hope your date goes well! If you're feeling the effects of the drought, I won't judge you if you fuck him.

Aaliyah: I'm not going to fuck him! I don't know him!

Nina: Well, the last time you hit your sex-drought threshold, you fucked Matthew, so . . .

Aaliyah: Please don't remind me. I will never hit that point again. Besides, I handled my own business, and I think I'm cool.

Nina: Well, if the date doesn't work out and you do need a release, there's always the bartender . . .

"What's the deal? What's the real reason you want a boyfriend by your birthday?" Ahmad asked just as I was about to text back.

Quickly locking my phone to blacken the screen, I looked up at him. "Huh?"

"You heard me." He smirked. "What's the real reason you want a boyfriend for your birthday?"

Shifting my eyes away from him, I licked my lips. "Because I want to celebrate in a very specific way."

"Mm-hmm."

His snarky intonation caused me to grin.

He crossed his arms over his chest. "So, who is it that we're meeting for this date tonight?"

I opened my mouth to speak, but he interrupted me.

"Let me guess . . ." He cocked his head to the side. "A dude with an ultra-perm?"

"What? An ultra-perm?" I snorted at the way he said it.

"An ultra-perm is—"

"I've seen *Coming to America,*" I interrupted, rolling my eyes. "I know what an ultra-perm is. I want to know why that would be your guess."

"I haven't gotten a solid read on what your type is because they've all looked different. You had that short one—"

"He wasn't short," I argued, knowing exactly which one he was talking about.

"He was short to me."

I rolled my eyes as he continued.

"And then there was the light-skinned one and the dark-skinned one and the one with locs." He shrugged. "I haven't seen one with an ultra-perm, so I feel like it was a solid guess."

With a serious expression, I held his gaze. "It's wild to me how funny you think you are."

"You're still denying how funny you find me." His eyes diverted to the man flagging him down a few feet away. "Duty calls."

He made a few drinks as more people poured into the bar. I was starting to think we wouldn't be able to finish our conversation.

"Now where were we?" he asked, drying his hands on a small towel.

My stomach fluttered as the feeling I'd been trying to push down fought its way to the surface. "I think you were about to tell me about your type since you were going in so hard on my type."

Our eyes were locked in a silent battle of wills. It was clear he wasn't sure where I was going with my question. I could almost see him riffling through information, deciding what he was going to share with me.

I quirked an eyebrow, waiting for information about his love life. "Who in this bar would you hit on if you weren't working?"

He cast his gaze around the room. Bringing his hands to his stomach. I noticed his black wedding band securely on his ring finger.

"That's easy—"

"Ahmad!" Asia called out.

When he looked away from me, I followed his stare and realized there were at least five people waiting for service.

He quickly jumped into action while I watched him, reflecting on what his answer could be. I looked around, trying to get a better understanding of his type. Even if he wasn't dating and he was still wearing his ring, I was curious.

Ever since he'd walked me home and we had that moment, I no longer felt like it was all in my head. He felt it, too.

That dick print proved he felt something.

But my curiosity was poking and prodding for more.

"Can I ask you something?" Ahmad wondered upon his return. "And be honest."

"I'm always honest," I replied with an indignant tone.

"What's really going on with this boyfriend-by-your-birthday thing? And I want to know the real reason. Because I know it's about more than proving something to your family."

I'd forgotten I'd told him that.

I cleared my throat. "Well, it is that. Mostly."

He shook his head, keeping his eyes trained on me. "That sounds like that's what *they* want—not what *you* want. Because if you just wanted a boyfriend for the day, you would've just picked any of these clowns from the app and brought them to the party.

But I think you're looking for something specific. So, tell me . . ." He took a step closer, bracing his hands against the bar. "What do *you* want?"

My pulse quickened. "I want the real thing. I want love."

He held my gaze for a beat too long. "Are you ready for it?"

"I am," I whispered. "I wouldn't be subjecting myself to these dates if I wasn't."

Clearing his throat, he took a step back and grabbed a rag to wipe his hands. "Who are you meeting?"

"His name is Lennox," I answered, shaking off the fluttery feeling that accidentally swept through me. "We've been talking since last week, and I'm actually looking forward to this one. I listened to the playlist, and I'm feeling pretty good about it."

His lips turned down as he nodded. "Okay, okay."

"And speaking of dates . . ." I leaned forward and rested my chin on my fist. "R&B concerts are great for date nights."

He nodded. "Yeah. But not for a first date, because you can't really talk to each other during a concert."

"True." I paused. "So, who was the woman with you at the concert?"

He gave me a weird look. "What?"

"I'm just curious. You have a front-row seat to my business, so the one time I see you out and about on a date, I feel like I'm entitled to know the details." I rubbed my hands together. "Let's hear it."

His lips spread into a slow smile. "And why are you so curious?"

"Because you're in my business, and it's time for me to be in yours."

Smirking, he stroked his bearded chin. "Interesting . . ."

I pursed my lips. "Never mind."

He looked deep into my eyes. "What do you want to know?"

"Everything you want to tell me."

" Okay for one, it wasn't a date."

"Well, you two looked like maybe . . ."

He shook his head. "Nah. That was Kayla's sister. We were always cool, and she gets tickets through her job. On the rare occasion her wife doesn't want to go out, she'll hit me up to see if I want in. She knows how I feel about India Davis so we went."

"Oh! That's nice you're still close to—"

A loud bang of barstools tipping over interrupted my sentence, and we both immediately darted our eyes toward the noise.

"Excuse me!" A woman flanked by two friends clamored against the bar. "We need shots!"

"Shots! Shots! Shots, shots, shots, shots!" the group chanted as Ahmad turned to serve them.

The ladies were flirtatious as he took their money. They didn't just catcall him; they were loudly objectifying him. When one of them asked for his number, he held up his hand, and they booed.

I giggled behind my hand as I picked up my vibrating phone.

My belly flipped with excitement as I read Lennox's text message letting me know he was at Onyx.

Taking a deep breath, I turned just as he walked in. With his dark skin and bright white smile, he caught the attention of a couple of women as he entered the bar. But once he locked eyes with me, he made a beeline in my direction.

"It's nice to finally meet you," he breathed, a starstruck look in his eyes.

I felt something.

"How can I help you?" Ahmad asked, breaking up the moment we were sharing.

Slipping onto the barstool next to me, Lennox flashed a smile. "Whatever the lady wants, the lady gets." He looked at me. "What would you like?"

"Malibu sunrise," I ordered.

"I'll try that, too," Lennox chimed in.

"It's sweet," I warned him.

"If you like it, I'm willing to try it. I trust your judgment," he assured me.

Ahmad tapped the bar. "I'll get those drinks for you."

Distractedly, we said *thank you* in unison.

For the next three hours, I hung on to every word Lennox said.

When we called it a night, I felt more positive about this date than I had about any other date all summer.

"Let me take you to your car," Lennox offered as we stepped outside of the bar.

A group of people were making their way down the sidewalk, so he shifted us to the side. Taking my hand, he moved me out of the way. Even though we were no longer moving, he didn't let go of my hand. The heat from it traveled up my arm and flushed my cheeks.

Over the time we'd spent at the bar, we'd brushed against each other and touched here and there. But his fingers intertwining with mine was the first deliberate touch we'd shared. And the way he did it was so smooth, it made me smile.

"No, it's okay. I didn't park far." I tilted my head to the side as I looked up at him. "But I appreciate the offer. Thank you."

"If you won't let me be a gentleman and ensure you made it safely home, will you at least promise me that you'll allow me to do it next time?"

"Next time?"

"I'd like to see you again, if that's all right with you."

My lips curled upward. "I'd like that."

"Good. Because like I said before, what the lady wants, the lady gets." He took my hand and lifted it to his lips. "Anything."

From the way his eyes pierced me, I knew he wanted to kiss me. And the way my body swayed forward made it clear I wanted him to kiss me. So, I wet my lips and waited.

The orchestra of city sounds consisting of people, vehicles, and music came to a halt when he tipped my chin. I let my eyes flutter closed, and I waited two long seconds until his full lips covered mine. Lennox kissed me gently at first. It was almost teasing as he wrapped his arms around my waist and deepened it. Kissing him back, I felt desire coil in my belly.

I needed to be kissed.

I needed to feel the warmth of hands on my body.

I needed to feel the urgency and desire in lips against mine.

But when his tongue slipped into my mouth, Ahmad's face flashed into my mind.

What?!

Startled, I pulled out of the kiss. I tried to blink away the image as I stared up at the eligible bachelor in front of me.

"I look forward to seeing you again, Aaliyah," Lennox whispered, stroking my cheek. "Text me and let me know you made it home."

"I will," I murmured.

He leaned down and let his lips lightly brush mine. "Good night."

"Good night," I breathed.

I was standing in front of a good-looking man who had the most potential to be elevated to boyfriend status of anyone that I'd gone out with all summer. He was single, educated, and entertaining. We hit it off, had lots of chemistry, and our conversations lasted for hours. He was on his way to making it to the elusive second date with me.

So why am I thinking about Ahmad?

17

Visions of Ahmad when I'd masturbated was one thing. I hadn't had sex in a while, and he was the last man I'd seen. It was an honest subconscious mistake. But thinking about Ahmad while kissing Lennox unsettled me. I was actively kissing a man, so there was no logical reason for me to be thinking of Ahmad when Lennox was *right there*. But after a good night's sleep, I came to the conclusion that because Ahmad was the only man I'd connected with and had great conversation with over the summer, the lines blurred. It meant nothing. And to prove it meant nothing, I made my time with Lennox more intentional.

And it worked.

Even though I knew we were in the getting-to-know-you stage, I felt like I'd known Lennox for years. There was so much about his life that he'd shared with me. Between texts and video chats, we were on the phone constantly. The more I learned about him, the more I wanted to know. I was so interested in him that I stopped engaging with other men from the app. I still set up a date for the last Friday before my birthday weekend, but I didn't talk to him much. That was my in-case-of-emergency-backup-last-ditch-effort meetup. My birthday was eight days away, and I was almost certain that I had found what I was looking for.

"And for our second time getting together and our first official date, this is the look I'm going for . . ." I announced excitedly as I turned my phone's camera to the mirror.

"Yes!" Nina exclaimed. "That's definitely the one."

The forest-green silk dress with the thin spaghetti straps had a slit exposing my thigh. The ruching in the middle accentuated my waist, and the shade looked so good against my mocha-colored skin. The strappy black shoes with the cute black clutch completed the look.

I propped the phone up and then backed up. "Do you think it's too much?" I wondered, striking a pose.

"For where he's taking you? Absolutely not."

Lennox was taking me to one of the trendiest spots in the city. It was hard to get a reservation, but somehow, he managed to secure us a table at Cloverleaf. With live music, cool vibes, and a celebrity chef, it was the premier place to be. Although it was expensive, I heard it was worth it. I'd never been there before, so my excitement was at an all-time high.

"You're ready early, aren't you?" she wondered. "I thought you were meeting him at eight thirty."

"I am. But I'm heading over to Onyx first."

Nina didn't say anything, but the smirk on her face spoke volumes.

"What?" I pressed.

"You're going to see Ahmad, the bartender you claim is just a friend, before you go on a date with Lennox, the man you claim to really like? Interesting."

"How is that interesting? Just like I called you before my date, I'm doing the same thing with Ahmad."

"Oh yeah, it's the exact same," she said sarcastically.

"It is! I'm just going to update him since he's been an integral part of my dating process."

"You could update him when you get back from your date . . . unless you don't plan on coming back home tonight."

I laughed. "I plan on coming back home because it's the first time we'll be on a real date. Last Friday, we met and had a great time, but this is the first official date, and I don't want to send the wrong message."

"And what message is that?"

"That I'm just looking for sex."

"But you two talk all the time, why would he think that? You two have been getting to know each other, right?"

"Yeah . . . I guess I'm just not ready to take it there yet."

I couldn't put my finger on why I didn't feel like I was ready to have sex with him. But I knew it wasn't time.

"What are you doing tonight?" I questioned, changing the subject.

"I'm pulling up to my parents' house right now," Nina answered. "I'm not going to be able to do dinner with them on Sunday, so I told them I'd make it tonight."

"That sounds nice!"

"Yeah, it will be. Dad put steaks on the grill. But let me tell you . . ."

She told me about her plans for the rest of the weekend and my jaw was on the floor. Nina was the epitome of fun; there was no doubt about it.

We concluded our conversation about fifteen minutes later, and five minutes after that, I was headed out the door. I still had about ninety minutes before my date with Lennox. And even though Nina's words swirled around in my head, I still felt compelled to go to Onyx. It had become my Friday-night routine.

Nothing more. Nothing less.

I pushed the door open to enter Onyx, and my eyes widened at the crowd that had already gathered. It was barely seven o'clock, and the place was packed. A man I didn't recognize greeted me when I approached the bar.

"Hi!" I flashed him a smile as I gestured around. "Something special going on tonight?"

"I'm pretty sure almost everyone here"—he pointed to the far corner—"works at that bank a couple of blocks up. They're having a happy hour meetup to celebrate something. What can I get you?"

"Oh, nothing, um . . ." I looked around. "Actually, is Ahmad here?"

"Nah." He looked down the bar at a man waving. "If you decide to order something, wave me down."

He left to do his job, and I was left confused.

I almost pulled out my phone to double-check that it was Friday. I looked around and finally caught a glimpse of Afro puffs moving through the crowd.

"Asia!" I called out as she grew closer. "Everything okay?"

"No. We're swamped, some of those bankers are assholes, and

I can't get ahold of my parents," she answered as she breezed by me and made her way behind the bar. "Sorry." She exhaled loudly, concern still etched across her face. "I didn't mean to dump all that on you. Hot date tonight?" She glanced at my outfit. "I love your dress."

"Thanks. I appreciate it! But I'm sorry you're going through it tonight." I looked around. "It's crazy how busy it is. I hope either it slows down just a little or you get some more help so you're not running around."

"From your lips to God's ears. Ahmad told me to look out for you." She gestured around as she forced a smile. "It may be a little harder tonight because of the crowd, but I'm here. What can I get you?"

"Nothing. Thanks, though. I was just looking for Ahmad to give him an update."

"He's not here." A woman waving money at her caught her attention. "He's at General," she added distractedly.

"General?" I repeated. My stomach plummeted as I connected the dots of what she'd said. "The hospital? Why? What happened?"

"He went to the ER. Car accident."

Everything stopped as her words echoed in my ears. "Is—is he okay?"

"I don't know. I mean, yes. I just got off the phone with him and he said he was. But"—she shook her head, blinking tears away—"he's fine." She moved down the bar to get to the woman. I followed her. "I can't get in touch with Mom and Dad to go check on him, so I told him to call me when he leaves." She shifted her gaze to the woman. "Sorry for the wait. How can I help you?"

I had so many questions.

I wanted to ask which hospital—General East or General West.

I wanted to ask for his phone number.

I wanted to ask if it involved another car.

The questions kept infiltrating my brain, but Asia was busy.

He's okay, I assured myself. *He's okay. She said he said he was okay.*

But I couldn't stop thinking about how she started to say something and then stopped.

But what, Asia?

I stared at the woman, who wasn't as bubbly as she usually was. Her normal chipper demeanor was clouded with concern, and maybe no one else would notice, but I'd spent enough time at Onyx to know her smile was off.

My mind was racing as I waited a couple of minutes for her to give me more information. But as soon as she finished one drink, someone else was ordering another. I had a date, so I couldn't wait for her much longer, and the way people were flocking to the bar, it was clear she wasn't going to have time to talk for a while. Wringing my hands, I shifted my weight from one foot to the other, unsure of what to do.

Do I wait around, or do I check back after my date?

Operating on autopilot, I ran out of the bar and crossed the street to my building's parking garage. I had a date with a man I was really enjoying getting to know, and we were going to a place I'd never been to before. Even still, I knew I'd be worried about Ahmad the whole time.

"I should've left my number with Asia," I muttered under my breath as I started my car.

Pulling out of the deck, I had every intention of heading to Cloverleaf. It didn't really register where I was going until I pulled up in front of the closest hospital.

Picking up my phone, I called Lennox. I sped into the parking deck and searched for the first open parking spot. The phone ringing only added to my anxiety. As soon as he answered, the words spilled out of me.

"A good friend of mine is in the hospital, and I'm so sorry to do this, but I'm not going to make it tonight," I blurted out instead of hello.

"What?"

"I'm sorry, Lennox. I just got to the hospital. I really do hate to do this."

"Aw, man . . ." He let out a loud breath. "It sucks, but I understand. Take care of your friend."

"Thank you. I'll give you a call later."

"Aight."

He disconnected the call without saying goodbye. It was the first time he'd done that, and it stung a bit. But I couldn't hold on to the feeling for long. The worry I felt in my core superseded anything else. Shoving the phone into my bag, I hopped out of the car and ran through the sliding emergency room door.

"Ma'am." The security guard stopped me. "You need some help?"

I guess I looked as frantic as I felt.

"I-I'm looking for a friend of mine," I stammered, casting my gaze around the waiting room. "He . . ." My voice broke and trailed off as I tried to get my words together.

"Okay." He pulled his pants up by the belt. "We'll do what we can to help. Just take your time. These floors can be slippery so"—he gestured to my feet—"just slow down."

Tears stung my eyes, and I nodded.

"Who are you looking for?" he asked as I turned away from him to scan the lobby. "What's the name? If they're here, the people at intake will be able to help you."

Loudly tapping against the desk, he drew my attention back to him.

"What does he look like?" he asked.

I blinked rapidly. "He's tall, muscular, sponge curls—"

"Was he wearing jeans and a white polo shirt?"

"I'm not sure."

He looked just above my hair. "Is that your guy?"

I whipped my head around, and the moment I laid eyes on him, I felt relief. He was walking away from the registration desk with his head down, staring at paperwork. Barely holding on to his jacket as he studied the papers in his hands. He didn't look up until I was a few feet in front of him. When I saw the huge bloody bandage high on his right arm, I stopped in my tracks.

"Aaliyah?" Ahmad's tone matched the shock on his face. "What are you doing here?"

"Are you okay?" I asked, taking a tentative step toward him. "Asia said you were at the hospital, and I just . . . Are you okay?"

"Just a little banged up, but I'm fine." His eyes swept down my body. "What are you doing here?"

"I . . ." My mouth went dry. I didn't have an answer that made sense. "I don't know," I answered honestly. "I just heard you were in the hospital and just . . ."

Our eyes locked, and he seemed to be trying to pull the rest of the sentence out of me. But I couldn't find the words. I couldn't find *any* words.

"Just what?" His voice was soft and his gaze questioning. "Why are you here?"

"You've been there for me all summer and"—I shifted from one foot to the other—"I just felt compelled to be here for you, too."

He lifted his hand to touch the bandage, and I noticed the black band on his finger.

"You've been such a good friend to me, so I wanted to show up and be the same to you," I explained in a rush.

"You didn't have to show up here to prove your friendship, Aaliyah," he replied quietly. "You're good." He reached out and let his fingers slide down my arm. "You're—"

Taking in a sharp breath, I took a step back.

His touch ignited my body, and electricity coursed through me.

"I-I'm-I'm sorry," I stammered. "I shouldn't have come. I should go."

"No, don't . . . don't be sorry."

"Ahmad Williamson?" a nurse called out from behind a set of double doors.

Breaking eye contact, he shifted his attention away from me, and I felt like I could breathe again.

"Go, go," I told him. "Take care of yourself. I shouldn't—I should go."

"Come back with me."

My eyebrows flew up. "What?"

"Come on."

"You want me to come? Why?" I whispered, unsure of what to do.

He twisted his lips and pointed to his arm. "Blood makes me squeamish, remember?"

Handing me his jacket, he started moving toward the waiting nurse. Without another word, I fell into step with him as we headed to the back.

Gripping the lightweight jacket, I quietly followed them to a small room with a curtain for a door. He sat on the bed in the middle of the room, and I immediately tucked myself into the farthest corner. As his vitals were taken, I tried to make myself as invisible as possible as he answered all her questions. I tried to make it seem like I wasn't listening, but I was.

She was finishing the last question when the doctor walked in.

After a quick introduction and some pleasantries, Dr. Myers eyed the injury on his arm. "So, tell me a little about what happened, Mr. Williamson."

"It was a car accident. I wasn't driving. I was in the back of a rideshare. Someone hit us, less than a mile from here, and I got cut with a piece of metal. The driver"—he shook his head—"man, he looked pretty bad. I just had this little opening on my arm, and once I got bandaged up, I didn't think it was that serious." He gestured to his arm. "But after the paramedics left, I was waiting for my sister to come and get me and I realized my arm might've been worse than we thought. So I told her to just head to work because I was heading here."

"How did you get here?" the doctor wondered.

"I walked."

I put my hand to my mouth and sadness tugged at me. The thought of him walking down the street, basically bleeding out, because he didn't drive was heartbreaking to me.

"I can't believe you walked," I said quietly.

"It wasn't that far from here," he explained. "I didn't want to get blood all over someone's car and it was only a few blocks."

"Okay, let's see what's going on. We want to make sure it doesn't get infected." The doctor peeled back the bandage on Ahmad's right arm, and blood gushed. "Oh! Okay!" He added gauze and quickly reattached the bandage. The nurse cleaned the blood that dribbled toward his elbow. "You are certainly going to need sutures. I need to get a couple of things to get started. Change into this gown for me, and we'll get you patched up. Then we'll get some blood and run some labs to make sure you're not infected. We'll also get you a tetanus booster shot. I'll be back."

As soon as they left, Ahmad turned to look at me. "Wow."

"Worried about the blood work?" I guessed.

He made a face. "I can show you the paperwork from my physical a couple weeks ago. I have a clean bill of health."

"I meant because of the fact that some random dirty metal pierced your skin."

"Ohhh!" He let out a light chuckle. "I'm trippin'."

I cocked my head to the side. "What did you think I was talking about?"

I knew full well what he was talking about, but I wanted him to say it.

"I might have a concussion," he stated, changing the subject abruptly. "What time is your date?"

"What makes you think I have a date?"

"That dress."

I posed. "What? This old thing?"

He eyed me from head to toe, setting my body on fire. "You look good."

My nipples hardened under the attention. "Thank you."

His gaze lingered, stirring desire within me and quickening my heart rate. I noticed him noticing my nipples pressing against the material and pointing at him. I noticed him taking in the sneak peek of my thick thigh, exposed by the high slit of the dress. But most notably, I noticed the unmasked want flit across his face as he took me in. Unable to take my eyes off him, I noticed a lot. And it only occurred to me after the fact that he could probably see the same longing on my face.

"I mean it. You look good." He watched me fidget under the intensity of his stare. "Really good."

I crossed my arms over my chest and pulled his jacket closer to me. His cologne hit my nostrils, and I inhaled deeply. A chill ran through me, and I shuddered. He licked his lips. "If you're cold, you can wear the jacket." He shook his head. "I'm sorry I didn't think to offer sooner. I mean, I don't know how it'll go with your . . . dress." He looked me up and down again. "But it'll keep you warm at least."

Needing an opportunity to breathe, I ripped my eyes away from him and I held the black jacket out in front of me. "Thanks."

I pulled it to see if it had a good stretch to it. Realizing it would fit, I slipped it on. I knew it wouldn't look good with the dress, but I was a little chilly in that cold, sterile hospital.

Looking up at him, I tried to make a joke of our moment and struck a pose. "How do I look? Am I making it work?"

"You look good. But if I'm honest, it's hard for you not to look good."

I gave him a suspicious look. "You know . . . that might be the first real compliment you've ever given me."

"I was just in a car accident and I'm probably not thinking clearly, so . . ."

Amused, I let out an exasperated sound. "Or maybe it just knocked some sense into you."

He let out a short chuckle before wincing, touching the bandage. "Too soon."

My hands flew to my chest. "Be careful."

"It's okay."

"But are *you* okay?" Taking a cautious step forward, I assessed him. "You didn't answer me when I asked before."

"Yeah, it probably looks worse than it is. I just need stitches, and it'll be fine."

"That's not what I meant."

He held my gaze, but he didn't speak.

"Are *you* okay?" I asked again. Getting a little closer, I reached out and touched his hand.

His brown eyes felt like they were burning into mine. "I'm fine," he said with just enough uncertainty to let me know he wasn't.

"Okay," I whispered, giving him a reassuring pat. "But if you weren't, I would understand."

He didn't take his eyes off me.

The silence between us wasn't uncomfortable, but it was tense. I knew he wasn't angry, but I couldn't place the emotion that was emanating from him. Whatever it was, it drew me in. My feet didn't move, but my soul did. I was in the moment with him, and there was something so open and vulnerable about it. The intensity of his stare was overwhelming, and as hard as I tried to look away, I couldn't.

I felt something. I felt it so intensely that it scared me.

My lips parted, and a huff of air escaped.

Clearing his throat, he reached his right arm up and grabbed the back of his shirt at the neck and pulled it over his head. When the fabric cleared his face, I saw him grimacing.

"You want some help?" I asked, stepping forward.

"Nah, I think I got it," he responded, pulling the shirt over his shoulder.

Ignoring him, I carefully helped him remove it from his injured arm without disrupting the bandage. It wasn't until I had the shirt clutched to me that I noticed how very shirtless he was.

It began innocently enough as I studied his injury on his very defined bicep. Slowly, my head moved, and I zeroed in on his muscular chest and ripped abs. His smooth, toffee-colored skin looked like candy under the fluorescent hospital lighting. It was the first time I saw his tattoos up close. My eyes followed the way they snaked down his arm from his shoulder. When my tongue ran across my lips, I realized I was no longer checking on him. I was checking him out.

And I was *very* attracted to what was in front of me.

Shit!

18

Ripping my eyes away from his body, I returned them to his face.

The way he stared at me felt like he knew what I was thinking, and heat started to creep up my neck.

He licked his lips, and then slowly, he eased into the hospital gown. "You had a date?"

Clearing my throat, I nodded. "I did."

Gesturing to the seat across from the exam table, he waited for me to sit. "And with only a week until your birthday, you're missing it?"

"I didn't really have a choice."

"Ah. I see. You were stood up again," he guessed with a slight smile tugging at the corners of his mouth.

"No." I rolled my eyes. "Such an asshole."

"There's no shame in getting stood up for *another* first date." He paused, squinting at me. "Well . . . maybe a little shame."

"You're enjoying the idea of me getting stood up a little too much. But for your information, I was coming to the bar to tell you that I was going on a second date."

There was a flicker in his eyes, and he shifted slightly. "Oh really? With dude from last week?"

I nodded. "Yeah. We hit it off."

He made a face. "The talkative dude from last week?"

"Yes."

"The one who kept talking?"

I sucked my teeth. "Ahmad, please."

"Are you happy?" he wondered.

I hesitated before answering, "Yeah."

His Adam's apple moved as he swallowed whatever he was going to say. With a slow nod, he asked, "Where was he taking you tonight?"

"Cloverleaf."

He let out a low whistle. "Oh, wow."

"Yeah."

He cocked his head to the side. "So . . . you and the talker?"

"Yes!" I snickered. "And why do you keep calling him that?"

"Because all he did was talk. I didn't see you get a word in. Every time I walked by, he was talking. He didn't take a break. I think I heard him talking and drinking at the same time."

I held in my laugh. "Can you stop?"

"You're not seeing it because you're stubborn and you don't want to see it. But that man talked from the moment he sat down. He asked you what you wanted to drink and then he didn't let you say anything else. I didn't see you get a word in."

"It wasn't like that," I argued, rolling my eyes. "Don't be a hater."

"I'm not hating. I'm just saying."

"Well, say less."

"Maybe if he said less . . ."

"I would beat you up if you weren't already injured."

He ran his hand over his beard. "If you two hit it off and it was all good, why'd you skip out on it?"

"Because I couldn't stop thinking about you—if you were okay," I clarified quickly. "I couldn't stop thinking about if you were okay. I went to Onyx to tell you about my date, and Asia said you were in a car accident." I fiddled with the hem of my dress as I crossed my legs. "You said the last one fucked you up, and I didn't want you to go through what you went through before."

Because of the significance of the first accident, I knew the second accident could be a trigger for him and I wanted to be there for him. There was no rational reason why I didn't stop to consider he had people to lean on in his time of need. It didn't make sense for me to show up to try to support him. It wasn't reasonable for me to track him down when our friendship was weeks old.

The longer he didn't say anything, the longer I had to sit with it. Looking away from him, I squeezed my eyes shut and thought about how I rushed to the hospital to be at his side. And one week prior, I found his address and popped up at his door.

This is unhinged behavior.

It took a few seconds before he responded.

"I appreciate that," he said softly. "For real, Aaliyah."

My lashes fluttered open. "You don't think it sounds crazy?"

"Oh, no, it's definitely crazy. But"—he smirked—"it's good crazy."

The curtain swooshed as Dr. Myers and a different nurse entered the room. They examined and cleaned his wound, remarking that it was deep but not critical. They gave him some pain medication, and after cleaning the wound, they proceeded to stitch him up. Someone else came in to draw blood and administer a booster shot as the doctor typed information into the computer. The whole thing only took thirty minutes.

When Dr. Myers finished, he went over some wound care instructions. "Tomorrow, you can start washing around the wound twice a day. But make sure you keep the area dry, clean, and away from anything that'll irritate it. Apply a thin layer of antibiotic cream. You don't want anything rubbing against it. Loose-fitting sleeves would be best for the next few days. These are absorbable stitches, and they'll dissolve in seven to ten days. If you see any signs of infection, come back immediately. We'll start you on some oral antibiotics. If there's anything of concern regarding your blood work results, we'll be in touch." He gave the bandaged wound a once-over. "But everything looks as good as can be. If you feel any discomfort, over-the-counter pain medication is fine. But you don't need anything but rest for the next few hours. What we gave you should get you through the night."

Ahmad nodded as he pulled his shirt back on. "Okay, thank you."

The doctor turned to me. "You are his ride home, right?"

"Yes," I answered automatically.

Dr. Myers nodded before turning back to Ahmad. "You may experience a little manageable pain, so"—the doctor gestured to me—"let your wife get you home and you take it easy tonight."

"Oh, uhhh . . ." He looked over at me and then down at his hand. "Right."

I immediately felt uncomfortable.

"We'll get you discharged and on your way. Give us a few minutes." The doctor left the room with the nurse in tow.

Ahmad was still looking at his hand.

"I'm sorry," I apologized softly, jumping to my feet. "I feel like I overstepped. I shouldn't be here. I'm going to go get the car and meet you out front."

"Aaliyah," he called after me.

I didn't look back.

I left the room just as the nurse asked, "Everything okay?"

No. Everything is not okay.

I couldn't put my finger on what I was feeling as I made my way to my car. But a series of emotions rippled through me, and all of them combined felt incredibly heavy. Like a weight was pressing down on me, and I couldn't do anything about it. I didn't know if it was fear, anxiety, tension, relief, desire, or regret. But in my myriad of feelings, guilt and disappointment seemed to level me.

I was disappointed in myself. I didn't once think about how triggering it would be for people to assume I was his wife. I didn't consider how he might have felt with my showing up at the hospital. I didn't correct the doctor when I was presumed to be his wife. But most of all, I felt guilty for how my mind, body, and soul continued to react to him. No matter how hard I tried, I was having difficulty shutting out my intrusive thoughts.

I had a tiny, insignificant crush on Ahmad because he was a genuinely good man. It was harmless because he wasn't ready to date. He still wore the ring his deceased ex-fiancée gave to him.

And yes, Ahmad and I had fleeting moments and that one almost-kiss. But he was not interested in me in any way. He actively helped me pursue other men. He gave me advice and encouraged me to not give up dating. He never made a slick comment to me or did anything that would make me think he didn't see me as just a friend.

And that's why the crush felt safe, insignificant, and a nonissue.

So, the fact that I felt something more disrupted my soul.

Thinking that something happened to him ripped something wide open. Because I had every excuse in the world to deny my feelings. I ignored my attraction to him. I disregarded the feelings he brought out in me. I wrote off the way we connected and shared with each other. I overlooked the way he cared for me. And I completely omitted the fact that I'd fantasized about him. But as my heart pounded in my chest, the truth was nagging me.

"Nina was fucking right," I muttered as I pulled out of the parking deck and headed to the emergency room entrance.

Now that I was cognizant of my not-so-innocent crush, I wasn't sure if it was possible to ignore it. He saw me and liked me for me, so of course I considered him a friend. And the fact that he was not in a dating headspace solidified the friendship as just that—friendship. I respected him too much to make him uncomfortable with my feelings. All I wanted was to go back in denial. Because if I couldn't, I would have to end the friendship. I didn't want to, but I didn't know if I had a choice. It all boiled down to respect.

But the minute I spotted him, all that confusion and conflict melted away.

He was my friend, and he was a good friend. I didn't want to end the friendship, and he didn't deserve for me to just drop the friendship like that.

It's fine. It's fine. It's fine. I repeated the phrase internally until I pulled up to the curb. I pushed the sleeves of the jacket up my forearms. *It's fine. It's fine. He's fine. It's fine.*

I slammed on the brakes as my mind acknowledged the little slipup I'd made.

When Ahmad opened the door, he gave me a look. "I texted Asia and then looked up to see you driving like you had a blindfold on. Let me find out you can't drive."

"Oh, you can walk," I countered, rolling my eyes.

He climbed in my car, adjusting the front seat so his legs had room. "You'd force me to walk all the way home?" He put on his seat belt and then frowned. "Well, actually, it might be safer than riding with you."

"Instead of worrying about my driving, worry about following the doctor's orders. You're already messing up."

"What do you mean?"

"He said not to constrict the bandaged area." I gestured to the shirt that showed off his impeccable body. "And you put your baby tee back on like it isn't two sizes too small."

The laugh he let out was deep, robust, and free. It filled the car with his energy, and I couldn't help but smile.

I checked my mirrors before pulling out.

"Just keep your eyes on the road," he commented.

When I glanced over at him, I saw the tension in his knuckles as he gripped the doorframe. Even though there was a smile on his face, I took his words seriously.

"I'm a safe driver," I assured him softly.

I kept my hands at ten and two. I kept my eyes on the road. And I double-checked my blind spots. I drove better with him than I did on my driving test fourteen years prior. I didn't realize until we were halfway home that it wasn't just about me wanting to make sure we got there safely. I also just wanted to make sure he knew he was safe with me.

That thought made my stomach knot.

We didn't say anything for most of the trip. I didn't even turn on the radio. In the quiet that filled the car, I couldn't help but wonder how he was really feeling. I wanted to ask, but I also knew how it felt to not want to or know how to process when you're in the midst of it.

"It was hard for me to go swimming after my sister died," I told him, interrupting the silence that had settled around us. "My sister loved the water. We were out on the boat every other weekend growing up. After she got too pregnant to feel like making the drive to the beach, she got her water fix at home. My sister and her husband had a house with a heated pool in the backyard. She swam every day, twice a day, to keep in shape. And one day . . . she overdid it."

"I'm so sorry for your loss, Aaliyah," he responded quietly.

"Yeah, thank you. This happened five years ago, so . . ."

"But still."

I glanced over at him and nodded. "Yeah."

We were both quiet for a moment.

"She drowned?" he uttered.

I shook my head. "She got out of the pool a little earlier than usual because she didn't feel well. She had sent her husband a text message to let him know. When he got home, he found her collapsed on the floor in the hallway."

I felt his eyes boring into the side of my face as I drove. Keeping my eyes on the road, I pushed myself to continue.

"Apparently, she had a fatal arrhythmia," I continued.

"Oh, wow."

"Yeah. She had an underlying heart condition, and with the pregnancy and the exercise regimen, it was too much, I guess. Every time she exerted too much energy or did too much, she was at risk. She was a ticking time bomb, and she never even knew it. None of us did." I paused, staring straight ahead. "And even though I knew what it was, and I understood what happened, I still couldn't go swimming. I just . . ." My sentence trailed off as I remembered the dreadful feeling that overcame me when I thought about swimming.

"You couldn't get past it," Ahmad said softly.

Biting my lip, I nodded. "I just couldn't do it. I was so focused on what happened to her that I wasn't able to focus on what was happening in the moment. It kept me stuck there. And then two years after she'd died, I went to a pool party, and someone thought it would be funny to push me in the pool. Now, he didn't know what had happened; I don't really talk to people about it. But I remember panicking as I went under, and I almost drowned."

"Oh, shit."

"I knew how to swim, but I froze. I couldn't do it. I wasn't ready. I wasn't ready to be in a pool. I wasn't ready to swim. I wasn't ready to deal with Aniyah's death. Someone pulled me from the pool, and the party went on without missing a beat, but I went home. It took another year and a half before I was ready to swim."

"What made you ready?"

I shrugged. "I don't know. Therapy. Time. Trip to Tulum. But I knew when I was ready. I knew I was ready before I was willing to test the theory of me being ready. And I recognized how much time I wasted because I was scared to deal with what really needed to be dealt with." I stopped at the light next to Onyx. "Trauma."

He didn't say anything, but he nodded.

"Being in someone's shadow is always hard. But when the person is no longer alive, it makes it worse somehow. Because I can never live up to the perfection of a memory. So even after dealing with my issues with water, there's still some trauma that remains . . ."

I let my sentence trail off.

I hadn't meant to say so much. The words just kept tumbling out of my mouth. I hadn't realized how much I was sharing until it was already out in the open. I hadn't really shared that with anyone. Nina and Jazz knew, but I never had to say it. Outside of the sessions with my therapist, it was the first time I'd verbalized it.

I cleared my throat. "So, I can understand how whatever happened today could retraumatize you," I whispered, hoping I wasn't overstepping with him.

Silence surrounded us again.

"How old was your sister?" he asked, breaking the silence.

I stared straight ahead. The sound of my turn signal clicked as I waited to turn onto our street. "She was thirty."

"Thirty?" he repeated in disbelief. "That's . . . young."

"Yeah." I cleared my throat. "It is."

I could feel him staring at my profile. His eyes on me made more of my truth tumble from my mouth than I anticipated.

"Her dying at thirty made me realize that life is temporary, and I want something to make it feel more permanent than it is. I want something . . ."

"Something real," he finished for me.

I nodded. "Yeah."

"So your birthday . . . ?"

"It's not just to prove something to my family," I admitted slowly. "It's for me, too."

We were both quiet as we entered the parking garage.

"I said all that to say that I understand how trauma can change you," I concluded softly. "How something can retraumatize you. And how there's no linear path to healing. I know how lonely that journey can feel." My voice was barely above a whisper. "I just wanted you to know you're not alone."

He waited for me to park before he spoke again. "Thank you."

"It's no big deal. We live in the same building. It's not like it's out of the way."

"No." He waited until I looked at him before he continued, "No, not just for the ride."

"You don't have to thank me. But you're welcome."

Just as I was taking the key out of the ignition, he reached over and touched my arm. "You came to the hospital to check on me. That's worthy of a thank-you—at a minimum."

With a gentle squeeze, he sent goose bumps across my skin.

I swallowed hard and shifted from his touch. "Well, when you put it like that, you're right. I'll accept my thank-you in the form of cash."

He let out a light chuckle. "This is why I give you a hard time. You always got something smart to say."

"I'm just matching your energy."

"I see that."

He held my gaze for just a little too long.

Almost simultaneously, we opened the doors to escape the car that suddenly felt too small. Neither of us spoke as we headed toward the entrance of our building. It wasn't until he opened the door for me and I thanked him that the silence was broken.

"I'm going to help you to your place," I told him as the elevator dinged, announcing its arrival.

"You don't have to do all that. I'm fine." He pressed the fifth-floor button.

"You are injured, Ahmad. I'm making sure you get to your place safely."

He smiled. "Okay."

"How's your arm?" I wondered as I noticed him rubbing it.

"It's a little sore. But it's not bad."

"Pain meds working?"

"Oh yeah."

"You look tired."

"I am."

The elevator opened, and he gestured for me to walk out first. When we entered his apartment, I looked around.

"I see you got the albums put away," I noticed.

"Well, when I don't have unexpected visitors, I have time to get things done," he countered.

Amused, I held in my laugh. "That's fair."

He put down his stuff and rubbed his shoulder again.

"I'm going to let you get settled and get in bed," I told him. "Do you need anything before I go?"

"Nah, I'm just going to take a shower and go to sleep. I'm tired. It's been"—he yawned—"a long day."

"I can understand that. Well, listen, if you need anything, I'm right downstairs." I turned to head toward the door. "I'll check on you."

He followed me to the door, and when I reached for it, he stopped me. "Aaliyah, wait."

I turned around expectantly. "Hmm?"

He stopped a foot in front of me. His closeness knotted my stomach and caught me by surprise.

"I appreciate you showing up to check on me. You blew off going to Cloverleaf to make sure I was good. You really didn't have to do that"—he rubbed his beard, and a slow smile spread across his lips—"but I'm glad you did."

The knot in my stomach grew. "I was just doing what any friend would do," I replied breathily.

His eyes held mine. "Any friend wouldn't do that." He reached out and touched my hand. "And I appreciate that you did."

The heat from his fingertips spread all over my body.

My back flattened against the door as I tried to create space between us.

"You're welcome," I murmured as we stared at each other.

The apartment was so quiet, if a pin dropped in the back bedroom, it would have sounded like drums. So when my phone started vibrating, it felt like cymbals crashing, breaking up whatever was going on.

I tore my eyes away from his and checked my phone as it continued to vibrate in my bag.

"It's Lennox," I told him. "I should go."

"Oh. Yeah. Okay." He reached around me to get the door. "Thank you again."

"You're welcome, Ahmad. Anytime," I whispered before putting the phone to my ear and answering the call. "Hey, Lennox!"

19

"I'm really sorry again about our date on Friday," I told Lennox as we sat on the patio of a chic restaurant, waiting for the food we'd just ordered.

The Wednesday-night crowd was tame, and the weather was perfect. My date looked great, I looked incredible, but something still felt off.

But maybe I'm just overthinking it.

"Don't apologize again. We're here"—he opened his arms wide—"enjoying happy hour together now, so don't worry about it, okay?" He leaned across the table and touched my hand. "And honestly, I think it's dope you care so much about your friends."

"Thank you—"

"Did I tell you about that time . . ."

He regaled me with the tale of how he didn't even tell his friends when he went to the hospital and that story turned into another . . . and another. Just before the food was placed in front of us, my mind started to wander. He was just as interesting and charismatic as he had been last week, but a little voice inside of me noticed how much he talked and how little he asked about me.

Fucking Ahmad.

He'd gotten in my head about how talkative Lennox was, and now it was all I noticed.

Lennox was handsome, funny, smart, and really charismatic—but he didn't ask many questions about me. I didn't realize that he didn't ask me much of anything, because we'd spent days exchanging stories. I was so caught up in our similarities and how charming he was, I didn't realize that the information that he knew about me was because I offered it up.

It wasn't because he asked.

"—and then I met the chef over at Cloverleaf . . ." He continued to talk without my input.

I knew he'd amuse himself, so I didn't feel too bad that my mind kept drifting. I found myself thinking about my dating journey and what I wanted in a man. I listed all of Lennox's amazing qualities and the things I enjoyed about him; but I couldn't stop hearing Ahmad's critique of him.

Ahmad.

And just like that, the pit in my stomach returned with a vengeance.

I'd spent the last few days in an emotional upheaval. Even though I was still reeling from Ahmad being in the hospital, I had a long conversation with Lennox when I got home. I felt good about it because it was a nice distraction from what had just happened. Once we got off the phone, I realized I still had Ahmad's jacket on, and the feeling returned. I wanted and planned to give him his jacket back; I just needed to do it while there were other people around.

I cannot be alone with that man.

A mixture of longing and confusion sat in the pit of my stomach. I'd hoped it would be gone by the morning.

It wasn't.

And until I had a handle on what I was feeling, I didn't want to see Ahmad or be around him. The energy between us was too powerful. He had me emotionally wide open, telling him things I hadn't verbalized to anyone else. He had me physically wide open, making myself available to him, showing up for him. And if I'm honest, he had me sexually wide open because I was ready and willing. And as much as our energy seemed to be mutual, what I was seeking and what he was seeking were on two vastly different planes.

So instead of pining, I overbooked my schedule and stayed busy. But for whatever reason, the knot in my belly whenever I thought of Ahmad just continued to grow. It remained through my solo brunch on Sunday, through my Monday-morning meeting at work, and even still when I met up with Nina for a Taco Tuesday meetup. I couldn't find the words to define my feelings, but it made me ready to distract myself with the company of a fine man like Lennox. So, when he asked me out for Wednesday night, I quickly agreed.

"You don't like the bruschetta?" Lennox asked, dragging me from my thoughts and back to the present.

"Oh, I haven't tried it yet. But it looks good." I picked up the appetizer and took a bite. I nodded as I chewed. "Mmm."

"Yeah, the first time I had bruschetta was actually on a work trip. Did I tell you about the time I went to . . ."

Two hours later, I was being driven home. The moon shined bright in the sky, the air-conditioning blew cold air in my face, and Lennox's incessant talking was grating on my nerves. I told myself I just needed a little break. I convinced myself that I just needed to get home and recenter myself, and then I could look at the situation with Lennox with a clear head. But as he drove me home, I couldn't help but feel like it was the last time I was going to see Lennox.

My birthday is in three days. Is this who I want to spend it with? This man would probably make the day about him. I closed my eyes momentarily. *He's very sexy, though.*

"—and that's why I think having a pet with someone you're not married to is risky. You know what I'm saying?"

I had no clue what the fuck he was saying.

Shifting my sights from the downtown traffic to the man next to me, I forced a smile. It didn't matter what I said, he'd continue with the conversation on his own.

"I have an early morning tomorrow," I told him as I directed him to stop in front of my building. It was just after ten o'clock, so it wasn't late. But I was ready to be by myself. I needed to decompress.

"I should at least walk you to your door," Lennox pointed out. "I want to make sure you get in safely."

I waved my hand nonchalantly as he turned on the emergency blinkers. "It's a hassle to park. It's fine. I'll be safe, and I'll text you when I make it inside."

"Okay," he relented. "But make sure you let me know as soon as you get in there. I want to make sure you're good."

"I will."

"I had a really nice time with you, Aaliyah. I leave tomorrow, but I should be back on Saturday night. I'd love to take you out for a late dinner when I'm back. There's this new lounge I found, and I'd love to take you for our third date. I want to show you a good time."

He doesn't even remember I told him about my birthday.

It didn't matter that he was good-looking and an engaging storyteller. Forgetting my birthday killed it for me.

"I have plans on Saturday," I told him. "You just enjoy your trip, and we'll have a conversation when you're back."

I saw the flash of disappointment in his eyes as he nodded. "Yeah, okay. That's cool. We'll talk when I get back in town."

I forced a bigger smile than I felt. "It was nice to see you today, Lennox. Thank you for dinner."

"The pleasure was all mine." He took my hand and kissed it. "Until next time."

With a final wave, I got out of the car and ran toward my building. The minute I had my back to him, the smile on my face disappeared, the enthusiasm waned, and the upbeat persona retreated. The farther I got away from Lennox, the more I felt like my true state of being came to the forefront. Standing at the elevator, I didn't have the energy to pretend I was in a good mood anymore.

Maybe Ahmad got in my head by pointing out how much Lennox talked, but Lennox forgetting my birthday was the dealbreaker for me.

I'm three days away from my birthday, and I'm no closer to having a man than I was at the beginning of summer. The only thing I had then that I don't have now is hope.

I turned on the piping-hot water and stepped into the shower. I tried to wash away the date with Lennox, the incident with Ahmad, and the uncomfortable nagging feeling that had been plaguing me for days. Unfortunately, it all was still waiting for me when

I stepped out of the tub. Wrapping myself in my towel, I'd only gotten one foot out of the bathroom when my phone rang.

I flew across the room to get it, hoping it was one of my girls.

It wasn't.

"Hey, Lennox," I greeted him with a frown. Trying not to sound annoyed, I continued, "What's up?"

"Hey. I was just checking on you." He paused. "You were supposed to let me know you made it."

"Oh yeah, I'm sorry about that. My mind was somewhere else, and I wasn't thinking about it. I just hopped in the shower and—"

"Oh, okay, no problem. When you didn't let me know you made it safely, I had to call and check on you." He let out a little chuckle. "I wanted to make sure nobody snatched you up on your way in."

I squeezed my eyes shut and took a breath.

"I'm fine," I assured him. "I just forgot to give you a call before my shower. But I'm good. Thank you. How are you? You made it home yet?"

"Yeah, I'm not too far from home. I started thinking about that time I went to the . . ."

I zoned out.

Going through the motions, I moisturized my body and then slipped into a shorts-and-tank-top set. I didn't even bother to twist my hair. I pulled on my bonnet and then stared at myself in the mirror as the story I was being told went on.

And on and on and on.

I knew I couldn't do another date with Lennox. I wasn't sure if it was the current conversation or how Ahmad made me feel about the conversations, but I wasn't feeling Lennox anymore.

Fucking Ahmad!

"I'm so sorry to cut you off," I interrupted as I saw Nina's name flash across my screen. "But my best friend is calling, and I need to take this call."

"Okay, that's no problem. Have a good night, Aaliyah."

"Good night!"

I ended the call with Lennox and connected the call with Nina.

"Nina!" I cried, taking a seat on the edge of my bed. "I'm so happy to hear your voice."

She laughed. "Well, okay, that either means the date went really right or really wrong!"

I groaned, falling back against my mountain of pillows. "It isn't funny," I complained.

"If dating is nothing else, it's funny," she replied. "Now, tell me . . . what happened?"

"Well, I took your advice, and I went on the date with Lennox—"

"No, ma'am," she interrupted. "I told you to go on a date with the other one—what's his name? Jerome?"

"Tyrone," I corrected her.

"I told you to go on the date with Tyrone so you could check out your other options because Lennox isn't working. You said he only talked about himself."

"I know. I'm going to let him down after he gets back from his business trip. I can't take another date with him. I can't believe I used to think that we had great conversations when it was just this man telling me his life story."

"Good! You need to see what's up with someone else and quick. What about one of Ahmad's friends?"

Just his name coming up unexpectedly made me clench.

"I wouldn't go there," I replied.

"Why not? You need to tell the bartender that if he puts you in the friend zone, you're going to end up in his friend's phone."

I laughed so hard. "What is wrong with you?"

"A lot, apparently. I had to tell this man that he needed to enjoy me while he had the chance because I'm a one-link wonder."

"Yeah, you have lost your mind," I snickered. "But I admire that about you."

"What are you going to do about Saturday, though?" Nina asked.

"I'm going to see what Tyrone is talking about, and if it works well, I'll just ask him if he wants to be my date for Saturday. If that doesn't work out, I will figure something out."

"I have no doubt you will. Oh, girl, let me call you back. My insignificant other is beeping in, and we have plans for Thirsty Thursday."

I love Nina so much!

"Okay, I'm going to bed, so call me tomorrow," I said.

"I'll call you nice and early. I want to know more about this Tyrone character, and I want to know the latest with Ahmad."

We said our goodbyes, and then I immediately went to sleep.

I woke up feeling much better than I had when I went to sleep. After a long, hot shower and a big bowl of cereal, I slipped into my favorite bright pink pantsuit and paired it with a sexy black camisole underneath. I spent an exorbitant amount of time on my hair, and I even glued on some lashes.

"It's a new day," I told myself, checking out my reflection in the mirror. "And I look good."

I took a step back and eyed my shoes. They were sexier than my typical work shoes, but they were comfortable, and I felt like being a little extra today. With a glance at the clock, I realized that I was going to be late.

Opening the front door, I was startled by an envelope sitting on my welcome mat. I looked around, not seeing anyone. Cautiously, I leaned down and picked it up. Opening it carefully, I caught a glimpse of a card. The sound of my heart thumped in my ear as I backed my way into my apartment. My body knew who it was from before my mind even registered it.

I peeked inside enough to see Ahmad's name at the bottom of the card, and I shut my eyes tight.

I can't do this, I thought with a shake of my head. *Not right now.*

I was already a few minutes behind schedule, so instead of reading the note right then and there, I stuffed the envelope in my bag. I wasn't going to get my emotions all stirred about. Rolling my shoulders back, I marched out of my apartment and to the elevator.

When the door slid open, it was a little crowded. If I hadn't spent that extra time on my hair, I would've just taken the next elevator. But I needed to get to work. I stepped inside and counted five people in there already—including Ahmad.

My eyes widened when I saw him in the back corner, almost directly behind where I was about to stand. Holding in a gasp, I immediately spun around and faced the front.

I've never seen Ahmad in my building, and all of a sudden, when I'm trying to avoid him, he's right here!

Even though there was someone between us, I could feel Ahmad's eyes boring into the back of my head. The hairs on the back of my neck stood up. I shifted uncomfortably and stared at the floor numbers as they lit up. Soft jazz music and the gentle buzz of the elevator descending were the only sounds that filled the small space. I shifted my gaze to the metal door that reflected the blank stares of almost everyone in the elevator—except Ahmad's.

His eyes were trained on me. His gaze swept up and down my body. I knew I was being watched, but I was unnerved as I watched him watching me. I took a deep breath and shifted my eyes to my reflection.

I've never gotten upset about a man not wanting me, and I won't start with this one. He doesn't want to date, and that's okay. I respect his decision.

I moved to the side as the elevator opened to the next floor. Two additional people hopped on, so we were packed tight. Somehow in the shuffle to accommodate more people, Ahmad was directly behind me.

I hated that I could feel his breath on my neck.

I hated the way my body reacted to his closeness.

I hated that I could feel him without him even touching me.

When the doors opened, I was the second one out of the elevator. I'd parked close and made a beeline to my car even though I felt a presence on my heels.

"Aaliyah!" Ahmad called out.

I wanted to continue walking and ignore him, but there were too many people around, and I didn't want to make a scene.

I glanced over my shoulder. "Oh, hey, Ahmad," I sighed, not even trying to feign surprise as he caught up to me. "I'm sorry. I'm running late."

"Aaliyah."

His voice sounded resigned, and I ignored the pit in my stomach that formed at the way he'd said my name.

Wrapping his fingers around my wrist, he slowed me to a stop. "Are you avoiding me?"

I inhaled sharply as the heat from his grasp spread through my arm. I hated that his touch made my pulse quicken. His fingers pressing into my skin made my panties wet.

"Of course not," I lied quietly before lifting my gaze to meet his. "This has been a busy week. Between work, dates, and pre-party duties, I have a lot on my plate."

"Okay, I understand."

"And I really can't be late today . . ."

Unfortunately, I made the mistake of looking him in his eyes before I opened my car door. Seeing part of the bandage peeking from below his short-sleeved shirt, I felt compelled to speak. "Are you feeling any better?" I gestured to his arm. "Are you okay?"

"Yeah," he replied with a short grunt.

I nodded. "Good."

I hopped in my car, started it up, and drove toward the parking garage exit like I was being chased. When I glanced in the rear-view mirror, I saw him waiting for the elevator. I exhaled loudly and then put on my seat belt.

"Okay," I muttered under my breath.

Just being in the confined space with him felt like it was too much too soon. But overall, I felt like I handled the situation with Ahmad well—and I looked good doing it. I'd hyped myself so much that I walked into my workplace with a renewed energy.

"Good morning," I greeted Ramona as we approached each other from opposite ends of the hallway. "How are you?"

"Hey!" She grinned, following me into the downstairs ladies' room. "I'm great! How are you?"

"A little annoyed that I rushed to get here and they pushed the meeting back an hour."

"Well, you look good! This pink is fierce! Where is this from?"

"Thank you! I ordered it online. I'll send you the boutique link when I get to my desk."

"Thank you. And"—she lowered her voice—"fix your eyelash and you'll be perfect."

My face fell. "What?"

"Your eyelash is coming off."

I rushed to the mirror. "No!"

"Yeah, it's like doing this"—she did a gesture with her hand that resembled a wilted flower—"and it just needs to come down a little. Actually, I think I have some lash glue in my bag if you want me to bring it down. I was on my way up to my office anyway, so I can run upstairs real quick."

Staring at myself with my left eye looking like a professional makeup artist did one side and a small child did my right side, I was in shock.

Please let this have happened on the drive.

"Is that okay? You want me to get it?" Ramona questioned, taking a step back and pointing over her shoulder.

I shook my head. "No, I'm just . . ." My words trailed off as I pulled the lash strip from both eyes. "I'm just going to add some liner and call it a day."

"Oh, okay." She nodded sympathetically. "That's much better."

"Thanks," I muttered under my breath as I dug for my makeup in my bag. It wasn't her fault that I looked like a clown, so I looked up and flashed a small smile. "But I appreciate it."

"Of course." She waved me off and then put her hands on her hips. "But one of the reasons I came down here was because I was looking for you." She took another step closer. "I wanted to talk to you about something."

I distractedly reapplied some eyeliner to disguise the morning mishap. "What's up?"

"So . . . you know how they've had me really busy with the new hires?"

"Yeah."

"Well, I haven't really spent much time catching up with friends, so, um . . . I just heard about Derrick."

"Who?"

"My friend . . . the blind date."

"Oh." I made a face as I dropped the eyeliner back into my bag.

"I had no idea he didn't show up. I figured you didn't say anything because it didn't go well, and I hadn't talked to him, so I had no idea. I'm so sorry!"

I shook my head and shooed the apology off. "It's fine."

"He said his car broke down, and he was stranded on the side of the road. By the time roadside assistance came through, he figured you were gone. You weren't waiting long, were you?"

Not willing to disclose that I ended up being there for a couple of hours, I simply said, "Long enough."

"He said he didn't mention it to me sooner because he felt like he blew it with you, and you wouldn't be open to giving him another chance."

I nodded, heading toward the exit. "He's correct."

She followed me out of the bathroom. "Really? He's handsome and successful and—"

"I'm not interested. I don't circle the block anymore," I explained.

"Are you sure? It was one little misstep, and I wouldn't want something small to derail what could be a really good pairing." She gave me a mischievous look and pulled out her phone. "I probably shouldn't show you his picture, but . . ." She turned her screen toward me. "I really do think you two would look cute together."

She showed me a picture of a handsome man who looked like he had common sense.

"He's cute," I commented. "But I'm good."

"For what it's worth, I believe him about the car issues. He just got a new car a couple weeks ago. You should give him a chance."

"I don't think so."

"Listen . . ." She lowered her voice. "He's a good one. He's good-looking, childless, never been married, and has a good job. That's a unicorn nowadays."

"He stood me up. That's not the type of unicorn I'm looking for."

"He didn't have your number to call," she reasoned as we stood outside of the IT office suite.

I placed my hand on the door handle. "Yeah, but he had yours.

When he was waiting for help, he could've called you to get you to call me. So, there was a way." I lifted my shoulders. "But he didn't do that. It might not mean much to you, but wasting my time is a deal-breaker."

She held up her hands in defeat. "Understood." She flashed me a smile. "I had to try."

"I get it. If it were my friend, I'd go to bat for them, too. But it is what it is. Everything happens for a reason."

"That's true." She gasped. "You have someone now, don't you?!"

"No—"

"You are looking extra pretty for a random Thursday . . ."

"Thank you." I grinned. "But I'm looking good today for me."

She pursed her lips. "There's a guy."

"Ramona, please," I scoffed.

"He's your soulmate, and Derrick would've just gotten in the way of that," she continued. Nodding, she took a step back. "It all makes sense now. You're in love, and that's why you don't want my friend. Got it."

"Goodbye," I laughed, pushing the door open.

The guys arguing over Steve's desk drowned out my amusement.

"You already knew him," she called after me as the door separated us more and more. "Oh, I know who it is! It's the bartender."

I froze mid-step, and I felt the color drain from my face. My heart slammed against my chest repeatedly before I realized I wasn't moving.

What did she say? What is that supposed to mean? Why would she even say that?

When I spun around, the door to the IT office had already closed. Rushing toward it, I swung it open and hurried down the hallway to Ramona.

She turned around, startled. "Jesus, Aaliyah!" She let out a little laugh. "You scared me."

"Sorry, I just—uh, why did you say that?" I asked in a panicky tone.

She made a face and her lips pulled downward. "What?"

"The thing about already knowing—what did you mean when you said . . . that?"

"When I said what?" She jerked her thumb back toward the office. "Oh, about—it was a joke," she confirmed. Ramona gave me a wary look before she took a few steps back. "What's going on?"

"Why would you say *bartender,* though?"

"I . . . didn't." Her words came out slowly.

"You said it was someone I know and that it was the bartender."

"Um, no . . . I said it was Bart Fender. My receptionist."

Bart Fender. Not bartender. I exhaled shakily, clutching my bag. *Dammit.*

I didn't need a therapist to work out how I jumped to that conclusion.

Ramona eyed me suspiciously. "I don't know what's going on with you today."

"Aaliyah!" one of the IT guys called out for me from the cracked door. "Meeting's about to start."

I glanced over my shoulder and then looked back at her. "I misheard you and got confused," I said in a rush. Backing away from her, I shook my head. "I'm sorry."

Her eyes were narrowed at me as I turned around and scurried back into the office. Feeling the knot in my stomach grow, I tried to focus on the itinerary that was handed to me. I participated in the meeting, but as soon as it was over, I went to my desk and plucked the card from my bag.

Words can't express how much I appreciate you, I read the card to myself. *Thank you.*

I stared at the scrawling script of his name, and my heart thumped in my chest.

What the hell is that supposed to mean? I questioned before shaking my head. *No.*

I told myself I wasn't going to give Ahmad any more time, energy, or attention, and I meant it. I needed to pour all of that into men who were available for me. But I could feel him lingering in the outskirts of my subconscious, so I buried myself in my work. When it was time for lunch, I ordered a pepperoni slice and a salad from my favorite pizzeria, and I ate at my desk. Spending my downtime on TenderFish, swiping on men I had no interest in getting to know.

Just before my lunch break was ending, I got another notification from the dating app. I almost didn't check it, because I didn't care about any of the men in my messages. But then I saw who it was.

"Let's see what's up with Ty," I said under my breath as I replied to his message.

By the time I was on my way home from work, I'd talked to Tyrone more that day than I had all week. I was so distracted by Lennox that I'd ignored him, and after a riveting conversation, I kind of wished I'd given him more of a chance sooner.

We'll see if he can keep this energy on our date tomorrow, I thought as I entered my apartment.

We ended up having a conversation after dinner, and he was charming enough to keep me focused on him and him alone. When we said goodbye, I swiped through his pictures. "You just might be my date to my birthday party," I muttered under my breath.

And I kept repeating that thought anytime my mind strayed.

"Hello?" I answered my phone an hour later.

"Do we all have to have a date for Saturday, or just you?" Jazmyn asked as soon as I picked up.

"Well, hello to you, too," I snickered. "Yes. But your date doesn't have to be a *date* date. It can be anyone you want to bring."

She cleared her throat. "Okay."

I eased myself into my oversize chair. "Is there someone you have in mind?"

"Is there someone *you* have in mind?" she countered, changing the subject. "Your party is in forty-eight hours, and last I heard, you were into Lennox. Is he still the one?"

I made a face. "Lennox is no longer a contender."

"What? Since when?" she reacted.

"Officially, last night."

I gave her a quick rundown of what happened over the past week, and she became quiet.

"He went out of town, and he'll be back on my birthday. But I'm going to let him know it's not going to work between us the next time we speak," I continued.

"Interesting . . ."

I slung my legs over the arm of the chair. "What?"

"So, you really liked Lennox, and then you blew him off to check on Ahmad?"

"I would've done the same thing for you or Nina if I heard you were in the hospital," I argued.

"Whaaaaaaaat? He's on the same level as me and Nina?"

"You know what I mean," I groaned. "I'm there for my friends, so of course I wanted to make sure he was okay. And I rescheduled with Lennox, so it was fine."

"But then you talked to Ahmad about him, and all of a sudden, you stopped being interested?"

"No, it wasn't like that. Ahmad may have pointed the flaw out, but Lennox talked himself out of things with me all on his own. But in other news, I have a date on Friday."

"So, you don't think there's more between you and Ahmad?"

"It doesn't matter one way or another." I explained his wedding band ruse and that he wasn't looking for a relationship. "So, no matter what type of chemistry we have, all we can ever be is friends."

"Are you trying to convince yourself or me?"

I frowned at her calling me out like that. "Both."

"Just checking," she clarified, laughing lightly. "So there's no Lennox?"

"Nope."

"And no Ahmad?"

"No."

There was a moment of silence before she replied, "Yeah, I'm not buying it."

"It's the truth!"

"Okay, yeah. I believe you," she said in a dry, sarcastic tone that made it clear she, in fact, did not believe me. "So anyway, you said there's some sort of date? With who?"

"His name is Ty. He's cute—he's thirty-five. And he owns his own trucking company."

"Are you going to ask him to be your date for Saturday?"

"I know he's free on Saturday, but it depends on how everything goes. We planned our date last week and we were supposed to meet at Onyx tomorrow, but that was before everything got weird with Ahmad. So, I'm going to have to change it to another place."

"Why are you changing locations?"

I let my head rest against the back of the chair. "Because I don't want to run into Ahmad."

"I thought there wasn't anything between you and Ahmad."

"There's not."

"So, what's the problem?"

"Ahmad and I have been having weird energy lately."

"Because you still have feelings for him, or because he has feelings for you, or . . . ?"

Her sentence trailed off, and the hint of a question hung in the air.

I lifted my head and cleared my throat. "I don't know. It's weird and not the energy that should be around my date."

"But if you're friends and just friends, it makes the most sense to go to Onyx."

I considered what she said. "Yeah, I get that. But I just don't want to deal with—"

"You're going to meet a strange man who drives long distances for a living somewhere random?" Jazmyn screeched. "Okay, cool, I guess I'll just pick out my outfit for the news when they come to interview me about you being a missing person."

"Come on, Jazz," I snickered.

"I'm serious! I'll be sure to let the reporters know that you had an alternative place you could've gone safely. But instead, you decided to meet Ty—that's his name, right? Ty?"

Shaking my head because I knew she was going to say something ridiculous, I answered, "Yes."

"I'll let the news reporters know that Ty has you in the back of his truck somewhere headed west. But it's cool because you didn't want to see some guy you claim to not have feelings for. Would you prefer we put your face on a milk carton or a billboard?"

Pushing myself out of the chair, I made my way to my bedroom. "Jazz, please!" I cackled.

"No, but seriously, if there's really nothing between you and Ahmad, there's really no reason *not* to go to Onyx," she reiterated.

I sighed. "You're not wrong. But . . ."

"But nothing! Now promise me you'll go to Onyx."

I squeezed my eyes shut. "Fine. I'll go to Onyx."

"Good. Now I feel better."

"Well, enough about me. What's going on with you? When are you coming back?"

Twenty minutes later, I was caught up on her life, and we were about to get off the phone.

"This is the longest I've gone without seeing you," I told her. "I'm going to give you the biggest hug."

"I'm looking forward to it," she said cheerfully.

She sounded different from how she had at the beginning of the summer. There was a lightness to her tone.

I smiled.

Time heals.

20

"Meet Ty's fine ass at Onyx and make the bartender have to eat his feelings when you flaunt your sexy ass tonight," Nina advised as soon as I picked up the phone.

I'd sent her a photo of Tyrone before leaving work for the day and let her know what I was wearing. I knew she was going to call me when she finished working, but I didn't expect her to launch right into it.

"Nina, I literally just got home," I giggled. "Please."

"Well, I just got wind that you were trying to duck out on an opportunity to rub your date in Ahmad's face."

I shook my head as I took off my shoes. "So, I take it you talked to Jazz."

"Yes. And she told me that you were trying to be featured on the eleven o'clock news."

I cackled. "Why are the two of you so dramatic? I already told her I was keeping the date at Onyx!"

"Listen, I'm down for you to go on as many dates as you want, with whoever you want, wherever you want. I'm just trying to figure out why you were going to let Ahmad run you from your spot. *You* chose that place before you even knew him. Yeah, he may work there, but *you* chose that spot because you're comfortable with it."

"You're right," I realized with my eyes wide. "I mean, his family owns it, so it's more his spot than my spot, but I see your point, and you're right. I *did* choose that place before I even knew he existed. It's been my first-date meetup spot."

"So, like I said from jump, put on your sexiest dress and flaunt your shit tonight! Best-case scenario, Ty is amazing, and Ahmad has to watch you get fawned over by that beautiful, muscle-bound truck driver. Worst-case scenario, Ty is a dud of a date, but you'll still make Ahmad jealous, so it's still a win."

I had a flashback of what Ahmad looked like shirtless. The sculpted frame of that man was a work of art. Even if we were just friends, I couldn't deny that he looked good.

Really good.

I shook off the thought and the mental image. "I mean, I don't think Ahmad's going to be jealous of Ty." I licked my lips. "He's pretty built. I mean, the body is giving."

"What? Have you seen the bartender shirtless? Aaliyah!" Nina reacted with delight.

"Briefly. But my point is that both men look like Sexiest Man Alive contenders. I don't think there's going to be any jealousy."

"We're definitely circling back to the fact that you've seen the bartender shirtless, but my point was that if Ahmad wants to just be friends, he should have no problem seeing you with that fine-ass trucker."

Shaking my head, I made a face even though she couldn't see me. "I'm not trying to make Ahmad jealous. I respect what he has going on. We're friends."

"Nah, it's more than that. I saw the way he was looking at you after that concert."

"You mean when he called me the Pink Panther?"

"Pink Panther!" Nina squealed, laughing a little too hard and a little too long.

I stopped and put a hand on my hip, glaring at my phone. "All right, that's enough."

She laughed so hard she snorted, which caused me to laugh along with her.

"Anyway, Ty seems cool," I announced, trying to shift the conversation. "He asked me ahead of time about my favorite drink and my favorite thing to eat at Onyx."

"Oooooh, a man who is thinking ahead? I like that!" Nina exclaimed.

"I said the same thing to myself when he asked!" I pulled my outfit from the closet. "We'll see if he actually comes with that energy."

"Either way, you're going to look good, and if it works, you'll bring his superhero-looking ass home."

"You know I don't fuck on the first date," I admonished.

"You were *just* telling me that you were tired of these first dates not amounting to anything because you were trying to get fucked on your thirtieth."

"Yeah, but I'm not going to bring Ty home just to get my needs met. I need to have an actual connection with someone."

"Well, all summer, you've been connecting, and that's not getting your needs met. And why not see what's up with a man who looks like a superhero?" She laughed to herself. "He looks like someone famous, but I can't think of the name."

My face twisted in confusion. "He does?"

"Yes! I'll text you as soon as I think of it, but in the picture you sent, I immediately thought of the guy I saw in a movie. He doesn't remind you of anyone?"

"No one I can think of. Hold on." I pulled the phone from my ear and clicked on the picture I'd sent her. "I can see what you're saying, though. He does have that really pulled-together, handsome look that a lot of actors have."

"No, he looks like someone specific. Ugh! It's going to bother me until I remember the man's name." She sighed loudly. "I'll let you know when I think of it."

"Okay, sounds good. And have fun on your date tonight."

"It's not a date. We're just linking up," she corrected me. "Unlike you, I plan to have my needs met tonight."

I smiled. "Mm-hmm. Well, have fun linking up with your *date* tonight."

"Goodbye, Aaliyah."

"Byeeeeeee," I sang in return.

I smiled. Nina could deny it all she wanted, but I knew she actually liked that man.

After the call disconnected, I took another glimpse at the photo of Ty.

With dark brown skin, bright white teeth, and a chiseled jawline, he looked good. But to me, he didn't look familiar.

But I'm looking forward to getting familiar with him.

After showering, I spent the next couple of hours doing my hair.

It was a mistake to start two strand twists prior to the date, but it was worth it when I achieved the final look.

Because of the time crunch, I didn't have time to overthink my outfit. I slipped into a black bralette bodysuit that showed off my breasts while still keeping them covered. It was sexy without going over the top. I paired the bodysuit with a short and flowy black skirt. Hitting a couple of inches above my knees, the skirt showed off my shapely legs and my strappy sandals.

With long dangly earrings and a deep red lipstick, I was dressed sexier than usual for a first date. But I didn't want to change. Part of the reason was because Jazz and Nina had made valid points. The other reason was because tomorrow was my birthday, and it was time to go big or go home. And if I were being honest, Nina wasn't wrong about how badly I wanted my needs to be met.

Between things falling apart with Lennox, realizing I had feelings for Ahmad, and my birthday in less than twenty-four hours, I was in need of mind-numbing, backbreaking, intensely passionate sex.

Or at the very least, I need to come.

Opening my drawer, I pulled out my vibrator and placed it on my bed. I wasn't planning on bringing Ty home since he was virtually a stranger. But I did plan to take care of myself when I got back.

I'm looking sexy, feeling sexy, and if the date is sexy, I'll be primed for a good time in bed by myself tonight.

Ty sent a message through the TenderFish app stating that he had arrived early but for me to take my time. With my clutch in one hand and my phone in the other, I made my way across the street. Taking a deep breath, I braced myself before following a group of women into the bar.

A nervous flutter moved through my belly as I walked into Onyx.

I scanned the room and was a little surprised by the size of the crowd. The murmur of the people mixed with the music. Pausing a few feet from the door, I swept the room looking for him.

He's not behind the bar. Or near the office door. Or near the booths. Or—

I froze.

Taking another deep breath, I shook off what was happening.

I'm looking for Ty, I reminded myself as I cast my gaze around the room again.

When a small group of men and women shifted out of the way, I saw a tall, dark, and handsome man get up from the bar and head in the direction of the bathrooms.

Is that him?

It wasn't until I saw a sleeve of tattoos running down both of his arms that I felt sure that the man I'd spotted was Tyrone. Seconds later, I felt my phone vibrate in my hand.

> **Tyrone:** I have two seats for us at the bar. If you come in in the next couple of minutes, look for the flowers. I'm going to wash my hands.

I glanced up and walked toward the far end of the bar and noticed a bouquet of yellow roses. With a small smile tugging at my lips, I approached the stool in front of the flowers.

"Hey, Aaliyah," Asia greeted me.

"Oh, hey!" I sat down and gently caressed a rose petal. "How are you?"

"Overwhelmed, but good! But just FYI, someone is sitting there." She glanced down to the other end of the bar. "But there's a seat on your regular side. I'm—"

The loud sound of a petite woman dropping a large bottle of liquor behind the bar interrupted her sentence. Asia immediately rushed in that direction without another word to me.

There were two new faces behind the bar. And although I wasn't *trying* to see Ahmad, I did notice he wasn't there.

"Aaliyah?"

I followed the sound of my name to my immediate right and instantly smiled. "Tyrone?"

His lips spread into a sexy smile, and he took the seat next to me. He extended his hand to me.

"It's nice to meet you." When my hand slipped into his, he

leaned forward. Staring into my eyes, he lowered his voice. "And I like it when you call me Ty."

"Well then . . . it's nice to meet you, too, Ty." Pulling my hand from his, I gestured to the bouquet. "And thank you for the flowers. They're beautiful."

"Not nearly as beautiful as you," he complimented as he checked me out. "You have really good taste."

"Thank you." I smelled the roses. "So do you, apparently."

"I wanted something that matched your energy." He leaned forward a little more and rested his forearm on the bar top. "So, I asked for roses because it's a classic and you're classy. I picked yellow, so they'd be different and stand out like you do. I had them wrapped in brown paper because they match your eyes. And I brought flowers to the bar because you have my attention and I wanted to put you on notice."

"Wow." I bit my lip and nodded slowly, contemplatively. I didn't know what to say. "Thank you," I whispered.

"Thank you for meeting me tonight. And for choosing this place." He stared at my mouth. "I like it a lot."

There was a lot of intensity in the way he looked at me and in his touch. The way his body was positioned toward me, with his long legs almost trapping me at the bar. The way he leaned close enough that I could smell his cologne but not so close as to violate my personal space. The way his eyes held mine and then lingered on my lips before returning to my eyes—and then doing it all over again. It was the way he licked his lips before each sentence. The sexual attraction between us was strong.

It was that mixture of sexy and dangerous that was typically a precursor to bad decisions.

It was hot.

He was hot.

But there was something about him that felt like he would blow my back out and ruin my life.

"Of course. I'm glad we're here tonight," I told him.

"When I got here, they said they have someone coming to perform live in a little while." He leaned closer to me. "Me. You. Live music." He licked his lips. "That sounds good to me. What about you?"

Oh, this could be promising . . .

I nodded. "Yeah. That sounds good."

Without taking his eyes off me, he lifted his hand to signal he was ready to place an order.

"What can I get you?"

Ahmad's deep voice made the hair on the back of my neck stand up.

I froze.

Refusing to turn my head and look at the man taking our order, I just stared at Ty.

"Yeah, let me get a Malibu sunrise and a Long Island, please," he ordered. "And do you think our table will be ready soon?"

"Yeah, give me a minute to check on it. You need anything else?" Ahmad asked.

"Aaliyah?" Ty asked.

I shook my head and turned to look at Ahmad. "No, thank you," I answered, my voice faltering a bit. "But we appreciate it."

Ahmad held my gaze for a second too long before he nodded. "Okay."

My stomach fluttered.

He looked good with his fresh lineup and trimmed beard. He was wearing another one of his tight-fitting shirts that I gave him shit about, but I couldn't deny how good they looked on him. Between his handsome face and sexy build, Ahmad Williamson always caught my eye.

But we are just friends, I reminded myself.

I squared my shoulders.

This is uncomfortable. But I was glad I kept the date at Onyx because if the energy was weird with Ahmad, seeing me on a date with a man should get us back on track.

He glanced at my date. "I'll be right back with your order."

My heart was racing as I shifted my focus to the flowers in front of me. Pretending the roses had my full attention, I tried to get myself together.

"They are quite beautiful, aren't they?" Ty asked.

Burying my nose in the roses so I could hide my face for a second, I bought myself some time. Exhaling, I smiled at him. "And they smell great, too."

"Speaking of smells . . . I have a thing about scents, and yours is doing something to me." He let out a light chuckle. "I don't know what soap or perfume you have on, but that's the one."

"Thank you. It's my signature scent. I went to one of those classes where you can create your own perfume, and I fell in love with the combo I created. I've been wearing this exclusively for the last three or four years."

"Where did you do that?"

"It was—"

"Your table is ready," a waiter I'd seen around before interrupted.

Ty stood and then extended his hand to me, helping me off the stool. "After you."

He whistled, not trying to hide the fact that he was staring at my body. I could feel his eyes on my ass as we made our way across the small establishment. But when we got to the table, he was careful to not let me catch him eyeing me sexually.

"Here you are." He pulled out my chair.

"Oh, thank you," I replied, allowing him to push me in.

"You're welcome. I want to make sure you're taken care of." He smirked as he took the seat across from me. "But I also can't sit with my back to the door."

"Ah, so you were really just doing it for you."

"Nah, it's not even like that." He pointed to the door. "What if someone runs up in here? I need to be able to jump up and defend you. I can't do that if I can't see them coming."

Laughing, I shook my head. "What kind of place do you think I brought you to?"

He lifted his shoulders comically. "I don't know. I think the dude at the bar got beef. Who knows who else could run up in here?"

I snickered.

"Here's our menu for this weekend," the waiter told us, handing us two small, laminated cards. "It changes every weekend, so let me know if you have any questions. I'll give you a couple of minutes before I take your order."

"Thank you," we said in unison.

As soon as we were alone, Ty picked up the menu and looked over it. "Have you ever eaten anything from here?"

"Just the burger and fries." I picked up my menu. "I don't even know what else they serve."

"Well, there's about ten things on here." He sat back in his chair. "Depending on how hungry you are and how much time you'll let me have, we can order everything."

Ty was saying the right things and being gentlemanly, but the man's energy was sexually charged.

Bemused, I gave him a look. "Everything?"

He nodded. "I have a biiiiiiig appetite."

"Is that right?"

He licked his lips. "Yes. And you can have whatever you want."

I wasn't sure if it was my level of horniness or if it was because of Ty's vibe, but everything he said sounded sexually suggestive.

I need to bottle up this energy for later tonight, I thought as I bit my bottom lip and stared at the menu.

Ignoring his flirty innuendo, I focused on picking my meal. "Well, I'll probably go for the burger sliders and fries."

"That's it?"

I placed the menu down. "For now."

"I'll get the wings, the onion rings, and mozzarella sticks. And I mean it, if you want anything else, order it. Please."

"Long Island," Ahmad said, setting the drink in front of Ty. The glass clanked against the table a little more forcefully than necessary. The wedding band caught my eye as he placed my drink in front of me. I felt a wave of emotion come over me as I made eye contact. "Malibu sunrise."

My stomach knotted, but I didn't look away. I squared my shoulders. "Thank you."

"Yeah, man, thanks," Ty responded. "Can we get two waters, too? And extra napkins?"

Running his hand over his beard, Ahmad paused momentarily. "Yeah, I'll let your waiter know."

I heard a bit of an edge in his voice. Grabbing my drink, I smiled into my glass as I took a sip.

He stalked off, and our waiter came back a couple of minutes later. We placed our order and then allowed the conversation to flow as naturally as it had over the last couple of days.

Glancing up, I caught Ahmad staring at me from behind the bar. My stomach flipped as our eyes locked. He was making a drink, but his attention was on me. Tearing my eyes away from him, I refocused on my date.

"—and that's how I ended up moving from Texas," Ty concluded.

I nodded as if I hadn't been distracted by another man. "Do you miss it?" I wondered, with a quick glimpse to the bar again.

Ahmad was smiling at a group of women. They were laughing excessively and flirtatiously as he made their drinks. But there was something different about him. He seemed rigid and tense. When his eyes met mine again, I saw something flash in them that I hadn't seen before.

Is that anger? Irritation? Jealousy? Regret?

I took a sip of my drink as I watched the way his face hardened, and his mouth stretched into a tight line.

Good.

"You want another drink?" Ty asked, interrupting my thoughts.

I nodded. "Sure."

He ordered another round of drinks when our food came.

Even though the crowd continued to grow throughout the night, there always seemed to be a clear line of vision between Ahmad and me. I felt him watching me as I ate and talked with my date. I felt his eyes boring into me as I laughed at Ty's jokes. I felt the intensity of his stare as I listened to Ty's stories. And I wasn't sure if it was the alcohol or the pent-up sexual energy coursing through my veins, but the fact that I was getting under Ahmad's skin made me feel all gushy inside. It wasn't just petty satisfaction anymore; it was something much deeper.

I shifted in my seat in an attempt to dull the ache.

"I'm going to run to the restroom," I yelled across the table. Covering my mouth, I hoped there wasn't something in my teeth.

"Want me to order you another drink?" Ty asked.

I rose to my feet. "Another water, please."

"Your wish is my command." He winked before picking up a wing.

I laughed lightly before maneuvering my way through the crowd. I tried not to look toward the bar, but as soon as I did, Ahmad's narrowed eyes were zeroed in on me. I smiled and then continued my way to the back hall where the bathrooms were located.

The first door on the right was the men's room, and the door to the left didn't have a sign. But the door at the end of the hall said WOMEN'S ROOM, and surprisingly, there wasn't a line.

Spoke too soon, I silently commented as I opened the door to see seven women waiting for stalls.

I stepped back out and decided to wait in the hall and not in the restroom.

I froze when I saw who was coming down the hallway.

His eyes swept down my body. His tongue ran from one side of his mouth to the other before he forced his eyes back to mine.

Swallowing hard, I pushed down my attraction to him.

"What are you doing?" Ahmad demanded.

My heart thumped in my chest. "What does it look like I'm doing? I'm waiting for the bathroom."

I saw how his black T-shirt clung to his muscular body earlier, but walking down the hall, I was able to take in his full form.

He is sexy as hell. Someone I need to keep at a distance. But sexy as hell. I licked my lips and then realized I was staring. *I should go. I should run back into the bathroom.*

Before I could make a move, he was standing a foot in front of me. "That's not what I meant. What are you doing with him?"

My eyes opened wide, giving him an incredulous look. "What?"

A group of women were passing by, and Ahmad grabbed my arm and moved me to the side.

"Can we go somewhere and talk?"

A chill ran down my spine. I hated how the throb in my chest made its way between my thighs. I looked beyond him at the man running into the men's bathroom. I needed to walk away.

"I only have fifteen minutes, and I need to talk to you," he continued.

I had every intention of saying no. I had a date—a very handsome and entertaining date—waiting for me, and it would be rude to keep him waiting for a man who lied to me.

But with Ahmad's fingers wrapped around my forearm, his eyes burning into mine, and the coconut rum running through my veins, my defenses weren't just down. They didn't exist.

"Fine," I relented softly. "What do you want to talk about?"

Another group of women, probably eight in total, came skipping and screeching down the hall.

"Not here," he grunted before tugging me with him through the unmarked door.

I gasped, my heels skating along the floor as I flew into the room. He had a grip on me that ensured I wasn't going to fall, but still.

21

"What are you doing?" I reacted, yanking myself out of his grasp after he slammed the door behind us. Looking around the small office, I put my hands on my hips. "Ahmad, what the hell?"

He stalked from the door to the desk and then back to the middle of the room where I stood. It was alarming how sexy he looked with his features hardened in anger. My taut nipples pushed against the lace top as I took him in. His ire fanned the flames of mine, but my body's reaction to him was totally unexpected.

"You're not falling for that fake Shaw Lockwood, are you?" he questioned, jaw tensed.

"What?" I sputtered, crossing my arms over my chest. "What's it to you?"

"That guy is not who you think he is. He ain't it."

My face scrunched up in disgust. "Says who?"

"He was being a little too friendly with Asia before you got here."

Well, that's a little disrespectful.

My face was unchanged even though I was slightly irritated by that bit of information. "Okay. It's a first date. And he's not my man."

"It's disrespectful," he pointed out.

"It's none of your business," I countered, squeezing my thighs together. "Why are you coming at me like this?"

"You asked me to look out for you and point out red flags if I see them."

"I didn't ask you to look out for me. You inserted yourself into my dating life."

"Well, I'm telling you that Salvation Army Shaw is not it."

I narrowed my eyes at him. "That's rich coming from you."

He frowned. "What is that supposed to mean?"

I rolled my eyes. "Never mind. What did you want to talk about?

You couldn't have followed me to the bathroom just to talk about my date."

"Fine." He pinched the bridge of his nose. "Why are things different between us?"

"I don't know, but it's weird." I paused for a second. "Why are you acting like this tonight?" I asked in return.

"Acting like what?"

"Jealous."

His jaw tightened and his eyes flashed, but he didn't reply to my comment.

He gestured between us. "I don't like the way things have been with us, and I want to clear the air."

"Okay . . . ?"

"You've been avoiding me since the night of the hospital." He moved so that we were only inches apart. "Why?"

The way his cologne infiltrated my nostrils caused a flutter in my belly.

Staring into his eyes, I cocked my head to the side. "I've been busy," I said simply.

Ahmad's head dropped back, and he let out a feral roar that seemed to come from the depths of him. My mouth snapped shut, and my eyes widened. I wasn't scared of him. I was surprised by his outburst, but I didn't even flinch. I'd never seen him raise his voice, let alone yell. I was more fascinated than anything.

Curling my lip in disgust, I gave him a look. "Are you done?"

"Are you? Are you done, Aaliyah? I mean, damn. I'm trying to look out for you."

"How are you trying to look out for me, Ahmad? By mean mugging me while I'm on a date?"

"Wow!" He exhaled gruffly, walking to the other side of the small office. When he turned to face me, his frown deepened. "I wasn't mean mugging you. I was mean mugging him."

My eyes narrowed angrily. "You have some nerve," I hissed.

A mixture of confusion, anger, and exasperation twisted his handsome face. He was only a few feet away, so I saw the way his eyes flickered before he replied, "Me?"

"Yes, you."

His long legs closed the gap between us, and he stood directly in front of me. "What is your problem?"

"You are my problem!"

"So why won't you talk to me?"

Searching my eyes, he leaned down. His face was inches from mine, and my gut twisted violently as he moved into my personal space.

I stepped back, ignoring the way my nipples tightened in his presence. I disregarded the way my panties dampened at his closeness. I couldn't stop the way my body reacted to him. But I was not feeling how dramatic he was being, and I chose to hold on to that.

"We've talked, and there's nothing else to say about it," I snapped, glaring at him. "We're *cool*!"

"Nothing else to say about what?" he questioned forcefully, continuing to move forward. "There's nothing cool about this."

I backed up with each step he took. He didn't stop until I bumped into the desk behind me. My heart raced as his gaze pierced me. It was like he was reading me, listening to my thoughts. It felt like he was hearing what I wasn't ready to say, and that made me uncomfortable. I wanted to look away, but I was stuck.

It was a bad idea to be alone with him.

When he broke the silence, his deep voice cracked with earnestness. "What are you doing to me?"

I pursed my lips but didn't say anything. The genuineness in his eyes and the gentleness in his tone were trying to get to me. I shifted my gaze so I could resist. I refused to let him get me in my feelings.

"There are some things I should've told you sooner, and I'm sorry." Cupping my chin, he turned my head so that our eyes met again. "But I'm sorry," he repeated gently.

Swallowing hard, I nodded slowly. "Okay."

"I should've told you I wasn't married, but I didn't think it mattered since you were on dates with other men."

We were both quiet for a moment.

"And now you . . ."

My brows furrowed. "And now me?"

"Yeah." He cocked his head to the side, and his hand fell from my face. "You don't think I deserve an apology, too?"

My jaw dropped. I felt my blood pressure rise as the question hung in the air between us. My body was physically shaking. "You think I owe *you* an apology?"

He looked taken aback. "Yes. You've been ignoring the fuck out of me—"

"I've been busy—"

"And you won't even keep it real and tell me why—"

"We're supposed to be friends!" I yelled breathlessly.

"We *are* friends!" he roared back.

I poked him in his chest. "And *that's* why!"

"I don't know—"

"It doesn't matter who I go on a date with, because we are friends."

"It matters to me," he growled, searching my face.

"Why does it matter?"

"Because you . . ." His voice trailed off. Bringing his face closer to mine, he exhaled. "Because you're you."

"And what's that supposed to mean?"

His words were slow and deliberate. "I want better for you."

"Better than what?"

"Better than the jackass you're with. Better than any of the men you were with this summer."

My heart thumped in my chest as I felt my resolve crumbling.

I need to get out of here.

"I'm going back to my date," I said in a huff.

Ripping my eyes away from his, I started moving toward the door.

He grabbed my arm and spun me around to face him.

My back was against the wall in seconds, and my breaths came out in short bursts. A chill ran down my spine as he towered over me.

Fear coursed through my veins.

But I wasn't fearful of him. I was fearful of how he was making me feel. The way he was looking at me made me feel like he knew too much.

Yeah, it's time to go.

He searched my face. "What do you want me to say?"

My lips parted, and I let out a trembling breath. My voice was barely above a whisper as I took in his words. "Whatever you want to say."

He studied me. His chest rose and fell rapidly as he seemed to read me. "You matter to me. Is that what you want to hear? You want to know that I care about you?" he questioned, releasing his grasp on my arm. "What do you want from me?"

"For the sake of our friendship . . ." My voice quavered slightly as it trailed off.

I want you to stop, I finished the sentence in my head.

He shook his head slowly, holding my gaze. "What do you want from me?"

As much as I knew I should've completed my thought, I couldn't bring myself to stop what was already happening. So, I didn't say anything. I just stood there. I tried to look away from him, but I couldn't.

"What is it, Aaliyah? Just tell me. What do you want from me? What do you need from me?"

"We're fine, Ahmad!" I retorted. "Our friendship is fine."

"You're just . . ." Staring into my eyes, he shook his head. "You're so fucking . . ."

"I'm so what?" I stepped up, getting in his face. "I'm so fucking what, Ahmad?"

His lips were tightened in an almost angry pout.

My gaze lingered on his mouth, daring him to say what was on the tip of his tongue.

His jaw clenched and unclenched. His nostrils flared. His chest rose and fell.

He silently stared at me, and I stared right back.

Without warning, Ahmad crashed his lips into mine.

I gasped as he backed me against the wall, kissing me hard. I was caught off guard, but instinctively, I returned the kiss. I clawed at his T-shirt, pulling his body closer to mine. Feeling his growing bulge pressing against me through his jeans, my body shivered. His hard body pinned me, and his soft lips moved over mine. His hands encircled my neck, brushed over my shoulders, and down my arms. But it wasn't until our tongues touched that I moaned into his mouth, fully giving in to him.

He was dominating me, consuming me, and I felt everything, everywhere.

I'd never been kissed like that before in my life.

I placed my hands on his chest and abruptly pulled out of the kiss. Staring up at him with wide eyes, I saw a mix of confusion and desire etched across his handsome features. His chest rose and fell as air escaped him in quiet bursts. His heart raced under my palm. His fingers flexed against my hips.

I'd stopped the kiss because I had to.

Ignoring the desire that churned between my legs, I opened my mouth to tell him I had to go. I looked into his eyes, ready to end whatever it was that was happening between us. But when he wet his lips and I caught a glimpse of his tongue, that yearning deep within me caused me to have a temporary lapse in judgment.

I knew I should've taken my hands off his chest. I knew I should've stepped away and created distance between us. If I would've given myself the space to breathe and think, I would've had a chance to resist. But the way he looked at me rendered me speechless. He was too close and too intoxicating. I couldn't think straight. But feeling the way his heart raced under my hand spurred something inside me.

Letting both hands move down his defined chest over his rippled abs, I swallowed hard. When I reached his belt buckle, his lips parted, but he didn't speak.

The desire I felt for him was too much, and I couldn't stop myself. I didn't care that I had a date waiting on me. I didn't care about the consequences of getting caught. I only cared about dulling the ache between my thighs.

His hands gripped my hips and then moved to my waist, up my torso, and then detoured to my breasts. His fingers found my rock-hard nipples, and my breathing became more ragged.

"Yes," I murmured as he pinched and tweaked my nipples through the lace.

"Why are you so fucking stubborn?" he uttered, bringing his face close to mine.

"Ahmad," I moaned as his mouth trailed across my jawline, down my neck, and then against my ear.

"Don't say my name like that," he warned, his voice hoarse.

My body trembled with want, and I held on to his belt tighter so I didn't tip over. "Like what?"

"Like you don't want me to stop." He kissed his way back to my lips and covered my mouth with his.

"I don't," I breathed almost inaudibly.

"What did you say?" he wondered as he slid the straps of my bodysuit from my shoulders.

"What are you doing?" I was nearly panting.

"Whatever you want me to do." He broke the kiss as my heavy breasts became exposed. "Whatever you need me to do." He looked down at my chest and then back into my eyes. "Whatever you ask me to do."

My stomach flipped. His words bypassed my ears and went directly to the apex of my thighs.

I had to get out of there.

Before I could make a move, his mouth covered mine again and my knees damn near buckled.

Spurred on by the combination of attraction and alcohol, my inhibitions were low and my desire was high. I was running on pure adrenaline and carnal lust. I was so lost in his kiss and in the way he toyed with my body, I didn't realize I'd unhooked his belt. It wasn't until I pulled on his zipper that I realized what I was doing.

"Aaliyah," he groaned softly.

The sound he made as he said my name made my toes curl.

I slipped my hand into his jeans and over the prominent bulge in his underwear. The moment my hand grazed the cotton fabric, his entire body tensed.

Sucking in a sharp breath, he froze. His hands stilled on my body. "Aaliyah . . ."

I responded by stroking him as best I could through his boxer briefs.

He groaned, bringing his forehead to mine and dropping one of his hands to my ass cheek. "Talk to me."

"I don't want to talk," I murmured before pushing my lips up to meet his. I continued stroking him inside his pants. "We've talked enough."

Without a word, he removed my hand from his pants and then grabbed my hips. His eyes bored into me with such an intensity that I didn't know what was coming next. He started walking forward, his body pressed against mine, moving me until my back hit the door.

I gasped, but I didn't truly feel the collision.

I was too far gone to feel anything.

I was lost in his eyes.

I was lost in my desire.

I was lost in the moment.

"Talk to me," he demanded.

I licked my lips. "Make me."

Breathing heavily, we continued staring at each other.

The way his eyes flashed gave me chills.

He let go of my hips and reached around me. As soon as I heard the click of the door locking, he cupped my face with both hands.

"You're so fucking stubborn, Aaliyah," he uttered before covering my mouth with his. Feeling the sweet heat of his lips and knowing it was going to go somewhere, my body curved into his. As he deepened the kiss, his tongue grazed mine, and I hit my breaking point.

The desire I felt for him was too much, and I couldn't stop myself. I placed my hand on his dick. I didn't care about consequences. My fingers slipped between us, and as soon as they slid across the front of his pants, something animalistic took over the both of us.

"Shit," he groaned into my mouth.

The rumble in his chest made the throbbing between my thighs intensify.

I ran my hand up and down his erection as it strained against his pants. The thought of his dick and how big it felt had my entire body on edge.

Dipping his head, he pinned my shoulders against the door, and he suctioned his mouth to my waiting nipple. The wet heat made me moan as he alternated from one nipple to the other.

"Ahmad," I whispered wantonly.

"What did I tell you about saying my name like that?" he growled, crashing his mouth into mine.

I slipped my hand in his pants again. This time, I went inside his boxer briefs. The palm of my hand ran down his shaft before I squeezed gently, applying pressure. "I don't want to talk . . ."

He closed his eyes and let his head drop back momentarily as I pushed his boxer briefs down. "Fuck," he growled under his breath. "What do you want to do?"

He was so thick that my fingertips didn't touch as I held him, caressing him on my way down and then back up his full eight inches.

"You're going to have to say it?" He grabbed my face and kissed me softly. He pulled away from my lips and started trailing kisses across my jawline, down my neck, and over my shoulder. "I know what you want, but you're going to have to say it."

Panting as his hands slid up and down my body, I couldn't get my mind to work properly, let alone my voice box. The only thing that came out of me was a moan.

"Was this what you wanted, Aaliyah?" He lightly bit down on my nipple. "Or do you want more?"

"More."

"I can give you more," he whispered, grabbing my skirt. Pulling it up and gathering it at my waist, he squatted in front of me. "Hold this," he demanded, giving me the hem. "Is this what you needed?" He kissed me along my panty line. "Is this what you need from me?"

Oh, shit.

"What are you doing?" I asked breathily.

Licking his lips, he unclasped my bodysuit and then hooked his fingers in my panties.

"I'm going to spell out my apology with my tongue and make

you come on it." Yanking the G-string down roughly, he removed it and then looked up at me. "Is that okay with you?"

Unable to trust my voice, I nodded.

Never shifting his eyes from mine, he placed my leg over his shoulder and nuzzled his nose into me, inhaling deeply. "Mmmm . . . I need to hear you say it," he whispered against my bare flesh.

"Yes."

I saw the desire in his eyes as he buried his face between my thighs. Using his tongue, he opened me up and ran it over my slit.

"Oh. My. God." I buckled against the door, and my knees shook. With one hand gripping my skirt and the other on the back of his head, I rocked into his mouth.

My response only encouraged him as his tongue strategically toyed with me. When he sucked on my clit, I almost collapsed.

Moaning something into my pussy, he darted his tongue in and out of me before lavishing my clit again. Pleasure shot through my body, and I was already on the brink of losing control.

"Ahmad," I exhaled sharply. I held his head right where I needed it. "Yes. Yes. Yes. Right there. Right. There. Right. Fucking. There."

His face was buried in me, and his fingers dug into my thick thighs.

When he swirled his tongue in a steady rhythm, I just knew I was about to come on his handsome face. He was going to send me over the edge in record time.

I was about to let him know that I was almost there, but he stopped and stood.

"I was so close," I whined, opening my eyes.

"I'm going to take care of you." He lowered his voice and brushed his lips against mine. "And you're going to talk to me."

"No, I'm—"

"Spread your legs," he demanded.

My entire body clenched.

The anticipation to have him fill me up was like nothing I'd ever experienced. My heart pounded in my throat as I widened my stance. Using his middle finger, he massaged his way into me. Sliding in and out of my wetness, he curled his finger into my G-spot. I moaned loudly.

"I'm going to take care of you. I just need you to be quiet for me," he started, his voice low. "Can you do that for me?"

He pulled his finger out and rubbed my clit.

"Yes," I moaned loudly.

"Are you sure?" He slipped his finger back inside me. "The music isn't as loud back here. You don't want people to hear us, do you?"

His fingers were magic. I could barely concentrate on the words he was saying. "No," I squeaked, squeezing his bicep as I maintained my balance.

Leaning down so that his lips brushed against the shell of my ear, he whispered my name as he applied pressure and rubbed me. My fingernails dragged across his T-shirt until I fisted the collar.

"Ahmad," I gasped.

My breathing changed when I felt myself approaching the edge.

"You want me to make you come?" he asked as he toyed with me.

"Yes." The word came out choppy as I tried and failed to regulate my breathing.

"That's it. That's all you needed. You needed me to take care of this pretty pussy. You needed me to make you come . . ."

"Oh, shit," I panted before letting out an octave that I didn't even realize I could hit.

"You like that right there, don't you?" he teased lowly, pulling his fingers out of me and rubbing my juices over my sensitive clit. "You want me to let you come?"

"Yes," I panted.

"Listen to how wet you are," he growled as he dipped into me. I gyrated against his hand. He sucked in a sharp breath. "Do you want me to stop?"

"No," I exhaled. "Please don't stop."

"Then answer my question . . . Why did you ignore me?"

"Ahmad," I groaned.

"Why did you ignore me?" he asked as he kissed me, caressing his tongue against mine. "Why did you switch up on me?"

My body was like putty in his hands, and he knew it. It was almost manipulative to ask me anything while he was stroking me. The way he was kissing me and touching me almost had me saying things I didn't want to say.

So, I moved one of my hands down the front of him.

He sucked in a sharp breath, and his fingers stilled as my hand brushed against his dick.

"Talk to me. Tell me why," he rasped, one of his hands leaving my body.

"I don't know," I whimpered as he lightly caressed my clit.

"You're not being honest with me," he murmured. "So now I'm going to have to make you tell me."

He moved his lips over mine, and we kissed with reckless abandon. I wanted him so bad that I was starting to lose control. I was so focused on watching him, he caught me off guard when he spun me around. Bending me so my head was against the door and my ass was out, he stooped down and ate my pussy from the back.

It took two and a half seconds for me to come on his face.

He rose to his feet and pushed me against the door. He pinned me with his body and whispered, "You taste so fucking good." He kissed my neck. "But I didn't tell you that you could come yet." He kissed the spot behind my ear before flicking my earlobe with his tongue. "You don't seem like you're done yet. You have another one for me?"

My body was on fire. My pussy was quivering. I wanted him in the worst way.

"Yes," I answered breathily.

"You're ready to give it to me?"

"Yes."

"Good."

My breathing hitched as I felt his erection against me. Gripping the jamb, I rested my forehead against the wooden door. The sound of the music and the people outside of the office were drowned out by the sound of my heart racing.

Forcing my skirt up around my waist, he palmed my bare ass. He moved so I could feel his dick against my skin. "Is this what you want?"

"Yessss." I swallowed hard. I was damn near salivating.

"You want me to fuck you?"

I trembled in response. "Yes."

"Tell me." He kissed the space right behind my ear before trailing kisses down my neck. His lips brushed against my shoulder. Taking a step back, he placed his hand along my spine and bent me over. He lifted my skirt, grabbed my exposed hips tightly, and pressed his dick into my soft ass.

I closed my eyes. "Ahmad, please," I begged.

"I already know you do . . . I can tell by how wet this pussy is," he breathed as I felt him lining up against me.

The head of his dick pressed against my opening, and my breathing hitched.

Ahmad reached around and squeezed my nipple between his thumb and forefinger. "But I'm not going to give it to you until you're honest with me," he whispered.

My eyes flew open. "What?"

"Tell me what you want."

Squeezing my eyes shut, I held in a moan as he pushed the head of his dick into me.

"Tell me what I want to know," he demanded, digging his fingers into my skin as he restrained himself.

I was so wet that the pressure of him stretching me was a delicious pain.

"I'm not going to let you come until you tell me what I want to know," he grunted. His fingertips moved over my flesh as he leaned forward. He pressed his mouth against my ear. "I know how bad you need to come, and I know you can feel how bad I want to make you come." He gently bit down on my earlobe. "Tell me what you want."

Afraid of saying too much, I shook my head. "No." My voice was small and timid.

"Why are you so fucking stubborn?" Ahmad wondered softly as he slipped another inch inside me.

I didn't recognize the mewling sound that came out of me. Rolling my hips, I tried to force him in deeper.

"Nah," he denied me, smacking my ass and then rubbing the sore spot. "I need to know . . ."

"Please," I begged.

He groaned, and I felt his big dick get bigger.

"I want to fill this pussy up so bad, but you're not being honest with me." He slid almost all the way out of me. Holding my hips steady, he prevented me from grinding on him. "Tell me what you want, Aaliyah. If you want to come on my dick, you're going to have to be honest with me. Tell me what you want, Aaliyah."

His words sent a chill down my spine, and I shivered.

"You," I panted. "I want you."

"Fuck," he swore.

I felt his resolve weaken at my words.

"Say that shit again," he growled in my ear.

"I want you."

"Good." He kissed the back of my neck and then stood up straight. "Now let me show you how bad I want you."

He worked his way inside me. After every inch he pushed into me, he paused to let me adjust. The deeper he got, the more I disconnected from reality.

The only thing that existed was him.

The only thing I felt was pleasure.

The only thing I wanted was to come.

"Ahmad," I groaned, my eyes rolling into the back of my head.

He let out a low, guttural noise and stopped moving. He ran his hands up to my breasts, pinching my nipples and then returning his hands to my ass. "You feel so fucking good."

I shuddered as I gave in to the ecstasy of being stretched out and completely filled.

Grinding my hips against him, I worked myself up and down his shaft. The rapid bursts of air from his ragged breathing coupled with the sound of my wetness, intensifying the moment for me.

With my palms flat against the door, I let my head dangle languidly. He moved in and out of me until I felt the tension tighten my entire lower body. Everything he said, did, and touched was exactly what I needed when I needed it.

"Dammit, Aaliyah." His voice was hoarse and needy. "Shit."

"Yes, Ahmad. Right there. Right there."

"Oh, shit," he groaned softly, flexing his fingers against my hips and picking up the pace.

He slapped my ass as it bounced noisily against his thighs.

"Please don't stop," I begged in the throaty purr that seemed to do something to him. "Please."

"Shiiiiiiiiiiiiiit."

His strokes consistently hit the right spot, and my body was loving each and every second of it.

"Yes, yes, yes, yes."

I wasn't doing a good job at keeping my moaning under control. I tried my best to hold it together, but I felt myself coming undone as soon as he picked up the pace.

"Please. Don't. Stop," I pleaded.

He sucked in air sharply. "Goddammit, Aaliyah," he swore under his breath. "You're so fucking wet."

As he continued to thrust his hips, I threw my ass back to meet him. Each swear, each groan, each grunt from Ahmad added to my building orgasm. Even though we were trying not to make any noise, our bodies were getting louder.

My knees buckled, and I cried out.

"Oh, you like that, Aaliyah?" he growled.

As I moaned in ecstasy, my muscles clenched, and I started clamping down around him.

"Fuck," he hissed as he continued to hit my spot. "That's it. Let me have it. Let me feel it. Come on this dick. Give it to me, Aaliyah."

I gasped as the fluttering feeling deep in my core detonated.

My back arched, and my body shook. The ache deep inside me exploded as I felt his throbbing dick and heard the raspy need in his voice.

My damp thighs quivered, and I collapsed against the door just as he pulled out of me.

A sexy guttural grunt burst out of him as he slumped against me. I watched as his seed splattered on the concrete floor between my legs. He spread kisses all over my back as he pulled me against him.

With our bodies still buzzing, our heavy, satiated breathing filled the room.

He kissed my shoulder and neck. "That was—"

The firm knock against the door reverberated through my body, and I was sure my eyes were as wide as his. Panic replaced the sexual high I was on as the sound of someone at the door startled us apart.

22

Scrambling away from the door, I frantically snapped my bodysuit in place and then pushed my skirt down to cover myself. Ahmad wiped my juices from his mouth and beard, and although his face appeared dry, his beard was shinier. Tucking his semihard dick back into his underwear, he yanked his pants up and buckled his belt.

Another round of knocks, and then the doorknob jiggled again.

Putting his finger to his lips, he indicated for me not to speak.

I made a face and nodded. *What else was I going to do besides be quiet?*

My birthday was the next day, and I had no intention of rolling into my thirties in jail. I had no interest in a public lewdness charge and being held in lockup on the weekend of my party. I wasn't even completely sure what we did was a crime, but I knew that if someone walked in on us, it would've been a problem. I glanced up at Ahmad and saw the contrition in his expression.

He grabbed a bunch of tissues and wiped the evidence of our lust from in front of the door. The damp spot on the floor no longer looked like what it was, but it certainly left a mark.

After tossing the tissues in the trash, he put his ear to the door. After listening for about thirty seconds, he turned to me.

Staring at my lips and then my eyes, he uttered, "Let's give it a minute."

Swallowing hard, I nodded. "Okay."

After a moment of silence, he said, "It drove me crazy to see you with him."

His admission made the air in the room seem thicker. Our mouths gravitated toward each other. His breath on my face made my skin tingle. His words made the rest of my body tingle.

"Is that why you followed me?" I wondered breathily.

"Yes." He nodded, his lips just barely brushing mine. "To tell you he's not right for you."

"Oh?"

"He's not your guy." His lips lingered against mine. "And I can tell by the way you came all over me that you know he's not your guy, too."

A rueful smile tugged at the corner of my mouth.

"And I saw him running his game on you, and that shit looked like it was starting to work," he continued. He shook his head, causing his nose to rub against mine. "I had to stop it."

His words hit me in layers.

The raw emotion and intense conviction in his words, his tone, his expression was sexy. But it felt like jealousy was all there was to it.

And that didn't sit right with me.

At all.

My best friends had pointed out that Ahmad seeing me with someone like Ty would make him jealous. And I knew that because I was keeping my distance, he was going to be in his feelings. But the idea of his jealousy that boosted my ego as I got dressed for my date and the reality of his jealousy spawning the best sexual experience of my life was vastly different.

The sinking feeling that consumed me was overwhelming, and my smile melted as the realization hit me.

I was about to respond when the door rattled again, followed by a knock. "Ahmad?!"

"It's Asia," he whispered, checking his watch. "It's been twenty minutes, so I have to get back out there. We still need to talk, though."

"Oh, shit," I hissed, my eyes widening. "Twenty minutes? I have to get back out there."

He leaned back and assessed me. "Back to imitation Shaw Lockwood? That's not your guy."

I quirked an eyebrow. "Maybe not, but it's still rude. I should at least—"

"You don't owe him anything."

My brows crinkled. "I know I don't. But it's common decency."

"So, you're going back out there? To him?"

"Yes. It's the right thing to do." I studied his face. My heart thumped vigorously as the wheels in my head turned. "You really pulled me in here just to get me away from him, didn't you?"

"Yes."

"So, you saw me walk away and you followed me, dragging me in here and . . ." I licked my lips as a chill ran down my spine as I thought about the sex.

Before I could finish my statement, he replied, "I had to stop it. I had to stop you from making a mistake. He's not your guy."

Flashing back to something he'd said before, I felt sick. "By any means necessary."

He nodded. "By any means necessary."

"Wow," I muttered under my breath, reaching for the door handle.

"Whoa, what?" He looked perplexed as he lifted his hands in surrender. "What was that?"

"Nothing," I told him, shaking my head. "It doesn't matter. I have to go."

"Aaliyah, we still need to talk—"

"I have to go."

"Aaliyah," he growled as I swung the door open.

Asia stood wide-eyed with her keys in hand. "I, uh . . . Oh, um . . . Well, damn!"

Surprised, I was frozen in place.

Looking from me to Ahmad, she took a step back. "A man in baggy jeans and a loose-neck T-shirt fell over and had to be escorted out by security. But don't worry, big bro, I took care of it while you were taking care of Aaliyah." She cocked her head to the side. "Very professional."

My face heated with embarrassment. I didn't know what to say, so I shook my head. "Sorry, I have to go," I said, finally getting over the shock.

"I knew you two had feelings for each other," Asia snickered.

"We were talking," Ahmad started to explain.

Ignoring them both, I quickly walked away. Maneuvering through the crowd, I found my way back to Tyrone.

"Hey," I greeted him, placing a hand on his shoulder. "I'm not feeling too well."

Ty's face went from annoyed to sympathetic. "What's wrong? It wasn't the nachos, was it?"

"I'm not sure, but I just want to thank you for a nice time. I'm going to head out. I have a car coming."

"Hey, hey, hey . . ." He stood up and pulled cash out of his pocket. "I'm not going to let you walk out of here by yourself. What kind of man would that make me?" Looking over his shoulder, he signaled for someone.

When I saw who it was, my stomach lurched.

"What's up?" Ahmad asked. "What can I get for you?"

"The bill," Ty answered just as the live band started playing. "We're about to head out."

"You're leaving?" Ahmad shifted his eyes to me. "Really?"

"Yeah," Ty answered.

"I need to get out of here," I said at the same time.

"I can send your waiter over with the bill," Ahmad replied through clenched teeth.

Ty shook his head, handing him three fifties. "It's cool, man. This should cover it. I need to get this beautiful woman home."

His face hardened as he took the money. "Okay, then."

I started to explain. "Well, it's—"

"The sooner we get this paid for, the sooner I can get you home," Ty interrupted me, grabbing my hand.

Before I could react, Ahmad was already stalking his way back to the bar.

I sighed, sliding my hand from Ty's. "I'm sorry. I need to leave now."

"I'm only parked a couple blocks that way." He pointed in the opposite direction of my building. "I'll get my change and then take you home."

"It's okay." I held up my phone. "My ride is already here, and I'm"—I put my other hand to my twisted gut—"not feeling well."

He nodded with understanding. "Okay, I'll get my change and settle up, and then I'll call you and check on you." He stepped up and brought me in for a hug. "It was good to put a beautiful face to a beautiful voice."

I hugged him back. "Thank you. It was very nice meeting you."

"You sure you don't need me to walk you out? If you give me five minutes—"

I pulled away from him. "I'm sure. My ride is right outside. You get home safely."

Our waiter came over with the check, interrupting our conversation. As Ty explained that he'd given the money to someone else, I said a quick goodbye and then darted out of the bar.

I didn't want Ty to come out and see me crossing the street, so I made a beeline to the first available taxi I saw. I needed to make a quick grocery run anyway, so I went to the store to clear my mind. Forty minutes later, I was being dropped off in front of my building with five bags' worth of snacks.

"Ayeeeeeeeeeee!" A woman who appeared to be about the same age as me held the door open as I approached. "Okay, outfit! Okay, hair!"

I grinned, nodding toward her dress because my hands were full of bags. "I see you, sis!"

"I see *you*!"

"Thank you," I told her as I passed her. "Enjoy your night!"

"I sure will. That's why I'm wearing these heels."

"And you look good in them!"

The brief interaction with the woman put me in such a positive headspace. I'd spent the last forty-five minutes stewing over my week. In a seven-day period, I'd had a falling-out with Ahmad, a pseudo breakup with Lennox, and a promising date with Ty that ended after I had sex with Ahmad in the middle of it. *Is it me? Am I the problem?* I wondered as I entered my apartment. *Because what is happening?*

Pouring a glass of wine, I put the groceries away and concluded that it wasn't me.

Ahmad pretended to be married . . . only to tell me that it was a decoy because he wasn't looking to date . . . only to fuck me in the back office because he got jealous.

Lennox liked to hear himself talk . . . and he forgot my birthday.

Ty seemed cool, and I still found myself distracted.

Ahmad was the common denominator. Ahmad was the problem.

He was supposed to look out for me. He was supposed to help me in my dating journey. He was supposed to be my friend.

"I should've just left the bar that day," I muttered as I poured a second glass. "If I would've gotten up and left after being stood up, I wouldn't be dealing with any of this bullshit."

The longer I thought about that, the madder I got.

But when I looked at the clock, I refused to enter my thirtieth birthday in a bad mood.

I inhaled, filling my lungs with air, and then I exhaled everything that was bothering me. I tried to expel the thought of Ahmad, but the soreness I was experiencing made it difficult. And even acknowledging the soreness made me remember how good he felt and how hard I came. The myriad of emotions he evoked in me made me feel off-kilter.

I needed to center myself.

I put on some music, drew a bubble bath, and lit some candles. Sinking into the water, I didn't have much room to lounge the way I wanted to. But the bubbles were nice, and the vibe was relaxing. When the clock struck midnight, I was bombarded with text messages and calls. Smiling, I responded to each of them.

"Happy birthday!" Jazmyn and Nina yelled in unison as soon as I answered the phone.

"Thank you!" I told them.

"We had a whole thing we were going to do on your voicemail," Jazz stated. "We didn't expect you to answer the phone."

I lifted my foot and used my big toe to add more hot water. "When have you known me to bring a stranger to my place?" As they agreed, I continued, "Besides, my date ended a couple hours ago."

"Okay, so details," Nina insisted. "How was the date with that fine-ass superhero?"

"Superhero?" Jazz laughed. "What did I miss?"

"I saw his picture, and he immediately reminded me of that actor Shaw Lockwood!"

While Jazz reacted and demanded a picture, the mention of Shaw Lockwood made me think of Ahmad.

"So, what happened?" Nina asked me. "I know you said you weren't going to bring Tyrone home tonight, but did he qualify for birthday dick?"

Placing my phone on the ledge of the tub, I reclined back so my head hit the tile behind me. "No. I don't think so."

"How did he blow it?" Jazz asked.

"It wasn't him . . ." I closed my eyes. Flashes of moments in that office with Ahmad flickered like a highlight reel. I shook my head, hoping to stop seeing it . . . and feeling it. I cleared my throat before I continued, "It was me."

"You blew it?" Jazz's confusion was evident. "How? Why?"

"It was the bartender, wasn't it?" Nina speculated.

Using my toe to add more water to the tub, I remained quiet.

"It was!" they yelled in unison.

"I don't know what happened," I began, my stomach twisting as I started to tell them the story. "Ty looks even better in person than he did in his pictures. He brought me roses." I gasped. "The roses! I left them at the table."

"He got you roses, and you left them? And you enjoyed talking to him, but you ended the date early?" Jazz paused. "Are you okay?"

"No!" I wailed, covering my face with my hand. "I was enjoying my date with Ty. He was saying the right things. He was being respectful, but he was giving me that look that let me know that he could get *real* disrespectful if I asked him to. He asked me questions, remembered things about me, and wanted to stay and enjoy the live music with me."

"This sounds like your dream date," Jazz commented.

"And then Ahmad happened," I continued.

"I knew it!" Nina yelled.

"The petty part of me was enjoying the fact that Ahmad was in his feelings," I admitted. "I was enjoying my date, enjoying the attention he was giving me. And then every time I looked at the bar, there was Ahmad—staring dead at us."

Nina cackled. "I love it. I live for it."

"So, what happened next?" Jazz probed impatiently.

"I was doing what I said I was going to do. I ignored him. I gave my time and attention to my date and minded my business. And then I thought I might have food in my teeth, so I excused myself before the performer came onstage. The line to the bathroom was long, so I walked back out and . . ." I squeezed my legs together and shifted in the water. "Ahmad was there."

"Oop!" Nina reacted.

"He wanted to talk. I told him we didn't have anything to talk about. He grabbed me and pulled me into an office down the hallway, and we got into it. I said some things. He said some things. He apologized. I didn't accept his apology, but I . . . I guess he made some points."

"Like?" Jazz pressed.

"Like the fact that he didn't feel the need to explicitly tell me about his marital status, because he only saw me when I was on dates."

"That's true," Nina agreed. "Shit. He's got you there."

"Yeah," I sighed. "So I don't know what happened, but before I knew it, we were kissing."

"Holy shit!" Jazz screeched. "You two kissed?!"

"And his hands were all over me and mine were all over him, and"—I squeezed my thighs to relieve some pressure—"then he asked me if I needed to come."

"What?!" Nina screamed.

"And I did." I shook my head in shame. "So, he made me."

I wasn't embarrassed to tell my friends what happened. They were my best friends in the world, and they wouldn't judge me. The shame I felt was because I made rash decisions that I didn't usually make. Even in the past when I was sexually frustrated, I would figure something else out.

I never had random hookups.

I never had unprotected sex.

I never had sex with anyone who didn't have feelings for me.

I never had sex with someone when I was supposed to be on a date with another man.

Everything I did was out of character. But from the way my pussy throbbed at the thought of what happened, I knew if I had it to do all over again, I'd do it in a heartbeat.

"You and the bartender? Holy shit! I see those pent-up sex consequences turned into successes!" Nina cheered. "I knew it! I knew it! I fucking knew it! I have questions . . . Was it good? Would you do it again?"

"Wait, wait, wait, wait, wait . . . I have questions, too. How did you two not get caught? Where were the other people who worked in the bar?"

"His dad owns the bar, and I think the only people with keys to that office are him and his sister. I don't know if anyone heard, but we didn't get caught. I mean, we kind of did. His sister saw us coming out of the office afterward, but she doesn't know for a fact what happened," I answered.

There was a moment of silence. "So, you're not going to answer my questions?" Nina burst out.

"I don't regret doing it, but that was so irresponsible and reckless. I should not have done it. And if I had better control over my body, I wouldn't have."

Jazz laughed. "I guess that answers one of your questions, Nina."

I closed my eyes as my best friends laughed at me. "It was the best sex I've ever had in my life," I confessed quietly. "I'm literally sitting in a tub now trying to forget the impression he left on my body."

They were loudly hooting and hollering, and if I wasn't in distress, I would've been amused.

I answered their questions, and when their excited confusion was satiated and their questions were answered, I finished the story. "And then he pulled out, and a couple minutes later, there was a knock at the door. It was his sister. His break was over, and she was looking for him."

"Wait, wait, wait, wait, wait . . . He pulled out? Does that mean you had unprotected sex?" Jazmyn asked, putting the context clues together.

"Not Aaliyah James," Nina hollered. "Not Aaliyah James getting it raw from the sexy-ass bartender! Not Aaliyah James getting it raw from the sexy-ass bartender while on a date with the sexy-ass superhero!"

"Not Aaliyah James having a Nina Ford kind of night," Jazmyn added.

"Hell yeah! That's my girl!" Nina cheered.

Begrudgingly, I laughed at their outbursts.

"But it won't happen again," I told them.

"You wanted birthday sex. You got pre-birthday sex," Jazmyn pointed out. "And you said it was good—"

"No, no," Nina interrupted. "She said it was the best sex of her life. The. Best. So help me understand, since this man you said was a great friend with great energy—and, Jazz, you haven't seen him, but the man is a ten—gave you the best sex of your life—which means the dick was a ten, too—how and why are you not going to do it again? Why are you starting your thirties off making bad decisions?"

"He only fucked me because he was jealous," I explained.

"I've seen the way that man looks at you," Nina countered. "There's no way he only fucked you because he was jealous."

I shook my head even though they couldn't see me. "He admitted that he only came and got me because he didn't like seeing me with Ty."

"He said that?" Jazz wondered skeptically.

"Yes." I pulled the plug to drain the water. "And I asked again for clarification, and he doubled down. He said he wanted to stop me from making a mistake or a bad decision or something like that. He said Ty wasn't the guy for me, because before I got there, he was hitting on someone. And then he proceeded to give me what I needed so I didn't get it from Ty." There was a tightness in my chest that made me uncomfortable. I cleared my throat. "So yeah, his sole reason for everything that happened was because he was jealous."

"Well, we knew he was going to be jealous," Jazmyn reasoned. "You'd been ignoring him, and he's been wanting you all summer. But do you really think that was the only reason?"

"Yes." I pursed my lips and sat up in the empty tub. "Mainly because he said so." I rose to my feet and repositioned the phone. "But also because he said he wasn't interested in dating."

"But how did it feel?" Nina asked. "He said what he said, but people can say anything. How did it feel?"

It felt good.

It felt natural.

It felt right.

Swallowing hard, I turned the shower on and let the water rain down on me.

"Hold on!" I yelled out as I closed the curtain to keep the phone dry.

I rinsed my body off as I listened to my best friends recap what I'd told them. When I turned the shower off, I opened the curtain to grab my towel and the phone.

"It doesn't matter how it felt," I finally answered. "The sex was good. But he and I are on completely different wavelengths. If he were interested in something more, it would've come up. It never did. And that's fine. But I know exactly what I'm looking for, and a random hookup isn't it. So, it won't happen again."

"What if—?"

I cut the question off before it could get started.

"It's my birthday," I announced. "I have some questions for you . . . Who are you bringing to the party? And what are you wearing?"

There was a pause.

"Not everyone speak at once," I joked.

"It's, um . . ." Jazz stumbled over her words.

"Oh, so when I was in the hot seat, questions were slipping off the tongue. Now that the tables are turned, the cat's got yours."

Nina laughed.

"You, too, Nina," I replied. "What's going on with you? Who are you bringing?"

"I'm just bringing a friend," she answered.

"A friend you're fucking?" I asked.

"It's complicated."

"Mm-hmm," I intoned. "All of a sudden, everything is complicated."

We laughed.

"Okay, before we give it a rest, serious question . . . What are you doing about your date tomorrow?" Nina wondered.

"Well, I guess I'm going to have to show up alone and entertain Marcus."

"Wait, wait, wait, wait, wait . . . Who is Marcus?" Jazz asked boisterously.

"He's the man my family has been trying to hook me up with," I reminded them. "He's the son of my mom's friend from church. Remember the guy from Aniyah's memorial party? My mom invited him to the party, and the family is still hell-bent on setting me up with him. It was a whole thing."

"Oh, I remember," Nina uttered.

"So, what are you going to tell your parents tomorrow?" Jazz inquired.

"My mom and I have our appointment to get our nails done in the morning, so I'm just going to tell her the truth."

"It's about damn time!" Nina clapped. "I'm proud of you."

"I'm going to talk to my mom at our appointment, and then you'll both be able to see the fallout when we get to the lake house."

"Birthday fallout . . . ?" Jazz quipped. "Let's not claim that energy."

"There will be no fallout," Nina said confidently. "It'll be a happy birthday."

"No, it will be," I whispered. "I feel it."

"I have one more question about the dick . . ." Nina started.

I sighed. "What?"

"You always said Matthew was top-tier dick. Was Ahmad better than Matthew?"

Throbbing, my pussy answered before I did. "Matthew who?"

23

I woke up before the sun on the morning of my birthday. Even though I was awake, I couldn't move. There was a weight on my chest that felt like it was pinning me down. Groggily, I tried to push myself up, but I was still unable to move. Fear started to nag at me, but then suddenly, a calmness washed over me, and my body relaxed.

Fuck what everyone else has to say. Never let anyone get in the way of you being you.

Gasping, I jolted up in bed. My bonnet was left behind on the pillow as I whipped my head back and forth. My heart pounded, and I put my hand to my chest to calm it down.

It was my sister's voice.

It wasn't a dream. Loud and clear, I heard my sister's voice.

The first voice I heard on the morning of my thirtieth birthday was hers.

Slowly, I reclined against the pillow and let Aniyah's words run through my head again and again. Her voice had faded, and it was only my voice in my head. But it was her words.

Fuck what everyone else has to say.

"You're right, sis," I whispered, teary-eyed.

It was my life. It was about me. It was about what I wanted. It was my birthday for goodness' sake.

I'd been internally counting down until my thirtieth birthday for the last five years. I'd been stressed to find a boyfriend for my party for the last two months. I'd been worked up about the situation with Ahmad for the last two weeks. So, to wake up hearing my sister's advice on my birthday lit a fire under me.

My mom and I had a birthday tradition of getting our hair and nails done followed by lunch on the Saturday closest to my birthday. But because we were on a time crunch and planned to get to the lake house by five o'clock, we'd planned to meet at a restaurant near the salon. Inspired by my sister, I arrived at the restaurant ready to get a few things off my chest.

Since Aniyah died, it was always just the two of us. So, I was surprised when I arrived at the restaurant and saw my father as well.

"Hey!" I greeted them, giving them both big hugs before sitting down.

"Happy birthday!" they cheered in unison.

"Thank you." I looked between them. "How's everything?"

We made small talk for a few minutes while we reviewed the menus. I already knew I was getting the chicken and waffles, but I still looked. We were all pretty much creatures of habit when it came to breakfast foods. Dad was getting the steak and eggs. Mom was getting the pancakes, bacon, and eggs. They were going to get coffee that they were going to complain about, and then they were going to reminisce about their trip to Colombia, where they had the best coffee of their lives, as they sipped their water with lemon.

"I know what I'm getting," my dad announced.

My mom nodded. "Me, too."

I looked between the two of them as they stacked their menus. "So, what's going on? Dad, you're coming to get your hair and nails done, too?"

"No, no," he chuckled. "Just haven't seen much of you lately, and I wanted to tag along for the breakfast portion of the day."

I smiled and nodded. "Well, I'm glad you're both here. There's something I wanted to talk to you about."

"What can I get for you folks?" the waitress asked.

We placed our orders and then we were left alone.

"What's on your mind, Aaliyah?" Dad questioned. A concerned look crossed his face as he sat up on his side of the table.

My mom leaned forward, reaching for my hand. "Is everything okay?"

I squeezed her hand, then clasped my hands in my lap. "I wanted to talk to you about today."

"It's about the boyfriend thing, isn't it?" my mom guessed.

I looked her in her eyes and sat back in my seat.

"I don't have a boyfriend," I started. "Part of the reason I told y'all I had one was because I was tired of the conversation, I wanted it to be over, and I wasn't happy that you invited Marcus to my party without my permission."

"Oh, Aaliyah!" Mom exclaimed. "You didn't have to lie to us about that. And you don't have to explain anything."

"No, we need to have this talk," I told them. "You mentioned how we hadn't seen much of each other this summer. And yes, I've been busy. But the main reason is because I need you both to heal from what happened to Aniyah."

"What do you mean? Losing a child isn't something you just get over," Mom argued tearfully.

"Aaliyah . . ." Dad started to say, but his sentence trailed off.

My eyes started to water, but I blinked back tears. "I don't know what it's like to lose a child. But I know what it's like to lose a sister. The pain may be different. The ways in which it affects your life are definitely different. But it's painful all around. And there's trauma with that. And trauma needs healing." I ran my palms over my jean-covered thighs. "I'm not saying you should just get over it and move on. All I'm saying is that you have to heal because I'm enough. All by myself. I'm enough."

"Oh, honey!" My mom's hands flew to her cheeks. "We know! We would never say otherwise. You're enough. You're more than enough. We love you."

I shook my head. "Please listen to me. I'm not saying you don't love me. I'm saying that I'm enough. How I live my life is enough. What I choose to do and not to do is enough. My choices and the timing of my choices are enough."

"We know that," my dad said slowly.

I shook my head. "I don't think you do." I exhaled. "For the last five years, you've been comparing me to Aniyah. You've been hoping that I give you what she gave you. You've been wanting me to fill the void that she filled. And I know you were looking forward to being grandparents. But you have to understand that I'm not Aniyah's replacement. I'm not going to get married and have children in order to replace the child you lost, the grandchild you lost."

I saw the tears in my mom's eyes, and I almost lost my nerve, but I continued.

"At some point over the last five years, you stopped wanting me to be me and you started wanting me to be Aniyah. And I'm not her. I'll never be her. And I want you to be okay with that."

My mom opened her mouth to speak, but I shook my head and kept going. "I don't have a boyfriend, and I don't know when I'm getting married. I don't know when or if I'm having kids. But I'm enjoying my life. I'm enjoying dating and taking my time. Aniyah found her person and then married him. She did things the way you would've done it if you were her. And that's fine. That's amazing. But that's not me. That's not for me. That's not my life. That's not what I want. And if this summer has taught me anything, it's that I'm not ever going to be Aniyah, and I was never supposed to be."

"We love you, Aaliyah. We just want you to be happy," Mom told me.

"Then let me be me. Freely. Without your commentary and judgment," I replied firmly. "And I'm going to be honest with you . . . what happened at the memorial really bothered me."

"Your uncle was out of line—" Dad started.

"Yes, he was. But I'm talking about what I found out about the two of you. It made me realize that I wasn't just imagining things or being sensitive. You've been wanting me to live Aniyah's life despite what I want. It didn't used to be like this. Over the last few years, I noticed the change, but I didn't think it was that deep. Until Uncle Al said what he said."

"I'm sorry it came across like we don't think you're enough. That's far from the truth," Mom noted. She looked at my dad, who was nodding, and then she looked back at me. "Our conversation was about us trying to figure out if being grandparents was in the cards for us. But you're right . . . even though our conversation was about us, it was centered around you and your choices."

"You two may have to come to terms with the fact that you may not be grandparents anytime soon. You have to grieve what you lost and then live in the moment. You can't put the pressure on me to be Aniyah's replacement, because that's not what I want and that's not going to be good for any of us."

The tears ran down my mother's cheeks as my truth hit her. My dad's glassy eyes seemed to hold back the emotion my mom couldn't contain.

"We want you to be you, Aaliyah," my dad choked out as he put his hand on my mother's hand.

"We love you, and we just want you to be happy," my mom added.

I took a deep breath. "I love you both so much, and I want you to know that my happiness isn't tied to being with a man or racing to the altar or having children. My happiness is tied to me living a life that I love and am proud of. My happiness is centered around me and what I want."

They nodded.

"So I need you two to heal from Aniyah's death." I swallowed hard. "Because I'm working on my own healing with her death, too."

Confusion flickered across their faces. "I thought you got over your issue with water," Dad stated in a low tone.

I shook my head. "No, not that."

My mom dabbed the corners of her eyes and then tearfully asked, "Is there something else going on?"

"I have a job I love, a life I love, and even still, I kept feeling like it was important for me to find the right man before today. Ever since Aniyah died, I've been feeling like I've had an expiration date on my head. For the last five years, I moved with the general thought that I had until thirty before it might be over for me, too," I admitted. "I didn't realize I felt that way until I was talking to someone about trauma and trauma responses."

"You thought . . . You thought you were going to . . ." My mom mouthed the word *die* before covering her mouth.

"I thought . . ." I let out a contemplative noise as I tried to sum it up for them. "It was more of a feeling than an expressed thought. It felt like I only had as much time as Aniyah, and I didn't know what life looked like beyond thirty." I looked between them and then started from the beginning. "But I realized the big, expensive party, the search for the boyfriend, the mental countdown that was ticking was all because I tied thirty to Aniyah . . . and her death . . . and . . ." I closed my eyes for a moment so I didn't cry. "My own death."

"Oh, Aaliyah!" my mom cried.

"I woke up this morning ready to release all of that baggage I was carrying. So I'm letting you know that I'm not bringing a date with me to my party. I'm not interested in a setup. I just want to live my life. And when I meet the man I want to be with, I'll let you know. Can you handle that?"

"We can handle that," my dad said with a firm nod.

"We can," my mom added quickly. "That's fair."

"And if Uncle Al—"

"I'll take care of Uncle Al," Dad replied. "Don't you worry about that."

I still planned on having my own conversation with him, but I appreciated the protectiveness.

I cleared my throat to keep my voice from breaking. "From now on, my life is about me."

"Now these plates are hot," the waitress said, placing the food on the table between us.

We ate breakfast rather quietly for the next few minutes. Although the conversation we had was heavy, it wasn't an uncomfortable silence. It was as if we were all just in a contemplative space. It wasn't until the waitress came back with the coffee for my parents that our conversation resumed.

"You know this coffee is terrible," Dad commented as he took another sip.

"No coffee will ever top the coffee we had in Colombia," Mom reminisced. Turning to me, she said, "You have to make a trip to Colombia for the views and for the coffee."

The rest of our breakfast resumed like any ordinary morning. When we finished eating, my father paid, and then we walked outside together.

Rubbing his belly, my dad yawned loudly. "Oh, man, I need to get a nap in so I can keep up with the young folks tonight."

I pointed at him. "You need to just worry about keeping up with Mom."

He laughed. "Shonuff." Pulling me into a hug, he held me tighter and longer than usual. "I love you, Aaliyah. Happy birthday."

"I love you, too, Dad. Thank you." I gave him a squeeze back and then released my arms.

He was still holding on.

"Dad?" I whispered.

Clearing his throat, he took a step back and nodded. "I'll see you tonight."

"See you tonight."

My mom was wiping her eyes when I looked at her.

"Don't make me cry," she stated, wagging her finger at me. "I'll meet you at the salon. Make sure Kim knows I'm here."

"Okay, I will."

I walked to the end of the block where the salon was located, and before entering, I glanced back at my parents. The two of them were hugging and comforting each other. If I were to guess, my mom was shedding tears and my dad was holding his back. It was hard to see them crying, but it was good to know that they heard what I was saying to them.

"Welcome to Hair Love," Kim greeted me as soon as I walked through the door.

"Hi!" I lifted my hand in a wave. "I'm here for Serena."

Four hours later, my hair was done, my nails and toes were done, and I was back in my apartment getting my stuff together to leave. I'd known what I was wearing for weeks, so it didn't take long to pack. It was the fact that I didn't realize until that moment that I still had Ahmad's jacket. Just seeing it caused my entire body to react. I tried to shake it off, but it was taking a little more time. It was much easier to shake it off when I was just imagining what he felt like versus having carnal knowledge of what he felt like.

I need to focus.

I put it back in the bag that I'd hidden it in and tossed it to the side.

"Okay, I have my shower stuff, my makeup, my dresses, my sleepwear, my shoes, my bag, my—oh!"

Rushing to the dresser, I grabbed a couple of cute bra-and-panty sets and also both bathing suits. I still didn't know if I was going to do more than dip my feet in the lake, but I remembered that there was a hot tub on the second floor.

"I'm all set," I whispered to myself.

Grabbing all the bags, I carried them to the car, turned up the music, and then made my way to my uncle's house. It was on the way to Dowdy Lake, and even though I didn't have much time, I didn't plan to be there long.

Pulling into the long driveway of the small home near the woods, I parked behind my uncle's truck.

"Happy birthday!" Uncle Al greeted me with a huge grin as he eased from his seat on the porch. "What are you doing here?"

"I just came to talk," I started, sliding my hands into my pockets. "Do you have a few minutes?"

"For you, of course. Come on up here." He waited until I climbed the steps to the porch before he added, "Sit in the rocking chair. It's sturdier."

I pursed my lips. "I'll stand."

He chuckled and shrugged. "Suit yourself." He sat down on the porch swing. "What's on your mind?"

"I didn't appreciate what you said at Aniyah's memorial," I blurted out.

His eyebrows drew together in confusion. "What? About you not really having a boyfriend?"

I nodded. "Yeah, and—"

"Well, do you?"

"No, and that's not the point—"

He chuckled and shook his head. "I knew it! I knew it!" He clapped his hands together. "You ain't have to come all the way over here to apologize."

Taken aback, I made a face. "I didn't come here to apologize to you. I came here to give you an opportunity to apologize *to me*. Because what you said was messed up."

"I—"

"No, I'm not finished," I interjected, my frustration evident. "Your jokes about my weight, your comparing me to Aniyah, your comparing me to Macy, your thoughts and opinions about my love life need to stop now! I'm not going to be made to feel uncomfortable about how I look, what I do, how I move, who I date, and the choices I make because you have a problem with it. This is my life!"

"I love you, and I'm trying to help you," he said gruffly. "I just want you to be happy and healthy."

"And who says I'm not?!"

He gestured to my body. "You're a pretty girl, but your weight—"

"Uncle Al, I weigh less than you," I snapped.

Putting his hand on his hip, he didn't say anything, but he frowned.

"So, not only are these comments unnecessary, but they're also hypocritical," I continued. "What I weigh is my business, so stop it!"

"I don't understand how you don't see that I'm just looking out for you. You're thirty now. You ain't got no prospects for marriage. If you don't lock something down now—"

"That's my business!" I yelled, throwing my arms up. Taking a deep breath, I exhaled audibly and calmed myself down. "Uncle Al, my life is mine. How I live my life is my business."

"I'm just worried about you."

"You should worry about yourself. I'm fine. There's nothing for you to worry about."

"You don't have no one to take care of you."

"I can take care of myself."

He let out a noisy sigh and waved his hand in the air. "That's what Macy said, too," he muttered.

"My life isn't over at thirty. My life doesn't revolve around me getting married and having children. When I meet the man I want to be with forever, I'll marry him. Until then, I'm fine."

"You're thirty."

"I would rather choose right the first time than just get with someone because I'm thirty." I gave him a look. "As someone who has been married three times, I thought you could appreciate that."

"That's even more of a reason to listen to me. I asked three women to be my wife. All of them slim—"

"And since their slimness didn't keep y'all together, I would say your points are irrelevant," I interrupted.

"But their slimness got them proposed to." He rubbed his hands together. "I'm just trying to look out for you. You don't solve problems by ignoring them," he said earnestly.

"Have you ever considered that I'm not the problem?" I narrowed my eyes at him. "You are."

"Well, I'll be!" he exclaimed indignantly. "You—"

"You are the problem. And if you can't admit that and change the behavior, you're not welcome at my birthday celebration tonight."

He looked offended and hurt. "I want the best for you, Aaliyah." I almost felt bad, and then he opened his mouth again. "And I'm scared being this"—he opened his arms out wide—"big is going to keep you from a good life."

"Keeping people around me who think like you do is the only thing that's going to keep me from a good life. So you can keep the yacht—"

"You need a man to be able to drive the yacht anyway."

I slow blinked. "You've got to be kidding me," I groaned in exasperation.

"You're being too sensitive."

"And you're not being sensitive enough. So like I said, you're uninvited." I turned on my heel and made my way down the steps. "Goodbye, Uncle Al."

"Aaliyah," he called out. "Don't be like that. I'm only saying this because I'm worried about you and I care about you."

Continuing to my car, I ignored him.

By the time I climbed inside and started the engine, he had made his way in the house. I had no doubt he was calling my mother or grandmother to tell them what had happened. And I was completely fine with that. I refused to celebrate my birthday with anyone who tried to make me feel bad about being me.

I reflected on the conversations I had with my family as I took the scenic route to Dowdy Lake. With each passing mile, I realized how much lighter I felt. A weight had been lifted from my shoulders. Saying what needed to be said to my parents and my uncle was the best gift I could've given myself. Because in my gut, I knew that no one would ever get in the way of me being me again.

With a huge smile on my face, I exhaled.

I felt a peace I hadn't felt since before Aniyah died.

"Oooooh," I murmured excitedly, looking around as I pulled onto the Dowdy Lake grounds.

The picturesque landscape was breathtaking. The houses that lined one side of the lake were beautifully crafted. The one I'd rented was a six-bedroom, seven-bathroom waterfront property with a firepit and the space for a table that seated thirty-two guests.

When I pulled up and saw the outdoor dance floor that had been constructed, I felt like it was worth the money.

"Happy birthday to me," I giggled to myself as I looked around.

I arrived early and placed all my belongings in the biggest bedroom located on the second floor. The two other bedrooms on the second floor were reserved for Nina and Jazz. I only needed three bedrooms, but I got one of the largest cabins for the number of bathrooms downstairs and the spacious living room and dining area. There were forty people who had RSVP'd for the dinner party and then about one hundred who said they were coming to the lake party at eight o'clock.

I hadn't thrown a big party since my high school graduation—and that didn't really count. That was more of a family reunion that happened to coincide with my graduation. But what was happening at Dowdy Lake was for me and about me. The decorator had turned the space into a shimmery black-and-green paradise. The caterer had the whole house smelling like my favorite foods. I looked at the clock impatiently.

Is it six o'clock yet?

"How many people are you expecting?" my dad joked as he walked through the door carrying bags at five o'clock.

"Well, if you and Mom hadn't announced I was having a party, maybe I could've shaved off twenty people," I retorted, grabbing a bag from his hand.

He laughed. "That was your mother."

"Why are you throwing me under the bus?" Mom's giggle followed as she teetered in, carrying a cake. "And I only invited six people—not twenty!"

"Are you guys sure you don't want to stay after the dinner?" I asked, pointing at one of the downstairs bedrooms. "If so, you can choose the room you want and put your stuff in there."

"No, no, no," Mom responded. "We will be getting out of here after dinner so you can enjoy your friends. We'll let you young folks do your thing. Your grandma wants you to come by the house tomorrow. Do you have plans when you leave here?"

"I can stop by for a few. How is she doing?"

"She still isn't feeling well. Your uncle decided it would be best for him to stay at the house and watch over her while we're here."

I pursed my lips. *That was* not *his idea.*

"And he gave us something to give to you," she continued. "I accidentally left the box at home. I called him and told him to bring it himself, but he insisted on keeping Mama company tonight."

"Mm-hmm, I think it's for the best," I pointed out. "Uncle Al's energy isn't the energy I need at my birthday party. I'm trying to celebrate."

"And celebrate we will." Dad started doing a little swivel of his hips. "I took my nap, so I can hang all night."

"We are leaving at a decent hour. I have to be at church very early tomorrow!" Mom protested. "If we're out all night, how am I supposed to explain that?"

"Well, God will already know why we're late."

"Darryl!"

It was clear he was trying to rile Mom up, so all I could do was laugh.

"Your hair . . . I like it!" my dad commented while Mom was

still huffing and puffing. He gave it a quizzical look and then smiled.

I touched the scarf covering the thick, long length of my natural hair in pin curls. My hair was going to give a lot of body once I removed the pins and styled it. But as it was, Dad couldn't see the vision.

"Once I take the scarf off and take these pins out, it'll look real good. But I appreciate the compliment, Dad."

"Okay, I didn't know what was going on," he chuckled good-naturedly.

Right after I showed them where to get dressed, I went upstairs and got myself ready.

My hair looked incredible. The emerald minidress with the plunging neckline looked good on my mocha-colored skin. The cut of the dress was sexy, but the structure was elegant. The dress I was changing into for the party after dinner was the exact same color but had a completely different vibe.

I twisted my lips, as I'd bought both dresses with the hope and expectation that someone was going to be ripping them off me. But since that wasn't the case, I needed the photographic evidence of how good I looked. I glanced from the dress that was on my body to the dress that was hanging on the door of the closet. Both dresses demanded for them to be pulled up or pulled off.

Like last night.

I shut my eyes and pushed the thought out of my mind.

I was about to be surrounded by my closest friends and family—plus Liz and Marcus. I was going to be celebrating the fact that I made it to thirty. I was about to be celebrating my new lease on life. I was about to be celebrating my newfound peace. I refused to let Ahmad infiltrate my thoughts and disrupt my peace.

"Today is about me," I reminded myself quietly as I heard my mom call my name.

It was six o'clock.

Showtime.

My four-inch crocodile-skin peep-toe stilettos weren't just the sexiest shoes I'd ever owned, they made my legs and ass look incredible. Unfortunately, they rubbed my heel. I just had to make it downstairs, pose, and then I'd be seated at the head of the table. But my heel felt rubbed raw by the time I hit the stairs.

Well, damn.

Mustering a smile, I made it down the staircase and to the landing. The applause I received momentarily made me forget that I'd lost my Achilles heel back on the third or fourth step.

"You look so good!"

"That dress is fire!"

"Okay, hair!"

"I see you!"

"Yasssssss, body!"

"You better show them how to do it!"

"Them shoes are it!"

"You better wear that dress!"

With laughter, I blew kisses and did a cute little curtsy. "Thank you, thank you, thank you."

I was swarmed by my family and friends. They were hugging me three and four people at a time. I couldn't stop smiling as I absorbed the quick hugs and abundance of love. I was being bombarded, so it caught me off guard when I turned around and saw him.

"We meet again," Marcus greeted me, pulling me into a tight hug. "You look beautiful, Aaliyah. Happy birthday."

"Marcus! Hi! Thank you," I replied. "Thank you for being here." I brushed his shoulder off. "You clean up nice."

He chuckled and then swept his hands down his light blue shirt. "I do what I can do. I appreciate you inviting me." He looked over to his mother, who was talking to mine. "I appreciate you allowing me to come even though our mothers have conspired for me to be here."

I snickered behind my hand. "Well, I hope you enjoy yourself, and I'm glad you could make it. That means I'm not the only one with my mom here."

He laughed. "True. And I'm not the only one with a mom who meddles."

"Facts! That's an absolute fact."

Someone walked by and grabbed my arm to tell me happy birthday. I thanked them, and when I turned back to Marcus, he was staring at me.

I smiled.

"Okay, so . . ." he started. "When we met a couple months ago, you were single. If that's still the case, I'd love to give you my number."

"Dinner service will begin in five minutes," the caterer announced. "Aaliyah, please report to the kitchen."

Everyone had scattered to different bathrooms to wash their hands before taking a seat at the elegantly set table.

"Go take care of what you need to take care of," he told me with a smile. "I'm not going anywhere."

Before I had a chance to respond, he winked at me and turned to walk away.

I didn't have a chance to really process the exchange, but his confidence was sexy.

Nina and Jazz grabbed me, and together, we walked into the kitchen.

"Who was that?" Nina scream-whispered, clutching my arm.

"I thought you didn't have a date," Jazz chimed in. "But it looks like you do."

"That was Marcus," I told them quietly.

"If this is the caliber of man your mom is trying to put you on with, let her know I'm single, too," Nina commented.

"Oh God," Jazz groaned with an eye roll. "Keep it in your pants, Nina. Let Aaliyah have something. It's her birthday, for God's sake!"

We all laughed.

After tasting the signature drink and confirming it was perfect, I headed to the bathroom on the other side of the kitchen with my two best friends.

"Okay, tell me about your dates," I demanded as soon as we closed the door behind us.

We did a quick update about Nina's date that she described as a friend with benefits. We did an even briefer update about Jazz's "friend." But from the few minutes I spent with them, I knew they both were in denial. There was more brewing between them.

I eyed them and pursed my lips. "You two were giving me such a hard time last night, and yet, here the two of you are . . . in love."

"What?" they screeched in unison as I walked out of the bathroom laughing.

"Love?! You have some nerve," Nina snapped, putting her hands on her hips. "You done lost your whole mind!"

"Your judgment is clearly clouded," Jazz assessed. She gestured to my hair. "I think that blowout blew out your common sense."

"It's my birthday," I told them, flipping my hair over my shoulder dramatically. "You have to let me have my predictions."

They shook their heads.

"Your birthday is over in six hours. We will be circling back to this blasphemy," Nina grumbled. "Love? Nonsense."

"Exactly. Just because *you* want love doesn't mean that's what I want," Jazz muttered just before we entered the dining room area.

Everyone was already seated and talking among themselves as the server finished filling the glasses. I'd had them remove the chairs that would've been occupied by my grandma, my uncle, and my date so there were no empty spaces. I got to the head of the table, and Nina sat to the right of me and Jazz sat to the left. I remained standing and grabbed my glass.

"Hi, everyone," I greeted the table to a round of cheers. "Thank you all for being here. You all look amazing. The men look dapper, and the women look gorgeous. I appreciate you getting all dolled up and coming to spend my thirtieth birthday with me. It truly means a lot to have you here. Tonight is a celebration of me. But more than that, tonight is a celebration of life." I made eye contact with my parents and exhaled. "Moving into this new decade of life, I am celebrating the fact that I am me. I am exactly who I am supposed to be. And I am so thankful to have you here celebrating that fact, too." I lifted my glass. "So, if you'll join me in blessing the food . . ."

That was my mom's cue.

She stood up and blessed the meal we were about to be served, and then the servers brought out the first course.

The hors d'oeuvres set the bar high, and then the appetizer raised the stakes. The salad was good, but it was the dressing that made it delicious. The chicken served with the main course was the juiciest and tenderest I'd had in a long time. By the time our plates were cleared, I wasn't sure if I was going to have room for dessert. But the lemon tart looked too good to pass up. The only reason I didn't finish it was because my dress was tight, and I didn't want to overstuff myself.

As seven thirty approached, the plates were starting to be cleared and photos were being taken. It felt like I'd said goodbye to my mom and dad, and then fifteen minutes later, everyone except for me was outside of the lake house getting the party started. The fire in the pit had been lit, the DJ had started playing music, and the well-fed guests were ready to burn off some calories. All the ingredients for the perfect night were there, and I was so excited to change into my sexy dress and enjoy myself.

So what if I don't have a date? I don't need one to have a good time. It's my thirtieth birthday!

"I'm coming. I'm coming. I'm coming. I'm just going to get changed, and then I'll be right out," I explained to Jazz when she came to check on me. "I'm just telling Chef Mason how incredible her food was."

"Hands down one of the best meals I've ever had," Jazz gushed. "I'm going to have to hire you for something, anything!"

"Thank you," Tiana Mason replied. "I don't cater private events anymore, but I'd booked this before I got my dream job."

I didn't know her personally, but I was happy to hear that she got her dream job. I was even more thrilled to know that everyone was going to be talking about the food for the rest of the year.

Jazz and I left the kitchen.

"It won't take me long to change," I assured her.

She went back outside, and I headed upstairs. It took me way longer than it should have because my feet were killing me. I'd just managed to get to my room and step out of my heels when there was a knock at the door.

"Give me about five minutes so I can change!" I yelled in a singsong tone, suspecting it was Nina.

I stripped out of the dress I was wearing, grabbed the satiny dress from the hanger, and then slipped it on. Where the first dress was structured with heavier material, the second dress was light, sexy satin that caressed my skin. The dress was clingy in all the right places. It was short. It was backless. It required me to be without a bra.

I did a little turn in the mirror before sliding into my crocodile flats. While the heels were more of a look, I wasn't going to be able to dance in them. I could barely walk in them. But I was willing to sacrifice for fashion. Stepping back into my heels, I grabbed the flats and carried them in my hand.

I'll make my grand entrance to the party in the heels, and then I'll change into the flats immediately after, I decided with a definitive nod.

Teetering down the steps, I rolled my shoulders back and held in my pain. I'd just dropped my flats next to the staircase when I heard a low whistle.

Glancing over my shoulder, I was surprised to see Marcus.

"You're ruining my grand entrance," I told him playfully as I let him catch up to me. "I thought everyone was outside."

"I had to use the restroom, but let me assure you"—he looked me up and down—"nothing was ruined. You look incredible."

He offered me his arm, and I took it.

"Thank you," I said, basking in his compliment.

He reached for the door and opened it. "Allow me."

Stepping back and smiling up at him, I held his gaze. *Okay, Marcus!*

"After you," he said.

I broke eye contact and allowed him to usher me out into the waiting crowd. Everyone started singing "Happy Birthday" as I walked down the sidewalk. Not wanting to fall, I held on to Marcus's arm tight as I approached the firepit. Looking around, I relished the celebration of me.

I let go of Marcus so I could stand alone and bask in the moment. He joined the crowd while Nina and Jazmyn carried the cake my mom had purchased with a big thirty candle.

"Make a wish," they said in unison.

I closed my eyes tight and took a breath.

I wish for continued peace. And love. Continued peace and love. I blew out the candle. *Amen.*

Everyone clapped, and I opened my eyes.

Nina and Jazz placed the cake on the table and then hugged me tight.

"Now meet me on the dance floor so we can show the birthday girl some love!" The DJ's directive caused a wave of movement. "Stand around the perimeter."

My stomach plummeted.

I'd forgotten that I was supposed to dance to my favorite India Davis song *with my date.*

Shit.

I stared at the dance floor while everyone got set. I felt the wave of panic as it dawned on me that I didn't have a date. I didn't have anyone to dance with, and I'd forgotten to tell the DJ to either cut that part completely or change the song to something upbeat so I could dance with my friends. My Cinderella moment where all eyes were on me in the middle of the dance floor with my prince was quickly turning into my *Black Swan* moment.

I've lost my mind.

Nina looped her arm with my left, and Jazz grabbed my right hand. Looking between my best friends, I felt comforted and reminded that I was enough.

It wasn't like I'd told the world that I had a man, and I was going to debut him at the party. But I hated that I'd planned a whole thing and forgot to cancel. I was kicking myself as we made our way to the dance floor.

The DJ was oblivious as he smiled and gave me a nod. Before I could respond, he started playing the song.

"We can dance together, or we can find Marcus," Jazz offered quietly as we approached.

I looked between them. "Stay with me," I whispered to them.

I didn't know that man.

I turned to the DJ to try to get his attention. I was going to have him change the song, but he'd started speaking.

"We're going to make sure all eyes are on Aaliyah right now. She's the birthday girl, and we're going to make sure she feels all this love."

Everyone clapped behind me, but I was still facing the DJ. My eyes were shooting daggers at him. He apparently wasn't picking up what I was hinting at or understanding that I was trying to stop what was happening, because he kept talking, pressed play, and then gave me a thumbs-up.

Sighing, I turned around and grabbed my best friends' hands as the most romantic song played. Onlookers observed in what I knew had to be quiet confusion. Closing my eyes, I blocked them out and just grooved to the music.

I felt my girls stop swaying before I knew why.

"Excuse me," a deep voice interrupted, catching me off guard.

My eyes flew open as the familiarity ran down my spine.

"Can I have this dance?"

24

My heart thumped in my chest, and my mouth went dry. Taking his outstretched hand, I looked over at my friends, who were gawking at him as they took steps backward. The shocked smiles on their faces seemed to be the opposite of the stunned expression on my own. I didn't know how I felt.

My heart was racing. My stomach was in knots. My hands were shaking. And my mind was spinning.

Refocusing my attention on the man who had just taken me into his arms, I allowed my mind to catch up with my body.

"You look . . . wow," he said softly.

"Ahmad," I breathed. "How . . . What are you doing here?"

"Happy birthday." Pulling me in close, he leaned down. "I'm showing up for you the same way you showed up for me."

A wave of emotion hit me, and my eyes pricked with tears. With my face buried in his neck, I inhaled deeply and took in his cologne.

He looked as good as he smelled.

Wearing a dark-green-and-black suit that seemed tailored for his muscular body, he looked good. The color didn't just complement what I was wearing, it looked good against his toffee-colored skin. I felt his thick beard brush against my shoulder, and I immediately had a flashback to the way my juices had glistened on his beard twenty-four hours ago.

Fuck.

The throb between my thighs was intense as I allowed him to lead us around the dance floor. My nipples hardened, and I tried to keep my body close to his so no one would notice.

He moved skillfully, much like when he was behind the bar. He floated around, and I merely held on and enjoyed the ride. We didn't say anything else the entire dance. We just existed in the moment together.

It felt good.

It felt right.

It felt overwhelming.

The song was starting to come to an end, and I swallowed hard. "Thank you."

"You don't have to thank me. You were there for me when I didn't know I needed you. Did you think I wouldn't be here for you?"

"I appreciate that, but you didn't have to. I didn't go to the hospital so you'd owe me. I . . ."

My tongue felt heavy, and my heart thudded as my sentence trailed off.

"Shout-out to Aaliyah, the birthday girl!" the DJ called out as the song came to an end.

"Can we talk?" Ahmad whispered against my ear.

I swallowed hard. "Not here."

"And shout-out to the brother in green," the DJ continued as we left the dance floor. "He was late, but he swooped in with style, didn't he?"

"Then where?" Ahmad countered.

"Follow me."

A popular song pulsed through the air while we made our way to the lake house. I had so many thoughts and feelings stirring within me that I didn't even feel my feet damn near bleeding inside my shoe. But when I got inside, I immediately went to the staircase.

He shut the door, muting the music. The sound of the catering team cleaning made the house sound big and empty.

"You look incredible," he complimented me again.

I took a breath. "Thank you."

Holding on to the railing, I slipped out of my heels and into my flats.

The hair on the back of my neck stood up, and I felt him close to me.

He cleared his throat, and I knew he had moved closer. "How has—"

"Why did you come?" I asked, keeping my back to him.

Wrapping his hand around my wrist, he turned me around. "Why did you leave?"

I opened my mouth and then closed it, unable to answer the question.

"I didn't like the way things ended with us last night." His thumb ran over my skin. "Talk to me."

I didn't want to have the conversation with him right then. We clearly weren't on the same page, and I wasn't trying to get into a big emotional argument on my big night. I'd just had my hair and makeup done for this occasion.

"I don't know what to say," I whispered. "It's my birthday, and I'm not trying to get into a whole thing with you, Ahmad."

"Just answer one question for me . . ." He searched my eyes and his fingers flexed against my wrist. "Was Asia right? Asia said you had feelings for me."

"Of course she did," I scoffed.

"And she said the reason I wasn't feeling your date was because I had feelings for you."

I swallowed hard. "O-okay."

"So my—"

"Birthday girl!" my nosy cousin Mecca called out as she entered the lake house. Her smile grew as she eyeballed my arm still in Ahmad's grasp. "You two looked good on the dance floor." She turned her sights on Ahmad. "How long have you been with my cousin?"

I started to deny that we were in a relationship, but he spoke first.

"We started seeing each other at the beginning of summer," Ahmad answered.

"Is it serious?" She wiggled her eyebrows suggestively.

"I can only speak for myself, but yeah."

I looked up at him, surprised by his responses. My heart skipped a beat when I found him staring at me. I inhaled slowly, trying to steady myself.

This man . . .

"Well, I guess I'll head to the bathroom and stop interrupting what you have going on." Mecca giggled. "Go, cuz!"

Ripping my eyes from him, I watched her as she continued down the hall to one of the bathrooms. Seconds later, two others came in to go to the restroom. They headed down the hall, and as soon as they were out of earshot, Ahmad began again.

"Do you—?" he started to ask as my cousin came out the bathroom.

Shaking my head, I cut him off. "Not here," I mumbled as I bent down and grabbed my heels. Ahmad followed me as I climbed the stairs. When we walked down the hall to my bedroom, I glanced over my shoulder at him. "My cousin will listen to our conversation and tell everyone. She's great. I love her. But she's nosy."

"Understood," he replied, removing his jacket and laying it over his forearm.

I opened the door, and he came in, closing it behind him.

"I still can't believe you're here," I expressed.

I placed my shoes on the floor next to my luggage and then turned around.

Ahmad tossed his jacket on the chair near the door and slipped his hands in his pockets. As he made his way to the middle of the room, my eyes coasted up his body. When our eyes met, the air left my lungs. The intensity of his gaze caught me off guard.

"I can't believe you left last night," he countered quietly.

I took a step back and bumped into the wall. Allowing it to hold me upright, I closed my eyes and shook my head. "I can't do this right now. It's my birthday, and we're in the middle of my party." I pursed my lips. "Why are you here?"

"You said you needed a date for your birthday," he explained.

"How did you know I didn't have one?"

"I didn't know for sure," he admitted, running his hand over his beard. "But I had to make sure you were good."

My stomach twisted. Shifting from one foot to the other, I broke eye contact. "Well, thank you."

"I told you I got your back. By any means necessary."

I gave a small nod. "You did say that."

"And I meant it . . ." He took a couple of steps toward me. "I still mean it." He paused. "But that's not the only reason I came."

I forced my eyes to meet his again, praying he didn't see the emotion in them. "What's the other reason?"

"Because you left. Because you've been ignoring the fuck out of me. Because I don't have your number. Because I didn't want to keep showing up at your place. Because of what happened last night."

"Last night is not a true representation of who I am or how I get down."

"But last night was real."

Exhaling audibly, I felt exposed. It felt like if the conversation continued, I was going to say something I was going to regret. It felt like if I didn't end the conversation right then, I was going to say too much.

Or worse, embarrass myself.

"I can't do this right now. I have to get back to my party." I made no attempt to move, but I wanted him to stop talking. "We can do this another time."

"When?" he questioned me. He kept his voice low and steady, but there was a fire in his eyes. "Because I'm tired of going back and forth with you."

"We've already talked. We aren't on the same page. We don't want . . ." I closed my eyes for a moment. "We're in different spaces in our lives, and that's okay. We don't have to get into it. I respect what you have going on. What more is there to say?"

"Oh, I think there's a lot more to say." He licked his lips. "About the ring—"

"I forgave you for that lie of omission," I interrupted. "I didn't like being misled, but I understood the situation, and I respect where you are with that." I glanced down at his hand and saw he wasn't wearing it. "You are—where's your ring?"

"I've only been wearing it when I bartend lately," he answered softly.

My mouth snapped shut.

I was *not* expecting him to say that.

He licked his lips and took a step closer. "And last night . . . last night isn't representative of how I get down either, but with you . . ." He shook his head slowly. "With you, it was different."

"Different, huh?" I scoffed softly. "I don't see how. I'm just the homie, right?"

He frowned. "What is that supposed to mean?"

"Never mind."

"No, what is that supposed to mean?" His voice demanded an answer.

"It means I'm just the homie. Isn't that how you described me to your friends?" I burst out, feeling like the emotional dam was breaking. "And you didn't fuck me because you thought I was different—you were jealous and didn't want me giving my time and attention to someone else. You told me that you wear the ring because you're not ready to be involved with anyone. You said you wanted to be friends. So, I don't know what you're trying to pull here—"

"Trying to pull?" He unbuttoned his shirt sleeves and forced them up. "What the fuck?"

"And last night, you could've just been jealous and looking for something to do—"

"If I was just looking for something to do, I would've kept condoms on me, ready and waiting for the opportunity. If I was just fucking you because I was jealous, I would've made a move after your second app date with ol' boy with the wife. I've known I've wanted you since then."

"And you didn't say anything! Between not telling me you weren't married and calling me your homie, it's difficult for me to buy that you think this"—I gestured between us—"is something different. Something that you're ready for."

"You think I would try this hard to get you to talk to me if I didn't think this was different? If I didn't think *you* were different?"

If you were bored.

He took a step toward me. "You think I would risk my dad's business to have sex with you in the back office if I didn't think this was different?"

If you were horny.

He stepped forward again. "You think I would be here tonight if I didn't think this was different?"

If you felt like you owed me for coming to the hospital.

He took another step. "You think I would buy this expensive-ass suit in your favorite color if I didn't think this was different?"

I stilled. "You remembered my favorite color?"

"Yes." He stopped a couple of feet in front of me and tilted his head slightly. "There's not much I don't remember about you."

My heart beat so loud that I was sure he heard it, too.

"You said you'd answer one question for me," he continued.

"What's the question?" I wondered.

He didn't say anything for a moment, and then he asked, "Do you have feelings for me?"

My automatic instinct was to deny what I felt. Even though I could feel the energy between us being reciprocated, and even though he alluded to his own feelings, it was hard for me to believe he felt something more than a physical connection between us. The sex was exquisite, so I understood the confusion. But the idea of me acknowledging my true feelings, while his feelings were based on how good the sex was, was laughable.

Not going to happen.

I opened my mouth to say no, but the word never formed. Instead, I shook my head.

He stepped into my personal space and searched my eyes. "No?"

Looking away, I clarified, "No."

He was quiet for a moment. "I'm calling bullshit." His voice lowered to just above a whisper as he placed his hands on the wall next to my head, caging me between his strong arms. "Look at me and say it."

I swallowed hard and forced myself to look him in his eyes. I wanted to deny it. The combination of self-preservation and pride was a hell of a drug. I was never one to run away from my feelings. But at the same time, I never invested in lost causes either. In that moment, I couldn't get my mouth to cooperate.

"It's bullshit, isn't it, Aaliyah?" His voice rolled over me like his touch did the night before, and I shivered. A ghost of a smile played at the corner of his lips. "Because you feel something between us, don't you?"

My heart drummed in my chest as I tried to bottle up my emotions. With each passing second of his question hanging in the air, I felt everything threatening to erupt out of me. I knew I needed to put some distance between us if I wanted any chance of getting my feelings in check. But I couldn't move.

Unfettered lust for Ahmad simmered inside of me, just under the surface, waiting to come roaring to the forefront. Overwhelming desire to feel Ahmad's lips on mine again sent a chill down my spine. I was barely holding it together.

The room was thick with tension. I felt like I was going to suffocate as we stood there staring at one another, breathing each other in. His breaths were coming more rapidly as his face hovered over mine. My eyes dropped to his lips just as his tongue ran from one corner of his mouth to the other.

That was a bad idea.

I shook my head slightly, trying to force my feet to move. I needed to put some distance between us. If I didn't, I knew I would end up saying too much, doing too much, feeling too much.

"Did you shake your head?" Ahmad brought his face closer, rubbing his nose against mine. "Haven't we been through this? Why are you lying to me, Aaliyah?"

My lips parted as I felt his breath on my face.

"Do you know how I know you feel something between us?" he murmured, taking my breath away. He waited, stretching the already tense moment out. "I know you have feelings for me because I could taste it."

I sucked in a sharp breath.

"I could taste it in your kiss," he breathed, brushing his lips against mine. "I could taste it when you came on my face."

I squeezed my thighs together and pressed my back against the wall. "Ahmad."

"I can hear it in the way you say my name," he continued. "I can see it in your eyes. But I knew for a fact when I felt the way you came on my dick."

"I don't . . ." My attempt at denying it was failing me as my feelings started to overtake me.

"You don't what?" he challenged.

My lips parted, and short, shaky breaths escaped. I couldn't answer him. I couldn't do anything. It was taking more and more effort to restrain myself.

"We don't want the same thing," I said finally.

"What is it that you want?" he asked.

"I want the real thing."

"And you don't think I want something real?"

"I don't think you want something real *with me,*" I choked out in barely a whisper.

Ahmad roughly forced me to look him in his eyes and pinned me with his body. "Something real with you is the only thing I want."

I trembled in response. My hands instinctively fisted his shirt. I wasn't sure if I was supposed to be pushing him away or drawing him closer. Either way, I was holding on to him. His closeness and his warmth hardened my nipples as they brushed against the satin of my dress, teasing me.

"Ahmad," I murmured.

"Let me be very clear about something . . . I want you. This isn't jealousy. This isn't uncertainty. This isn't a rebound. This isn't anything but the fact that you walked into that bar and changed my fucking life." His mouth moved over mine teasingly, seductively, and just when I was about to give in and kiss him back, he pulled away. "But I need you to tell me what you want," Ahmad demanded.

Pulling away slightly, I peered up at him through my lashes. "You haven't been clear."

"How can I make it clearer?" Ahmad grunted before he let out a low, rumbling breath. "The fact that I'm here should make it clear. The fact that I drove up to damn near every lake house looking for you should make it clear."

My eyes widened slightly, and my voice trembled. "You drove?"

He nodded. "I needed to get here, and I didn't know exactly which house it was."

"You *drove*?" I repeated.

His chest rose and fell. "For you, yes."

"I thought . . ." I gaped at him.

"I had to do what I had to do. If there was another way, I would've found it. But it was for you. I wasn't going to miss your birthday. I wasn't going to let you be here without someone. And I wasn't going to let last night be it. Aaliyah, I—shit!"

He swore, and his eyes closed as the palm of my hand applied pressure against the bulge in his pants. I rubbed him through the starched fabric that separated his skin from mine. My fingertips traced his erection, and from his facial expression, he could've exploded right at that moment.

"You did that for me," I said more to myself than to him as I unzipped and unbuttoned his pants and reached inside. Wrapping my hand around his girth, I squeezed. "I can't believe you did that for me."

He sucked in a sharp breath and opened his eyes. "I'd do anything for you."

His words caused desire to rip through my body.

I blinked up at him. "Anything?"

"Anything." He kissed me softly. "I know you want this"—his hand covered mine as I continued stroking him—"and I know you want me. But until you tell me how you feel, I'm not making a move."

Something tightened deep in my belly, and I let out a huff of air instead of the moan that was caught in my throat.

Unable to hold out any longer, I admitted it. "I want you." Rising up onto my toes, I brushed my lips against his ear. "I want all of you."

A deep, sexy groan rumbled from his throat. "Say it again," he demanded, taking my hand from his pants.

"I want all of you," I told him as he ran his fingertips down my neck, along my collarbone. When he got to my shoulders, he took the straps of the dress down with him. The satin material dragged along my skin, giving me a chill as my breasts were exposed. He tugged the formfitting garment down my body until it pooled at my feet. "I have feelings for you." Tipping my head up, I locked eyes with him. "And not just because last night was the best sex I'd ever had."

He licked his lips but said nothing.

"I want you, Ahmad."

Without warning, he crashed his lips into mine, kissing me hard. He was rough, the force of the movement making me tremble with want. I felt his kiss all over my body, and I knew if I didn't get some relief soon, I was going to explode.

"Tell me what you want," Ahmad demanded.

Pulling away slightly, I peered up at him through my lashes. "I want you."

"Tell me how you feel," Ahmad grunted before he let out a low, rumbling breath.

"I want you the same way you want me," I answered as I slid his pants and boxer briefs down and then cupped his balls.

He sucked in a sharp breath and opened his eyes. "I didn't ask you to tell me what you wanted. I want to know what you feel." He kissed me softly, restraining himself. "Tell me how you feel."

I licked my lips, running my tongue from one corner of my mouth to the other, silently begging him to kiss me again. "I want to feel you inside of me."

His chest rose and fell as if he were taking in my answer. "I can see it in your eyes, Aaliyah."

My skin burned with anticipation as he leaned forward and trailed kisses down my neck. His fingers gripped my hips as he kissed his way to my breasts. Looking up at me as his nose nuzzled my hardened nipples, he smirked.

Biting down gently, he swirled his tongue around. I sucked in a sharp breath before sighing his name. I was already turned on from the way he kissed me, but when he suctioned his wet mouth around my nipple, I wasn't just damp. I was soaking wet.

"Ahmad," I moaned. "I feel—oh!"

My sentence was cut short by his finger sliding across my slit. The damp lace underwear was no match for how wet I'd gotten the material and how skilled Ahmad's hands were. As he toyed with me, my head rocked back against the wall, and my eyes fluttered shut. Without warning, he slipped a finger past the lace and ran it over the length of my slit.

"All of this is for me?" he asked, finding his way inside me. He added another finger, and I almost came on contact. "You're this wet for me, Aaliyah?"

"Yes, yes, yes, oh," I panted. "Yes."

He grunted his approval of the sounds he was pulling out of me before he covered my mouth with his own. His tongue played with mine as his fingers did the same.

I was in heaven.

"Shit," Ahmad swore under his breath as he pulled out of the kiss and increased the pace of his fingers.

"I want to feel you. I want you inside me."

I reached for his dick, but he grabbed my hand and held it against the wall.

"I've imagined how you look when you're coming, and I missed it last night," he uttered before kissing me. "I'm not going to miss it again. I need to see you . . . I need to see this pretty face as I'm playing with this pretty pussy. I need to see you come for me. I need it." His rough tone combined with his gentle touch was causing a tingling sensation. "Are you gonna give it to me, Aaliyah? It sounds like it. Yeah, that's it. Listen to how wet this pussy is. It sounds good. This pussy sounds so good. And all this juice is for me? I can't wait to taste you again. I can't wait to slide right in this pretty—that's it."

"Oh God!" I cried as the orgasm snuck up on me and caused me to buck against his hand.

"Yeah," he grunted before his mouth covered mine hungrily.

I put my arms around his neck and deepened the kiss. Never taking his mouth from mine, he unbuttoned his shirt and stepped out of his pants. I thought he was bending down to move his pants out of the way, but he stooped down, grabbed my ass, and then lifted me without warning.

"Ahmad!" I gasped, clutching onto his neck. "You're going to drop me."

"I'm not going to drop you." He moved across the room with surprising ease. His fingers dug into my ass as he traveled the short distance; carrying my two-hundred-plus-pound body didn't seem to faze him at all. When we got to the bed, he met my gaze. "You doubted me. You should never doubt me."

I touched his still-bandaged wound. "You're going to hurt yourself even more. Is your arm okay?"

"My arm is good," he assured me. "I'm good. You're good. We're good."

I bit down on my bottom lip. "Ahmad, what are you doing?"

He ran his tongue from one corner of his mouth to another. "Making sure you know this is real."

My gut twisted, and my heart pounded in my chest.

There was nothing and no one I'd ever wanted more than him in that moment. As he slid me down his muscular body, he placed me on the bed. With his dick hard and heavy at eye level, it was impossible to look anywhere else.

"Aaliyah," he whispered as he stroked himself.

When I finally met his gaze, he looked as if he wanted to devour me.

"You know I want you," he groaned.

Mesmerized, I watched his hand move over his thick eight inches. I nodded. "I want you, too," I assured him.

I held his gaze as I slinked my way to the top of the bed. I made a show of removing my G-string. Keeping my eyes on him, I tossed it off the side of the bed. Running my hands over my breasts, I rolled my nipples between my fingers. Reclining against the stacks of pillows, I let my legs inch open. Propping myself up with one arm, I let my other hand move over my soft belly and stopped at the apex of my thighs.

"I think I made it really clear that I want you," I reiterated.

Ahmad's eyes were trained on my hand and the subtle movement of my fingers as he climbed on the bed.

My eyes closed in anticipation. I let my head sink deeper into the pillows, and I inhaled sharply. I could feel him staring at me as I played with myself. A moment of déjà vu gave me goose bumps as I flashed back to the fantasy I'd had weeks ago.

Remembering how hard I came then, combined with the reality of him watching me now, my teasing session turned into a real masturbation as I strummed my clit.

The thought of him filling me, stretching me, taking me the way he did the night before made me heady.

I moaned.

The second the sound escaped my lips, Ahmad was on top of me. Positioning himself between my legs, he parted my lips with his tongue, kissing me with a passion I'd never experienced before. My legs wrapped around him, pulling the fullness of his weight on top of me.

Breaking the kiss, he grabbed my hips and repositioned me at a tilt, spreading me open wider.

I licked my lips when I felt him pressed against me. My body was practically begging for him, but seconds passed, and he hadn't pushed his way in. I opened my eyes to find him staring at me.

"Aaliyah . . ." Ahmad rubbed his dick in my wetness before moving it over my throbbing clit.

Closing my eyes again, I exhaled roughly. Excitement rippled through me. "Yes."

"Tell me what you want." The sexy grit in his tone gave me chills. "What do you want from me?"

"I want you to fuck me. I want you to stretch me out." I rotated my hips. "I want you to make me come on your—oh, shit," I cried out as I felt him push the tip in me.

"Look at me."

I tried to focus on him, and as soon as I did, I felt myself become wetter. I watched him, sexy and determined as he took me in. Groaning, he ran his hands up and down my thighs as we stared at each other. His fingers dug into the meatiness of my legs as he set me in position.

"When I said that I want you, I didn't just mean because you're sexy as hell and your pussy is perfect," he told me just as he gave me another inch of dick. "I mean . . . I do want your perfect pussy. I want your beautiful body. I want to watch you come over and over again. Can I have that? Can I have what I want?"

"Yes," I panted, hoping my gyrations would give me more.

He put his hands on my hips and held me in place. "But I also want your conversation. I want your mind. I want your heart." He gave me another inch. "Can I have that?"

My eyes started to roll back in sheer ecstasy. "Yesssssssssssssss."

"So I'm going to ask you again . . . what do you want from me?"

Seeing the sincerity in his eyes, hearing the genuineness in his tone, and feeling the earnestness in his touch, I was wide open for him. My body was still buzzing. My erogenous zones were on fire. My heart was beating wildly. A thin sheen of sweat was on my brow. But my soul felt peace.

"I want you," I answered honestly. "I want all of you. I want to be with you."

"That's what I've been waiting to hear," he growled. His voice was louder, clearer, and full of want.

My head tilted back, and I cried out again as he applied more pressure. "God, yes . . ."

"Do you know how long I've been waiting to hear that from you?" he uttered as his grip tightened on my hips. I could hear and feel his restraint as he gave me one more inch.

I let out a muffled grunt as I struggled to maintain eye contact. "No."

"Weeeeeeeeeeeeeeeeks." His voice broke sexily as he inched his way in. "God, you . . . are so . . . fucking . . . wet. This pussy . . . Fuck." With each inch, he filled me, stretching me out deliciously. "I love how perfect your pussy is."

I moaned in response.

He leaned forward, and his tongue played with mine. He broke the kiss only to watch my reaction to his touch. I sucked in a sharp breath as his hands slid from my hips to my aching nipples. He rocked into me, and a fresh wave of chills ran down my spine as we adjusted to the tight fit.

Staring into my eyes, he started slow stroking me at first. We both let out a strained moan as we settled into our groove. He leaned forward again, but this time, he kissed me softly.

Working himself as deep as he could go, he held the position. "Are you mine, Aaliyah?"

"Yes." My answer came out in a short, hot burst.

"Is this body mine, Aaliyah?"

"Yes."

"Is this pussy mine?" Ahmad asked.

The feeling of fullness felt so good that I almost forgot to answer him. "Yesssssssss," I cried.

Our faces were close, and I felt a flurry of emotions. I clenched around him.

"Shit," he growled. "You like that, huh? Say it. Say the words."

"This pussy is yours."

He somehow felt like he got bigger, wider, deeper. "I love hearing you say that." His lips met mine and when he pulled away, he whispered, "You're going to let me take care of it?"

"Yes," I panted.

"Tell me again," he demanded, pulling almost all the way out and then working his way back in.

"This pussy is yours."

The low, guttural groan he let out curled my toes.

I loved the feeling he gave me, and I loved watching his face twist in pleasure. My lips parted and a sound that was part moan, part cry, escaped.

My feelings for him combined with the yearning in my body, and I felt exposed—in the best way.

I didn't try to hide it. I didn't want to hide it. I wanted him to see me, all of me.

And he did.

I felt it, and I knew he felt it, too.

It wasn't just his dick rubbing against my walls; it was his soul rubbing up against my soul.

With each stroke, I felt closer to him, connected with him. With each stroke, I felt like I was falling in love with him.

My heart thudded in my chest and knots coiled in my belly as the accidental thought entered my mind. His dick moved in and out of me with precision, holding the thought in place for a minute longer than necessary. Each time he bumped into my cervix, he tapped into something spiritual within me. He was making me think about a future with him. He was forcing me to fall for him. He was rushing me to orgasm.

Everything was moving fast.

As if something snapped inside both of us, he pushed my legs as far back as they could comfortably go, and he lifted my hips before he started ramming into me. To heighten my pleasure, he toyed with my aching clit, causing me to whimper.

"You like that, don't you, baby?" he uttered so softly I had to read his lips. "I want to know everything you like so I can take care of this pussy. Because it's mine."

"Yes, yes, it's yours. All yours," I panted.

It was so hard not to come when the most distinct pleasure was pulsating through my body.

"Yeah, that's it. That's it, baby. I want you to come for me. I want you to milk my dick as you get yours, baby. I want to feel you come. I want to see it and feel it. I want all of it. You good with that?"

His voice was low, gruff, sexy as hell.

I breathed heavily, unable to answer.

"You good with that, Aaliyah?" He brought his free hand to my nipple and pinched, causing a new sensation and a new wave of heat to course through my veins.

I nodded. "Y-yeah." I was breathing heavily and starting to lose it.

He stared into my eyes for a beat too long. "I can feel how bad you want to give it to me," he uttered thickly.

"Oh God," I groaned loudly.

My eyes fluttered closed as each moan grew louder than the one before it. I clawed at his arms as he pounded into me over and over again. I felt so full as he touched spots I'd forgotten existed. I was at my breaking point, but it was his voice that pushed me over the edge.

"Let me feel it, Aaliyah," he begged, using long, deep strokes to make sure no part of me went without being massaged. "Give it to me."

"Oh, shit . . . Oh—I—oh God," I began, unable to get the words out as I worked my hips harder, meeting him thrust for thrust.

When I hit the point of no return, I started bucking, lifting off the bed.

"Let me—oh, shit," he groaned as I started to shake.

I had no control of my pulsating body as I gave in to the ultimate pleasure. My mouth opened, yet no sound came out as I succumbed to my orgasm.

Hearing his deep guttural moans spurred me on as I gave him full ownership of my body. His impending orgasm extended mine as we thrust into each other with reckless abandon. Each stroke more intense than the last. Feeling him lose control was it for me. I had an IUD in place, so I wasn't worried about him coming inside me. But feeling his restraint wane and him succumbing to desire made me crave it. Wrapping my legs around his waist, I pulled him in deep and held him in place.

"Come inside me," I panted.

"Aaliyah," he grunted, his body becoming rigid. "Fuck!"

A second round of that tension that had been building released from deep in my core and spread throughout the rest of my body. I feverishly gyrated against him as we climaxed together.

I experienced the most intense back-to-back orgasms I'd ever had.

Our heavy, satiated breathing filled the room as our bodies came down from the high we were riding. Collapsing beside me, Ahmad lay in sated silence for a few minutes before pulling out.

"When I started to realize I felt something for you, we'd already established our friendship, so I was willing to fall back and help you get what you wanted. You said you were happy, and that's what I wanted . . . for you to be happy. Now that I know what's between us is real, I'm not willing to let you go." He paused, pulling me closer and pressing his lips against my shoulder. "You said your body was mine. But is your heart mine?" he asked quietly.

Turning to face him, I stared into his eyes and felt nothing but affection, desire, and peace.

"Yes," I whispered.

25

I didn't get blowouts often because the slightest bit of water or steam guaranteed my hair would be back in a 'fro in no time. So when I climbed out the bed and saw my hair in the mirror, I froze. There was no evidence of pin curls. My hair was no longer showing off my stretched strands. It was shrinking up by the second.

"My hair," I gasped as I stared at myself in the bathroom mirror.

"You look beautiful," Ahmad said, coming up behind me. He kissed my cheek and then stared at our reflections. "You definitely need to do something about your hair, but you look beautiful."

"Shut up!" I wailed, swatting at his arm. "I have to go back down there, and I can't go out like this."

"How can I help?"

"One hundred and twenty dollars down the drain," I marveled. "It was worth it, but damn." Glancing at him, I smiled. "You can help by giving me a repeat performance later."

He smirked. "Oh, I got you."

While he went to get dressed, I went ahead and spritzed my hair with water. As I watched it reappear as subtly looser-than-normal coils, I smiled. I didn't have any products to really style it, but my natural 'fro looked good.

I just hope it doesn't frizz when it dries completely.

When I strolled into the bedroom, Ahmad was dressed in his dark green pants and black button-up. He was holding the jacket over his arm. I went to my suitcase and pulled out a new pair of thongs and then slipped on my dress.

"You look good in green," he complimented me.

A smile pulled at my lips. "Like a sexy M&M?"

Nodding, clearly amused with himself: "Like the sexiest M&M."

"You play too much."

"I'm serious though." He pulled me into his arms and turned me around toward the mirror. "Look at you."

His hands slowly moved over my thick waist and rounded hips. Situating me so that his dick was pressed against my ass, he stared at our reflection. My nipples poked through the material, giving the dress a more explicitly sexy look. I wasn't trying to go downstairs with my nipples on display, but they seemed to always be on high alert around Ahmad.

"You look good in this dress," he started, dragging the word out seductively as he stared at us together. "But I can't wait to get you out of it again. I can't wait to be inside you again."

Turning around, I wrapped my arms around his neck and puckered my lips to get a kiss. "As soon as the fireworks are over, I'm ready to come up here and create our own."

"That's some corny shit, but I'm with it."

I giggled. "Come on. I've been gone for an hour."

"Then let's go out and celebrate your birthday with your people."

We headed toward the door, and then I stopped. "You want to leave your jacket up here?" I wondered, gesturing to how he had it draped over his arm.

"Does this mean you're inviting me to stay the night?"

"Yes."

"I don't even have your number yet, and I get to spend the night? You must like me or some shit."

Grinning, I looked up at him. "Where's your phone? I like you enough to give you my number *and* let you spend the night."

"I like that deal." He leaned down and pressed his lips against mine. "I like it almost as much as I like you."

Hand in hand, we walked downstairs. There were a handful of people milling around. We'd barely made it out the front door when Jazz spotted me. She hurried over to us.

"What do we have here?" Jazz grinned, looking between us. "Hello. I'm Jazmyn," she introduced herself.

He reached out and shook her outstretched hand. "I'm Ahmad. It's nice to meet you, Jazmyn."

"It's nice to finally put a name to a face. You've been holding my girl down this summer, and I appreciate that."

Nina walked up just in time to hear her response. "From the look of Aaliyah's hair, Ahmad has definitely been holding Aaliyah down."

My jaw dropped. Jazz didn't even try to hold in her laughter. I was too stunned to look up at Ahmad for his reaction.

Nina shifted her attention to me. "You traded your blowout to get blown out." She nodded appreciatively. "I respect it."

"Nina!" I cackled. "Will you stop?"

"Am I wrong?" Nina put her hands on her hips. "The bartender swooped in to drop off dick as a birthday gift."

Bringing my hand to his lips, Ahmad kissed it. "I have more to offer Aaliyah than just dick. I promise you that."

"Well, you better, because she deserves the world," Jazz responded.

He looked over at me. "And I plan to give it to her."

Nina gave him a look and quirked an eyebrow. "Oh, I'm sure you do plan to give it to her."

We all burst out laughing.

"I'm going to get a drink and let you ladies talk," Ahmad announced. He turned to me. "What can I get you?"

"The signature drink," I answered. "Malibu sunrise."

A slow smile spread across his face. "Malibu sunrise, huh?"

"I like what I like."

"Good choice."

He turned to my friends. "What can I get you?"

"I'm good, but thank you," Jazz said.

"Your brother's phone number," Nina joked.

"I only have a sister," he chuckled. "But I can get you a drink instead."

She sighed loudly and dramatically. "I guess I'll take the signature drink."

"Aight, I'll be right back." He took a step away from me and then came back and planted a tender kiss against my lips. "Happy birthday."

Ahmad had only gotten a few feet before my girls started talking at once.

"You weren't kidding when you said he was fine," Jazmyn commented.

"And did you see the way he was looking at her?" Nina chimed in. "Ahmad is in love!"

"And Aaliyah's in love, too," Jazz pointed out.

"Yes! She was smiling so hard I could see the sockets where her wisdom teeth used to be."

I snickered. "I can't stand y'all."

"He is a smooth talker, though." Jazz tapped her chin and then looked over toward the makeshift bar on the dock. "Are we sure he's cool? He was saying all the right things, so I'm wondering if he practiced beforehand or if he's just that good."

"He's just that good," I answered. "He's not like other dudes."

"Any dude that tells you he's not like other dudes is the team captain of the other dudes," Nina quipped.

We all laughed.

"Nah, he's good," Jazz relented. "I like him. And I like the way you two look at each other. I like how he showed up today."

Nina smiled. "I knew he was going to be the one you ended up with. I saw it at the concert. There's so much chemistry between you two. I don't think he's the team captain. He's got the look, but I think he's legit."

"He is legit," I assured them with an uncontrollable grin. "Now before he gets back, what's up with your dates? I want to get to know them."

"It's not a date," they both argued in unison.

I pursed my lips and gave them both looks. "Mm-hmm."

They gave me brief, largely downplayed stories about the men they brought to the party before Ahmad returned with our drinks. We were joined by Nina's date first and then Jazmyn's date. Then as a group, we went to the dance floor.

The music thumped loudly, but not at the level that would damage eardrums. The songs were hits, and the DJ managed to put together a mix that kept the dance floor packed. Conversations floated through the air from the people in the yard, under the tent, and lakeside. And at midnight, we all stood in awe as the fireworks went off.

It was a good night.

When the party ended, I said goodbye to almost everyone. My cousins Mecca and the man she brought with her, Tamara and her wife, and Jonelle and her husband stayed in the three downstairs bedrooms. My best friends were in the upstairs bedrooms with their dates. And once I'd said good night to everyone, Ahmad took me upstairs to my room and had his way with me.

For hours, we ebbed and flowed between making love and fucking and back again. My body ached from physical exhaustion and complete and utter satisfaction. By the time we wore ourselves out, it was the wee hours of the morning, and we were starving. We were exhausted, but we couldn't sleep because we were so hungry.

"You want to go get food?" Ahmad wondered, running his hand over my stomach.

"I don't think anything is going to be open around here," I murmured.

"Then let's go get something."

His incredible smile seduced me, and somehow, I let him convince me to leave the lake house. Showering together, it took us twice as long to get ready to go. But at almost five o'clock in the morning, I walked out of the lake house for our first official date. We headed to my car.

"It's our first date. I can drive," he insisted.

"I'm right here"—I pointed to my car—"and you're all the way over there. It'll be seven o'clock before we make it to your car," I joked. "Let me just drive."

He chuckled under his breath. "Aight," he relented. "But you know this isn't a real date, right?"

My eyebrows flew up. "Because I'm driving?"

"Because we're probably picking something up at a convenience store." He took a look at my outfit. "And we're not dressed for going out."

I looked down at my black leggings, lingerie top, denim jacket, and sneakers. “You don’t like what I got on?” We climbed into my car, and after I started it, I looked over at him. “I didn’t pack anything for a late-night run, but I think I pulled this together nicely at the last minute.”

“Yeah, yeah, yeah, yeah, yeah, you look good,” he replied with a playful sarcasm. “But when we go out on a real date, I want you to at least match.”

“Not this coming from the man who, outside of tonight, mostly wears tight-ass T-shirts and jeans,” I scoffed. “Tonight is the exception, not the rule. So I know you’re not trying to be the fashion police! Ain’t no way in hell you got one good suit and now you’re policing my wardrobe?”

He chuckled. “I got more than one.”

“Prove it.”

“I will. And even when I don’t have on a suit, at least I always match.”

My eyes bulged emphatically. “What doesn’t match with jeans?”

He pointed to my outfit. “Whatever this is.”

My head tipped back, and I let out a loud cackle as I eased down the road.

“You’re parked so far back,” I said as he pointed out his car. As I continued down the street, we were both silent until I got to the main road. “I still can’t believe you drove here.”

“Yeah.” He was quiet for a moment.

“How did it feel . . . ?” I glanced over at him, briefly studying his expression. “How did it feel to be driving again?”

“It wasn’t easy.” He shook his head. “I didn’t think I was ready. But”—he reached out and caressed my arm—“I had the right motivation to get me behind the wheel again.”

“Well, I’m glad you made it to me safely. The fact that you even attempted is just . . . wow.”

“I needed to get to you, and it was the only way. Once I realized how many lake houses there were and how long it was going to take a driver to get me here, driving was the only option if I was going to make it.”

“Did you go to every lake house?”

"Not all of them. But there were at least ten that I hit up before finding the right one."

"Wow . . . I can't believe you did all that to make it to my party."

"I knew how much it meant to you. And I didn't want another day to go by without me telling you how much you mean to me." He paused and in a low tone continued, "I would do anything for you."

Butterflies moved through my stomach. "That's really sweet." I bit my lip. "You definitely made me feel special."

"You *are* special." His hand slipped into my lap, settling between my legs as he gripped my thigh. "So, if I had to drive here to tell you, to prove to you that what I feel is real . . . and that you're the first thing I think about when I wake up and the last thing I think about when I go to bed, it was worth the trip. Because I don't want there to be any confusion about how I feel about you."

My heart skipped a beat as I approached the stop sign.

"If you keep talking like this, I'm going to fall in love with you," I joked, even though I was serious. The way I was feeling, there was enough evidence to conclude that I was already there.

But I wasn't ready to admit that yet.

I felt him staring at me, so I met his gaze.

"That's exactly what I want," he uttered.

Heat spread across my skin at his words, and in that moment, I knew Ahmad Williamson was in love with me.

It was in his tone. It was in his eyes. It was in his touch.

He squeezed the meaty flesh of my thigh as if to corroborate my realization.

With our seat belts on and my foot on the brake, an attempt at a kiss wasn't as smooth as I'd hoped. But as soon as we got enough slack for our lips to meet, the kiss confirmed everything for me. The way he smiled against my mouth let me know my feelings were apparent to him as well.

Soft, sensual, and expressive, our mouths and tongues said everything we weren't ready to say and more.

A horn blared from behind us, startling us both.

"Oh, shit!" I exclaimed, seeing the car behind us at the stop sign.

Looking both ways before making a move, I stepped on the gas.

I felt Ahmad tense as we eased onto the main street, so I kept my hands on the steering wheel and my eyes on the road. Our destination was only a mile away, but we took the trip in silence. Ahmad didn't seem to relax again until we pulled into the parking spot.

I placed my hand on top of his. "You good?"

He raised my hand to his lips and nodded. A few seconds later, he asked, "You good?"

"With you? Always."

Out of the corner of my eye, I saw his smile.

We went to the gas station closest to the lake and grabbed some snacks and a toothbrush. We devoured the chips and pastries on the way back to the house. By the time we got back into the room, we were ready to crash.

Sleeping naked, my back to his front and his arms around me, I drifted into the best sleep of my life.

Until a loud banging woke me up hours later.

"What's that?" Ahmad wondered groggily.

"I have no idea," I responded, pushing myself up into a sitting position. Rubbing my eyes, I looked around, feeling a little discombobulated. The sun was pouring into the room, and I had no idea what time it was or where the noise was coming from. I grabbed my phone.

"Oh, shit," I reacted, eyes wide.

"What? What's up?" Ahmad's deep voice was etched with concern.

"It's eleven o'clock. We have to check out at noon. The cleaning crew is here now." Jumping out the bed, I threw on the first thing I saw to cover myself, and then I ran downstairs. Giving them directions to start outside and then work their way inside, I went around to each bedroom to make sure everyone was up and getting ready to get out. Two of my cousins had already left. Mecca was in the process of leaving. Jazmyn was up and packing. Nina had just woken up. When I made it back to my room, Ahmad was in the shower.

So, I joined him.

The decision put me fifteen minutes behind schedule, but it was worth every single minute.

"What are you doing today?" Ahmad asked after placing my suitcase in my trunk.

"I'm stopping by my parents' house to see my grandmother. She didn't end up making it to the dinner last night because she wasn't feeling well. After that, I'm pretty open," I told him. "What are you doing?"

He shook his head. "I was hoping I could have a few minutes of your time later so I can give you your birthday gift."

I placed my hand on his crotch. "I'm quite fond of the gift you gave me."

He snickered, pulling me into his arms. "I'm glad to hear it, because I'm trying to give you more of that, too. But I'd like to give you an actual birthday gift."

A smile tugged at my lips. "What is it?"

"You'll see. Can we link up tonight?"

"We absolutely can."

He brought his lips down to mine and kissed me softly. "Good. Let me know when you're on your way home so I can set things up."

"You're not going to give me a hint?"

"The hint is that it's your birthday present."

"That's not a hint."

He laughed, kissing me again before letting me go. "You'll have to wait and see." He opened my car door for me. "You'll find out tonight."

I eyed him suspiciously. "You can't tell me because you don't know." My eyes widened as it hit me. "You haven't gotten it yet."

He laughed harder. "In my defense, you weren't speaking to me, and the last gift I gave you, you tried to return to sender."

I nodded as I got into the driver's seat. "That's fair."

He leaned into the car and kissed me again. "Let me know if anything changes on your end."

"I will. But what are you doing?" I wondered, looking around. "Get in so I can drive you to your car."

"It's not that far . . ." He looked far into the distance where his car was parked. "You right."

I laughed as he climbed in on the passenger side.

"Let me know when you make it home," I told him as we pulled up to his car.

In the light of day, I was able to get a good look at it. His car wasn't necessarily flashy, but it looked expensive. I didn't know cars, so I just knew it was pretty.

"And let me know when you make it to your parents' house."

"Thank you . . . for showing up and making my birthday everything I wanted it to be."

"I was always going to show up for you." He searched my face. "I will *always* show up for you." Leaning over the middle console, he kissed me. "God, you're beautiful," he whispered.

I felt warm all over.

And that feeling stayed with me as I arrived at Mom and Dad's. I saw my uncle's truck, and not even his bullshit attitude was going to bring down the high I was on. Pulling out my phone, I sent Ahmad a text.

Aaliyah: Just made it to my parents' house. Looking forward to 7pm.

Ahmad: I can't wait to see you again tonight.

"Hey, hey!" I yelled, announcing my arrival. "It's me."

"Aaliyah!" Mom called out from the kitchen. "I'm in here."

I followed her voice to see her whipping up something that smelled delicious. The closer I got, the more I realized I was hungry.

"Hey, Mom," I greeted her. "What's that?"

"I'm making a beef stew for your grandmother so she can put

something hearty on her stomach. Well, I'm making it for everyone, but at your grandmother's request."

"She still not feeling well?"

"She seems to be recovering well. She's downstairs in the den." Mom put the ladle down and gave me a hug. "How is my birthday girl?"

"I'm great," I told her honestly.

"You look great."

The yellow dress I was wearing was cute, but she'd seen it before and told me it was too loud. My hair wasn't as pulled together as I usually had it because I didn't have any products with me, and she hated it when my hair wasn't neat.

"Thank you . . ." I stretched the word out as I tried to figure out what was going on. "You hate this dress."

"Yes, it's too bright. But I'm not talking about the dress." She gently jammed her pointer into my chest. "I'm talking about you. You're glowing."

"Am I?"

"You were glowing last night, too. I told your father when you did your toast at dinner. There's something happening with you."

"I'm in a good place," I admitted, my smile stretching across my face.

She shook some seasoning into the pot, and then she turned back to me. "Does it have anything to do with that man of yours?"

I froze. "What?"

She went to the kitchen table and grabbed her phone. "You told me and your father that you didn't have a date and that you were happy on your own. So imagine our surprise when we leave your party and wake up to this." Holding out her phone, she showed me picture after picture of me and Ahmad—dancing on the dance floor, kissing on the dock, sitting on the bench. Random photos of us being taken without our knowledge.

"Who—?"

"Mecca," she answered.

"Does she work for the tabloids?" I grumbled.

"Now don't get mad at her. She thought we knew."

"No, she didn't. She was just being her nosy self."

"Her mother was the same way," Mom admitted with a smirk. "But don't try to change the subject. Who is this young man, and when do we get to meet him?"

"His name is Ahmad, and I will let you know," I told her begrudgingly.

Her smile was a little too excited. "He's the one."

Just her saying that caused my stomach to knot. "Mom, I need you to chill."

"How long have you two been dating?" She studied the pictures on the phone. "You two look really comfortable together."

I let out a short laugh. "Mom, I'm not doing this."

She put her phone down and went to the sink to wash her hands. "Not doing what?" she questioned innocently.

I saw right through her.

"Mom."

She sighed loudly. "Fine!" She snatched a paper towel and dried her hands. "But will you answer one question for me?"

"One question."

There was a flicker of sadness that moved through her eyes. It was brief, but I saw it. "Why didn't you tell me the truth? Did I make you feel like you couldn't tell me?"

"I did tell you the truth. When I had that talk with you and Dad, I had no idea Ahmad was going to show up at the party. Up until this weekend, we were just . . . friends."

"So yesterday morning, you didn't know he was going to be there?"

"I didn't know he was going to be there until he showed up. He wasn't even invited. It was a whole thing."

I saw the relief smooth the wrinkles from her face. "Oh, thank God." She grabbed her cross necklace and kissed it. "I was thinking we'd alienated you and that you didn't feel like you could be honest with us." Her eyes watered. "I prayed about it last night and again this morning at church after getting the picture. I don't ever want to make you feel like you can't share your life with me. And the fact that I thought that means that I have to do better. So, I'm sorry, Aaliyah. I'm so sorry."

"Mom." I embraced her, squeezing her tight. "Thank you for saying that."

The oven timer went off, and we broke up our hug. She pulled twelve delicious-looking cinnamon rolls out, and I washed my hands to help her glaze them.

She plopped one on a plate for herself and then put the others on a serving tray. "Will you take these to the den for me, please? There are plates already down there."

"Not a problem."

I grabbed a bottle of water and went downstairs to the den. My father, uncle, and grandmother were relaxing and watching preseason football.

"Aaliyah!" Dad greeted me when he saw me. "Cinnamon rolls!"

The cheer for the cinnamon rolls was a bit louder than the one for me. I set the plate down on the coffee table with the rest of the food items, and I decided to not be offended by his excitement. As I took a bite of the gooey goodness on the plate, I understood where he was coming from.

He gave me a big bear hug and then stepped around me so he could see the instant replay of the interception he'd missed.

I said hello to my uncle and grandma as I finished chewing my bite.

"I heard I owe you an apology and you actually did have a man with you at your party," Uncle Al said. "There's no guarantee he isn't someone you hired to play the part, but if I'm wrong, I stand corrected."

I opened my mouth to say something petty, but my grandma spoke first.

"Don't pay him any mind," she intervened, rising to her feet. "But come outside on the porch with me for a minute."

I took my bottle of water and cinnamon roll with me.

"How are you feeling, Nana?" I asked her as she took a seat in the rocking chair.

"I feel good."

"Was it like a twenty-four-hour bug or something?" I wondered, sitting in the chair next to her.

She shook her head. "No. I wasn't sick. I wanted to be at your birthday party, but I didn't think Al deserved to be. Not the way he's been acting. I didn't do enough to protect your mom from his ways when they were coming up. I didn't know the type of things he was saying to her or the reason why she was so obsessed with her weight. I didn't know. And by the time I found out, they were grown. But seeing how he acted at Aniyah's party, I wasn't going to let him ruin yours."

"Thank you, Nana." I gave her another hug. "I wish you were there, but I appreciate you taking one for the team. I had already uninvited him, but I'm glad you were there with the reinforcement."

"For you, my beautiful granddaughter, anytime."

"So, you're really not sick? Because Mom's making beef stew so you'll have something hearty on your stomach."

"I'm fine. I'm better than fine. I feel great. But I wasn't going to turn down homemade beef stew."

I tipped my head back and laughed. "I love you."

"I love you, too." She leaned forward. "So, tell me about this man that gave you your Cinderella moment."

"How did you know about that?"

"Who do you think? Mecca!"

I shook my head. "Of course."

After a two-hour visit and a bowl of beef stew, I told everyone goodbye. They were mostly distracted by the close game. I would've been interested in the outcome because it was neck and neck, but I had something better to do.

Before I backed out of the driveway, my uncle came out the house, flagging me down.

Rolling my window down, I sighed with pursed lips.

"Aaliyah," he called out.

"Yes?" I replied.

He handed me a box the size of a book. "Happy birthday." He took a step back. "I'm sorry."

"Thank you—for the gift and the apology."

"I hate that I missed your party. I told your mom to give it to you before your dinner, but she forgot it. But I, uh . . . I have to say that I'm proud of you for standing your ground." He pointed at the box. "Open it when you get home."

I nodded. "Okay."

"I love you."

"I love you, too."

Backing out of the driveway, I waved and then sped off. I waited until I got to the first stop sign and curiosity got the best of me.

Tearing open the wrapping paper, I opened the book-shaped box, and my eyebrows went up. Slowly, a smile pulled at my lips.

Wow.

A horn beeped behind me, so I placed everything in the passenger seat and then got on the road. As soon as I got to the next stop sign, I pulled out my cell phone and called Ahmad.

"Well, hello, Aaliyah." His deep voice put a smile on my face as it boomed through the speakers of my car. "I was just thinking about you."

"Oh really?" I replied. "And what were you thinking?"

"It was about your gift. I had to reach out to Asia for some help. That was a mistake."

"What did Asia say?"

"Well, first, she said she knew something was between us from day one and just a whole lot of 'I told y'all so.'"

I laughed. "I'll give her that."

"Oh, don't let her hear you say that! She's been insufferable all afternoon."

"What else did she say?"

"Well, she kept saying how she knew we would end up together because we spent the summer pretending we weren't in love with each other. And for that reason alone, I needed to pull out all the stops since it's our first real date. She said I needed to take you to a five-star restaurant and then bring you home and do the rose petals, expensive wine, and gourmet chocolate thing to end the night. Then she said"—he changed his vocal pitch to imitate Asia—"'If you love her and you want this to work, you'll listen to me,'" he concluded.

"Oh, wow, okay," I giggled. "She was laying it on thick!"

"She thinks she knows everything now. Can't stand her ass sometimes."

I smiled, knowing how much he loved his sister. "I bet!"

He was quiet for a second. "So yeah, thanks to some strings my family pulled, we have a reservation at seven o'clock at Cloverleaf."

I burst out laughing. "So, I see you took her advice about the five-star restaurant."

He let out a light chuckle. "Well, she was right one time before. It couldn't hurt to see if she was right about this, too. What's the worst that could happen?"

Butterflies rippled through my belly, and I bit my lip. "Famous last words."

"How was your visit with your family?"

"It was nice. Mostly watched football. But my uncle gave me a pretty cool gift."

"What did he give you?"

I glanced over at the ownership paperwork, manual, and keys. "A yacht."

acknowledgments

To Marvin, the love of my life: Thank you for your love and support in life and throughout the writing process. Your love is the stuff that romance novels are made of, and I am blessed to experience life and love with you. Publishing my first traditional release would've been a lot more stressful without you rooting for me, supporting me, encouraging me, and loving me. I love you, and I am thankful for you.

To my family: I love you, and I thank you for always shrouding me with love. From a very young age, you've always told me that I could do any and everything I put my mind to. You've always nurtured and supported my creativity, my imagination, and my vision.

To my best friends, Ashley, Christina, DaShauna, Noelle, and Joe: I love you, and I thank you for the bonds we've created, established, and maintained throughout the years. My life wouldn't be the same without you making your distinct mark on it. Thank you for showing me the definition of true friendship. You're the reason my heroines have such great friend groups. Some people go their whole lives without experiencing friendship in its most pure form. I am blessed.

To my agent, Ashley Antoinette Coleman: I am so thankful for you. I appreciate how you have opened doors for me and rooted for me to win. I have nothing but love and respect for you.

To Monique Patterson: Thank you for your time, patience, encouragement, vision, and support. I appreciate it, and I have nothing but love and respect for you.

To Bramble and everyone who worked together to make this happen for me: THANK YOU! I have so much respect for every step of the process, and I thank you all for your hard work.

To everyone who has read this and any other Danielle Allen novel: From the bottom of my heart, thank you. Every story is personal to me, and there's so much love poured into them. When you take the time to buy, read, and review my work, it feels like that love is being poured right back. It means so much. Your love and support over the years have meant the world to me. I appreciate each and every one of you. THANK YOU!

about the author

Danielle Allen is an author, an educator, and a life coach. Living authentically has been the key to her living her best life. With a background in social sciences, helping people better understand themselves so they can become the best version of themselves is one of her passions. She aims to write contemporary romance novels that change the status quo of the genre.

Facebook: DanielleAllenAuthor
Goodreads: Danielle Allen
Instagram: @authordanielleallen
TikTok: @authordanielleallen
BookBub: @authordanielleallen